FALL
THE
SHE SH

BY
FIONA McARTHUR

DR CINDERELLA'S
MIDNIGHT FLING

BY
KATE HARDY

MILLS
BOON

FALLING FOR THE SHEIKH SHE SHOULDN'T

BY
FIONA McARTHUR

To Trishabella—who makes me smile.

First published in Great Britain 2012
by Mills & Boon, an imprint of Harlequin (UK) Limited.
Harlequin (UK) Limited, Eton House, 18-24 Paradise Road,
Richmond, Surrey TW9 1SR

© Fiona McArthur 2012

ISBN: 978 0 263 89158 4

Harlequin (UK) policy is to use papers that are natural, renewable and recyclable products and made from wood grown in sustainable forests. The logging and manufacturing process conform to the legal environmental regulations of the country of origin.

Printed and bound in Spain
by Blackprint CPI, Barcelona

A mother to five sons, **Fiona McArthur** is an Australian midwife who loves to write. Mills & Boon® Medical™ Romance gives Fiona the scope to write about all the wonderful aspects of adventure, romance, medicine and midwifery that she feels so passionate about—as well as an excuse to travel! Now that her boys are older, Fiona and her husband Ian are off to meet new people, see new places, and have wonderful adventures. Fiona's website is at www.fionamcarthur.com

CHAPTER ONE

THE lift doors opened. Prince Zafar Aasim Al Zamid stepped inside and to his disgust his heart began to pound.

Someone slipped past him into the elevator and he couldn't help the deeper breath he took as the doors shut. A drift of orange soap vividly recalled the memory of fruit-laden trees in the palace grounds as a child, and, by association, the memory soothed him.

Thoughts that calmed were an excellent idea. Life had been much less complicated then. He opened his eyes as the lift shifted under his feet.

Lately he'd been acquiring phobias like new shirts. Since the crash it had been heights, now elevators—worse every ascent—until even a closing door caused symptoms. Perhaps it was a sign the claustrophobia in his life had worsened since he'd been forced to give up his work in favour of royal duty.

He would address his inner calm with the solitude of a retreat as soon as he sorted this latest mess. The vastness of the desert always made his problems seem less significant.

For the moment he was cramped and palpitating in a lift with the painful reminder of all he'd lost. This particular enclosed space held a fragile-looking new mum with a baby in one arm, a beaming new father clutching a balloon, and thankfully the orange-scented woman as well, dispensing an aura of tranquillity.

The metallic 'It's A Boy' helium balloon bobbed towards him and Zafar leant closer to the wall and regretted his decision to stay at this hotel. A baby hotel. The last place he needed to be. The image he carried of his tiny son's body flickered in his mind and he forced it away. Such happy families were constant reminders he could have done without but the stakes were high.

He had hoped to find Fadia, his estranged cousin, prior to the birth but time was against him. He'd discovered she planned to convalesce here instead of hospital if he arrived too late to find her beforehand.

The lift jerked and his pulse thundered in his ears.

The balloon wielder tugged on the string as the proud new dad hailed the woman. 'Carmen! We didn't get a chance to thank you.' He grabbed the woman's hand and shook it vigorously. 'You were amazing.'

The woman retrieved her hand and smiled at the young mother. 'Hello, again, Lisa, Jock. Lisa was the amazing one.'

Her voice soothed like a cool hand to his forehead and, infinitesimally, a little more of his agitation drained away as the phobia receded. Thankfully. It would be useful if his psyche finally accepted the obscenity of irrational fears.

'It was a beautiful birth.' She cast Zafar a swift apologetic look for their exclusive conversation, and the unexpected impact of her one glance collided with his, as if that ridiculous balloon had bumped him, before she turned back to the father.

Medical background, he concluded, and dismissed the stab of frustration the loss of his career left him with. Midwife probably. He'd met women like her before—those natural soothers who could create a rapport with strangers without effort.

He lifted his head and glanced over her. Anything was good to take his mind off the ascent through the lift well.

Thankfully his phobia retreated by the second as he studied her. She had thick black hair coiled on her head like rope. An Irish accent. Carmen seemed more Spanish than Irish yet she suited her name.

He watched her mouth as she said, 'How is young Brody?'

Jock laughed, loudly, and Zafar winced as the noise jarred his ears. 'He's a bruiser.' The father's pride resonated within the four walls as the lift stopped at the fifth floor with an extra jolt. The cage floor fell six inches and bounced before it came back to the level. Everyone laughed nervously, except Zafar. He closed his eyes and swallowed.

There was rustling and movement as the lift emptied and the father's voice, a little further away now. 'We'll see you soon, then.'

'I'll be down as soon as I have handover report from the morning midwife.' So Carmen was still in the lift. He opened his eyes as she waved at the couple.

'That's great. We'll see you then.' Zafar noted the relief in the father's face and his mind clutched at the distraction of wondering about this trend of moving postnatal women from the hospital into hotels to recover from birth.

Not something he was familiar with but it made sense

when he thought about it. A place of quiet comfort, fewer germs, useful for the hospital to have quick turnover and quite appropriate if your health fund covered it.

The lift doors closed silently, though the cage remained stationary, and he returned to contemplate the lights on the panel above the door despite the insidious desire to study the woman called Carmen more closely.

She stepped back and seemed to lean into the wall.

He knew she was tall because her head came above his shoulders and her knot of hair had been near his nose as she'd drifted orange blossom his way. The lift still didn't move. Seconds to go and he would be able to breathe properly again.

He glanced at her from under his lashes and saw her eyes were shut. He frowned. Not a usual occurrence when he shared space with a woman. In fact, he couldn't remember the last time he'd been ignored. In repose she appeared weary. Too weary?

His concern increased. 'Are you unwell?'

Her eyes flew open and she straightened. 'Good grief.' She blinked at him and then focussed. 'A micro-sleep. Sorry. I've been on night shift. It's been a busy week.'

Suddenly he felt empathetic to a perfect stranger because he could remember that weariness from a string of busy days and nights during his internship. Lack of sleep he'd grumbled about, but now the choice was no longer his, he'd love to suffer from that inconvenience again.

That was the problem with returning to Sydney. It reminded him that he wasn't living the life he'd once loved. Made him feel frustration he shouldn't feel towards his duty to Zandorro.

The elevator jerked, ground upwards for a few inches. The sooner the better, he thought, then the lift bounced suddenly as the cable stopped.

His breath caught as he waited. The doors didn't open and the light sat on neither five nor six. Midway between floors. Stopped.

This was not good. He felt his heart rate shift gear, double before his next breath, his chest tightened, and air jammed in his lungs.

'I am so not in the mood for this.' Zafar heard her in the distance as he tried to loosen his throat. He sank down onto his haunches and put one hand on the wall to give himself more blood to his head. With his other he loosened his collar.

The lift was suddenly the cabin of the private jet. His family would plunge in a few spiralling seconds and there was not a thing he could do about it. So now it was his destiny to die. It was almost a relief. And he'd complained about being in line for the throne.

Distantly he realised she'd picked up the phone and spoken to the operator. When he heard her re-seat the instrument she bent down to him. 'You okay?'

He didn't refocus his eyes off the floor until he felt her hand on his arm—warm, firm, comfort personified—and not letting go. He had the bizarre idea he couldn't fall anywhere while she held him. Yet all she did was share touch without moving. He breathed with difficulty through his nose and inhaled drifts of orange. Incredibly steadying, like a shot of Valium through his bloodstream.

He sucked air through clenched teeth and the light-headedness faded a little. This was ridiculous. Irrational. Acutely embarrassing. He forced himself to look into her face. She had dark golden eyes, like burnt twisted treacle, calm and wise and filled with compassion. Mesmerising up close. 'You're a nurse?'

Her eyes crinkled and his chest eased a little more. 'Sort of. I'm a midwife. Do you need some deep breathing?'

'I'm not in labour.' But this was hard work. He shut his eyes again. 'Possibly.'

'Do you have a phobia?' The same gentle conversational voice as if she'd asked if he needed sugar in his tea.

The demons from the past battered against him. He strove to keep his voice level. 'So it seems.'

She sank down. He heard the rustle of fabric and felt the slight brush of her leg as she settled herself beside him on the floor. Her hand rested still on his arm, not moving, as if to transfer energy and calmness from her to him. It seemed to be working. 'What's your name?

He had many. 'Zafar.'

She paused and he felt her appraisal until he opened his eyes again. Her golden interest captured his. 'Well, Zafar. I'm Carmen. I've been stuck in this lift three times this week. Big, deep breaths should help.'

Deep breaths might be difficult. 'It is a battle with small ones.'

Coaxing. 'You can do a couple.'

He wasn't sure but the fact that she'd lived through this three times did help. He was feeling faint again. 'A rule of threes?'

'In through your nose…'

Intolerably bossy woman. 'Out through my mouth. Yes, I know.'

Her voice firmed. Like his mother's from the distant past. The time of orange trees. 'Then do it.'

He humoured her. And felt better. Actually, quite a lot better so he did it again. With her sitting below him he had a delightful view down the valley between her breasts. He glanced away politely but could feel himself improve every second with the picture in his mind. Surely a harmless medicinal remedy.

Imagine if the lift had still been full. He mentally shuddered. There was just her to see this weakness. Thankfully he'd sent his bodyguard and secretary to the suite. In future the stairs would be good for his fitness. Once free, he'd never see this woman again. A good thing, and a shame.

At least it seemed his brain had accepted death was unlikely.

And she had the most incredible breasts but he wasn't going to look again—his gaze travelled back to her face—and a delightful mouth. Those lips... His body stirred. A mouth designed by angels and plump for surrender if he was willing to risk life and limb for it. She may be calm but she looked very capable of protecting herself despite the weariness. His lips twitched.

'Are you feeling better?'

'Much.' Better than she knew. He watched with some amusement as she slowly recognised the direction of his fascination until she stared straight back at him and raised her brows.

She removed her hand from his arm and she shook her head. 'Tsk tsk.'

The lift jerked and resumed its ascent. Zafar shut his eyes briefly but the panic had gone.

It seemed she was good at her job. He straightened

until he stood with his feet firm beneath him, reached down and took her hand to help her up. Such a lovely hand, but workworn. She rose fluidly into his space, as he'd intended.

For that moment as their glances met he forgot the lift, the heights, the strain his life was, all except this unexpected awareness between them that swept away their surroundings, so enmeshed in this unexpected connection that when he said, 'Thank you,' the words hung in the air between them like mist.

An imp of mischief drew his head closer. He expected her to pull away. 'You're very kind…and incredibly beautiful.' He stroked her cheek, his gaze drawn once more to her ripe and luscious mouth.

She did the unpredicted. 'It's okay. I understand.' He heard it in her voice, a note of sympathy that horrified him. Pity?

He recoiled. He needed no one's compassion.

The elevator jolted and the doors opened on seven. They'd missed six altogether. She turned away from him with a frown on her entrancing face.

There was some consolation in the way she compressed her lips together as if to hide the way they'd plumped and reddened in anticipation…of what? The almost brush of his lips on hers? So she had felt something too?

'You certainly look better.' Her comment made him smile again, the dryness hiding undertones he couldn't identify, but there was a subtle flush of colour to her cheeks and her wide eyes searched his face as if seeking a hint of what had passed between them during the last few frozen moments.

Despite his urge to throw himself out of the lift to

safety, Zafar stretched his hand across the doors to allow her to precede him. 'My apologies for my weakness earlier.'

She assessed him with a clinical scrutiny he wasn't used to getting from a woman and strangled back a half-laugh. 'I doubt you're a weak man so I'm sure you've good reason.'

He inclined his head.

She glanced around. 'And I should have got out at level six.' She turned swiftly out to the left of the lift and pulled open the door of the fire escape to go down a flight before he was fully out of the lift himself.

He started to hum. The day was not as bad as it had started out.

Carmen moved quickly to reach the door to the stairwell but she could almost feel the eyes of the man in the lift on her back.

What had just happened? Her lips tingled as if still waiting and she could detect the unusual spicy aftershave from his skin so close to hers. And what a mouth! Sinful was too tame a word. She couldn't pretend she hadn't been tempted.

Not the sort of encounter she'd expected today and she wasn't entirely sure she'd behaved properly. Hopefully she wouldn't see him again.

When the fire-escape door shut with an echoing clang she breathed a sigh of relief as she leant back against it. Cold metal against her back was lovely to counter the heat everywhere else in her body. She glanced around.

Appropriate name. Fire escape.

She definitely felt a bit singed on the edges—like a

ragged sleeve too close to a candle—ragged and breathless. She touched her lips. Burnt and hot without even touching him.

She glanced around again, reassured in a dark stairwell with unpainted concrete stairs and the echo of empty walls, but there was no doubt she was glad of the sanctuary afforded her.

One would have thought she'd learnt her lesson from her ex-husband about smooth-talking men in expensive suits who seduced you and then destroyed your life.

Still. One almost slip didn't make a disaster. She hoped.

Eighteen hours later Carmen O'Shannessy admired the gifts Mother Nature had bestowed on her at five that morning with a soft smile. She knew there was a reason she loved night duty, apart from the fact it allowed her to do two jobs.

Twins. Dark-haired cherubs with skin like dusky rosebuds. Her patient, Fadia Smith, rested back in the armchair like Madonna with her sons poking out under her arms like tiny bundled wings. It had taken a little juggling, a few attempts, and almost an hour of patience, but with both boys feeding well this moment was a very satisfying end to a drama-filled morning.

It had been a long time since Carmen had seen twins born with so little fuss but, then, Fadia hadn't left them with much choice. Her cumbersome arrival alone and a bare five minutes before her first son appeared had left Carmen literally catching the baby. By the time the obstetrician and his entourage had arrived, number two had also decided to greet the outside world and Dr Bennett had waved her on with an incredulous smile.

To continue their no-fuss arrival, both wee boys had

cried and then settled on their mother's skin. While they appeared small, there were no signs of prematurity or respiratory distress.

That would be unlike the breathless-from-running neonatal staff, who'd drifted back to their unit unneeded shortly afterwards. Carmen still smiled over their shock when she'd rung for help.

Two hours later Carmen should've been feeling ready to hand Fadia over to the day staff and go home. 'You sure I can't phone someone for you?' Something niggled.

Fadia seemed very sad. On cue with the question, Fadia jumped in the chair and the two babies stopped their sucking with startled eyes before resettling to their feed.

Their mother forced herself to relax. 'No, no. My babies are fine. I really don't have anyone else to call. I'm a widow and there's just a friend of my husband who's been helping me until my relatives arrive.'

Fadia seemed determined nothing was wrong and hurried on. 'We're all safe.' It seemed a strange thing to say.

'Well, your boys weren't waiting for anyone.' She leaned over and stroked a tiny hand that rested on his mother's neck. 'You're amazing, Fadia. Congratulations. Tilly will be looking after you today. I have to go home to my bed, and I'll see you when you move to the baby hotel in a day or two. Have you decided on names?'

'Harrison and Bailey. My husband's names.'

'Lovely. I'm sure he would have loved that.'

'He didn't even know I was pregnant when he was killed.'

Was killed? Not died. How horrible but not the time to ask. 'I'm sorry. But I'm sure, somewhere, he knows. Do try and get some sleep as soon as they do.'

'Thanks, Carmen. You've given me so much strength in all of this. It means so much that you weren't cross with me for leaving it so late.'

'You were always strong, Fadia. So amazing. And we know babies come when they want.' Carmen grinned. 'You must have a guardian angel. And that makes sense. Thank you for a lovely end to my night.' She waved and almost bumped into Tilly, the day midwife, passing the door.

'Finally going home?' Tilly glanced at her watch.

Carmen knew she was nearly an hour late getting away already. 'At last.'

'You working this afternoon as well?'

'Doing the one p.m. at the hotel till seven. I get to sleep in my bed tonight.'

Tilly shook her head. 'Don't know how you do it. I'd be dead doing those hours as well as night duty.'

'I get around four hours' sleep.' Carmen shrugged. 'It's short term. But I'm starting to come down from the night's euphoria. But I am tired now.' She did not want to talk about this or the reason she was almost killing herself. She'd never taken help from anyone and she wasn't going to start now.

Thankfully Tilly wasn't slow on nuances because she changed the subject back to Fadia. 'Well done, you, with this morning. Lucky duck. Catching twins is hard to do without a cast of thousands trying to help these days.'

'And your Marcus didn't push me out of the way.'

Tilly's cheeks went pink and Carmen felt a tug of wistfulness at her friend's happiness. A fleeting picture of the man in the lift intruded again before she pushed him away.

She hadn't given him a thought for hours. Been far too busy. Which was a good thing. 'It must be great to have everything in your life going well.'

Tilly said, 'I'm fostering Marcus's faith in midwives. I think it's working.' They smiled at each other.

'And Fadia was lucky.' Carmen's smile dropped. 'Her friend's coming in at lunchtime. She's very quiet but, then, she did lose her husband fairly recently. There's no one else listed under "Next of kin" from her booking. Look after her, Till. We need to make sure she has somewhere to go after she's discharged.'

'Yes, Mother Carmen.' Tilly's answer was light but the look they exchanged reassured her that her friend would be extra vigilant. Tilly would be just as determined as Carmen to be there for any mother, let alone one with twins who had twice as many reasons for moments of unusual interest.

After too few hours' sleep it was time for Carmen to dress for work again. This time she would be providing postnatal midwifery in the baby hotel, a pet name the medical profession used for the five-star beach resort that catered for a few privately insured postnatal mothers. It was another warm and fuzzy part of her job and the women she supported often existed on less sleep than she'd had so a few yawns between friends was quite acceptable.

It was even better if she'd been with the women in labour and could follow their progress until they went home.

As she pressed the lift button in the car park she couldn't help thinking of the man on level seven. Zafar. Mysterious name. And what would have happened to him if she hadn't been in the lift that extra floor? The memory of their close encounter burned brightest.

She screwed up her face. 'Go away.' The words hung quietly between her and the closed lift door and she twisted her head uneasily to make sure nobody had heard.

There'd been something incredibly vulnerable about such a virile and powerful-looking man sweating over a stalled lift. Which maybe explained a little why she hadn't backed off more quickly.

There had been nothing vulnerable in the way he'd crowded her after, though. Or the way she'd almost dared him to kiss her. She couldn't help the curve of her lips at the return of that memory and thought ruefully that he'd never want to see her again.

Which was fine. Her husband's underhand conniving had taken her home, undermined her self-respect—though she supposed she should thank him because she was tougher than ever now—and taught her to reserve judgement for a long while yet.

But Zafar's face seemed indelibly stamped in her memory. Dark, tortured eyes under black brows and a firm yet wickedly sexy mouth that captured her attention with such assurance—a mouth that looked used to command. Everywhere. She felt the re-kindling of awareness low and hot in her belly. Outrageous. She shook her head. She wasn't going there.

The guy embodied everything she hated about men. Power and prestige. She knew he had it despite his aversion to a stalled lift, and she had no doubt he could be as cynically ruthless as he looked.

He had to have extreme wealth, of course. The very expensive watch and the suit that shrieked of a tailor her ex would have killed to find were dead giveaways.

Though why he was out in the beach fringes of eastern Sydney was a mystery.

She really needed to stop thinking about him, but once inside the lift she could picture him across from her easily, too easily, in fact, for someone she'd met for five minutes twenty-four hours ago.

The lift stopped on six and she stepped out onto the main baby floor and made her way to the midwives' room. To work, woman!

As she discussed her patients with the morning shift midwife she was surprised to hear that Fadia had already been moved to the hotel. Occasionally a very well woman with her second or subsequent baby would move across after four hours but for a first-time mum with twins it was very unusual.

'And the paediatrician said it was okay? And Tilly's Dr Bennett as well?'

'They'll both be visiting daily here and a mothercraft nurse transferred across with her.'

Special considerations, then. Not the first time wealthy clients had brought their own nurse but she hadn't envisaged Fadia being like that. 'That will help.'

'Not any more. Fadia sent her away as soon as she was settled. Apparently didn't like her.'

Carmen raised her eyebrows. 'Curiouser and curiouser.'

Fifteen minutes later when Carmen knocked on Fadia's door, the last person she expected to open it was the man from the elevator.

Zafar.

Her pulse jumped and he captured her gaze easily and held it, just as he held the small smile on his lips. Heat flooded her cheeks.

CHAPTER TWO

'AH. THE midwife. Come in.' As if she was always turning up on his doorstep.

She hoped her mouth was closed because he looked jaw-droppingly handsome when he wasn't terrified. He seemed ten times taller and broader than before but she guessed her first real impression must have been coloured by his distress.

'It seems I must thank you for your magnificent skills at the delivery of Fadia's twins.'

'Being there was a privilege. Fadia did all the hard work. I was just catching.'

He smiled sardonically. 'Yet some skill is required with multiple birth.'

He leaned casually against the door. Funny how she had the idea he was as relaxed as a tiger about to spring.

Fadia, perched on the edge of the chair with one of her sons, looked anything but calm and Carmen's fluttery surprise turned to bristling protection of her patient.

Was the lift almost-kisser the person Fadia was scared of? 'Is this your husband's friend?'

Fadia shot a startled glance at Zafar and then back at Carmen's face. 'No. Goodness, no.' Carmen couldn't help the relief. That saved a bad lack of professionalism and would be a sorry pickle.

'No, this is my cousin. From Zandorro.' Fadia sent another glance his way—this time slightly less anxious. 'He's come in response to a letter I sent to my grandfather and to see if I need help.'

Zafar inclined his head. 'Ensuring you and your babies are well. So I can pass the good news onto your relatives, yes.' He turned to Carmen and raised one sardonic eyebrow. 'So you haven't met the elusive friend of our newest family members either, then?'

'No.' Carmen had no plan to elaborate. She shrugged to let him know that family dynamics were none of her business. 'But perhaps you could excuse us while I spend a short time privately with Fadia?'

'Is that totally necessary?' Such surprise when she'd said it and obviously a request uncommon in his experience. Carmen bit back her smile at his shock. So, we don't like being asked to leave, she thought. How interesting.

Just who was he? But it didn't really matter. She'd had four hours' sleep, she was worried about Fadia, and wasn't in the mood for tantrums. 'Yes. Afraid so.' Tough. Out you go, though she didn't say it out loud.

He frowned down his haughty nose and thinned those sexy lips until they almost disappeared, which was a shame, but proclaimed this man expected obedience, not orders.

Welcome to my back yard, buddy. Carmen squared her shoulders and fixed the smile on her face. She could be as tough as he was. Or tougher, if needed.

His eyes clashed with hers. It seemed he was going to cross his arms and flatly refuse.

What would she do then? She had no idea. Figure something out. Mentally she crossed her own arms. Bring it on. Never hassle a woman off night duty.

He didn't. On the brink of refusal he hesitated, gave her a mocking smile that actually made her feel more uncomfortable than a flat refusal—almost a promise of retribution—and annoyingly her satisfaction at the win dimmed.

She didn't like that look. Or the feeling it left her with. Who was this guy?

'I shall return,' he said to his cousin with a stern glance in Carmen's direction, 'when your midwife is finished with you, Fadia.'

Fadia nodded, twisted her hands, and Carmen inclined her head politely. She couldn't wait to ask Fadia what the problem was.

'We won't be long,' she said sweetly as she opened the door for him. The lock shut with the heavily finality hotel doors had and thankfully the room returned to a spacious suite.

Amazing how much breathing space one man could take up. Carmen looked at her patient. 'You okay?'

'Yes.' The young woman hunched her shoulders and tightened the grip on the baby in her arms. Fadia didn't look okay. She looked shattered, on the brink of tears, and Carmen just wanted to hug her.

'And your babies?'

'Fine.' Fadia glanced across at her other baby asleep in the cot and visibly shook. 'I can't believe he actually left. You told him to go!'

'Of course.' She wasn't wasting time on him, she was worried about her patient. Something was badly wrong here.

'Zafar wasn't listed as next of kin?'

'I didn't know if the family recognised me.'

'So his arrival was unexpected?'

'Yes. No.' She lowered her voice. 'I wrote to my grandfather last week but Tom said I would be sorry when the family took over my life. But I'm glad Zafar is here while I decide what I wish to do.'

'Well you have a few days to think about it before you have to go anywhere.' She took Fadia's pulse. It was faster than normal, she hoped just down to agitation and not a postnatal problem. 'I'm surprised to see they allowed you out of hospital so soon after birth.'

'They said I could come across to the hotel today as long as I brought the mothercraft nurse. My cousin visited me soon after you left this morning and arranged one when I asked.'

Carmen glanced around the otherwise empty room but didn't comment on the fact the mothercraft nurse was nowhere to be seen.

Fadia shrugged. 'We did not get on. So she left.'

'Oh.' Not a lot she could gather from that. 'That's very quick transfer for twins. Because of your over-extended uterus you're at risk of bleeding. We need to watch for that. And you'd get much more help if you stayed on the ward. I could have you readmitted back there.' Especially if your cousin helped you leave, she thought.

Fadia shook her head. 'Now that he's found me, I'd prefer to be here. Apparently the paediatrician will visit me as well. I hate hospitals, which is why I was so late coming in. Zafar wants me to have private nurses. I said I knew you and was comfortable without.' She looked up and pleaded, 'That is my biggest concern. I want to care for my babies myself, not with some nurse taking control as soon as they cry. Which is why I am unsure if I wish to return to Zandorro.'

Carmen could understand that but she wasn't so sure Fadia knew how much work two small babies could be. 'Well good for you, but it will be exhausting, even if it's a great way for a mother to feel.'

Fadia nodded with relief. 'Access to the baby hotel is why I chose your hospital. Tilly said you were working here today so I wanted to come across now.'

'Okay, I can understand preferring to be here than hospital.' But that didn't explain her cousin's agreement when most people would realise the twins needed more observation too.

'I do feel a little less alone now Prince Zafar has arrived.'

'Prince Zafar.' Carmen blinked. Prince of what? 'Like Prince Charles?'

'From the desert. Zafar is fourth in line to the throne of Zandorro.'

'A sheik?' That explained a lot. 'So you're from this Zandorro, too?'

'My family were from a small but powerful country in the desert. My father is dead, my mother left five years ago and brought me to Australia with her, but she sadly passed away not long after we arrived.'

So much drama and tragedy for one woman to cope with. But why was Fadia so unsure it was a good thing her cousin had found her?

She'd known Zafar was someone out of the ordinary, but it wasn't an everyday occurrence to run into a prince. Or be trapped in a lift with one. Or be almost kissed by one.

No wonder he expected to be obeyed. And she'd coolly told him to leave. She struggled not to smile. Too funny.

She needed to think about this. 'So if he's your cousin,' Which made Fadia…? 'Does that make you a princess?'

'Yes.'

She pointed to her sons. 'I'm guessing they're princes too, then?' She looked at the babies. 'And you walked into the hospital at the last minute alone to deliver twins?'

A cloud passed over Fadia's face and her voice lowered until Carmen strained to hear her. 'Unfortunately, when my husband died, I was alone and pregnant and the only help I've had has been from friends of my husband, but I'm starting to think I don't really trust them.'

'Tom told me I was being followed and I moved out of my flat close to the hospital into a hotel for what turned out to be the last day of my pregnancy. The poor driver was beside himself that I would have my babies in his taxi.'

Carmen could imagine it. She'd bet he was terrified. 'You were lucky they weren't.' Crikey.

Fadia's eyes filled. 'I think Tom didn't want Zafar to find me. Zafar is here to take me back to his country, and I am starting to think that is a good thing, but it will separate me from the memories of my husband and mother. Yet my sons need their heritage. Tom said he will help me stay in Australia.' Her voice became a whisper. 'But I'm not sure that is what I want.'

'So when is your husband's friend—Tom, is it?— coming?'

'Today. And I'm scared for my sons.' Fadia began

to shake and Carmen frowned as the woman struggled to pull herself together. 'I hate being weak. But I seem to have lost my strength since my husband died.'

Poor Fadia. And, boy, she was really in the middle of something here, Carmen thought. Then the twin in his cot screwed up his face and let out a blood-curdling wail as if aware of the tragedy of his mother. At least she could do something while her brain raced.

She unwrapped the little boy and checked his nappy before she re-wrapped and lifted him out of the crib. 'Don't be cross, little prince.' Then she tucked him into her neck and gently patted his bottom. The unconscious rhythm soothed them both.

She needed to understand how she could help Fadia. 'So do you want me to keep this Tom away?'

Fadia's eyes widened. 'Can you do that?'

'Midwives are very good at screening people without upsetting them.' Carmen shrugged. 'Lots of times a mother's labour is going slowly because of an inappropriate person in the birthing room.' She grinned. 'Like a scary mother-in-law or a friend she couldn't say no to.' She smiled. 'We suggest they have some time out and they don't get them back in until the mother asks us to.' She spread her hands. 'I could hold Tom off for you. But isn't your cousin better for that?'

Fadia stroked the bed sheet with her fingers. 'No. The situation could escalate more than I want'

A strange thing to say but Fadia's fingers twisted and turned and Carmen held her tongue. 'Or Zafar might do something to him.'

Carmen barely stopped herself from rolling her eyes. Oh, come on. This isn't the Middle Ages.'

'You don't understand.'

'Okay. So, this Tom? Have you got a photo of him?'

Fadia thought for a moment and then nodded. She reached for her purse and removed a photo of a smiling couple, the woman Fadia.

'Your husband?' Fadia nodded. Carmen looked at the third person in the photo and there was something about him that reminded her of her ex. Carl. A hardness around his eyes, a sleaziness in his smile. She was good at picking that up now.

Fadia was shaking and Carmen felt for her. That was enough emotional drama for this exhausted mum. 'Fadia. Can I borrow this? I'll copy it and give my friend downstairs a copy. We'll keep an eye out and and nobody will be hurt. But for now…' she held the baby towards his mother '…we could get these boys fed because this little one is going to bring the roof down if he really gets going. And you're not going to have time to worry about annoying Toms, or frowning Zafars, because these boys will keep you on your toes without them. And after that you get to rest.'

Fadia nodded and some of the strain left her face. 'You're right. Thank you.'

An hour later, when Carmen opened the door of Fadia's room, a tall man in a flowing robe stood up from the chair at the end of the corridor and stared at her as she hesitated in the doorway. What was going on here?

Good grief. This was getting worse. She was guessing Zafar had put a guard on Fadia so maybe there was more she needed to know.

They were infecting her with their dramas but the last thing the new mum needed was more tension and Carmen needed to know what she was up against.

Carmen stiffened her shoulders, let the room door shut behind her and marched up to the guard. 'I'm assuming you're Prince Zafar's man?'

He bowed his head, though his expression remained anything but subservient. 'Yes, madame. I am Yusuf.'

'Then, Yusuf, perhaps you could take me to your prince, please.'

'No.'

'No?'

'I think not.' The guard raised his eyebrows, looked her up and down, as if to say she was only a woman and a servant at that, and Carmen's usually dormant temper flickered. She glared at him. This was really beyond a joke.

Any minute now Fadia could poke her head out and see she was under guard.

Her voice firmed. 'I think so. Right now, thank you. I'm quite happy to use the stairs.' She smiled sweetly. 'The prince and I do know each other.' A white lie. Serve Zafar right for flirting with her.

She and Yusuf, her new best friend—not—stared at each other for a moment and she could see a faint scar running the full length of the man's face. He was probably extremely used to defending his prince.

There was stalemate as the silence went on and she threw caution to the winds. 'I'd hate to have to pass on my displeasure.'

The man's face tightened and he shrugged fatalistically. 'As you wish. This way.' He opened the door to the stairwell and allowed her to precede him. Carmen could hear the swish of his robes behind her, even though his footsteps were silent.

'Please wait.'

She glanced back and Yusuf held up his hand.

She paused at the top of the stairs and the guard leaned forward and opened the heavy door for her. That second of waiting gave her time to realise she had no clear agenda for her visit with the prince when she arrived. Was it enough of her business to barge in? What on earth was she doing here?

On the seventh floor Carmen could see another guard standing outside the door to the presidential suite and the reality sank in a little further about how different this man's life was from hers. And how out of her depth she really was.

She paused to say she'd changed her mind but one glance at the cynical face beside her told her dear Yusuf had picked up on her discomfort. Great to know she was providing him with amusement.

That decided her.

Yusuf glanced once more at her determined chin, nodded at the man standing guard, then knocked on the large wooden door.

A few seconds later a tiny robed woman appeared and they spoke a language Carmen didn't understand but it wasn't hard to guess what was said—something along the lines of stupid woman annoying our prince, no doubt.

The woman glanced over Carmen, shrugged and stepped back to allow them to enter.

The room opened into a window lined terrace and the magnificent blue vista of Coogee Bay curved like a sickle seven floors below. The scent of sandalwood was strong and quiet discordant music played discreetly in the background.

Several low armchairs were grouped together and

there were heaped cushions on colour-rich carpets, all facing the entertainment centre on one side of the room, and a boardroom table with a dozen comfortable chairs took up space on the other.

She'd been in this room before and the furnishing had changed dramatically. It seemed Prince Zafar travelled with his own furniture. A tad different from her bedsit with a rickety bed.

A door leading off into another room opened and Zafar came out—no, she thought, he made an entrance. Dressed in white traditional robes of an Arab, with his head covered, she couldn't help a little more gaping.

His brows drew together when he saw her but he came forward until he stood in front of her. He looked even bigger and more formidable surrounded by his servants but this time it was not only his physical presence, more the scent of distinct power.

'You wished to see me.'

She felt the pressure from interested eyes, and he too glanced around. He spoke three short, sharp words that cleared the room like magic.

Despite herself, she was impressed and to her irritation couldn't deny a little nervous thrill now that they were alone.

'Please…' he gestured to the lounge chairs '…be seated.' He gestured to the tiny kitchen. 'Would you like a juice or water?'

'No, thank you.' Despite her dry mouth. Maybe she should have had one to give herself time to think of something to say.

He sat when she did. 'In that case, what can I do for you?'

She had no idea. 'I wish to discuss your cousin.'

He inclined his head and she suspected a fleeting crinkle of amusement before he assumed a serious face again. 'I had guessed that was the case.'

Now she felt silly. Of course he did. She wasn't here because he'd almost kissed her. Was she? The thought brought a tide of pink to her cheeks and she felt like sliding under the gorgeous carpet or pulling one of those cushions over her face. How did she get herself into these situations?

Another flash of humour. 'Let me help you.'

She blinked. It wasn't where she expected help to come from but she'd take it.

'You're wondering if I am an ogre, or some medieval lord who drags around unwilling women and their babies…' he caught her eye and she was sure he could read her agreement in her face, but he went on, '…back to being imprisoned in their homeland.'

Just making sure it's not something like that. 'Not quite so dramatic but yes.'

'Thank you for your honesty. Let me explain. Apart from things you cannot be aware of, I think to clear the air between us could save us both some time.'

He smiled at her and she could feel herself soften. Even lean slightly towards him until she realised what she was doing. He seemed so reasonable and she was starting to believe she'd done the right thing to come here in the first place. This guy had serious charisma when he turned it on. She needed to remember that.

A random worry niggled and jostled with her hormones for attention. Please, don't let me fall again. Carl had been this smooth. This 'open' and friendly at first. Before she'd agreed to marry him and discovered how dark his soul really was. She was too easily sucked in by smooth guys. Guys she almost allowed to kiss her in elevators. She felt her shoulders stiffen with the thought. Good.

'By now you have discovered who I am, although I imagine my title would mean little to you?' The inflexion made it a question and she answered like the puppet she was trying not to turn into.

'You're right. No idea.'

'So…' He smiled at her and there was no way she couldn't smile back, damn him. 'I am from the small Arabic state of Zandorro that has, by the blessing of Allah, found itself abundantly supplied with oil and precious gems.'

There seemed to be a lot of those around, Carmen thought cynically, but she nodded to show she was paying attention.

'Our grandfather, King Fahed Al Zamid, is ruler, though his health is not good. Fadia's father, my uncle, was second in line to the throne until he died.' He looked at her. 'Unnatural causes.'

Unnatural causes. She fought to keep her eyebrows level. He went on when she nodded. 'It was thought Fadia had passed away with her mother several years ago, and as the succession passes only to a male child her wellbeing unfortunately slipped beneath the family's radar.'

He didn't explain that but went on. 'My eldest brother is next in line and I too have become closer to the throne because of these misfortunes.'

He paused, a short one, to see if she understood, and she was glad of the respite while she filed the succession order away in her brain.

She nodded and he continued. 'But now, with Fadia's

children being male and healthy, they are automatically next in the line of succession.'

She thought about that. Next in line? Major succession. Then he carried on. 'Unfortunately, this also increases their risk from certain elements once their birth is known, and that is something I have tragic personal experience of. Naturally I am concerned that my cousin and her sons remain safe. And she did ask for help.'

'Safe. Physical danger? Do you mean kidnapping?' This was a little more complicated than Fadia had led her to believe. If she believed him, that was, a calm inner voice suggested.

Zafar went on in that reasonable tone that seemed to flow hypnotically. 'At best. Hence my urgency to find Fadia once we knew she was alive and return her to our country before the babies' birth in case all of them were in danger away from the palace. At least until we can settle the dangers once and for all. A goal I have been working on.'

'Do you think there really is a risk of danger?' She couldn't help thinking about Fadia's concerns about Tom.

'Certainly. Her eldest son is next in line to rule when he comes of age and the younger brother is the next in line after that. Fadia's sons could provide leverage over the monarchy, which unfortunately is not an uncommon occurrence with our hostile neighbours.'

She was starting to get that.

He shrugged philosophically. 'Fadia needs to come home, at least for the time being, for her and her sons' safety, now she is a widow.'

'I don't suppose it's easy for her. I think she has some friends and a life in Australia.'

His lip curled. 'The friendship of a man who has plans to control a royal widow? A man who pretended to be a friend of her husband, who has helped her remain cut off from her family now she has no husband to protect her?' She could see the implacable intent in his expression. 'What sort of man preys on a young woman like that?'

So he knew a little about this Tom. Okay. But wasn't it Fadia's final decision they needed to wait for? She stamped down her initial unease over saying something. 'She seems to have relied on him in the past.'

His gaze sharpened and she could almost smell the briny scent of storm to come. 'So she has mentioned him?'

She looked away. 'No.' She really didn't think she'd get away with her pitifully thin denial but he wasn't looking at her.

He'd focussed across the room at the windows. 'But has he already found where she is?'

She wasn't touching that assumption. 'Is that why you have a guard in her corridor?'

His gaze returned to her but he declined to answer that question. 'Her marriage and the birth of her sons has been an unexpected development for our family.'

His eyes bored into hers. 'She must come home. But even I would not whisk a new mother with twins away until she has had a chance to recover.'

'And is that your intention?' She could see it was.

His look measured her. 'Yes.' There was no doubt in his mind anyway.

Now they were down to the real thing. Was he the type of man, like her ex-husband, who saw only his own wants and needs? Did he even care about Fadia the person or just her sons? 'Even if she's not a hundred per cent sure she wants to go?'

'I believe it is in her best interests, and the best interests of her babies to return to Zandorro.'

Controlling creep, then. It seemed Fadia's wishes were not in the equation at all. 'You didn't answer my question.'

'Again, you do not understand. It is my prerogative to not answer any question.'

Well, that was straight out. She was on Fadia's side until the young mum definitely decided what she wanted to do. She stood up and he did also. 'I see. Thank you.' Her voice was dry. 'And thank you for seeing me.'

He studied her. Intently. And she felt he could see not just her but right through her. Into her brain. Hopefully not through her clothes. It wasn't a comfortable feeling. 'I found our conversation to have been most illuminating.

'Yes.' Well, she had learned a little. 'Some of it was.'

'Good day, Miss Carmen.' He bowed and a small smile teased at the side of his mouth. The air in the room seemed suddenly more heavily scented, the music dimmed, and his eyes burned into hers. She knew he was thinking of that moment in the lift. She was too. She could feel the flush in her skin, her neck warmed, and yet she couldn't look away. His perusal drifted down and swept the full length of her. And it was as if he'd trailed a feather down her skin. She shivered and his eyes darkened even more.

She needed to get away. 'Good day, Prince Zafar.'

'My word, it is, Miss Carmen.'

CHAPTER THREE

ZAFAR accompanied her to the door and watched her walk away up the corridor. Actually, he couldn't take his eyes off her, even toyed with the idea of calling her back until he realised what he was doing.

Her shapely legs would show to advantage in traditional dress and her formless tunic still did not disguise the lushness of her body. He could quite clearly remember his view from yesterday and had even recognised the scent of her skin next to his today.

Unexpected recognition when he barely remembered any woman since his wife had been killed.

The memory saddened him and pulled his mind away from Fadia's midwife.

Poor, sweet Adele. Theirs had been an arranged marriage, she younger than him, eager to please and expecting her husband to keep her safe. Her broken-hearted family had entrusted him with their precious daughter and he'd failed. The burden of that guilt still weighed heavily on him, the picture of her frightened eyes before the plane crashed haunted him in his sleep.

He hadn't looked at another woman since. Had lost himself in his work until recalled to royal duty.

Now his task was to ensure Fadia and her sons were

safe. Nothing else. But he feared it would not be easy. That was his real problem. He feared. Feared he would not be able to stop something terrible happening. Feared he'd be unable to save Fadia and her sons like he had been unable to save his own family.

Prior to two years ago he's been afraid of nothing. Evil had arrived and until it was conquered he would not be distracted.

His eyes strayed to the empty corridor. Perhaps the midwife could help, though. And so his concentration returned to Carmen as he turned thoughtfully back into his suite. She had braved the lion in his own den. He admired her courage. And she amused him with her determination not to be cowed by his prestige. But she'd lied about Tom.

So the dog might be here in the hotel. He would have Yusuf investigate. And delve into the delightful Miss Carmen's past too. Perhaps she could help his cousin more than they knew, and such information would be useful.

He needed Fadia and the twins well enough to travel as soon as possible. He would feel better when he had them back in Zandorro.

Zafar strode across the room and out the doors onto the balcony, punished himself with the rise of gall in his throat from that height, forced himself to grip the rail and glance down. His gut rolled and he stepped back as he drew breath.

His mind roamed while he stared out over the rolling sea. If he cut off the bustling town below, the ocean seemed not dissimilar to the rolling dunes of his desert, and he could feel a lightening of his mood that normally only came when he retreated to solitude.

A whimsical thought intruded where none normally went. He wondered what Miss Carmen would think of the desert or the ways of a desert prince. It was an unexpected but intriguing scenario.

Carmen clanged the door behind her. Her favourite place. The fire escape. He'd burnt her again. It was criminal to be that handsome and mesmerising. But at least she'd found out Fadia was just a pawn on his gold-embossed chess set and she, Carmen O'Shannessy, didn't like the idea. Or him. If Fadia needed an ally, Carmen was her girl.

It brought back too many unpleasant memories. The way Carl had turned, as early as their honeymoon, swearing at her, keeping her awake with tirades when she'd needed to sleep, wearing her down, demeaning her after a year of desolation until she'd finally accepted the enormity of her mistake and run away. Had moved jobs, states, lost friends until finally she rebuilt her life.

Domineering men did not have a place in her life. She straightened off the door and began her descent. Unfortunately, she could picture this man's wicked smile so easily and the warmth she'd felt.

No. No trust, especially for men who could cool and heat her body with just a glance. So why did she want to run back and relive the sensation? How did that work?

When Carmen opened the door on the sixth floor, of course her friend the guard was still there. He rose from his chair when she appeared and nodded coldly as she walked past him towards her own room at the end of the corridor.

Made a good little enemy there, she thought as she stared past him to the rooms of mums and babies that looked out over the beach. When she reached the end of the corridor the midwife's room welcomed her with a sanctuary, which she couldn't help embracing, from his beady eyes.

So what if her room only held spare supplies? At least she could shut the door—which she did firmly—and lean back against it.

Unfortunately, the barrier didn't stop the thoughts of Zafar that followed. She couldn't remember ever being this unsettled over a man and that loss of control brought unpleasant reminders of her marriage.

Carmen pushed herself off the door and straightened the empty baby cots before energetically restocking the linen from the trolley into her shelves. Still needing distraction, she wiped over the bath equipment and scales she used to weigh the babies.

'Done. Hmm.' She rested her hand on the computer at the desk, but she didn't see any of it. She could see Prince Zafar, though, in her mind's eye, and recalled the way he made her feel.

On Tuesday, refreshed after a full night's sleep, Carmen welcomed the new mothers recently arrived from their birth at the nearby hospital. When she'd finally made it to her room the phone shrilled with neglect.

'Midwife. Can I help you?'

'Carmen? It's Fadia. I've been trying to reach you for ages. There's a new pink rash on Harrison that's a bit pimply. Can you come to my room when you get a minute, please?'

'Sure. Everything else okay?' No word from Tom, she hoped.

'The boys and I are fine otherwise, if that's what you mean.'

Carmen relaxed. 'Is it okay if I check on one of my other mothers first?'

'Oh?'

Carmen smiled into the phone. 'I'll be as quick as I can but might be ten minutes, unless it's urgent.' A little of the privilege she was used to had crept into Fadia's voice. Interesting family. 'That way I can spend longer with you when I get there.'

'Of course. No problem. I'll see you soon.'

The time Carmen spent with the other young mum seemed to fly and she glanced at her watch as she waved goodbye. She needed to arrange times for weights for those who were going home that day but she'd better check the princess first. She made her way to Fadia. With two babies to care for, she needed the most help.

Carmen knocked, then opened the door with her key, and almost walked into Zafar who again was with his cousin.

His black brows rose in disbelief. 'You have a key?'

Carmen shared her own frown. That tone. That arrogance. She wasn't sure why it goaded her so much but thankfully she wasn't one of his underlings. 'Yes. To all the mothers' rooms so they don't have to get up to let me in.'

She tilted her head at him. 'Of course I always knock first.'

Now inscrutable, his 'I'm sure you do' left Carmen seething again. What was it about this man that pressed her buttons? Normally the easiest-going person, just a glance from him was enough to raise her blood pressure, and yet his actions were almost reasonable in the circumstances. So why wasn't her response more tranquil?

She narrowed her eyes at him. Did he think she was in collusion with Tom? 'I hope Fadia is able to rest between feeds. Having you come so often, that is.'

'My cousin would be able to rest if the midwife came immediately when she was asked.'

So now we get to his Excellency's displeasure. Tsk, tsk. Real world. 'Unfortunately, your cousin is not my only patient.'

His lips tightened and he glanced at his watch. 'Then I will arrange it to be so.' There it was, his red rag to her bull.

It's not all about you, buster. 'You will do no such thing, Your Highness.' She stressed the title, more to calm her own urge to throttle him than out of respect. Was this guy for real? The most annoying part was that she couldn't let it show because drama was the last thing Fadia needed. She smiled at her patient before she turned back to the royal pain.

'Perhaps this topic is best saved for a time that isn't taking up your cousin's.' She moved past him. 'Now, Fadia, would you like to show me your baby's rash?'

Zafar's voice floated over her shoulder, blandly. 'I have already told her it is erythema toxicarum, a rash very common in the first three days in newborns.'

Carmen blinked but didn't turn to look at him. Obviously he had a medical advantage he hadn't mentioned. Typical.

'My cousin is a paediatrician and established the new children's hospital in Zandorro before he was recalled to his duty to the monarchy,' Fadia explained.

That would explain his knowledge and also a little

more about why they'd let the twins out so early. She looked at the red pimply rash on Harrison's neck and arms. So he knew what he was talking about.

'He's right. And mums are naturally concerned.' She smiled at Fadia. 'You might find that the rash moves with heat. So if you were to hold Harrison's leg while you changed a nappy you might find the rash had suddenly become more prominent there and less prominent from where it showed a minute ago.'

Zafar was over harmless rashes. 'I agree that my cousin looks tired. Is there a nursery where the babies can go while she sleeps?'

And who had made it easier for her to leave the hospital ward too quickly? Carmen thought. Hmm. 'I'm afraid we don't have that option here. This facility is for transition to home. If Fadia wanted to have the babies minded she could return to the hospital or have a relative stay in the room while she rests.'

She spread her hands. Her look said she doubted Fadia would relax while he was watching over her.

'Or I could hire a mothercraft nurse for you again. Surely that would be easier?' Zafar queried his cousin, but Fadia's eyes pleaded as she shook her head. 'No. Please.'

'For the moment we will do as you wish.' Zafar frowned and Carmen wondered if he was regretting he'd hurried her here.

She watched his face but he gave nothing away. 'I will discuss this with your midwife later today.' It seemed Zafar was choosing to leave this time or was he wary of her asking him to go. Either way, Carmen was pleased she didn't have to fight about it.

Left to their own devices, the women had the babies

fed and settled within the hour. Despite a tantrum from Harry that rattled the windows and an inclination from Bailey to sleep through the feed, finally the curtains closed so Fadia could have a rest.

'You can ring me if they wake and I'll help you get sorted for the feed.'

Fadia nodded sleepily.

'Ring the midwife's room if you get stuck. If I get tied up, the other midwife will be here and I'll see you tomorrow.'

The day seemed to stretch for ever, not unusual after Carmen's run of night duty was finished, but tonight was the second of the four in her week when she could fall into bed and sleep the night through.

As seven o'clock drew closer, she found herself looking forward to a break. Handover took longer than normal for the night midwife because the intricacies of Fadia's case involved so many layers. Finally she was riding down in the lift to the basement on her way home.

'You look exhausted.' Zafar was leaning against her car.

Was that a coincidence or did he really know it was her vehicle? Tiredness suddenly took a back seat to nervous energy. 'I'm feeling a little wired after today. Strange men who recognise my car make me even more cross.'

He smiled, unperturbed, but offered no explanation as he watched her.

She tapped her foot with irritability—not nervous energy. She wished he'd go away. Almost. 'Did you want something, Prince Zafar? Apart from to tell me that I look tired, which was very kind. Thank you.'

Zafar pushed himself off her bonnet and loomed in

front of her. 'I wish to invite you to walk with me. Even tired, you are lovely.'

Yeah, right. Lovely with little sleep. She resisted the urge to step back. A walk? 'Now? It's almost dark.' She narrowed her eyes. Kidnapping had been mentioned. 'Why?'

He shrugged. 'Because it would be good to get out of the hotel. Walk along the cliff top. What is it you say? Blow away the cobwebs? That is one of the things I miss most about Australia. The graphic expressions.'

So he'd lived here before. It had been an endless twenty-four hours but his background and history couldn't but intrigue some part of her. Had he lived here before he was a prince perhaps? A young doctor? That made him more normal. She met those every day.

The idea of walking in the fresh air before driving to her solitary flat was tempting. Let the stresses of the day be whisked into the salty breeze that blew a mere hundred metres away. It held some attraction, as did the idea of hearing a little about this enigmatic man in front of her.

'Perhaps a short one. I sleep better with exercise.'

'So obliging,' he mocked gently.

Carmen glanced at her car, shrugged her shoulders, and added, 'Or I could go home now.'

He smiled. And what a smile. The most spontaneous grin she'd seen. 'I am walking. Would you care to accompany me?' Still optional, and it seemed she did want to go because her legs made their own decision and followed him up the ramp like she was on a string.

It was still light, towards the last before sunset, but the salty tang of ocean breeze made her glad she'd ventured out.

She didn't know what made her look back—in truth, she'd forgotten about his bodyguard—but Yusuf was there in the lee of the building, watching them. His eyes met hers coldly.

Zafar saw her frown and with a flick of his wrist banished the man from sight.

He wasn't sure why it had been so important to spend time with this woman. His brain had suggested a discussion about Fadia but his mood had lifted as soon as she'd stepped out of the lift. How did she do that? And did he want her to?

They waited at the traffic lights and strangely the silence was not heavy between them. His interest in the companionship of a woman had been absent for the last two years and yet her company made him feel light and free.

They chatted about his homeland and his love of the desert until the 'Walk' sign propelled them across the road and down to the cobbled path that ran around the headland.

'I've never been to the desert.'

'It is very beautiful and harsh.' He smiled down at her. 'Like some Australian women.'

What was it about her that captured his interest? He glanced at her. Perhaps it was the genuine empathy she could feel for his cousin. Perhaps her obvious lack of ulterior motive. Or her transparent emotions that enticed him to savour her moods, even when she annoyed her. He felt his mouth curve until he realised what he was doing. He was not here for this.

Carmen ignored the teasing inherent in that remark and stamped down the excitement she could feel growing at his company. This was not good. They were worlds apart and she didn't need to fall for another domineering man. But she could enjoy her walk and satisfy her curiosity. No strings attached. 'So, if you are a prince, do you have a palace?' A little tongue in cheek. He probably lived in a nice house in the city.

'My brother and I each have our own palace in the mountains, and share service to our grandfather at his palace in Zene, the capital of Zandorro.'

Oh. She hadn't actually thought he was that grand. It was all too fairy-tale but it made her feel safer that he wouldn't be interested in an ordinary midwife. 'What about an oasis in the desert with tents?'

It was as if he'd read her mind. 'Absolutely. You would not believe it.'

'Lawrence of Arabia?' They smiled at each other. 'Tell me.'

He shrugged, amused. 'A true Bedouin camp is a little earthier than mine. My oasis belonged to a tourist company that went bankrupt. I bought them out when I could have just waited for them to leave but the karma is good. I use it for business negotiations when Western wives accompany their husbands. Their fantasies are always good business. Bathing in oils, traditional dress for the meal. I think you might enjoy it.'

It could be fun. 'Are you saying Westerners are easily swayed by that fantasy?' She was having a few pretty pictures of her own. She smiled at him. 'I'm all for fantasies as long as I can get off when I want to.'

Zafar watched her face. Saw the dreamy expression in her eyes change as she thought of something unpleasant. He felt his own mood lower in response.

He realised he'd like to see this kind woman pampered, cosseted, cared for. The worries of the world removed from her lovely shoulders. Perhaps one day, when he was not called to royal duty and all this was over, he might come back and search her out. See if she still wanted to see the desert.

It was an intriguing idea he shouldn't consider and it seemed her curiosity was greater about his time in her own country. 'So you've lived here before?'

He looked across at her as they walked past the old baths. 'My mother was buried in Sydney.'

'Did she leave Zandorro late in life?'

He put his hand on her elbow to steer her safely aside as a pushbike rider pedalled past. Her skin was like silk yet taut with youth and vibrancy. He could feel the impact of her arm on his fingers.

Touching her skin was too distracting. Zafar let his hand drop. Too soft yet supple, too enticing, and he had no right to touch her. Guilt swamped him. How could he forget his wife so easily? Just two years and for the first time he was burdened with the beginnings of lust. For a woman so different from his beloved.

So why did he want to capture this woman's hand and bump his hip against hers as they walked? Why now, suddenly, did he see Carmen as attractive when for ages he'd barely acknowledged other women existed? What was it about her? He glanced at her animated face as she waited for an answer. What had she'd asked? Ah, yes. His mother.

'Yes, my mother left Zandorro when my father died. She married an Australia diplomat a few years later.'

He didn't want to think about how she'd left him and his brother behind in their grandfather's care. How much they'd missed the brief chances to feel her gentle love and support, which they'd taken for granted in their busy lives. It hadn't been until he'd demanded he come to university here that he'd learned the truth. She'd had no choice if she'd wanted a life for herself and the hour or two each day she saw her sons hadn't filled the gap his father had left.

Her face was turned to him. Not passive attention but real empathy in her gaze. 'So where did you live when you were here?'

And he was allowing her truths he shared with no one. 'With my mother and her husband all through university. Then I bought a house near theirs until I completed my time as registrar three years ago.'

'So you worked here as well?'

'I studied under Dr Ting at Bay Hospital.' They had been good years and he'd taken innovative ideas back to Zandorro and set up a state-of-the-art paediatric hospital in Zene. He'd been bitten by passion, obsessed with creating a better place for sick children, research for hope, and he had achieved a lot of that dream.

He had the sudden urge to tell her but that had all been before he'd had to hand it on and take over his royal duties.

Dr Ting? Carmen was stunned. 'So you're a consultant?' If he'd been under the eminent paediatrician, he was no slouch. No amount of money would have secured the radical but brilliant Dr Ting's agreement unless Zafar was worthy. She looked at him with new respect. 'I'm impressed.'

He frowned. 'Don't be. I'm unable to practise as much as I wish.' Such was the despair in his voice she backed away from the topic. This guy could create tension with just a word and she wasn't used to that. More layers she didn't understand and more reasons for her to be careful.

The silence had a bite to it now. Something had happened to stop his work. She wondered but shied away from digging. 'The view is spectacular along this path.'

The darkness in his tone made the water in front lose its sparkle. Such was his presence that the idea didn't even seem too fanciful. Maybe night was just coming on more swiftly than she'd anticipated?

They walked quite briskly along the cliff past the steps to the ladies' baths and onto the wide grassed area near the playground. Suddenly she noticed the families gathering blankets and children under their arms. She turned curiously to survey the way they'd come. A summer storm threatened, and she lifted her hand to point it out when she was distracted by a young woman in a pretty sarong, kneeling on the grass. At first Carmen thought she was praying.

As she drew level the woman moaned and they both stopped. The woman's glittering, pain-filled eyes made Carmen draw breath and they both crossed over to her.

Carmen rested her hand gently on her shoulder. 'You okay?'

The woman moistened her lips. 'No. My baby.'

Must be the month for pregnant women to be out and about alone in labour, Carmen thought as she glanced around. In fact, the busy park lay almost deserted as the cooler breeze sprang up. 'Are you in pain or have your waters broken?'

The young woman laughed, a little hysterically. 'Both.' She turned her head and she, too, realised they were the only people left. Her eyes sought Carmen's. 'I'm so scared. The pains are coming like a freight train.

You won't leave me?' The woman stopped and moaned as she tried to catch her breath.

'Ambulance, please, Zafar?' Carmen glanced at her companion, who nodded and raised his phone to make the call, and Carmen knelt down beside her. 'What's your name?'

'Jenny.'

'I'm Carmen, Jenny. And this is Zafar. Is this your first baby?'

The woman nodded. Carmen's shoulders relaxed a little so hopefully they'd have time to transport. 'Can you stand? We've called an ambulance. Would you like to move to the bench?'

Jenny looked at the short distance to the bench. 'No. I'm too scared to move. I need to stay like this.'

Carmen's eyebrows rose. She glanced at the roomy sarong. It was one of those tube ones held up by elastic, and she decided the woman was probably as comfortable kneeling as she'd be anywhere and at least she was covered for privacy.

Carmen smiled to herself. They could probably have a baby under that sarong and nobody would notice.

At work most of her births were in the semi-dark and by feel anyway, but surely it wouldn't come to that.

'That's fine. Your comfort's the most important thing while we wait for the ambulance.'

She exchanged glances with Zafar and he nodded. She had support. All was good.

'So I'm guessing the contractions are pretty powerful?' The girl nodded. 'Well, you're breathing really well. It's so important not to get scared.'

'I'm freaking here,' Jenny ground out. 'It should not be this quick.'

Carmen pressed her hand into Jenny's shoulder. 'You're doing great. They say fear's your worst enemy. I try to remember that when things happen that scare the socks off me. Birth isn't an enemy—it's nature's way. Everything will be okay if a little unusual in setting.'

Jenny shook her head. Emphatically. 'It still shouldn't be this quick.'

'Sometimes that happens,' Zafar said reassuringly. 'Carmen's a midwife and I'm a paediatrician. We know babies.'

'So someone up there's looking after you.' Carmen sent Zafar an ironic glance that she hoped she was ready. 'And babies are spontaneous and pretty tough. Do you want to slip off your underwear in case? Might be tricky otherwise.'

Zafar compressed his lips to hide his smile. The woman was clearly terrified but Carmen had it all well in hand. He could only observe, uselessly. There wasn't a lot he could do without interfering and he was afraid he couldn't achieve the same degree of calm she had with so little time. But he was more than willing if there were complications with the newborn.

Jenny shook her head. 'I don't want to move from here.'

'And we can work with that if we have to.' Carmen tilted her head down lower so the woman could see her face. 'If your baby is born, I'll catch and pop him or her through your legs to you at the front. Do you understand?'

The woman moaned and then a look of surprise and horror crossed her face. 'This can't be happening.' Her eyes darted around as if the ambulance would suddenly appear.

'It's about to happen.' Carmen looked at Zafar to back her up if needed. She knew an imminent birth when she heard one. Her voice was serene as she repeated, 'Afterwards, just lift your baby and put it against your skin under your dress and pop your baby's head out the neckline. The length of the umbilical cord will tell you how high to lift it. Okay?'

'Oh, no-o-o-o,' Jenny wailed, then groaned as she suddenly she eased her panties off.

Carmen rolled the woman's underwear up neatly as it appeared under the dress and Zafar decided that no doubt she had a use for that too.

He was reminded of her calmness in the lift and it was the same here. As if she was saying that having a baby in the park was no big deal. She was very focussed and even the woman looked as though things might be fine after all.

A mindset that had seemed a pretty big ask two minutes ago. Why wasn't he surprised?

He should really say something more but he was only a spectator at the moment, an appreciative one, unless his skills were required. He hadn't used them enough lately. 'We'll be here for you and your baby until the ambulance comes.' He copied the same calm tone Carmen used then stripped off his jacket and bundled it up like a pillow to keep the warmth inside for the baby when born. He had no doubt Carmen would manage most of the impending birth.

It had been several years since he'd worked on a neonate and a nice natural birth was not something he'd expected along a cliff path. He hoped this baby was well because he didn't fancy resuscitation out here in the freshening breeze, but they would manage what they had to. The ambulance wouldn't be too far away.

The woman groaned and he focussed back on the present. Carmen had shifted around behind Jenny, shielding her from the path and lifting her dress slightly. 'Head-on view,' she murmured, and held her hands either side of the baby's head. He wished he'd had gloves he could have given her but doubted she'd give it a thought at this moment.

The sound of the ambulance in the distance overlaid the sound of Jenny's breathing. All the while in the background the crash of the surf on the cliffs melded with the moment of expectation and added to the surreal, amazing, incredible moment he hadn't anticipated.

'Here it comes,' Carmen said calmly. 'You're doing beautifully.'

Jenny moaned, the baby's head appeared, and then slowly the little face swivelled to face the mother's thigh. Seconds later a shoulder and then two arms eased into Carmen's hands in a tangle of limbs and cord and water and the baby gasped at the cold air on wet skin and cried loudly as his legs and feet slid out.

Zafar smiled at the swollen scrotum. Definitely a boy. 'Hello there, young man.' Then the memories rushed in. His own son. Limp and lifeless.

Zafar quickly wiped the little boy over with the warm inner lining of his jacket to dry him a little so he wouldn't be chilled and then Carmen fed him between his mother's legs into her waiting hands.

Zafar listened to her voice from a distance as he shook his head to shut out the clarity of the past. His own joy at Samir's birth. The look between he and

Adele at the moment of birth. The summit of their expectations. His family.

Then family lost. Both dead and buried. The bleakness of loss washed over him until the newborn cried
again and he shook himself. This was not his son. This
baby was vigorous and healthy and beginning life on a
windswept headland.

'Oh, well done, Jenny.' Carmen's voice. It was over.
Incredible.

He heard Carmen mumble, 'Nice long cord, that's
handy.'

Handy, he thought. Such a handy length of cord, and
suddenly his mouth tilted, the painful memories receded
and the miracle of new life made his lips curve into a
smile he wouldn't have believed possible a moment ago.

Women amazed him, these two in particular, and the
memory of the last ten minutes would no doubt make
him smile for years.

Carmen glanced across at him and his smile broad-
ened. 'Very handy,' he said.

She frowned and then remembered what she said.
He mouthed, 'Handy cord,' and she grinned at him then
back at the mother.

Within fifteen minutes the ambulance had arrived,
the officers took over, and he and Carmen stepped
back. Zafar was glad to see the officers offer towels
and hand steriliser to Carmen, who blithely washed
herself down. His jacket had been bagged for cleaning
because Carmen wouldn't let him put it in the bin.

'You could reminisce when you put that on,' she'd
said. He doubted he'd wear it but she had a point. His
mouth curved again.

Soon mother and baby were tucked into the back

of the vehicle with blankets, everyone was happy with their condition, and with the air-conditioner set on warm they were ready to go.

Zafar dropped his arm around Carmen's shoulder and pulled her body in next to his as they watched the flashing lights disappear. She fitted into the side of his body too well and he fought to keep the moment platonic because for him something had changed. Not just in the way he felt about this amazing woman but about the colour of the world.

The idea of new life in unexpected places, perhaps even the easing of the pain he'd carried since that fateful hijacking two years ago when he'd lost so much, and now for the first time he felt hopeful.

He frowned. Because of Jenny's birth? An unknown woman's son? Or because of the midwife? Perhaps he did owe some of this amazing feeling to this woman. And again, outside his usual experience, she genuinely didn't want anything in return for the blessings she'd given him.

CHAPTER FOUR

'It's almost dark,' she said.

Zafar, too, had noticed. 'Indeed, I fear we're in for a storm.'

'Good grief, look at that.' While they'd been busy a new weather front had rolled towards them and looked worlds nastier than a summer storm.

He glanced up at the wall of cloud that rolled like dark oil off a cliff, grey and black clouds with angry faces shape-shifted as they lit.

Zafar gestured her to precede him. 'I think we should return more quickly.'

'You think?' she muttered, and scooted along in front of him, but it was too late.

He pulled her into the lee of a bull-nosed iron picnic shed just as a sheet of rain blew across the path. They were instantly splattered with pea-sized drops followed by a deafening crack as a bolt of lighting exploded into the ground on the cliff edge. Carmen jumped and he tightened his arms around her. Felt her shudder beneath his hands.

Zafar loved storms but it seemed Carmen had her own phobias. At least he wasn't the only one with irrational fears. 'Shh. We'll be fine here.' It seemed so long since he'd held a woman to comfort her, felt his chest expand with the need to protect, set his feet more firmly as if to ward off anything that would threaten her.

The briny scent of ozone seared his nostrils and two seconds later thunder directly overhead rattled the roof of their shed like a giant hand had slammed their pitiful shelter with a baseball bat.

Carmen shuddered. Zafar's arms felt so safe around her and instinctively she tucked her forehead into his chest. His shirt was fine but thin and she could feel the corded muscle rock solid beneath her cheek, warm and welcoming, and the steady thud of his heartbeat in her ear.

The spice of an exotic aftershave, one that made her think of souks and incense, made her bury her nose and banished the smell of rain and ozone with a big shuddering inhalation. It was just that she hated storms. She'd always been afraid of storms.

'I'm not enjoying this thunder,' she mumbled shakily into his shirt when finally the ringing in her ears made talking possible. She ignored the tiny voice inside her that wondered if this time she told the whole truth.

He leant down and even the warmth of his breath calmed her as he spoke into her hair, 'We will stay until the lightning has passed.'

There was no sign he would loosen his embrace and she was quietly pleased about that. There was something primal about the extreme force of nature around them and she knew about the danger of reckless exposure.

She should distract herself from the storm and think about Jenny and her new baby but, come to think of it,

Zafar's arms kept the outside world at bay like a force field, a zone she was very happy to be within.

To her disgust she snuggled deeper into the haven he afforded. It was so darned reassuring to be wrapped firmly in strong arms against this amazing wall of masculine strength and, to be honest, that first bolt of lightning had given her the willies. 'Just let me know when you're ready to move,' she mumbled into his chest.

He shifted his mouth until his breath was warm in her ear again. 'I was thinking of making a move now.' And squeezed her arms with teasing pressure. His voice was low and with a distinct thread of humour she couldn't miss, along with overtones of seduction. She felt the tug of her own smile.

The guy knew how to make the most of situations. She unearthed her nose from his shirt and looked up at him, but she had to lean back in his arms to gain some distance. 'No cheating.'

'Third time lucky?' Dark and dangerous eyes were brimful of wicked intent. 'I won't ask for anything you're unwilling to give,' he murmured as his head descended. 'But I will ask...'

The heat. That was her first thought as her traitorous mouth accepted and then returned his kiss with precocious enthusiasm. What was this recognition, as if she'd been joined to this mouth many times before? How could that be?

He bent again, less gently, and the kiss deepened, became more sensual than she'd imagined, more insidiously addictive than she'd bargained for.

Carmen merged into the burning pressure of his lips against hers, the drugging assault as their bodies melded, and the rising heat between that mocked the puny storm around them. Then the coolness of his leaving as he skimmed her neck with hot lips, leaving his own trail of electrical activity where before there'd been the chill of sleeting rain.

When he bent to brush his mouth between her breasts she felt her nipples jump like bobbing corks in a sudden sea of arousal. She had to hang on or she'd fall down. Her fingers slid up to bury themselves in hair like strands of silk beneath her fingertips, until she forgot that sensation in a host of new ones as he tipped her backwards over his arm like the marauder he was and suddenly she felt like ripping open the buttons of her shirt to give him access.

Then he was back at her mouth and she was drowning.

A scatter of drips from the leaking roof splashed her hair and annoyingly penetrated the fog of arousal. Good grief. She'd kissed him back as wildly as he'd kissed her, for heaven's sake.

If she wasn't careful, he'd take her on the picnic table behind them and she'd blithely wrap her legs around him with delight. She pushed her hand against his chest and eased at least her chest out of his embrace. What was she turning into?

'Whoa there, cowboy.'

He stopped, looked down at her, stared for a moment and then to her surprise he threw back his head and laughed. Really laughed. And if she'd thought him a handsome man before, this laughing god was a million light years ahead of any man she'd seen before.

He eased her away slowly, almost unpeeling her from where they were plastered together at the hip, and with both hands he straightened her shirt. 'I'm sorry.' He raised his brows with amusement still vivid in his face. 'Cowgirl…' He put her from him. 'You are without doubt the most original woman. It is fortunate one of us has their wits about them.'

'You're pretty special yourself,' she muttered as she increased the distance between them. Where had that sensual onslaught come from? And no little peck. Good grief. She couldn't remember a kiss like that, ever. A year of marriage hadn't prepared her for that. That mother of all kisses and she'd let him. Encouraged him. But what else was a girl to do when snuggled into a man such as Zafar in a picnic shelter during an electrical storm? Not that!

She needed to get clear of this guy because already she was like one of those puddles the storm had just dumped. Wet, formless, muddied with lust.

She glanced around and the inky front was noticeably lighter above them as it rolled out to sea. 'It seems to be passing. Let's get out of here.'

He'd distanced himself from her too. She could feel it. Good. Maybe he regretted their ignition as well. He removed the phone from his pocket, dialled, spoke, and then tucked it away. 'Yusuf will pick us up from across the grass.'

'We can walk.' As she finished speaking a long black car pulled up opposite the park. So the henchman had been out there waiting in the storm anyway. She shivered. So now she was cold without Zafar holding her? What the heck was she doing when she got close to this guy? Apparently whatever he wanted.

She needed to remember he was from his own world, with his own rules. Rules that differed from hers no matter that he'd worked here for a while.

Zafar pondered Carmen's silence and staunch independence as he slid into the car after her but he pondered his own response more. What had happened? The heat they'd created between them, the shock of unexpected connection had rocked him. But perhaps it had just been his body requiring sex. Either way, it was not something to rush. As was the change he could sense in himself. Very unsettling. He filed away the fire between them in the storm for future thought.

For the moment he had decided he needed to secure her services for his cousin. And he did not want her caring for other women, only available for them. This was certainly a new direction for his usually solitary thoughts.

'I believe we were going to discuss the possibility of you caring for Fadia as your only client.'

She shifted beside him and avoided his eyes. 'There is no discussion.' Her words were clipped as if her mind was elsewhere and did not want to be disturbed.

Almost in panic? Why did that amuse him? So she could sense the strangeness of the shift too. 'That is not an answer. More a knee-jerk reaction, I believe they call it.'

'I have a knee if you want one,' she muttered, and he wondered if he had been supposed to hear that. Such a physical woman. More clearly, she said, 'I'm afraid I can't help you.'

Why was she so sure of herself? She did not know him. Still, this woman could be most annoying.

He restrained himself from correcting her. 'Because…?'

What was so absorbing outside the car that she must look past him out the window?

'Because I have two jobs already.'

Of course. She worked at the hospital. Fadia had said Carmen had been her midwife at the birth. No doubt that's why she looked so tired. The money answer would be the simplest one. 'And why have you two jobs?'

'That's none of your business.'

He caught Yusuf's eye in the mirror and his driver nodded. Not yet but it soon would be. Perhaps Yusuf already had gleaned some information.

She went on, militantly, so he had annoyed her with his questions. He suppressed his smile. 'If you wish Fadia to have a personal mothercraft nurse, of course you can arrange that, but it won't be me.'

'I was thinking a professional midwife to act as flight assistant for Fadia for the trip to Zandorro and to help her settle in.' Such a prickly woman.

'No. Thank you.'

'A week or two only?' The look she gave him suggested a change of topic. 'Let's leave that for the moment. Tell me how this baby hotel works. Do all the midwives work at both here and the labour wards at the hospital?'

She frowned as if collecting her thoughts. 'How did you know I worked at both places?'

'My cousin told me, remember?' He liked her off balance.

She narrowed her eyes at him but then looked away past him again before she said, 'I do the occasional night shift at the hospital as well as this. Yes.'

She was lying again and he wondered why. Fadia had said she worked nights every Friday, Saturday, Sunday, and worked day shifts on the five weekdays. That meant two double shifts a week. She had to be exhausted.

Every time she did not tell the truth she looked away. A hopeless liar. Then again, that was not a bad thing.

She answered a question he'd moved on from in his head and it took a moment for him to refocus.

'We have eight beds on floors five and six that are kept in the hotel for the private patients who transfer from the hospital. Most new mothers stay two to four days before they go home.'

Ah. His question about the baby hotel. He was interested in the concept. It could work in Zandorro. Perhaps even for the children's hospital. 'So after the birth, when they wish, mothers transfer here?'

'That's right. As Fadia did. If their birth was uncomplicated. And their doctors will visit. The beauty of the hotel as opposed to the hospital is the mother's support people can stay. Friends can visit less rigidly than in a hospital.'

She hurried on as if to avoid the topic and he had no difficulty understanding why. She looked away again. He fought back a smile. Her complicity with Fadia was not something he wished to bring up now.

'In fact,' she said, 'up to two other children could also stay with the parents in their rooms, and the access of the midwife means the transition period to home is less stressful than a busy ward in the hospital or the return to full household duties at home.'

'And the midwife provides what?'

'Help with feeding problems, settling techniques and to talk about postnatal needs out of the hospital environment. The hotel provides food and housekeeping.'

She shrugged. 'The lovely part here is the view. Mums can gaze over the beach from their balcony. It's a great place to regather their resources before they go home.'

His attention was caught. Regather their resources. He liked that. Just looking at Carmen regathered his resources. He hadn't realised just how low his reserves had fallen until the lift incident and the more he saw of this woman, the more alive he felt.

It seemed some time with the delectable Carmen could even be as beneficial as the solitary sojourn in the desert he'd prescribed himself. He would see what Yusuf turned up.

'That is all very interesting.' He glanced ahead to where they would pull in as the car glided to a stop. 'We are back. Thank you for accompanying me and my apologies for your exposure to the weather.'

'I doubt even you have control over the weather.' She gave him a little mocking smile he did not appreciate then raised her hand to open her own door.

He was pleased to see her start of surprise when it opened from the outside. She would learn a woman should be cared for and protected.

Carmen didn't like this henchman of Zafar's. This man with a scar who did his master's bidding unsettled her. Judging by the cold expression on Yusuf's face, the feeling was mutual.

Still, another two or three days and the lot of them would be gone. She hoped Fadia decided sensibly but it was none of her business.

She glanced back inside the car but Zafar had exited and moved to her side. 'Oh. Here you are. Goodnight.'

He reached, took her hand, bowed over it briefly and then deliberately turned her fingers to expose her wrist before he lifted it to his mouth.

The kiss lingered, with subtle eroticism, and her response to the intimate caress was totally unexpected. Still not fully recovered from the passion in the storm, his mouth sent shock waves surging back through her that weakened her knees. She hoped that explained the absolute melting of every bone in her body as soon as his lips touched her skin. Good grief.

She turned away shakily, ignored the expressionless face of Yusuf, and passed through the doors into the lobby to use the lift to the car park. She doubted her suddenly wobbly legs would be able to traverse the steep driveway down to her car without her falling over.

Her wrist burned like a brand and she rode down the lift with it covered with her other hand. Get a grip, she warned herself fiercely. He's just a man. You're just out of practice and your hormones pulled the rug out from under you.

The drive home passed in a blur, automatic pilot obedient, as her brain whirled and her eyes strayed to her wrist near the steering-wheel. What was she doing? What was he doing? Did he have intentions of seduction and if so, why? Did he want his cousin watched so badly he thought she might be useful?

Was she tempted?

When she arrived at the door of her block of flats a group of youths called out and weaved towards her. A bottle smashed into the gutter across the road and, not surprisingly, she fumbled with the lock. The outside light had broken and she dropped her keys in the dark. She hated it when that happened.

Someone approached the youths and spoke to them. Whatever was said worked because they turned and walked hurriedly back the other way. Her neck prickled and she resisted the urge to peer into the gloom at her good Samaritan across the road. Which was ridiculous, wasn't it?

She glanced uneasily over her shoulder before bending down and scooping the keys from the cold tiles. Her eyes were scratchy with tiredness and she just hoped that blasted Zafar hadn't interfered with her ability to sleep.

Managing the next four days depended on this good night's sleep before she started work at lunchtime tomorrow and Thursday, then after work on Friday night duty would begin again.

She felt frustration gather as she contemplated the unrelenting schedule. As Tilly had said, working seven days a week was crazy but it was only for another six months until she'd paid all the debts her husband had left her with and she'd be free. She wanted her credit rating back.

That was when she'd been offered the baby hotel job, which paid well, and for the moment she had her head above water. If she needed to work seven days a week for another few months, at least she loved both her jobs.

Carmen stripped off her clothes, hurriedly showered and fell into bed.

Lord, she was tired.

Carmen slept despite being seduced by her dreams, wonderful, stretch-like-a-cat-and-purr dreams, and the wisps of memories remained when the sun rose and left her with a small kink in her lips that peeped out while she brushed her teeth.

'You need a swim,' she admonished the sultry-eyed woman in the mirror. 'In fact, you need a freezing cold shower.' But her skin belonged to a womanly her and not the machine-like work person she'd turned into, even if her 'admirer' was some nebulous dream man with a magical mouth. She rubbed her arms. Scrummy dreams, whatever they'd been.

Life seemed a lot more interesting than it had two days ago and she couldn't pretend it had nothing to do with a certain dark-eyed sheikh.

She glanced out the cramped window of her room to see the sun shining onto the road, enticing her to play. She hadn't done much of that for a while either; more work and worry than play. The morning stretched ahead before her baby hotel shift at one p.m. and she decided to pack a small lunch and head to the beach.

Coogee glittered with tourists. Sun-loving mums toted babies to play in the waves and reminded her why she'd preferred to live in a bedsit here than a unit somewhere else.

Carmen dropped her towel and bag on the white sand and shed her sarong, along with the cares of the last few months. Life was too short and the waves beckoned with their walls of cheeky fish daring her to join them. The fish scattered into white wash as she splashed through the tingling freshness of the surf with a grin on her face.

Zafar watched her run in his direction. She hadn't seen him because her smile was carefree, oblivious, and outshone even the brightness of the sparkling bay.

So this visceral response was not from the emotions of an unexpected birth or a wild storm.

His body quickened with the promise of her bare skin close to his. There was no doubt this woman drew him like mythical mermaids drew sailors to rocks, attraction destined for disaster if he wasn't careful, but still he pushed through the wash towards her. Why he felt so alive posed a threat to his peace of mind. But that was for later.

She surfaced and wiped the sea water out of her beautiful eyes, squeezing and shaking her hair like a boisterous puppy, but it was the jiggle of her body that deepened his voice as he hailed her.

'I had forgotten the delights of an Australian beach.' He watched her face change from carefree to careful and the sight saddened him. He didn't know why, just that in the last two years he would never have noticed such a thing.

Obviously he'd startled her. 'Prince Zafar?' But she recovered quickly. He was beginning to think this woman would recover in any circumstances.

'We are not in a formal situation. Please, Zafar.'

He saw the crinkle of amusement in her eyes as she glanced around at the water and the frolicking children. 'No. Not formal at all.' She might even be laughing at him and he didn't mind if she was because it was worth it to see her expression become more relaxed. How strange.

'Is this what you do before work?'

'Not enough. But I'm going to make concerted effort to do it more often.' She looked away from him and spread her arms. 'Isn't it glorious?'

His blood thrummed despite his intent to retain his self-respect. 'The view is indeed spectacular.'

He needed to direct his energies elsewhere or he would pull that delicious body against him and who knew where that would lead? 'Do you swim well?'

'Better than you,' she tossed over her shoulder as she dived into the next wave and struck out for the centre of the bay.

A challenge. We will see, he thought with satisfaction as he followed her with a powerful overarm stroke that soon had them level out past the breakers. They stopped and floated. 'You were saying?'

She grinned across at him and a wave slapped her in the cheek. She choked and coughed. He laughed back at her and she trod water until she had her breath again.

She tossed her head. 'You might have speed but I could swim all day.'

He raised his brows and his voice lowered. 'In my youth I was famous for my stamina.'

To his delight she blushed. So she had been thinking of him. A delectable warning of danger for both of them. 'A race to the beach, then.'

She didn't answer. Just turned and swam, and this time he outpaced her so that when she arrived, breathless, he was waiting for her. She swam well. As well as any woman he'd seen, but she'd pushed herself hard to catch him. A hint of competitiveness he admired. He couldn't help teasing her.

'Such rapid breathing.' And a delightful sight he enjoyed as her breasts rose and fell. 'Perhaps you would like me to carry you up to your towel?'

She stood up and rested her hands on her knees to catch her breath. 'Never. I would rather crawl before then.'

'I believe you.' He inclined his head. Then words came unexpectedly. 'Perhaps we could share lunch before you go to work?'

She shook her head. 'I don't think it's a good idea to have lunch with one of my patient's relatives.'

Or for him to give in to the temptation to know this

woman more. Yet… Ridiculous. Who would presume to judge? 'I see nothing wrong with it.'

She tilted her head at him as if he were some object from outer space. 'Of course you don't.'

Truly, other people's opinions of him were the last of his worries. 'You are afraid?'

She narrowed her eyes at him and he withheld his satisfied smile. She didn't like that. Baiting this woman warmed his cold soul when it shouldn't.

'Then only if I pay my share.' Capitulation, though not complete, was sweet. It had been a long time since he'd tasted sweet.

But he did not charge women for food. He shrugged. 'Not possible.'

'Then you eat on your own.' She began to wade through the water towards the beach, not looking to see if he followed. He wondered if she knew she drew him like magnet as he watched the swing of her hips. It was indeed an unexpectedly glorious day.

'Perhaps you would wish to pay for my meal.'

She stopped and looked back at him and a small throaty chuckle delighted him. 'You're on.'

Fanciful thought.

CHAPTER FIVE

AT THE baby hotel later that afternoon in midwife hand-over, Carmen heard that Fadia and her babies were managing splendidly.

They went on to discuss the other mothers and their plans for discharge. As she took over the care Carmen left Fadia until last, because no doubt that'd be the longest visit. That way the other families would know where she was if they needed her urgently. One mention of twins and the mums were instantly sympathetic.

Yusuf was not at his usual post and outside Fadia's door she knocked and waited a moment for Fadia's call to come in before she used her key. A tall, swarthy man approached her and Carmen instantly recognised him from the photograph.

'Excuse me? You are the midwife?' He smiled, eyed her up and down, and she didn't feel flattered.

'Yes?' She withdrew her hand from the door lock.

'I wish to visit my friend, Fadia Smith. Can you tell me which room she is in?'

'I'm sorry.' She smiled at him. 'Or I could, but then I'd have to kill you.' Not the time for levity. As soon as the words left her mouth she regretted them. His face darkened and he looked even more like her ex-husband. She could feel the menace. Ironically appropriate?

Before anything else could be said, Zafar appeared from the fire escape and the man took one look at him and turned to disappear down the corridor in the direction of the other lifts.

Fadia's voice floated through the door. 'Come in. Is that you, Carmen?' Carmen looked at Zafar and his frown as he came towards her and decided discretion was the better part of valour.

She swiped the card and opened the door. 'Yes.' She stepped inside and held the door for Zafar as if nothing had happened.

His eyes held hers. 'Did he threaten you?'

'No. But he might have. I think your timing was good.'

'I hope it continues to be so.'

He opened his mouth to say more but she shook her head as she mouthed, 'Later'. He walked past her into the room and nodded at his cousin. 'You look rested.'

'Thank you.' Fadia smiled at them both and looked much happier. 'They've been perfect. They're sleeping now.'

'I will return shortly.' Zafar nodded and swept out again and Fadia raised her brows.

'Zafar was coming down the corridor just as you called for me to come in. Maybe he thought I was going to throw him out again.' They both tried not to smile. 'So tell me. They've both been sleeping?'

'Since just before lunch. I managed by myself. I can't believe it.'

'They'll wake up soon and maybe even for the next twenty-four hours will want lots of feeds. Be prepared.

Then it will settle down. You're doing amazingly well. It'll soon be easier.' She was talking to Fadia but her mind was elsewhere. Judging by the expression on Zafar's face, he'd taken off after Fadia's thwarted visitor.

It was all unsettling but as long as Fadia was not unsettled then useless speculation wouldn't help anyone and it was her job to help.

Carmen went through the bath routine and by the time they'd finished it was almost time for tea.

'I'll be off to see the other ladies. Just give me a ring if you need me. Maybe you could sit out on the veranda afterwards. That way you can enjoy the view over the beach.'

Fadia nodded. 'One day my boys will be big enough to run on the sand.' They both smiled at the distant future.

The whole shift passed without Zafar since that brief sighting in the corridor, which she would have liked to discuss, but the opportunity didn't arise.

She noticed Yusuf in the limo as she drove out of the car park on the way home. What went on in the henchman's head? she wondered, and then decided she didn't want to know. Whatever it was, his master had ordered it.

The next day, as Carmen approached Fadia's room, she could hear distressed babies and their mother's sobs through the door.

'Fadia?' She used the keycard that hung around her neck to get in. The noise dumped on her like a wall of sand from a collapsed sandcastle and hastily she shut the door.

'Fadia? You okay?' She could see she wasn't.

The young mother lay face down on the bed, shuddering into the mattress, the twins bellowed, red-faced and in unison as they waved tight little fists in their cots. Locked in with them for a moment, Carmen felt every minute of lost of sleep from the last two months. Then her brain kicked into gear.

Babies first to lower the noise level seemed a good place to start. She unwrapped Harrison, deftly changed his sodden nappy, which slowed the high-pitched roar to a hiccough, and re-wrapped him in a new bunny rug, before placing him back in his cot.

Then she did the same for Bailey and popped him in with his brother so the two tiny wrapped bundles lay facing each other with little frowns.

'Fadia. Sit up, honey. What's happened?' The young woman sobbed more dramatically into her sodden pillow and Carmen glanced around. 'What's happened?'

'The boys have fed every two hours since yesterday evening, I had little sleep, and Tom sent a note this morning to say he wouldn't come back.' She sniffed. 'I'm just so tired and I was going back to Zandorro anyway, but he was my last link to my husband and it makes me so sad.'

Carmen wondered if Zafar had had anything to do with Tom's blessed absence but the lack of sleep was definitely taking its toll. 'Of course I understand.'

Fadia wasn't listening. 'It will be good when I get to Zandorro. I'm not managing as well as I thought I would.'

Poor Fadia. And it was day three after two babies. 'You're being hard on yourself. Yesterday was too good and it's payback today. You've had a very tragic start to your family. On top of all that you have two babies that need you twenty-four seven. I think you've been amazing.'

Fadia sniffed tragically. 'But yesterday everything was going so well.'

'And today is a difficult day for you, plus after birth day three is a notorious time for getting the blues. We talked about that. With twins, the boys are hungry and feeding more often to bring your milk in. There's twice as many hormones floating around and with so little sleep of course you're going to feel fragile. You need help.'

'I thought I could manage.'

'And you are. But perhaps help from family is a good answer for now. Try not worry. I'm sure the last thing Tom wants is for you to lose sleep over him.' Though if Tom was as like her ex-husband as he looked, she doubted he thought of anyone but himself.

There was a knock on the door and Carmen's heart sank. Visitors were the last thing they needed now. When she opened the door it was Prince Zafar.

He narrowed his eyes at his cousin's red face and puffy eyes. 'Yusuf says there is a problem?'

'Good old Yusuf,' Carmen muttered under her breath.

As if to support his comment, both babies began to cry again and Carmen sighed. She wasn't even going to go near the Tom fiasco. 'Babies need feeding, mothers need sleep. It's a day for feeling blue.'

She looked at Fadia, who teetered on the verge of casting herself into her bed again. 'Fadia, perhaps you could wash your face while we mind your sons?'

Reluctantly, she heaved herself off her bed. Carmen picked up Harrison and handed him to Zafar. 'Here. See how you are with princes. I'll go you halves.' Then she picked up Bailey, tucked him into her shoulder and patted the little bottom.

She shouldn't have been surprised when Zafar did the same, calmly and confidently, and even cross little Harry seemed to understand the command to settle. He even twitched his mouth in a windy smile. 'You're very good at that.'

His look mocked her. 'Should I not be?'

She shrugged. Actually, she was surprised but the guy had to love kids if he'd studied paediatrics. She had the feeling this man could do anything. And do it well. 'I'd forgotten you specialised in paediatrics.'

'And will again, one day.' When my duties allow and I can stand the pain, he thought. Zafir stroked Bailey's bunny-wrapped back in slow, steady waves and stared down at the baby's soft dark hair. 'I had personal experience with children. I had a son. Samir.'

He could feel her eyes on him but he didn't look. He did not want her sympathy. So he kept stroking Bailey and speaking to the little downy head.

Still he didn't look at her. 'My wife and small son died in the same hijacking that almost killed me.'

He glanced out the window and added flatly, 'Of course I wish I too had died. You can imagine my horror when I actually woke up.'

Zafar felt the tightness of grief again in his chest. He wished he'd never come here to be reminded so forcibly. Why on earth was he telling her? His hands tightened as he looked down at the baby. 'I remember his weight in my arms.'

Carmen suddenly understood the bleakness she often saw in his face. 'That's terrible. I'm sorry.' She moistened her suddenly dry mouth. How much tragedy did this family hold?

He looked her way but he wasn't seeing her. His voice remained devoid of anything she could offer sympathy to, but the depth of his suffering reached out to her. 'Two years ago now, but I remember how to care for a baby.'

Fadia returned from the bathroom and Zafar ended the conversation as he spoke to her. 'You are exhausted. Now will you have a mothercraft nurse?'

Fadia looked at him, turned and ran back, sobbing, into the bathroom and shut the door.

Carmen didn't say anything. She patted her baby's back once more and laid him back in his cot before she turned to Fadia's bed and straightened it. She needed to do something with her hands or she'd strangle him.

'What? Nothing to say?'

She glared at him. Oohhh. She counted to three and at least her voice came out calm. 'Nothing you don't already know. You may have skills with babies but you're not that hot with new mums.'

He frowned. 'I do not understand her wish to be without help when she has had such difficulties.' His next comment she didn't expect. 'Or yours. I wish to speak of something else…'

His voice changed, heralding something she knew she wasn't going to like. Her instinct proved correct. 'Forgive me, but I have been told your husband proved a poor choice? This is correct?'

He looked anything but apologetic.

How did he know that? She felt sick. She didn't even want to think about how. 'Not something I wish to discuss.' Just what had he been doing poking into her affairs?

His gaze didn't waver. Mr Arrogance was back and of course he didn't stop there. 'And swindled you out of your home and left you with debts.'

This wasn't happening. 'Who told you that?'

Again he ignored her comment. 'You live in a slum area. Live alone, unprotected? Yusuf spoke to men who accosted you the other night.'

Carmen shook her head in disbelief and incredulous anger at his intrusion into her private life simmered up from her stomach and into her throat. The men in the alley. The smashed bottle. She did remember that incident. But it didn't matter. She would have managed. He'd had her followed? Carl had done that after she'd left him.

'How dare you? Neither of you have the right to intrude on my privacy.'

The wet washer of reality. Another horror of a man. And she'd be attracted. He didn't think like normal people. Never would. She wasn't sure who she was angrier with, him or herself, for being drawn to him.

He shrugged. 'Privacy can be bought.'

'Not my privacy, buster.' And to think she'd kissed him with abandon in a shed.

The arrogant sheik stood very much in evidence and she reminded herself he was just as high-handed about Fadia. No wonder she had misgivings about returning with him. No wonder she wanted Carmen to come and stand up for her. She lifted her head and glared. 'What an attractive person you are.'

His eyes narrowed. 'Sarcasm does not become you, Carmen.'

'Funny.' She couldn't remember being this angry. She sucked in air, trying to calm herself so that her words came out low and biting. 'Yet bullying suits you very well.'

Despite her low tone, anger vibrated in her voice and she wasn't sure she could contain it. She still wasn't sure if she was more wild with him or herself. A bitter exchange carried on in quiet voices. The air quivered with tension.

He brushed that off. 'I am not ashamed of my actions.'

She almost laughed in his face. 'Why am I not surprised?' She rolled her eyes.

He didn't like that. 'You would be wise to hold your tongue.'

So, she'd pushed him too far. Carmen stamped down the cowardly urge to do what she was told. Tough biscuits.

'Hold your own tongue, buster. I've met men like you before. I married an arrogant, self-important bully. And I won't be bullied again. Ever!'

She spun around and walked to the door before he could comprehend she'd actually walk out on him. 'I'm no woman in your harem. And I'm not in your employ.'

She called through the bathroom door, 'I'll be back later, Fadia,' and let herself out before he could stop her.

As she walked down the corridor to her room, anger bubbled and popped like a little lava pool from sudden volcanic eruption. She didn't do loss of control. Someone had to remain rational. She rarely did anger because she liked to be level-headed. That was how she'd escaped her marriage. Level head. Planning. What was it about this man that pushed all the buttons of high emotion?

Her eyes narrowed as she concentrated on any sound behind her of pursuit. Listened for the sound of the door opening again, but it didn't. She could feel Yusuf's frown follow her as she increased the distance between them, could admit she was ridiculously glad his chair was near the lifts and not positioned at her end of the corridor.

She should have shut the door to the midwife's room but she refused to have them think she was scared. She really did like the mums to feel they could poke their heads in any time. It wasn't quite the same when Yusuf appeared. She couldn't help the jump in her pulse rate.

Yusuf folded his arms. 'Prince Zafar wishes to see you in his suite.'

She didn't stand from her chair. 'Tell him I'm busy.'

His eyes narrowed and he took a step towards her. 'You will come now.'

And you are dreaming, Carmen thought. She stood up, casually reached for her handbag and rummaged around inside. 'Should I comb my hair?' She removed the small can of attacker spray a friend had given her when she'd first divorced.

'Do you know what this is? Paint. It won't hurt you but they say it takes a week to wash off.' Her voice remained pleasant. 'Please tell Prince Zafar I'm busy.'

Five minutes later her phone rang. Zafar sounded amused. She doubted Yusuf was.

'So I must come to you?'

'Or not. I really am busy.'

'I apologise. I did not intend to bully you.'

'Well, you tried!' An apology? She hadn't expected

that. She may have overreacted a tad. But the pain was still there from her shattered illusions in the past and perhaps a few from the present. 'I'm touchy on the subject of pushy men.' But she did feel less tense that he didn't seem angry at her defiance. And an apology was something her ex had never mastered.

Zafar went on. 'I wish to apologise more fully. And I still need to discuss Fadia with you. Perhaps we could find a time that you are not busy. Dinner? If I were to arrange a table in my suite for seven-thirty? That would be half an hour after you finish your shift tonight.'

Didn't he realise he was being arrogant and pushy again? Perhaps it was a failing with royalty as well as creeps. Shame he couldn't see her sarcastic salute.

'That would give you time to change.'

Unbelievable. Like she had a cocktail dress in her handbag? 'Change? From my uniform into my sarong and swimmers, you mean?'

There was silence. 'Whatever you wear will be acceptable.'

'Gee, thanks. But no thanks.'

He sighed. 'You are tiresome with your objections.'

'Heaven forbid.' She swallowed the hysterical laugh that wanted to escape. She needed to shut the lid on the box of memories he'd opened and a cosy dinner wouldn't help.

There was silence on the end of the phone. It went on until she was the one who felt like a petulant child. Not fair. To her own disgust she thought of poor Fadia, how much she needed her support, and relented. 'Oh, very well. I'll see what I can find.'

She put the phone down gently but her heart pounded

in a way that wasn't gentle at all. She should not have agreed.

But she had.

She could just picture herself sitting in the suite in her uniform, or her sarong, and she couldn't deny the fact that she didn't like the picture.

The last thing she needed to feel was at a disadvantage dressed like an employee or a beach bum.

She picked up the phone again and spoke to the best concierge in Sydney, Donna, her friend from downstairs, always good value and someone guaranteed to know the quickest place to buy anything.

'A cheap dress that looks good? There's a great specials bin in the boutique at the moment. I'll send something up in your size. No worries. Do it all the time for guests.'

The clock seemed to be going twice as fast as normal as the afternoon sped by in a blur of breastfeeding issues, baby weights and newborn bathing demonstrations.

When she visited Fadia the young woman seemed to have recovered her composure and Carmen wondered if, now that Tom was absent, Fadia would come into her own. Carmen had no doubt that Fadia had strength that would astound her cousin.

Perhaps Tom had played up to Fadia's emotions to keep the girl dependent. She hoped Prince Zafar didn't intend to continue the trend. Again she thought of her own marriage.

Her mind twisted and turned as she prepared to take blood from the twins for their newborn screening tests. Fadia grimaced for their discomfort and breastfed them one at a time to help distract them from the sting of the lancet prick.

When it was over they tucked the boys back into bed and Fadia shook her head in disbelief. 'But they didn't cry.'

'Because you fed them at the same time.'

'I'm glad it helped.' Then another worried frown creased her brows. 'When I go to Zandorro, if the results come back bad, how will they find me?'

So she'd decided. It would be hard here with her babies on her own and she couldn't help her instinct that Zafar was a much safer bet than a man like Tom. 'The results go to your doctor. We would find you and follow up.'

Fadia put her hand out. 'Are you sure there's no chance you could come with me? Just for a while?' Her dark eyes pleaded. 'You help without fuss. I would not be as nervous if you were with me. Once I'm back I know the older women will try to take over.'

Had Zafar told her to ask? 'I'm sorry, Fadia. I can't. I have my job here. But you will be strong.' Carmen gestured to the sleeping babies. 'For your boys. You're amazing and nobody can ever take that from you.'

She hugged Fadia. 'Maybe a mothercraft nurse from here isn't such a bad idea. Someone whose loyalties lie with you? I'm sure Zafar would agree.'

She shook her head. 'I want you. Just for a few weeks?'

Such imploring eyes and Carmen could feel herself weaken. Then she thought of Zafar. Of her response to him. Of being under his 'rule'. A disturbing thought.

But then so was Fadia without a champion if she needed one. 'I don't think I can. It's a long way to go for something a lot of people could do. I'll think about it but it's unlikely. I'm sorry. I'll see you in the morning. Make sure you ask the night midwife if you need help.'

By the time she'd written up her notes and handed over to her colleague, it was seven-fifteen.

Carmen used the midwife's bathroom to wash and pulled the new dress from the bag to check out the tag. Slashed price, non-iron and machine washable. She loved Donna.

Carmen shivered with the silky slide of fabric down her body and she hoped it wasn't an omen. Maybe she should wear her uniform. What was she doing anyway, trying to impress a prince with her bargain-bin clothes?

She shook her head at herself. No. She was dressing for herself and it looked good. Maybe the maroon fabric did plunge a little into her cleavage but that was fixed with the cream silk scarf Donna had added. The pair of slip-on half-heels were perfect and she'd even thrown in costume jewellery. God bless her favourite concierge.

At least she didn't feel like the poor relation any more.

Mascara and lipstick would do if she didn't want to be late. Carmen paused with lipstick in hand in front of the mirror. Did she want to be late?

She smiled at herself. She'd probably pulled enough tails today. In fact, she'd take her attacker dye.

'Evening, Yusuf.' The man's eyes glittered at her as he stood up to accompany her. 'I can find my own way.'

He bowed impassively. 'But I will accompany you.'

He didn't have to ask her to wait while he opened the heavy door at the top of the stairwell. It was funny how they all opted for the stairs now. She guessed she'd learned some of the rules at least.

While she waited she remembered the first time she'd stood here like this. Had it been only three days ago? So much had happened.

So much that her world might prove a little flat when all these unusual people moved on from her life.

In the hallway the other guard, still standing like before, watched them approach. She doubted he even leant against the wall when he was tired.

Yusuf knocked and the same woman opened it. *Déjà vu.* Except this time Carmen wondered if the woman was Zafar's concubine. She banished that thought because for some reason it spoiled her evening.

As she walked past the woman inclined her head in deference. Carmen frowned. She was pretty sure she hadn't done that last time.

She was still pondering when Zafar's door opened and he came through—in tailored slacks and a silk shirt. A very poor attempt at not looking like a million bucks.

'*As asaalum al aikum.* Peace be with you.' He smiled.

Nice of him to translate for her. 'Good evening.'

'Now, why did I think you would be late?'

Carmen shrugged. 'Because you don't know me?'

'But I will,' he said quietly. He gestured to the cushions spread on the carpet beside a low table or a table and chairs on the balcony, then said more conversationally, 'Would you prefer to sit inside or out? Fatima will lay the table.'

She glanced out the door to the balcony, screened from other guests by a metal lattice and with a northern view over Coogee it would be criminal to waste.

Lots of air space around them if not physical distance. And she'd rather be at eyelevel with him on a chair.

'Outside.'

He nodded to Fatima, who picked up a wicker basket and moved outside, where she proceeded to produce everything needed, like Mary Poppins or, more appropriately, an Arabic genie, out of the bag. When the table was set she disappeared into the tiny kitchen and wheeled out a trolley with dishes of food.

Zafar picked up a bottle from a stand of ice. 'Perhaps I could pour you a drink while we wait. Champagne?'

Something to settle the butterflies that had landed in her stomach perhaps. It seemed he wasn't a strict Muslim, thank goodness, for the way she felt at the moment… 'Champagne would be lovely.'

He held the glass and she reached for it carefully, ridiculously anxious not to touch his fingers, until his eyes met hers. He knew. And with that one glance she knew he knew. She frowned, decided not to play the game and took it firmly. His fingers tingled against her own.

'Thank you.'

He turned away, but not before she could see his amusement.

Carmen looked at Fatima and took a couple of calming breaths. The servant had arranged dishes of food and napkins beside a huge flat dish of white rice, another with sliced lamb roast. She recognised the bowls of stuffed tomatoes, a dark and aromatic stew with lime-green beans wafted an amazing aroma her way, along with several dishes she didn't recognise. Surely far too much for just the two of them. Carmen looked away.

'Ah. Fatima is finished.' He tilted his head at his servant. 'Leave.' The woman bowed and left the room.

'Now, I find that offensive.' She'd thought she was talking to herself as she moved out to the balcony but apparently not under her breath enough.

'And you think I should care what you think?'

Carmen threw her head up but his eyes were crinkled with amusement. It seemed she was hilarious, Carmen thought mutinously.

She must have looked murderous because he held out is hands. 'I'm sorry. Couldn't resist. I can almost see you with your can of Mace pointed at Yusuf.'

She narrowed her eyes at him. 'Mace is illegal. This is dye for self-defence.'

This impossibly handsome man, ridiculously wealthy, accustomed to his servants obeying his every command and probably accustomed to women falling at his feet. He must find it strange to be less revered in another culture. It must be strange when he was with her.

He was watching her. Still with amusement in his eyes. 'Did you bring it?'

Now what was he talking about? 'I'm sorry?'

'Your pressure-pack protection.'

She smiled. 'You'll never know.'

For a moment she thought he was going to ask to see her purse. He didn't and it felt as though she'd won a small victory.

It made her wonder why he didn't become more impatient with her lack of amenability. 'How can you be normal at times and so arrogant at others?'

'With you?' So he had read her mind again. 'I'm still working that out. It is novel for me. I was born into privilege, which I assure you comes with responsibility, but I studied in England and latterly Australia. You have very good schools, a school system that levels a young man so he understands your abhorrence of our feudal system.'

He shrugged. 'I understand a little of the differences between you and the women in my culture.' He pulled out her chair and waited for her to sit.

'But I am first of all a prince of my country and second a travelled man. I was angry today and not without power. Perhaps it would be wise for you to remember that.'

He sat opposite and she took a sip of her drink to fill the silence between them. When she put her drink down she did have something to say. 'I don't like it that you had me investigated.'

He nodded. 'I noticed.' Well, at least she'd got that point across. He went on. 'It is as well we discuss this now.'

He leaned across to top up her glass but she covered it with her hand. 'I need my wits with you.'

He put the bottle back and she noticed he wasn't drinking. 'I'm flattered.' He didn't look it.

'Don't be.' She thought he was going to follow up on her comment but in the end he changed tack.

He hitched the sleeve of his right hand and gestured to the food. 'Eat.'

Carmen carefully transferred some rice and a tomato to her plate with her knife and fork. She couldn't bring herself to use her fingers.

There was something erotically earthy about a man eating slowly with his fingers. Zafar watched her. 'Try this.' He picked up a sliver of something that turned out to be aromatic lamb, which she obediently tasted, but the taste was nothing to the feel of his fingers against her lips and her stomach kicked at that sensation.

'Please don't feed me.'

Zafar could not take his eyes off her. He savoured the play of light across her skin as her expression changed like the ocean in front of them. Her sense of humour amused him—she made him smile more than he'd smiled for a long time—and her anger was transparent because she made no attempt to disguise it when he had annoyed her. A new experience for a woman to show her displeasure and probably good for his soul. No doubt a concept that would have amused his departed mother.

The change in his thinking had continued since he'd witnessed Carmen help that woman give birth in the park. He was touched by the way she had cared for the frightened young woman. He wasn't sure why it had made such an impact on him. Then she spoke of it. 'I rang the hospital today to see how our mother and baby are doing.'

Had she read his mind? If she had, she would have read more than she'd bargained for. He bit back a smile. 'And are they well?'

She smiled at him and he took the gift of that and stored it away in a corner of his cold heart.

'You know they are. You checked as well. I understand they haven't seen a flower arrangement so exotically expensive for years. Jenny feels very special.'

He watched her taste the rice and an expression of unexpected pleasure crossed her face at the subtle tang she would not be used to. 'I'm glad she liked it. I am not just the arrogant bully you think me.' He held up his hand. 'And I do beg your forgiveness for that. Holding my nephew brought back the reality of my loss and I behaved badly towards you. I apologise.'

She looked less than convinced but inclined her head. 'I accept your apology. So what else do you do when you're not being an ogre or having people investigated?'

'Tsk. So hard on me.'

She shrugged, unrepentant, and to his horror he wanted to pull her into his arms and seduce her bravado away. How could he forget the pain from the past? The time was not right for that, could never be, while his role lay in the royal household.

Where were his barriers? His safeguards from creating a relationship?

He should be thinking of more important things. 'My investigation of you was carried out because I wish to offer you a short tenure as Fadia's assistant.'

CHAPTER SIX

SOMETHING was going on in his mind that was outside the conversation. Carmen could sense it. Physically feel it. Even discern his slight withdrawal. She opened her mouth to refuse but he held up his hand and to her utter disgust she waited obediently.

'And I need to be sure she and her sons would be safe with you.' Now he paused to wait for her comment.

'So I can talk now?'

He nodded good-naturedly and she realised she was in danger of sounding ill-tempered. How did he put her in the wrong when he was the chauvinist?

Carmen straightened the scarf around her shoulders as if to gather her control closer to her chest then counted to three. She spoke in her usual calm voice. 'I see her need. But I'm a midwife, not a mothercraft nurse. I'm afraid you've wasted your money on investigations.'

'You are good at your job. Fadia likes you and needs a friend.' He shrugged. 'So that is enough for me. I wish to secure your services.'

'It seems she lost a friend today.' She tilted her head at him.

'Did she?'

'I gather Tom is not in the picture any more?'

Zafar questioned her blandly. 'Is he not?'

She decided he looked lazily ruthless. And disgustingly attractive with it. So now she was attracted to dangerous men? What was happening to her? 'I'm asking you. He is conspicuous by his non-appearance since the one time outside Fadia's door.'

No answer to her question. Just one of his own. 'So you assume I have done something?'

She just raised her eyebrows. 'Don't look so surprised.' As if. He didn't look surprised at all.

He shrugged. 'It is my intention to be aware of things that are my concern.' He added some lamb to her plate.

Now they were down to the nitty-gritty. 'Then be concerned for your cousin's state of mind. With Tom off the scene she will be alone again and she has already lost her husband. Safeguards need to be in place. She's frightened she'll lose control to the palace servants and maybe even access to her sons.'

He leaned forward and pinned her with his full attention. 'I thank you for sharing that.' He shook his head, obviously pained. 'I would not do that. I have learned the difficult choice my mother had to make. I've lost my own son and know that feeling of emptiness.' His sincerity made her throat tighten.

He went on. 'I will champion Fadia and only want what is best for her in this difficult time. Hence the real need for you to consider my request that you accompany her.'

And Fadia had pleaded as well. Carmen pushed temptation behind her and looked away. There were too many variables for that course. Too many dangers, and one of the most dangerous sat opposite. 'I've already told you I have two jobs.'

He brushed that aside. 'And you're almost too tired to do either. You work at least seventy hours a week on mixed shifts. Why? For money. Ridiculous.'

See, she admonished herself. He'd been checking up again. 'That's none of your business.'

He ignored that. Perhaps he ignored everything people said that he didn't agree with. 'I believe you have holiday leave owing?'

Yes, but none she could take without a big drop in pay. Why was she discussing this? 'I suppose you have that in writing from my employers?'

'I have verbal confirmation, which is sufficient.' He shrugged that inconvenience away. 'What if I offered to clear all your debts for the sake of two weeks work in Zandorro with Fadia?'

She'd forgotten he'd known about the debts. It was obscene to have that much money to tempt people with. He was forcing her hand.

Or was she a fool to throw away the chance of a new life for two weeks work with a woman she wanted to help?

Could she leave Australia? Go to a country where she couldn't even speak the language or understand the customs? Could she trust him? Her nerve endings stood up and waved in distress.

'Well, what would you say?'

'I'd say I sold my soul to the devil.'

He tossed his head. 'You are being dramatic.' His eyes no longer smiled. 'But would you say yes?'

She stared back at him. Could feel herself weakening under his gaze. Bowing before his will when she didn't want or mean to. She knew how this could end. 'No.'

'Why not.'

She knew the answer to that one too. 'You're arrogant enough while you have no power over me. I imagine you'd be intolerable as my employer.'

His gaze bored into hers. The food lay forgotten between them. 'You don't know that.'

'I'm not stupid.'

He smiled at her and she almost smiled back. 'No, you're not, but what is it most that worries you?'

Everything, nothing, nothing she could pin down. 'I could find myself adrift in a strange country without any job.'

He didn't deny her fears. Just rang a bell and Fatima reappeared and began to clear the table.

Carmen was left in limbo. Confused at the sudden halt in the conversation.

No doubt it was all a part of the Eastern customs of taking one's time with negotiations. She was more of the thrash-it-out-and-finish-it kinda gal but there wasn't much she could do.

Time passed as options kaleidoscoped in her head in confusing patterns. She was no nearer to a decision when Fatima had finished and poured small gold cups of thick coffee, which she placed beside them. At Zafar's command she left a jewelled coffee pot in the centre alongside a tray of tiny baklava.

'Coffee?'

She nodded and he poured. 'Please, finish the conversation.'

He took a sip and held his cup. 'If I promised that wouldn't happen? If I paid what I promised into your bank account here, now, and you would keep that even if the job didn't work out? Plus a return air fare you could use at any time.'

Stop tempting me. Ridiculous offer. Carmen bit her lip. Surely he was joking. 'Nobody would pay that.'

'You say I am a nobody?' The cup went down and his chin went up. Oops. Insulted him again. Every inch the prince. Too easy to offend. She watched him regather his patience and go on.

'Supplying money is not hard. Finding people to trust is.'

She could see his point. But that was the crunch. She didn't trust him. Or perhaps herself. 'You may have decided to trust me but it's not mutual.'

He brushed that side. 'That is not necessary. I have given my word.'

She didn't laugh. Could see he meant it. Just wondered if his interpretation differed from hers. What was she thinking, even considering this? She wouldn't fit in. Then again, what did she have to fit in with? 'And what of your henchman? Yusuf hates me.'

That perplexed him. 'This worries you because…?'

She guessed it was unlikely Yusuf would do anything his master wouldn't like. But she didn't need any more pressure. Doing it for money was bad enough. 'Let's not talk about it any more. I'll think about your offer.'

To her relief, he agreed to leave the subject for the moment.

Night had fallen. She wasn't sure when that had happened. A ship with lights blazing passed across the horizon out to sea. Heading off to who knew where. Did she want to do that? Even contemplate leaving everything she knew to accompany these people she didn't really understand?

They carried their coffee inside and talked desultorily about where they'd both travelled, and of course the things he'd seen were different no matter if the destinations were the same.

Time passed insidiously. She grew more comfortable with him, though she seemed to do most of the talking. He made her laugh with stories about his internship in Sydney, and she with her midwifery escapades returned the favour, until it was unexpectedly late.

She glanced at her watch. He saw her eyes widen, and she jumped to her feet. 'I must go.' As if suddenly woken from a dream, she needed distance from.

Zafar, too, glanced at his watch. He'd savoured her company, understood her a little, wondered about the destructive power of her bad marriage, could admit to himself there was danger in knowing too much and that it was not just a culmination of abstinence. The moral issues of being attracted to a new woman, someone other than the woman he had vowed to stay faithful to, and where it led—that was what worried him.

He needed to think this through. Maintain distance. Especially if she agreed to join them. 'I apologise for keeping you late.'

He believed she would come. Probably not for him but because she would worry about Fadia. And that was where he would apply the pressure. 'One question.'

She paused and turned on her way to the door as he caught up with her. 'Do you have a valid passport?'

'I haven't agreed to go but, yes, I renewed it last year. I used to travel a lot with my parents when I was young.'

'Very well. You have less than a day to decide. We leave for Zandorro tomorrow afternoon at four. If you do decide to help Fadia, there are things we must arrange.'

'Don't count on it.'

'We will see.' He lifted her hand and she realised what he was going to do before it happened. Tried to pull her hand back but he held her firmly and she didn't tug—actually, couldn't tug because her arm wasn't listening. Her mouth dried and she tried not to lean towards him. Head down, still watching her face with his dark eyes, he turned her wrist and brushed her skin with those wicked lips. Goose-bumps scattered like drops from a fountain until her body overloaded and she shivered.

He smiled as he straightened. '*Fi aman illah*. Go in God's keeping.'

'Goodnight.'

Carmen didn't know who to turn to. She never asked for advice, something her mother had quizzed her on all through her childhood and later in her teens, but this was too big a risk without some insurance and someone knowing where she was. And she was running out of time.

As soon as she left the presidential suite she rang Tilly. Her friend lived within walking distance of the hotel and they agreed to meet in the bar for a nightcap to discuss the job.

Tilly arrived with her fiancé, Marcus Bennett, head of Obstetrics and the man who had been there for Fadia's second son's birth. Carmen decided it was a good thing having friends in high places.

Marcus dived straight in. 'Tilly says you've had a job offer you're not sure of. With Zafar.'

'Yes.' She hadn't expected this. 'Do you know him?'

'As well as someone can know him. Sure. We did uni together, he worked at the Royal when I was there, then specialised in paediatrics. He may be a prince but we usually meet for a meal when he's in Australia.'

Tilly's jaw dropped. 'You didn't say he was a prince.'

Carmen brushed that aside. 'He's a sheikh. There are lots of desert kingdoms and he's not directly in line for the throne.'

Marcus smiled. 'I think he is but not in the first instance. So he's our twin lady's cousin?'

'Estranged. Apparently the twins are too close to succession to be unmonitored. He's here to help Fadia get back to her country.'

'She's a widow, isn't she?' Marcus looked at Tilly, who nodded.

Carmen's chair faced Reception, unlike the others', who had their backs to it, and she saw Zafar walk in through the front door with his henchman. So he'd gone out after she'd left. To do what? She let the conversation flow around her as she tried to halt the colour in her cheeks.

She put her head down but he'd seen her and even from this distance she could tell he was studying who she was with. She glanced at Tilly.

Marcus's voice drifted back in. 'Wasn't there a friend involved, helping Fadia?'

'Umm.' Carmen concentrated on the conversation. 'The friendship cooled, I think. Either not a good friend or I did wonder if Zafar may have bought him off.'

Tilly, oblivious to Carmen's discomfort, was relishing the idea. She hunched her shoulders and lowered her voice theatrically. 'Or he could have threatened him.'

'No.' Carmen shook her head. 'I think there was more to it than that. Zafar has power.'

Marcus laughed. 'You girls watch too much TV. Zafar's a bit stiff but he's an honourable man. One who's had his share of tragedy.'

Carmen listened to the absolute belief in Marcus's voice and let her breath out. That was lucky because he was coming that way.

She'd just needed to hear the words before the topic of their conversation came within hearing. 'So you're saying his job offer would be genuine and reliable.'

'I would say so. Yes.' Marcus nodded emphatically.

Carmen wanted it spelt out. 'And if I don't come back, you'll ask him where I am and he'd tell the truth?'

He nodded again. 'I believe so.'

That was it, then. She couldn't not take the offer because it would solve all her money problems in a couple of weeks. She'd just hope she didn't inherit other dilemmas worse than money issues. 'Thank you. I really appreciate your advice.'

Tilly rubbed her hands. 'So when do I get to meet this prince?' Just in time for Zafar to hear. Carmen winced and looked up.

'Perhaps you could introduce me to your friends?' Zafar stood above them, quite splendid in black. Yusuf, three steps behind, watched Carmen impassively.

Marcus stood and turned and Zafar smiled with delight. He held out his hand. 'Well met, Marcus.'

'Zafar.' Marcus gestured proudly. 'Allow me to present my fiancée, Matilda. Tilly's a friend of Carmen's.'

Tilly was blinking and Carmen smiled sourly to

herself. She knew how that felt. Zafar lifted her hand and kissed Tilly's fingers. Not her wrist, a little voice gloated, and Carmen frowned at herself.

'Congratulations on your engagement. You are both fortunate people. Of course any friend of Carmen's is a friend of mine.'

Yeah, right. Carmen watched Tilly's eyes glaze over and felt slightly better that even a woman deeply in love could be knocked askew by Zafar's charisma.

Marcus filled the awkward silence. 'Carmen says you've offered her a position for a couple of weeks in Zandorro until Fadia's babies are settled.'

Zafar glanced at Carmen. 'I am glad she is considering my offer.'

She met his enquiring look with a bland face. 'I'm setting up a safety net.'

Zafar raised his brows and spoke to Marcus as if the girls weren't there. 'These Australian midwives are feisty, are they not?'

Marcus smiled down at Tilly. 'I'm living dangerously and loving it.'

The conversation moved on between the men and Zafar and Marcus became immersed in the topic of hospitals. Tilly caught Carmen's eye as they both sat down. She winked and Carmen had to smile.

'So?' Tilly whispered. 'You going?'

'I guess so.' She shrugged. 'I feel better that he knows Marcus and there's a big bonus that will clear my feet and then some.'

'I'm glad. You're killing yourself here and you've always enjoyed travel.'

'Not in the royal entourage.'

Tilly grinned. 'Why not?'

Carmen had to laugh. Maybe it was exciting to think about being whisked somewhere without effort.

Suddenly it was easier to let go of a little of the responsibility to work everything out for herself, something she hadn't done for a long time, and when she glanced across at the men Zafar was watching her.

She wondered what he was thinking.

So these were her friends. Zafar wanted to drop his arm around her shoulders like Marcus was doing with his woman. He wanted to take her wrist and savour the feel of her skin, the scent of orange on his lips, and pull her back into his body.

These thoughts shouldn't intrude when the information he'd found out tonight was of such national importance and here he was fantasising about a woman.

Such poor timing to feel alive again.

A time of great danger approached and he had failed to keep those he cared about safe before.

CHAPTER SEVEN

THE next day proved hectic after a whirlwind of formalities made more intricate with Carmen joining the party at the last minute. Carmen only had time to glimpse Coogee beach recede in the distance as they drove away she was too busy checking her handbag to make sure she had everything. Her leave from work had been smoothed by the fact she hadn't taken any holiday for so long. She'd been waved away with little censure of the short notice. Carmen couldn't help but wonder if Zafar had spoken to them.

The baby hotel had said to return when she could. All too easy. Or maybe nobody would miss her?

Even Donna had said, 'Enjoy, lucky thing'.

Carmen couldn't help feeling she'd been manipulated by a force that was stronger than she'd realised. Zafar.

They'd left the hotel in two cars, which shouldn't have surprised Carmen, and maybe added that tiny hint of needed reality, being relegated to the secondary car with the twins and Fadia. What did she expect? To ride with Zafar? Of course she was a glorified nanny.

Thankfully the babies were remarkably settled and Fadia seemed mostly relieved with her decision.

Now the decision had been made, Carmen was glad

she'd come to support the young mother and help her as she became reacquainted with her homeland. Despite Zafar's assertion that he would not force the widow into anything she didn't want, Carmen knew Fadia was worried.

They both knew, though, that he would have other matters to distract him.

Carmen tried to put herself in the young mum's shoes. 'Are you worried about returning to Zandorro?'

Fadia nodded. 'A little. It's been six years. And I'm nervous about meeting my grandfather again. He is a powerful man. But Zandarro is becoming a more progressive country, not as traditional as our neighbours, which causes friction between the two countries. I hope it continues that way.'

They both pondered the differences between a monarchy-ruled Arabic state and the relaxed vibe of Coogee.

Carmen smiled. 'Might be a little removed from what we've been used to.'

The short trip to the airport passed silently and once they arrived in Zafar, or more likely his staff, had arranged for them to slip through diplomatic transfer to their private jet.

'Would you like something to drink before take-off?' The exquisitely dressed hostess appeared from nowhere and Carmen looked at Fadia.

'No, thank you, we're fine.'

The woman inclined her head. 'We'll be taking off in ten minutes.'

Not too long to ponder her decision, then. Surely she was doing the right thing. Carmen shivered as last regrets surfaced. It was momentous to allow herself to be whisked off to an unfamiliar country with people who played by their own rules.

Fadia seemed disinclined to talk and Carmen let her be. All she could do for the moment was check the babies and later through the flight ensure they were fed, changed and settled.

Carmen glanced across at the boys in their capsules strapped to the opposite seats. Two little heads tilted towards each other, matching frowns as if they were squinting to see through the hard plastic sides of their beds to see each other. Maybe reassure each other during their first trip in a plane.

She smiled at flights of fancy and gradually she realised she was actually relieved to be there, and even excited by the prospect of visiting a new country and finding out more about these fascinating people. Just so long as she wasn't focussed on a particular fascinating man.

Zafar had fulfilled his obligations and now it was for Carmen to fulfil her own. And she would, diligently, and she was certain Fadia would be better away from the horrible Tom.

'So why did your mother leave Zandorro?'

'When I was fifteen she divorced my father. She never wanted to go back and here I am doing just that. I hope it's the right thing to do.'

'Did you never want to go back at all before this?'

'Perhaps but it is a big thing to lose my new identity in a country I loved. I see the advantage for my sons in Zandorro, but wonder what is there for me. I am constrained by my station. When I left last time I was betrothed to a man I never saw. Thankfully my mother paid back the bride price from Australia so he has no hold on me.'

Carmen struggled to understand the concept of arranged marriage, something well outside her experience. Everything Fadia spoke of was new and interesting. She encouraged Fadia to talk. 'So where did you meet your husband?'

The girl smiled sadly. 'At university in Sydney. We were both studying pharmacy and he was three years older than me.' She shrugged tragic shoulders. 'We fell in love but now he has gone without even seeing his babies. Killed by a hit-and-run driver. Without even knowing I was pregnant. All I have left of him are my sons.

'I think I will try to sleep.' Fadia rolled over in the pod the hostess had prepared for her and Carmen gazed thoughtfully at her back. Good idea.

Zafar was in for an interesting time with his cousin and she just hoped he had some plan for long-term support.

They arrived in Dubai twelve hours after take-off for refuelling and the high temperature shimmered off the tarmac outside the window. Robed figures seemed to float around their plane, maybe on flying carpets of heat, Carmen thought fancifully as the engines and fuel tanks were tended too.

Zafar had alighted without glancing at her and she stifled disappointment, not for his company, honestly, but for not having a chance to at least see the airport. She consoled herself that she would see that on her way back in a couple of short weeks.

Both women had slept well between feeds. Fadia

and the boys' routine had become swift and efficient at feeding time with Carmen's help, so despite the distance travelled Carmen at least felt rested, pampered and ready for her first sight of the desert.

Mid-afternoon Dubai time they prepared to leave for Zandorro, and Zafar boarded the plane just before they took off.

Fadia followed her gaze. 'He does not even see us now that he has achieved what he came for.'

Carmen glanced at her. 'Wasn't that the only reason he was in Australia? To find you?'

Still she watched her cousin. 'And bring my sons home. He is a man who gets what he wants.' Now she looked at Carmen with warning in her eyes. 'My mother used to say a Zandorran man uses any means needed.'

Carmen glanced away from the concern in Fadia's eyes. 'Do you really think that?' She didn't share Fadia's concern. She was fine and not afraid of Zafar. She stared out the window but all she could see was the reflection of her own face. She knew Zafar's will was strong, but so was hers.

They'd left the azure blue of the ocean and soared over mountains craggy with rock and then the golden desert stretched as far as the eye could see, undulating like a sleeping monster, shimmering with stored sunlight that would cool quickly.

'It's stark yet beautiful.' Carmen began a new topic, shelving her own unease in the relief that at least she and Fadia had each other.

'The desert has great majesty. But it is a furnace by day and freezing at night. I think I prefer the sand of Coogee Beach.'

Fadia's comment revealed her ambivalence about

her return. Then she winced uncomfortably because her bodice was bulging at the front of her dress and Carmen just wanted to hug her—carefully. No problems about the boys going hungry but it looked very tight and painful in Fadia's body at the moment.

'Another twenty-four hours and you'll be much more comfortable again. I'll ask for another cold pack.' She raised her hand and the hostess appeared within seconds.

They'd been sliding cold sports packs down the front of Fadia's dress and Carmen had even managed to draw a smile at least once at the relief against poor Fadia's hot and aching breasts.

'Is it nearly time to feed them again?'

'Not quite. Both boys have their eyes closed. Probably another half an hour before they wake.' Fadia nodded and closed her eyes as well.

Carmen glanced at the boys tucked into their travel capsules sound asleep, and looked out the window again. She'd travelled a little with her parents but those happy days seemed from another century. Everything had changed when she'd married and her parents had died. She just wished she'd chosen more wisely or at least chosen a man of honour.

Did Zafar have honour? Marcus had seemed to think so and Carmen doubted she would be there if her gut feeling hadn't reassured her. Why did she feel reassured by a man she didn't know well? Was that how she'd made her last mistake? She winced. No. It wasn't like that because she wasn't getting involved with Zafar. She knew better now.

There was no doubt Zafar had changed since they'd left the hotel and not only into flowing white robes. He'd distanced himself from her, created a barrier through which he didn't see or hear little people like her.

She wondered if there'd been more to the Tom saga than she'd been told. Big surprise there she hadn't been included. She was really having difficulty with this servant attitude she needed to get. Since they'd left it was more obvious she had slid down the totem pole.

His persona of Prince who travelled with entourage, immersed in business documents at the front of the plane, was daunting even for her. It seemed obvious his plan was that she'd take the whole problem of Fadia and her sons off his hands until the girl settled into Zandorron life.

Then again, who was she to complain of that because he'd paid handsomely for just such a purpose? And she'd sold her soul to clear her debts and start a new life. As long as she didn't throw her body—or her heart—into the bargain, it was worth it.

Carmen wished she didn't feel so unsettled by the man underneath the trappings yet that attraction seemed to grow insidiously despite her reluctance. Those wild unplanned moments in the storm were hard to banish, especially when she could see him up at the front of the plane.

Her gaze strayed to the back of his head, the glimpse of his aristocratic profile as he turned to speak to the stewardess, the distant deep timbre of his voice. She felt herself warm at the memory of the way he'd kissed her, held her in his arms. Was she mad? What possessed her to have followed him to a land where his power was absolute? She breathed in and out slowly, three times, and reminded herself to relax. Calm. She was still in control and would just have to be careful. She was just feeling a little overwhelmed.

It was all such a surreal experience, travelling with Zafar. Her father had been worldly but Zafar was princely and there was a huge difference. She suspected that clothed even in rags he would still be commanding, and she couldn't deny she felt drawn to the man regardless of his station. She dragged her eyes away from him again. Drawn but immune.

She'd be totally professional, cool and collected. And she was not going to think about the way he had kissed her or why.

Zafar put down the papers he'd been battling to concentrate on and tried not to think about kissing Carmen. Or summoning the midwife to his on-board bedroom and seeing just what could happen. As if stepping onto the plane meant the time of pretending he was not fiercely attracted to her was past.

While most of his attendants had dozed during the long flight he'd prowled the cabin, had looked down at her as she'd slept in her pod, realised it was the first time he was privy to that view and vowed to himself he would have at least one night where he could drink his fill of the sight.

He could picture her now, her thick lashes curled on her cheek, that beautiful mouth soft in repose instead of militant the way he often saw it. The blanket, fallen to her waist, had left her vulnerable, but that strangely only made him lift it to cover her. Not like him at all.

He smiled at the memory and then other memories flickered like an old-fashioned movie. That first drift of orange blossom from her skin in the lift. They said that scent was the only true memory. He could very easily remember that first glance of hers, a basic recognition he hadn't been able to deny, and that wild kiss in the storm had rocked him. He remembered that with clarity.

Then the cameo moment she'd hugged the woman in the park—imparting her strength to her like she had to him during his weakness in the elevator, a moment he still didn't understand.

Interesting, phobia-wise, this morning when he'd unconsciously pressed the button and descended to check out of his suite. It seemed that his aversion to lifts had been put to rest. Because of her? Or because he was moving on and creating new moments of life instead of dwelling on death? Even his fear of heights had receded a little.

Not huge events but remarkable and requiring thought.

Still, there remained a lot on his mind. Fadia's ability to settle in Zandorro, the kidnap attempt Yusuf had discovered with Fadia's 'friend' just a weakling pawn in a larger plan. He'd quashed that risk but information had been gained that put his grandfather—in fact, his entire family—at risk as well.

Yet a corner of his mind had been building with anticipation for the moment he had Carmen in his country, his palace, the chance to show her the sights and sounds and scents of Zandorro. To see her smile.

Normally he worked right through these flights.

'Can I get you anything, Excellency?' Yusuf hovered.

'No. Rest yourself.' Yusuf nodded and subsided but

when Zafar glanced once more at Carmen he noticed his manservant's eyes follow his.

Another memory clicked. She was right. She was not a favourite with his man. He would need to watch that. He fixed his gaze on Yusuf's face and spoke softly and clearly. 'But I will hold you personally responsible if she is not happy in the palace.'

Inscrutable, Yusuf nodded. His man had allies in the palace but Zafar had many more.

They landed not long before the sun set above the surrounding mountains outside the main city. The waiting limousines, complete with baby capsules, whisked them through several miles of desert hills to the massive gates and into the turreted city tucked behind a towering stone wall.

Dark faces peered at them from doorways as the vehicles climbed curved alleys and Carmen acknowledged with a sinking heart it would be difficult to find the way out again. She turned away from the window. That was okay. Really it was. She would be fine. She'd be able to leave any time she wanted. Zafar had promised.

Thankfully she was distracted as they rounded a bend and there ahead of them shone the palace as if positioned to receive the final light in the country through a break in the mountains. She couldn't help her indrawn breath.

Rooftops shimmered in a blanket of precious metal vying for space in the skyline with domes, towers and minarets reflecting the sun. Golden turrets glistened and one soaring tower in the middle with arched windows and a spire that reached for the sky watched over all.

'It's beautiful. Look at that tower.'

Fadia actually smiled at her enthusiasm. 'Yes, it is lovely.' They both glanced again at the magnificent building.

Harrison stirred and yawned and Bailey opened his eyes and blinked. Even Fadia's tiny sons seemed touched by the moment.

'Your babies sense something's happening.' Carmen leant over and patted their blankets but it was unnecessary. The boys didn't cry. Just lay in their capsules awake and alert as their car pulled up behind Prince Zafar's and a solemn manservant, accompanied by two older men, opened their door.

Two older women stood behind the men and Carmen could only guess they were there to help with the babies. The castle steps loomed away to the huge front door at the top and a long line of servants stood waiting to catch a glimpse of the royal heirs.

'You take Bailey, I'm taking Harrison.' Fadia had decided no stranger would carry her boys and Carmen was glad to see her eyes brighten with intent. 'They can take the bags.'

Carmen obligingly leaned across and extricated Harrison from his capsule and handed him to his mother then lifted Bailey for herself. 'No problem.'

'How did my cousins and their mother travel?' More softly. 'And you?' Zafar stood outside the car, waiting for them to alight. He was looking at her, not the others, and she could feel her cheeks warm.

Had he grown taller again or was it just the backdrop

of the palace that made him seem larger than life? He was waiting.

'We travelled well.' He didn't look convinced. 'We were very comfortable.

'I am sorry I did not speak to you.' His cynical smile lifted the hair on her arms. 'I had things on my mind.'

His scrutiny pinked her cheeks more. Maybe she was wrong and she wasn't invisible. She felt herself blush and frowned at him.

He nodded. 'We will discuss this later. Rest today. We visit the King tomorrow.' He moved away to be greeted by the dignitaries lined above them.

Carmen looked across at Fadia, who was only now alighting, and the young mum's wary mood seemed improved by the excitement of their arrival. Perhaps she'd have a chance to talk to Zafar about that later. For the moment it seemed they had to run the gauntlet of the stares.

To Carmen's relief they were whisked in a huddle past the greeting party and into the palace while Zafar remained behind. Carmen wondered just how powerful this man was.

Carmen, Fadia and the boys were shown to a whole wing of the palace that had been turned over to them. Carmen's room was sumptuously decorated, pleasantly cool, and looked out over a tiled courtyard graced by a tinkling fountain. It was much grander than she had anticipated and with a sinking feeling she realised how small her voice would be amongst these people who didn't have to speak in her language if they didn't want to. Just what had she got herself into?

Then she straightened her shoulders. Not the right

attitude if she wanted to help Fadia keep control of her boys and her life. And that was why she was there.

She thought wryly that she'd never had a room so huge or opulent. The boys' room took up almost a quarter of their floor, nestled as it was between those of the two women.

A maidservant dressed in flowing chiffon pants and overshirt bowed and offered to put away her clothes. Carmen glanced down at the one small case she'd brought and shook her head with a smile. 'I think I'll manage, thank you.'

She knew her few toiletries would be lost in the marble bathroom and her clothes would hang pitifully in the cavernous walk-in closet. She needed to remember they'd all fit back perfectly into her one-bedroom flat when she went home. A much-needed dose of reality.

When she crossed the expanse of the room to peer into the closet there were half a dozen silk camisoles in varying lengths, sleeveless, short-sleeved and long, all loose with matching trousers in soft shades of blue and green and lemon, and even a longer black version.

'His Excellency said you may wish for more comfortable clothes. Until the palace seamstress has your measurements she has sent up these.' The girl cast an expert eye over Carmen. 'I'm sure they will look very pretty.'

'I'll probably wear my own clothes.'

The young girl smiled and bowed her head. 'As madam wishes. Excellency said it is the young nursemaids who will help so it is I and my sister who will be your assistants whenever you wish for the young princes.'

'Thank you. I will tell Princess Fadia.'

When the girl left Carmen peered through the open door to the boys' room where Harrison was yawning and Bailey lay wide awake in his huge cot. Her feet sank into the luxurious carpets that overlaid each other like pools of shimmering colour. It seemed sacrilegious to walk on them.

'At least you boys can spend a bit of time lying next to each other. Your beds are huge.'

Deftly she undid Bailey's nappy and popped him in Harry's bed unwrapped and legs kicking while she did the same for his brother. Then she laid them side by side and watched them turn their heads towards each other. Harry touched Bailey's face and Bailey seemed to smile as Harry kicked him.

Fadia's room door opened and the new mum came in. She looked tired but a small smile lit her face as she saw her boys together.

Carmen gently drew her over to the boys. 'Look. I swear your sons are more handsome every day. And there's only us here and two young girls who will do as you wish. Everything will work out perfectly.'

'I hope so. I'm glad you're here but when you go I will be alone. I hope they won't marry me off like a parcel.' She clutched Carmen's sleeve. 'I miss my husband. I miss my life.'

So Fadia was feeling the weight of the palace too. 'Of course you do. But perhaps for now this is better than being alone on the other side of the world. Anything could happen to you there.'

The girl nodded. 'My boys are safe. That is good.'

'Zafar promised you would have choice in your future. I believe him.' He hugged her. 'You're a wonderful mother. Your husband must be smiling at your beautiful boys.'

'I agree.'

They both turned at the unexpected empathy from Zafar as he entered the boys' room and crossed to Fadia. Kiri, the maid, followed him with a tray of light refreshments. 'I am sorry for your loss, Fadia, and know it is hard for you to come back here.'

Fadia turned tear-filled eyes towards him and nodded. 'We will see how good your word is.'

Carmen winced and glanced at him, not sure what he would do. She couldn't help feeling uneasy. It was blatant disrespect for his authority—in public—and the maid's gasp ensured that more than those in the room would hear of it.

Since her arrival she'd become more aware by the hour of the difference in power in the palace. From what the maid had said, Zafar's authority seemed almost as great as his grandfather's and at this moment his face seemed chiselled from the same stone as the mountains she'd seen on the way in. His eyes narrowed as he watched his cousin escape.

Unable to stop herself, Carmen dived into the breach of protocol. 'She's been away from Zandorro a long time. Of course she is upset about being here.'

He raised haughty eyebrows then clapped his hands and the maid ran from the room. He turned back to Carmen. 'She does not need your championing. She is as royal as I.' His brows dropped lower. 'Why look at me like that? As if I would throw her in irons?'

She couldn't help being a little relieved that had been said out loud. 'You should see your own face in the mirror. Pretty scary.'

To her surprise he smiled, though grimly. 'First I am a cowboy and now I have a scary face? You are the strangest woman.'

'No. Just different.'

'No doubt of that.' Zafar strode to the window and then turned back to her, exasperated. 'You of all people should realise I am a civilised man.'

'I'm sorry.' She smiled. It had been a silly thought. 'Thank you. It's reassuring. But this place can be a little overpowering...' she glanced around and then back at him ruefully '...and I don't like the feeling of being overpowered.'

He shook his head and the last of his anger faded from his face as he crossed the room until he stood a few feet in front of her. 'I do not fully understand you, Carmen, but I doubt the strength of an empire could overpower you if you felt strongly enough.'

Did this man really think that about her? It was a hefty compliment out of nowhere and she couldn't help the glow it left her with.

'Once I was overpowered, and I vowed I would not let that happen again.'

He nodded and she felt he really did understand. 'That has made you strong. I respect that.' He went on. 'Tomorrow, when we return from my grandfather's audience, and after the boys are fed, Kiri can mind them for an hour or two while I take you both for a tour. It will be good to remind Fadia how beautiful Zandarro can be. Help her to settle in.'

'That sounds sensible.'

He didn't look pleased at her response. 'I had hoped it would be less sensible and more enjoyable?'

Despite his flippant comment, he still seemed to be

worried about something and she hoped it was nothing Fadia should know. 'And when she has settled, you promise not to arrange a marriage for her.'

He looked past her and his voice dropped. 'You may not think so but I do feel her pain. The loss of loved ones.'

He lifted his head and stared at her as if determined to say the words to her face. 'I buried my son. Prepared his body and laid him on his side with my own hands, facing Mecca in the warm earth. I knew then I could never face the fear of that loss again. Could not face the failure of keeping those I love safe. Who am I to ask another to do the same?' His voice dropped. 'Of course I understand.'

She believed him. But it hurt, when it shouldn't matter to her at all, to see him still so badly wounded by his past. 'I'm glad.'

'I will do what I can. But she should know I do not have the final say.'

She let her breath out with relief. 'She's no girl now. She's a widow with children. And a princess. Life has been hard on her but she is strong. She just needs time.'

He sighed. 'Again it is not I who has to give her time. Already there has been some talk of an alliance for her. Our grandfather believes the sooner she has a man to care for the better she will be. I have disagreed and believe I will prevail. He is not an unreasonable man. We are to discuss it again tomorrow morning before the audience.'

Ouch, but still, Carmen thought, with Zafar on her side Fadia would have a strong champion. She had faith in him, unsure where such faith had come from, but didn't doubt his intent to protect his cousin.

She shook her head and crossed to the boys. 'She says she feels safe here. I hope that's true.'

'As she should. We discovered her Tom had hoped to hide Fadia away while he bargained with me for her whereabouts. He was part of a cell that seeks to bring down our government.'

She couldn't say she was surprised but it gave her the shivers to hear it out loud. 'He's not my Tom. I barely met him.'

He raised his brows at her. 'But you would have hidden their plans from me.'

'Not hidden.' But perhaps she would not have tried to prevent Fadia if she had wanted to run away.

He shook his head at her foolishness. 'You do not understand. It is different here. Risks are greater. I believe Fadia's husband's death was no accident. What if she was expected to die with him?'

And Tom had been in on that? Who were these people they could discuss death and murder so easily? 'So you didn't pay him off?'

'It was suggested he leave my cousin alone. But I believe we have not seen the last of his family. They are eager for a chance at the kingdom.'

She was coming to understand that. 'But what if Fadia decides to return to Australia?'

He dragged an exasperated hand through his hair. 'For the moment she needs to stay here.'

'You can't make her stay if she's unhappy.'

'A woman's view.' He looked away and again she felt there was something he was keeping from her. 'Now, I do not know why I am discussing this with you.'

She straightened. 'Because I'll tell you the truth when everyone else is too scared to.'

'That's right, Carmen.' The way he said her name lifted the hairs on her neck. His words were gentle but his eyes darkened as he closed the gap between them. 'You are not afraid of me.'

Just a tinge of danger and perhaps she should choose her next words a little more carefully. It was different here. Marcus had suggested she tread carefully until she understood the culture more. She should have listened. Zafar wasn't finished.

'Not afraid from the first moment we met, were you?'

And suddenly it was back. That tension between them, like the glow from a hundred candles slowly lighting a room, like a storm overhead in a picnic shed, a moment in a lift, the brush of his lips on the inside of her wrist. 'But, then, you have not been in Zandorro long enough to learn our ways.'

CHAPTER EIGHT

HE'D made her uneasy. Zafar understood her more than she realised, had learnt a lot while he'd attended university in Sydney about Western women, had enjoyed the company of many before he'd married. But this woman was different.

He could see her zeal for her work, her integrity, and most of all he could see the fire within her. Perhaps a fire she had no idea she held or the passionate woman she could become for the right man. A fire that matched his in a way he had not expected.

He watched her search for words to lessen this pressure between them and it amused him that she who lived by defusing tension had momentarily lost her touch. Bravado was all she had left.

'No. I'm not afraid of you.' She only just held eye contact and they both knew it a lie. 'You were the one who said the strength of an empire would not overpower me if I felt strongly enough. I do feel strongly about protecting Fadia. That's why I'm here.' Her voice remained firm—on the outside anyway.

He stepped closer. 'Perhaps you should be. Afraid of me.' A slow, leisurely perusal of her—head to foot—her posture taut with defiance, and he wondered just how angry he could make her, and what would happen if he did. 'Are you not here for the money?'

Her eyes flashed. 'Apparently money was the only way you could get me here!' There it was. So she had given up holding her tongue.

He watched her regret the words as soon as they left her mouth. What had happened to the usually placid Carmen? It seemed he did something to her too. Incited her. Well, she incited him, and he could barely keep his hands by his sides with the need to pull her against him and quieten that mouth of hers with his.

She hurried into speech. Aware of more peril now. Happy to clutch at any straw to avert a difficult situation. 'Your friend, Marcus, said you were a man of honour.'

'That was in Australia.' His eyes travelled over her again with deliberate scrutiny, watched the pink rise in her neck, watched her lick her lips for the taste of danger. 'We are not in your country now. Here honour and law interchange. Here my word is law.'

He closed the last space between them, captured her gaze with his and held it with the easy power of generations of royalty.

Carmen could feel her heart pound. He'd stopped a hairsbreadth away, just short of the fabric of her shirt, fabric she could suddenly feel caress her breasts as she breathed in and out more quickly to calm the agitation caused by his invasion of her space.

'Your law is not my law.' Some foolish pride, some devil inside, refused to allow her to step back.

His voice hardened. Became emphatic. 'You are in Zandorro now. It is my law.' Then softly, 'Come here.'

She blinked. Was he kidding? 'I doubt I could get

much closer without bumping into you.' And some evil twin inside urged her into his arms. She wasn't sure who was the more dangerous to her safety—him or her inner temptress.

He raised his brows. 'Indeed.'

She could feel the aura between them. The air shimmered, thick with vibration that wasn't all words and power struggle, more at stake here than pride and stubbornness. Her brain screamed of danger and her body dared her to walk into him. Give in. Submit.

She unstuck her tongue from the roof of her mouth. 'You might be living under ancient rule but I am not.' She stepped back. She met his eyes unflinchingly and then, to her eternal gratitude, Harrison cried. Actually, almost lifted the roof of the palace with his demands. Thank you, dear, dear baby Harry.

She took the few steps to the ornate cradle, picked up the baby and lifted him like a shield. 'If you'll excuse me, Prince Zafar—' her voice was very dry '—I will take Prince Harrison to his mother.'

He watched her, even with a glimmer of a smile, and nodded once. 'We will return to this subject another time.'

'I don't think so.' She said it as she walked away but she had no doubt he had heard her and she could feel his eyes on her back until the swish of his robes told her he was gone.

She looked back and the room was empty. She leant heavily against the doorframe with a sigh of relief and clutched the baby. What had she fallen into? Just how reliable was his honour? And how reliable would hers be if he took her into his arms again?

* * *

Zafar walked away. He was annoyed with Carmen, annoyed with himself for playing cat and mouse and having a ridiculous argument when what he wanted to do was feel again the rapport they'd had in the park in Australia. All he'd succeeded in doing was alienating her. Of course she was there to stand up for Fadia if she thought her badly done by. What did he expect?

But he was doing the best he could. Had used all his persuasive powers with his grandfather. He would just have to try harder for Fadia. And be more patient with Carmen—and with himself.

Fadia went to bed early. Carmen decided bed was a safe place, a haven, and a good option for herself as well. She didn't sleep well.

The next morning after breakfast she received a message via Yusuf that Prince Zafar wished to see her. The manservant and the midwife eyed each other and she thought of her little can of dye. Yusuf smiled grimly.

She was taken to the library off the huge tiled entry and through a massive studded door. The room had long, arched windows that opened onto a terrace and inner courtyard with the largest fountain she'd seen yet. The tinkling of falling drops filled the room with a background symphony as she crossed more carpets that shimmered and glowed like pools of coloured light, each more beautiful than the last. At the back of the room ceiling-high bookshelves circled the wall.

It could have been an overpowering room with murals and giant urns, except none seemed to have the magnificence of the man standing front of her in full traditional robes. He suited the room too well.

'How did you sleep?'

How did he think? After the first two hours it had taken her to banish their last encounter. 'Fine, thank you.'

'And the boys?' So he was to be solicitous this morning?

She answered calmly. 'We have a routine. Necessary with twins that are breastfed. They sleep longer at night.'

Still he watched her. Did she have a smut on her nose? 'And they are growing well.'

She glanced around the room, looking for clues to this conversation. 'They certainly seem to be. I don't have scales but as long as they're giving us plenty of wet nappies a day, they're fine.

He nodded decisively. 'I will have scales sent to the nursery.'

'As you wish.'

He allowed himself a small smile. 'Now, was that so hard to say?'

She glared at him. 'Am I allowed to ask what happened with your communication with the King this morning?'

'The king has agreed to leave Fadia in my hands for the moment. Which is why I have summoned you.'

She let him get away with summoned because this was much more serious. 'Does she know?'

'I will inform her this afternoon before our audience.' He walked to the window and looked out. 'We meet to postpone our tour tomorrow. Of necessity our time away from the boys will be short. I wish to know if you have a preference for the souks or a drive around the city to see a broader example of the sights?'

'Perhaps the sights, and at least then I may understand the city better.'

'As you wish. The city, then. Taqu, my friend, wishes to accompany us. Do you mind?'

'Why should I mind? But I'm not sure about Fadia. Does she know him?'

'No. Though he was originally betrothed to Fadia before her mother left. He is a good man and wishes to see her.'

'So at least she knows him?'

'They have never formally met and since then he did marry but is now a widower like myself.'

'So he's the one her mother returned the bride price for? Is this a trick to have them meet?'

'What little faith you have in me.' She did have yesterday. Before their discussion.

Then he calmly said, 'No. This allows my grandfather some face and to take pressure off Fadia.'

'What's he like? What makes you think she'd even talk to him?'

'He is not old or unsavoury.' He smiled as he turned back to face her. 'Though, in fact, as a friend of mine, perhaps he is a little old in my cousin's eyes.'

She had to smile back. 'Not too old, then.'

'My thanks. Prince Taqu lost his wife in childbirth, which for someone in our profession is perhaps just as horrific as a hijack.'

Her breath sighed out. She wondered where Zafar's tragic hijack had happened but she should be thinking of Taqu and his loss. 'I'm sorry to hear that.' She watched his face. 'When you say "our profession", is Prince Taqu a doctor too?'

'He is. But I was referring to your midwifery as well.

Taqu has taken over the running of my children's hospital. He also has a young daughter who needs a mother and he knows Fadia is a kind woman.'

Carmen's brain connected to the next thought. 'Should the unlikely happen, and Fadia and this Taqu fall in love and marry, then have children, doesn't that mean you will be further from the throne? Fadia's new husband would act as guardian of her sons, and your brother Prince Regent until Harry comes of age?'

'That is correct.'

'And you don't mind?'

'Not at all. It places me another step further from the throne. A step closer to return to my work. Zandorro has already lost a future king. Now, when the time comes, if Fadia does not remarry, my brother will act as regent until Harrison is fit to be king in his twentieth year. When Harrison has children then I am further removed.'

'Don't you want to be ruler?'

He shook his head. 'It was never my place. If my country needs me I will be there, of course, but I long to return to my work.' She watched his face change.

His eyes brightened and she felt a kinship towards him for a passion shared. 'One day soon I would like to show you. I have great plans for my oncology research. Sick children can never have enough chances of cure. If it is my destiny I will be able to return to the world I love.'

Then he became a prince again and the light died. He pinned her with his gaze. 'So tell me how you think Fadia will take this?'

'Unimpressed.'

He smiled cynically at her. 'Succinct.' And paced some more.

Carmen sighed. 'She's brilliant with the boys but she is worried about how much control she will have over her life.'

He stopped and considered her words and tried to see what she was seeing. He remembered Fadia as a quiet but cheerful girl, watching him from afar, with shy smiles and even shyer laughter. There had been a time when they had been close.

Before he'd had to learn to be a man. Before his mother had left. 'She was always a happy little thing.' His cousin had suffered the same pain he had and he didn't want her to suffer more. He just wished he knew the right thing to do.

Carmen rubbed her forehead. 'This could really upset her.'

He knew that and he needed Carmen to watch over her more than ever. 'Then it is for you to be vigilant.'

He sighed and as if in slow motion his hand came up and he tucked a strand of thick black hair behind her ear. 'Between us we will see if we can return the smile Fadia's face. But for today my grandfather wishes to see his heirs. I will send ceremonial robes for them to be dressed in before lunch. The audience is at one o'clock.'

She'd bet that wouldn't be fun. 'Of course. I will see they are dressed.'

'I would like you to come.'

Carmen smiled and he felt the day improve with just one lift of her mouth. 'If you wish,' she said, tongue in cheek.

'As you appear to be compliant this morning, is there any chance you would wear the clothes in your room?'

She glanced down at her tailored slacks. 'Not appropriate for a royal audience?'

'I'm sure my grandfather would understand if necessary. Of course that is your choice. The palace seamstress was glad of the extra income. If you do not wish to accept clothing from me, you could always wear them while you are here and leave them behind when your tenure is complete. We would donate them to the needy. I will have her informed you do not wish the rest that I ordered.'

'So if I don't wear them I ruin a poor working woman's wage with my pride.' She looked at Zafar and he wasn't smiling so why did she think he was amused? 'Of course, if I may leave the clothes here, I'm happy to fit in with everyone else.'

He didn't look at her as he replied, 'You may even find our style of apparel is better suited to our climate than yours. Everything has a reason in Zandorro.'

Dryly. 'I'll remember that.'

'Tonight you are both expected to dine with the women, who are all anxious to meet you. They are very happy to dress well for the event.'

The women. The harem? Or the female relatives? Either way, she was the hired help. Oh, goody. 'And you?'

'I?'

She raised her brows. 'Who will you be dining with?'

He smiled as if he knew she wouldn't like it. 'Of course I will be dining with the men.' He inclined his head.

She kept her face bland and saw he was even more amused. 'After the meal tonight, I will bid goodnight to my nephews and I expect you to be there. There are things we need to discuss.'

And she was expected to wait around for that? 'Perhaps it could wait until tomorrow?'

'Tomorrow we will see the sights we discuss tonight.'

The King sat on a gilded throne at the end of a long hall. From the breadth of his shoulders Carmen gathered he must have once been a warrior like Zafar but his hands and wrists were twisted and thin with the passage of years beneath his flowing black robe.

To her surprise, his face, though lined, looked wise and compassionate. She hadn't expected that.

Two guards, surely Yusuf's twin brothers, stood on either side of him, wearing the curved swords she'd always thought Yusuf lacked.

Zafar headed their party. Fadia stood proud and tall beside him. Zafar carried Harrison and Fadia carried Bailey.

'Show me the heirs!'

The king gestured for them to approach and much of what followed Carmen didn't understand.

Zafar took Bailey from Fadia so that he held both. He stood tall and imposing, with a tiny baby in flowing gold robes in the crook of each arm. The twins blinked and gazed about as if searching for each other. Fadia watched her sons. Carmen watched Zafar. She saw the fleeting shadow of pain as he held the boys up.

Of course he would feel his own loss, his own investment in the future gone with his family, and she almost took a step forward to comfort him before she remembered where she was. That would not have gone over well.

Carmen closed her eyes. So much pain in this family. It seemed she didn't hold the franchise on that one.

After a few minutes of discussion with Zafar and Fadia in their native language the King waved his hand at the boys.

'Hmph.' The old man sighed. 'I congratulate you on your fine sons, granddaughter. They look healthy but must be renamed. In respect of your wishes and in honour of their father I name the future king Hariz, meaning strong, a ruler's name, and for the second born Ba Leegh, meaning eloquent and level thinking, to support his brother.'

He waved his hand at Zafar. 'They may go.' Zafar signalled to Carmen to approach and between them she and Fadia carried the boys from the throne room.

'I will see you later,' he murmured before he returned to the King's side.

So it was over, great-grandsons checked and accepted, and she and Fadia could just toddle off while the big boys talked. How her life had changed since she'd met these people.

So how much input had their mother had into her son's names? Perhaps Fadia did wield some power. An effort had been made to compromise. Hariz for Harrison and Ba Leegh for Bailey. She wondered whose idea that had been and hoped secretly it had been Zafar's.

She followed the royals back to their quarters. Every hour she realised more how insignificant she was here and became more determined not to be overwhelmed. Her sympathy lay even more strongly with Fadia. In a moment of trivial thought she wondered what Zafar's name meant. Probably big of chest or something.

She chuckled to herself and Yusuf turned and

glanced at her. She smiled at him and he stared stonily back.

'Please to come this way. I will return for his Excellency this afternoon.'

They followed Yusuf obediently back to their wing of the palace. She couldn't help wondering what she'd do if Zafar went away. Apart from Fadia, she had no other allies in the palace.

Fadia fed the boys and they removed their robes then Carmen went for a walk to the palace garden to gather some fruit for her and Fadia's afternoon tea. The sticky almond cakes didn't hit the spot as much as a freshly picked orange did.

Soon it would be time to prepare for dinner with the women and then be ready for her audience with Zafar. She would do as she had been bidden on the small things—it was the large issues she wanted to win.

Like making sure Fadia was happy, and that she, Carmen, made it safely home when all this was over. With her debts paid and her heart intact.

That night after the meal, a learning experience she actually enjoyed with the women, Fadia stood nervously twisting her hands as they awaited Zafar, upset at the idea of seeing the man she was once betrothed to during tomorrow's excursion.

To Carmen's relief, when Zafar came to bid the boys goodnight he was quick to see his cousin's distress. She watched as he soothed her, his voice calm and gentle against her pain. 'You need a friend as well and he is a good man to keep others at bay. You can deal well together without pressure. I give you my promise I will protect you.'

Fadia nodded before she pulled away and looked

with distress at them both. 'I'm sorry. I'm so emotional lately. My poor babies will think their mother is always crying.'

'It is early days. Less than a week. You have been through much. Be gentle with yourself.'

She turned and walked quickly from the room and Carmen moved to follow.

'Wait.' Zafar put his hand on her arm and motioned for Kiri to follow his cousin.

She sighed. 'I'm still so worried about her.'

He shifted until he could look into her face. 'As am I. But Yusuf will stand guard for the time being and Kiri will help with my nephews. Do you not need a moment to think of yourself?'

'I'm fine.'

He shook his head. Lifted his hand as if to move that strand of hair again but didn't complete the action.

'It will all be as it should. Trust me. One day she will be happy again. Tonight I will discuss with Taqu tomorrow's excursion. He is my friend and a good man, and knows we are keeping the King happy. I will ask him to come just for company. I must go away for a few days soon and you will both be alone until I return. At least ask her not to worry and try not to think about reading anything into his presence. Then we will talk again.'

Carmen nodded and Zafar went on quietly, 'Will you walk with me?'

'Now?' She tried not to guess his purpose but she could feel the nerves building as she waited.

'Why do you always say "Now?" when I ask you that?'

'Because you ask at the strangest times.' And I don't trust myself not to follow you into a deserted bedroom somewhere, she thought. She said, 'I'd hate to compromise myself.'

He smiled. "Now is not the time. When it comes there would be no compromise.' No matter how hard she tried, there was no doubt about his meaning.

So there was to be a time? Did she have no say? She looked down at the sleeping babies and pretended to herself she was affronted by his assumption yet inside the temptress stirred and smirked. 'Their mother is still unsettled. I need to be here.'

'Kiri is here. As is her sister. They will watch over them. And Yusuf will stay so he can find us if we are needed. I wish to show you something. I won't have a chance tomorrow and after that I will be busy until I leave.'

So he really was going. 'Very well.' She dropped her pretence and glanced down at her palace clothes, worn for dining with the women, filmy swathes of fabric that made her aware of her own curves and left her with little armour to shield herself with against this man. 'I'll get my coat.'

He saw her glance and held out his hand. 'Your clothes are perfect. It is too warm for a coat.'

He took her through the palace, through a dozen different turns she would never remember until they came to a courtyard, the tinkling of the fountains the only sound as they stepped out into the moonlit night.

'Where are we?'

'At the south wall. The vehicles enter by the north gates and climb the hill.' He strode to a gate and selected a large brass key from a ring of many such keys. 'This is the other side of the palace and there is no descent to the desert from here.'

He gestured for her to precede him and they came out onto a walled ledge that hung over the cliff. The shimmering moon-bathed desert lay before them hundreds of feet below.

In front lay miles of undulating dunes, expanses of sand and rocky outcrops, all ghostly silver in the night so that she felt they were the only living beings as far as the eye could see. As if they themselves were on the moon.

She slowly turned her head and sighed. 'It's incredible.'

'When I can't get away, this is where I come. In the past it was the place I could find some peace, even if just for a short time.'

He lifted his arm and she followed the direction in the silvery light. 'Can you see that small hill under the moon to your right?'

It was surprisingly easy to distinguish. 'Yes.'

His voice lowered. 'There my family lies. I tell you not for your sympathy but because I am more at peace than I have been since the day I awoke. It began that day in the park, with new life unexpected yet beautiful, and you have helped me to heal.'

'Thank you for sharing this with me.'

'I know our ways are different, and I know you try hard to understand. But I want you to know that I see you. If it seems I am ignoring you, or have forgotten you, that is not true. I owe you much. When I am gone for a few days, you may like to come here and find peace for yourself.'

It was as if finally he was allowing her to see a tiny part of his mind. And his heart. She wondered how hard it had been for him and how much the darkness out here had helped.

She took his hand and laced her fingers through his, and when he bent his head she lifted her lips and kissed his cheek. She wanted to do more than that but it was time to go before she did something she regretted.

'Please take me back to Fadia.'

For a moment she thought he would protest but he didn't. Just nodded. 'As you wish.'

CHAPTER NINE

WHEN Carmen woke to the sound of Harry in the morning, it wasn't his usual royal demand. It was fear. A primal bellow that made her throw the covers and slip from the bed more swiftly than normal.

'What's wrong, little man?' She picked him up and glanced across at Bailey just as Fadia arrived. Harry's twin brother lay pale and still in the bed and Carmen's heart thudded with fear as she thrust Harry into his mother's arms, scooped little Bailey from his bed and tipped him over her arm to tap his back.

'Lights,' she called, and Fadia hurriedly switched them on. 'Get help. Tell them to get Zafar!'

Fadia ran from the room, her other son clutched to her chest, and Carmen laid Bailey down on top of the padded dresser and tilted his chin up a little to open his airway.

There was no chest movement but his pale skin felt warm as she searched swiftly for a pulse in his neck. Faint and slow, less than sixty, so obviously not her heart rate, she felt, but such a relief to have something.

She puffed three quick breaths over his mouth and nose and began to compress his little sternum with her first two fingers. One, two, three, breath, one two three, breath, all the while the pounding of her own heart threatening to drown out the world as her fear rose.

Zafar swung through the door, Yusuf and Kiri on his heels, and he moved in smoothly beside her and took over the cardiac massage.

Fadia arrived with Harry just as Bailey's little body twitched and he coughed and began to cry weakly. Carmen bit back her own tears as she stepped away, her hand covering her mouth as the restrained fear rose in her throat like bile.

She opened her arms for the distraught mother and hugged the shuddering Fadia as they stood clutching hands and watched Zafar. Yusuf handed Zafar a stethoscope and Carmen bit her shaking lip as she waited. Zafar bent and examined the little chest front and back and both sides.

Carmen chewed her lip as Bailey's cries grew louder and she hugged Fadia, her own need for comfort almost as great as hers.

Then she saw Zafar's face. Saw his cheeks suck in and his mouth work before sound came out. 'Good air entry now. Probably a choking episode.' He paused and blinked and inhaled. It was much harder to be calm now that it was over. 'We'll take him for an X-ray, though.' His eyes sought Carmen's. 'Tell me what you found.'

She ordered her thoughts in her head, strangely more focussed now she knew Zafar needed her control. 'Pale, blue face, not breathing. But skin warm and heart rate around sixty.'

'Too close.' Their glances met. Zafar shuddered, it was subtle but she saw it. She didn't think anyone else did but this had rocked him. Both of them knew how close it had been. 'Well done.' He took another deep breath. 'So fortunate you were here.'

Carmen looked up at him and he drew strength from her support. No doubt his own face was as white and strained as hers. His own eyes just as wide with shock. He knew later he had to hold her close, alone, so that he could banish the fear that would live, like the pain from the past, but for now he needed to reassure his cousin.

Carmen was saying something. 'Harry's cry was frantic. That's why I jumped up.'

'I, too.' Fadia sniffed and wiped her eyes and hugged her eldest son and kissed him before she handed him to Carmen, who hugged him into her chest with her own need for comfort. 'Harry saved him. I've never heard him cry like that.'

The two women looked at each other and Zafar placed Bailey gently in Fadia's arms and gripped his cousin's shoulder. 'It seems he is fine. Obviously your sons are designed to give us all grey hair.'

'Thank you, Zafar.' She turned to Carmen. 'And you, my dear Carmen.' She squeezed Carmen's hand in gratitude.

Carmen just nodded and stepped back further, bumping into Kiri, who was shaking like a leaf. The little maid slipped her hand into hers and Carmen, juggling Harry, hugged her to stop the shudders. She felt frozen on a treadmill of mental pictures. Couldn't help imagining if she'd been too late. If they'd been unable to save Bailey.

She squeezed Kiri's hand and turned away, and Zafar had no doubt she wanted to hide the tears he had seen spring to her beautiful eyes. They were so fortunate she had been here, had been so quick thinking, and he closed his eyes for a moment at the horror that could have been.

Zafar followed her and turned her gently to face him, saw the streaks of tears across her skin and the trembling of her mouth. He took Harry and handed him to Kiri and then drew Carmen in until she was against his chest. 'Let me hold you.'

Zafar searched her face, could see that shock had set in and needed to feel her against him and show her how much her quick thinking had saved them all. How bravely she tried to control the shudders that rolled through her body in the aftermath of horror. His brave Carmen. 'Thank you,' he whispered against her hair. 'Again. For caring for my cousin and my nephews.' He closed his eyes as the scent of her stirred memories of another time, of other comfort, and the strange way this woman felt so right in his arms. 'And for me.'

He spoke into her hair. 'We will take Bailey to the hospital and check his lungs more thoroughly. Would you like to come?'

Of course she would. She nodded under his mouth and he couldn't help the kiss he brushed against her hair.

'Then go. Dress. We wait for you and Fadia. We can bring Harrison.' He smiled. 'No doubt he too has concerns for his brother.'

The next hour proved reassuring as Bailey was X-rayed and examined again, this time by the head of Neonatal Intensive Care, and Carmen was surprised when Zafar suggested they leave Fadia and the doctor to talk while they minded Harry.

'Distressing episodes like this need discussion, and

she needs to ask everything she can. I think she will listen more if it is not I who tells her that all will be well.'

So Carmen walked around the children's cancer ward with Zafar, and tried not to think of those few moments in Zafar's arms. To feel him around her when death had been so close made her realise how precious life was. How easily lost. She shuddered as Harrison slept on Zafar's shoulder as they watched the children have their breakfast.

Inquisitive little faces peered at them from beds and highchairs. 'It's a lovely ward.'

'We tried to make it more like a pre-school than a hospital. And also so the mothers can sleep comfortably in their children's rooms.'

'And you designed this?'

'With the help of Dr Ting in Sydney. We had many discussions but it is a first for Zandorro and our staff are very dedicated.'

'And you gave this up when Fadia's father died?'

'It was my duty.'

She could tell he missed it. 'Perhaps one day you will be able to return.'

'Perhaps.' He slanted a glance at her. 'I'm hoping soon now. Another time, perhaps we could discuss the baby hotel concept and if it would work for sick children. If the whole family could come, and the sick child could visit the hospital instead of being admitted.'

'Of course. I'll look forward to that. For children on cancer treatment I think it would work well. I'm sure it would be less daunting for them without the separation of siblings.'

'Good.' He smiled down at her and she could see how passionate he was about this. 'We will discuss this again.' He looked up as a nurse approached and spoke to him. 'They are ready for us to return.

It seemed Bailey's all-clear had come through and she had an idea Zafar had been trying to distract her from the stress of the morning. Or perhaps distract himself. She couldn't rid herself of the idea he was still in shock and no doubt either of them would ever forget the image of that moment.

The ride back to the palace was quiet but there was a feeling of unity and support for each other that had previously been missing. Fadia kept her eyes glued to her sons and every now and then tears would well and then her glance would sweep between Zafar and Carmen and she would sigh and relax back in her seat.

Zafar and Carmen spoke quietly about the idea of building a child-friendly hotel next to the hospital for families and soon they were back at their rooms in the palace.

But always at the back of his mind Zafar could not lose the memory of Carmen's support in his moment of need, her quick thinking in Bailey's crisis, and as quickly as possible he finished the multitude of tasks he could not put off before he could return to check on them.

The female servants hovered around Fadia and her boys, and Carmen vibrated with a restlessness that was probably due to the stress of the morning, but it made his brows draw together as his glance lingered on her face.

'Would you like to walk with me?'

His heart warmed as he watched her struggle not to give away her relief at his request. She did need to lose the edginess that possessed her. 'I shouldn't leave Fadia.'

'Go.' Fadia waved her away. 'We are fine here and perhaps a walk will help you settle. You have stood and sat a dozen times these last few minutes.' She smiled at Carmen. 'No doubt your nerves are as bad as mine. The girls are here.'

Zafar nodded. 'Come. I will leave Yusuf here and he will phone me if we are needed. We will return in a while.' He smiled. 'Or maybe longer.'

Carmen followed him through the palace until they came to a part she hadn't seen before. The furnishings were more ornate, grander in the hallways, until finally they came to an entrance with a carved wooden door flanked by giant pots, then he stopped.

She knew. 'Your rooms?'

'We will have peace and privacy here.'

She nodded and he drew her through the doors and closed them behind his back. 'I need to hold you.'

She couldn't say no because her body still felt frozen in limbo and somehow she knew that Zafar could make her feel again. And she could help him. When she moved into his embrace he pulled her in against his chest and the strength of him made her close her eyes with the wash of comfort and relief.

'Thank you,' he whispered against her hair. 'Again. For saving Fadia, for saving me from another tragedy.'

She closed her eyes as his warm breath stirred memories that lingered of her times in this man's arms.

She sighed. 'It was such a shock.'

He shifted until he could look into her face. 'Yes. Yet you managed. But Yusuf will watch them all for the moment. I too need time to soak in the fact that all are safe. You need to let yourself be comforted for once.'

'And perhaps you do too.'

'I know you saw that. But for you we would just be at the beginning of more pain.'

'No. Anyone would have done the same.'

'Perhaps, but not as magnificently.'

He shook his head. Stroked her face. 'We were blessed the day Fadia met you.'

'Fate.'

'Perhaps. My brave Carmen, I just wish I knew what fate had planned for both of us.'

His hand rose and cupped her cheek then he leant down and kissed her. Firm lips tightly leashed with control yet full of dark emotion as he took her mouth and showed her he had been truly rocked by the morning's events. In return she couldn't help share her own horror and both grasped the lifeline, and a promise that they could forget how close they'd been to disaster.

For a moment sanity surfaced and she pulled back reluctantly. 'Can you let the pain go? Please. From now— and from the past?'

His eyes burned into hers. 'At this moment I need you held against my heart.' If only she could, and as if she'd spoken out loud he drew her back against him. 'The horror if you had not been there...'

'Let it go, Zafar.' She didn't want to think of horror in this moment. She saw his need. Answered it. 'You were there too. You made it happen.'

He tightened his grip. 'For once. Take the comfort I offer.'

But what if she lost herself? 'And will you take mine?'

That was all she wanted to do. Feel every glorious

inch of him against her; be crushed by his power and reborn with his possession. Stop fighting, for once, against the magnetism of this man who drew her like no other. Put away her fears of the ramifications she knew would follow.

His mouth came down and she sighed into him, let herself go, savoured the defeat of her fears, absorbed his pain and ached to heal it. Her shirt buttons fell away, as did his; she tasted his skin, dug her fingers into his corded muscles, soaked his strength into hers and gave freely and openly of her own. He lifted her and she wrapped her legs around him as she held his face against hers.

The world shifted under her as they turned as one, skin against skin, his eyes adoring as they skimmed her body. Then a shift, a shrugging off of more clothes, and she could do nothing but glory in his possession as she opened herself to him, her back against the wall, the rhythm of their need pounding in her heart until both were lost in the maelstrom. Soaring into the light. Suffused with heat like the desert that stretched away on the other side of the drapes.

Lost in a sandstorm of sensation she'd never imagined. Clinging to the centre of her world. Until slowly they returned to earth like the blown grains of sand outside.

They rested, panting against the wall, eyes wide and stunned at each other and the storm they had created between them, until Zafar carried her across and lay down with her still cradled in his arms.

When Zafar lifted his head the world had changed, along with his acceptance of the inevitable. He needed her. Loved her. Was endangered by her in his very soul, for how would he let her go? Staring into the shadows of his room with Carmen's cheek resting on his chest, Zafar inhaled the scent of her. He stroked the thick silken strands of her hair and a part of him died inside to think of her gone. What had he done?

A magical connection that had smashed into a million brightly jagged shards his foolish idea of perhaps loving her once and banishing her hold from his heart.

The most glorious foolishness of it all was he could not regret his heart's decision. He'd had no idea this was how it was meant to be. Or what price he would pay. All he knew was that if he did not return tomorrow, he could not regret this knowledge.

When they woke she shifted against him. 'I must go.'

Her forehead leant into him as his hand touched her cheek. She turned her head and with her own hand she stroked his fingers. With such tenderness she held his heart.

'Go to Fadia.' Yet even as he said it his hand tightened to keep her in his arms 'And later I will come to you.'

He sighed, captured her hand, and drew it to his mouth. 'We are going to regret this.'

'Perhaps.' So she realised that, too. 'But thank you.'

So he was already regretting it. Carmen understood because her mind had already accepted that this man was no ordinary man. Zafar the prince made her feel like a queen, more woman than in her whole year of marriage, more girl than a decade of flirtation, and, no matter what, she would always remember this time of mutual need as part of her destiny, even if their future could not lie together.

Later that night he did come to her but he didn't stay.

He pressed a key into her hand. 'I leave tomorrow. If I am detained...' he glanced away at the windows and then back at her, and she couldn't deny the flicker of unease his words caused '...perhaps unavoidably, then I would like you to remember there is magic in Zandorro as well as the things you don't understand.'

He sighed. 'I tell you that if I do not return shortly I have arranged for you to fly back to your own country as soon as possible. But in the meantime you may use the east courtyard as your private sanctuary.'

'I don't understand.'

'To have you here is a gift but difficult times lie ahead and I wish you back in the safety of your own country. As it stands now, there is no future for what we have.'

'Are you in danger?'

'I have safeguards arranged but I will be safer if I do not have to worry about you.' Unable to argue with that, she nodded reluctantly.

The next morning the sun was shining in through the windows when Kiri opened Carmen's blinds. 'Good morning, Miss Carmen.'

No. It wasn't. Zafir had gone. Probably into danger.

Carmen felt cold. Which was ridiculous. She was in the middle of a desert city. Eggs could fry on car bonnets. It seemed her heart lay packed on ice for its own protection.

She hated that here, as a woman, she had no power; she was not allowed to help Zafar. But, then, would Zafar even want her help? He'd hinted that they had no future. The uncertainty was stretching her heart to breaking point. She couldn't live like this. To be here was to be helpless.

She needed to believe that for her own safety. The safety of her heart. She was just a pawn like Fadia and the twins and even Zafar himself. As soon as Fadia was settled she would go home. The sooner she went home to the world she understood, the better.

Zafar was away for days and Carmen told herself she was glad. The distancing effect of time allowed her to see how powerless she was. How ridiculous her attraction to Zafar was in the royal scheme of things. How little future they had, no matter how she felt.

Thankfully every day Fadia seemed to recover a little more of her self-confidence and enjoyment of the simple pleasures in her life grew as she became more comfortable that Bailey would be fine in the long term.

Contrary to her fear, the older ladies in the palace were kind and helpful and doted on her babies and her. But the biggest change in Fadia was that from victim to advocate against Tom, against people who could so coldly plot the death of her husband, perhaps her babies. And Carmen began to see the fighting spirit of Zafar's family.

When the babies' feeding had settled into a routine and Fadia became more confident and her boys began to develop personalities that made them all laugh.

Hariz truly was the leader. Along with his demanding roar his little clenched fists waved impatiently when he wanted to be fed, while Ba Leegh would lie quietly, watching the world, observing, secure in the knowledge his needs would be met.

Carmen grew fonder of the young maid, Kiri, and her sister and the way they cared for Fadia and the twins.

And so the days passed but Carmen began to fret at being stuck in the castle. She never did get that tour.

Often she was superfluous in the boys' care now and took to spending an hour at the hidden eyrie Zafar had shown her as she prepared herself to return to her old life.

On the third day after Zafar left, word came to their wing that Prince Taqu, who had arrived in the palace the day Zafar had left, wished to take Fadia and Carmen for an outing to the souks.

'I do not want to go,' Fadia said as she wrung her hands and Carmen tried to calm her.

'Of course you don't have to go. We can say that.' Carmen peered out the window but she couldn't see the forecourt. 'Is that what you want?'

'Yes.'

'Aren't you a little curious?'

'No.'

'Fine.' She walked to the door. 'I'll go down to apologise and say you're too tired today.'

Fadia twisted her hands. 'Do you want to go, Carmen?'

'I'd like to get out, yes. But I can see the souks when Zafar comes back.'

'You could go.'

Carmen laughed. 'I'm sure the prince would love that. A strange foreign woman instead of you.'

'Let me think. Perhaps he could come back tomorrow and if Zafar is not back we could go out for a short time. I do not like leaving the babies.'

'Of course. But I won't promise anything in case you change your mind.'

Carmen's first sight of Prince Taqu reminded her

how much she missed Zafar. The man was tall, not as broad across the chest as Zafar, but a truly impressive specimen, and with a smile that promised kindness, not greed. She wished Fadia could see that she didn't need to be afraid of this man.

He came towards her. 'You must be Miss Carmen. Zafar has told me about you.'

'Prince Taqu. I bring apologies from Princess Fadia.'

He didn't look surprised. 'And they are?'

'That today she is tired. And her sons need her.'

'I am here for a few more days. Perhaps tomorrow.'

Carmen couldn't help her smile. It was too early to be sure that Fadia would but she liked this man. 'Perhaps. But the princess thanks you for your kind offer.'

'Does she?' Too polite to disagree with her. He shrugged. 'Or perhaps you do out of kindness. It does not matter. I will return this time tomorrow and ask again.' He glanced at his watch. 'Please tell Princess Fadia I await her pleasure. Assure her we will go out for a short time only and perhaps a change of scenery will assist in her recovery. And for your entertainment too, of course.'

'Of course. Thank you.'

On the fourth day, despite Fadia's misgivings, she and Carmen visited the souks, accompanied by Prince Taqu. Vendors bowed respectfully as they showed their wares, much less vociferous than Carmen had expected. No doubt their escort helped with that. Although the first day proved very formal, by the time the two-hour visit was over Fadia looked less strained and had agreed to another foray.

The next day, the fifth Zafar was away, saw them examine all the mosques in the city, along with a leisurely lunch at a city restaurant. Prince Taqu had studied at the same university as Zafar and his stories of their escapades had Fadia giggling in a way Carmen had never seen.

On the sixth day, the day Prince Taqu was to leave, they went back to the souks to search for more treasures for Carmen to take back to Australia. This time the prince brought his daughter and afterwards they all returned to the palace to show the young princess the twins.

It proved to be a delightful day and by the end of it Carmen's presence was barely necessary. Unobtrusively she drifted further away from them.

She was glad to see Fadia more relaxed and there was no doubt that Taqu had planned a concentrated assault on the princess's defences. His promise to return the following week seemed to be greeted with pleasure by Fadia and already there was rapport between his daughter and Fadia.

Carmen realised her need to be in Zandorro was drawing to a close, which was a good thing. Carmen just wished watching them didn't make her feel so alone.

On the seventh day Zafar returned, and even the sight of Yusuf coming towards her made her smile in anticipation.

'Prince Zafar wishes to see you.'

'Where is he?'

'The library.'

Zafar waited. Pacing back and forth over the carpets. Unseeing as he strode from side to side. Every morning and every night of the last six he'd looked forward to this day. The day he would return to Carmen. But now the day filled him with dread. Taqu had discovered a spy in the palace and unearthed plans to kidnap Carmen and Fadia.

Imagine if he had not asked his friend to come and watch over the women while he had searched for the rebel stronghold. He needed to have Carmen safely back in her own country before the final coup attempt. If he'd realised how dangerous the situation would become so quickly, he would never have brought her here.

The door opened and she was there. Her face shining, her eyes alight, looking at him as he'd dreamed she would look at him. How had all this happened without his knowledge? To give his heart to a woman from the other side of the earth when his world balanced on the edge of danger.

To fall for a woman who did not understand the dangers. Who unwittingly exposed his own throat and hers. Who could prove his next failure to keep those he loved safe. A failure he could not bear to repeat. She was so fragile. So unprepared. So precious.

When she entered the library she didn't know what to expect but the distance between them came as a shock. Zafar nodded in greeting but there was no smile in his eyes, no move towards her, and she halted inside the door. Yusuf let himself out and closed the door.

'Is everything all right?'

'It is time for you to leave.'

CHAPTER TEN

THE words flew like darts from an unexpected ambush and punctured her euphoria. Destroyed her dream of him opening his arms to her. Mocked her anticipation until it fell in tatters around her slippered feet.

'Fadia's fine now and the boys are settled. It's time for you to return to Sydney.'

She heard the words, glanced around at the opulence of his office and unconsciously rubbed her arms. 'Today?' Go home. It would be soon but...leave them all right away? 'Why the hurry?'

Zafar's dark brows drew together as he looked past her shoulder. 'Your job is done. Your time here is over.'

Carmen looked away herself. To hide the shine of tears she could feel. She was such a fool. So she'd slept with him and that was that. And she'd been like a damsel in the tower, waiting for her prince to return. More fool her. Huge fool her. 'As you say, you want me gone. There is no reason for me to stay.' Still she wouldn't look at him. Couldn't.

She heard him move and her heart leapt. She turned her head and he was pacing, but not towards her.

Fool again. What did she think? That he hadn't really meant it and she could stay? That the royal family would greet her with open arms because she'd kissed him a few times? Slept with him once.

She lifted her chin. Well, damn him. That was that. And she felt remarkably, frozenly calm. It proved he wasn't to be trusted. She had reason to hate him now, which was so much safer than that other emotion. Why was that?

It all happened very fast after that. Her clothes were packed when she arrived back at the children's wing, Fadia was stunned and white-faced, Kiri sniffed and hid red eyes as she gathered all Carmen's things. In the background, waiting, Yusuf stood, arms crossed, impatient for her to say goodbye.

She was bundled down to the car, and when Yusuf opened the door he seemed surprised Zafar was already seated. 'I will accompany you to the airport.'

Yusuf stared at his master for a moment and then inclined his head before shutting the door. Carmen became more confused. The car started and within minutes they were leaving the palace behind. 'What is going on here?'

'I need you out of the country. For both our sakes.'

She thought about that and couldn't help a glimmer of foolish hope that he didn't really want her to go.

As he sat beside her in the limousine the darkened windows kept the interior dim and intimate. He didn't speak so she looked out the window as they drove through the winding streets. She never had got to explore on her own. She should have.

'I understand you saw the souks with Prince Taqu and Fadia?'

'Yes. I enjoyed it.' How could he carry on a normal conversation after the last half an hour?

She looked away again and a woman dressed in black with all but her eyes covered disappeared into a doorway as they drove through the big gates out into the desert. 'It's very difficult for a woman like me to understand your culture and customs.'

'But not impossible?'

'No. I should thank you that I had the chance to set out on an adventure to an exotic land in the company of exotic people.' Once started, she couldn't stop. 'Just as long as I remembered this was a job that would end…' she glanced away from him to the sand that stretched into the distance and her mouth hardened '…suddenly. But, of course, I am only the hired help.'

'Have you finished?'

She inclined her head mockingly. 'Of course, Excellency.'

He ran his hand through his hair and she smiled grimly. At least he wasn't immune to how he was treating her. 'Listen to me. You are at risk and I need to have you safe. I will not be responsible for harm befalling you.'

'I can look after myself.'

His eyes burned into hers. 'You will leave now and be safe.'

She narrowed her own, sifting through the mixed messages, reading between the lines. 'You said I could never be bowed.'

'Listen to me, Carmen. At this moment—'

A sentence he never had the chance to finish as gunshots rang out. Disjointed cracks like stones hitting the side of the car. She'd never heard them for real before but she'd watched enough movies to get the gist of what was happening.

Yusuf swerved the car onto a side road and suddenly they were airborne as they crashed through the scrub beside the road and into the desert along a barely discernable track.

The window between Yusuf and them wound down as Zafar pushed her onto the floor and he slid lower in seat with his phone out. His eyes held hers as he spoke rapidly into it and for some crazy reason she was too angry to be frightened.

'Three vehicles. They will catch us.' He nodded to Yusuf. 'Support is coming. They will meet us at the valley pass.' Then he turned back to her.

'I have arranged for us to be picked up in an armoured vehicle in fifteen minutes. We wait by the rocks in the crevice. We must quickly hide ourselves. It is too late to get you away. We must return to the palace until it is safe.' She shook her head. She didn't understand.

'If anything happens, and we get separated, keep quiet and unobtrusive and I will find you.'

'Why is this happening?'

'It is almost done but I feared this last assault. The last of the rebels have nothing left to lose. They wish to capture me but do not worry. Safeguards are in place.'

Now she was scared. 'I'm not letting you out of my sight.'

'Nor I you.' He grasped her arm and eased her up beside him. 'This is my world and when this is done it will be done.' He dropped a swift, hard kiss on her lips. 'Do as I command and you will be safe.'

For the moment the other vehicles were out of sight as they passed a large outcrop of rock and before she realised what was happening the car slowed. Zafar reached in front of her and pushed open the door on her side. She could see the sand rushing by.

'Go,' he said urgently, and pushed her so that she slid across the seat and out of the door onto the sand in an ungainly heap. He followed her and Yusuf in the car accelerated away from them in a spray of sand and dust, and suddenly the car was gone. She was in the middle of the desert, at midday, and Zafar was pulling her towards a crevice.

Zafar cursed his own stupidity as he crawled across the sand towards her. He'd known trouble was brewing but he'd thought they'd had another twenty-four hours before it escalated enough to pose a threat. And he'd dragged his woman into danger because he'd wanted to have her safe on a plane.

He froze. His woman.

It would be best when the fog that weakened him flew out from Dubai until all this was settled. His Carmen was a resourceful woman but the worry gnawed at him like a rat in the palace dungeons. All she had to do was lie low and wait to be picked up. Why did he worry she wouldn't?

The hurt he'd seen in her eyes would pursue him. She didn't trust him and he couldn't blame her. He had missed her like a limb for the last seven days until the communication they had captured had outlined the revolt. And the plan of kidnapping Carmen to force Zafar's hand had driven him back to the palace.

But the plan of shifting her to safety had backfired so now there was no time for thinking. Only surviving.

Carmen heard the growl of approaching vehicles and her heart thumped in her chest in time to the revs of the engines.

'Go.' Zafar's voice was urgent behind her. Spurred into action, she crawled inelegantly across to the outcrop and there was a crevice, sand crusted and pushed a couple of feet back into the rock, just as Zafar had said, which afforded some protection from the road. When she pulled herself in, it was deeper than she'd thought and she fell several feet down into a heaped pile of sand. It was dim, and something scuttled away from her hand as she tried to steady herself. Carmen shuddered and pulled her hands in close to her chest. Zafar fell in beside her.

The roar of the approaching vehicles seemed to vibrate through her body and she blocked out the animals or reptiles she'd disturbed to worry about later as she jammed her head down into his chest and squeezed her eyes shut as if she could squeeze the whole crazy ten minutes away. This was not happening.

That thought at least brought her some sanity. And Zafar's arms around her helped.

'Fear's your worst enemy.' His voice in her ear. She'd heard those words before, the woman on the headland, a test by solitary birth that Jenny had had to go through, and she'd said that to Jenny. Well, fear was in this dark and dismal hole right alongside them both, and she wasn't happy.

'Who are they?'

'Friends of Tom's.'

The cars roared past and the sound bombarded her more than the sand that flew into their crevice and coated their hair and cheeks. Her heart thumped in her ears, staccato thumps, and then she realised it was not her heart but the sound of a battle not too far away. An explosion. Then the whoosh of heavy fire and the rattle of machine guns. Then the distinctive sound of vehicles driving off.

Now beneath her own dread was her fear of what had happened. And even a little for the annoying Yusuf. Who was attacking them and why? And just how out of her depth was she?

Zafar stood and pulled himself up. 'Stay here. You are safe here.'

And then he was gone. The previous tenants scuttled against her hand and she shuddered. Zafar's footsteps faded.

She shifted onto her knees and peered over the ledge. He'd told her to wait there but she'd never been good with orders. The sound of fighting over the rise had been quiet for ten minutes now and she had a bad feeling about it.

The tenant brushed past her hand again and that decided her. She was out of there. If need be, she could come back to get out of the sun but she had to know that Zafar wasn't in danger.

It had been easier to fall into the crevice than climbing out, but with a skinned knee and three broken nails she finally crouched on the outside of the opening. She shuddered as she glanced back into the dark interior. It would take a fair incentive to get her back in there.

The hot breeze dried the perspiration on her face and she licked her lips. Sand grated against her tongue and she could smell the smoke that was rising from ahead. Thirst was an issue already but not one she could worry about just yet. Keeping low, she scurried to the next outcrop and stayed crouched as she listened. No sound from over the hill and no vehicles that she could hear.

When she made it to the top of the sandy ridge she

could see the remains of the battle. She gasped when she saw Zafar's car teetered on its side next to another burnt-out wreck of a Jeep. A collision with consequences, and then she saw Zafar edging towards the car. Yusuf!

She scanned constantly for movement as she skidded down the hill from outcrop to outcrop until she was ten yards from where Zafar crouched. He turned and looked at her; his eyes flared briefly then he sighed and shrugged. 'Of course you came.'

The low groan made her jump and she flattened herself against the rock and twisted her head from one piece of wreckage to another. It came again, guttural, weak and definitely masculine.

They crawled across the open ground to Zafar's car and peered through the smashed rear window. Yusuf. The man seemed trapped. Crumpled against the steering-wheel. The smell of fuel reeked. The burning Jeep smouldered too close for comfort. They slid around the chassis of the car until Zafar could stretch up and peer through the driver's window. 'Yusuf?'

With a struggle he opened his eyes. 'Leave here. It is too dangerous.' He closed his eyes and whispered, 'It is the will of Allah.'

Typical. She was getting so sick of men giving orders. 'Not until we get you out.'

Zafar was concentrating on the task ahead. 'Let us see if Allah wants you out first.'

He turned to Carmen. 'I cannot budge it alone. If we put weight on this side that teeters, maybe the whole car will fall back on its wheels.'

Away from the flaming wreck beside it. Neither mentioned that. 'Not easy to do that without getting closer to the flames.'

As they circled the car the tyres began to smoke as the building heat encouraged the fire to cross the distance between cars.

'We need a wedge, something to give leverage. We're running out of time.'

'Yusuf.' Zafar's command snapped the man awake. 'Reach the lever for the boot.'

'Leave, Excellency. Take the woman.'

'Not without you. Do it.'

She heard keys rattle and then the boot latch clicked. Zafar scooped out a large coil of rope and a tyre lever. And her suitcase, which she thought strangely thoughtful.

'We can do this.' He glanced around. 'That rock. Can you tie it there?'

She estimated the length of the rope and the nearest outcrop, and Zafar took his own end of the rope and tied it quickly around the doorframe next to Yusuf.

She ran and circled it until she had tied the car to the rock with as much tension as she could. She'd always been lousy with knots but the granny would have to do. The rear tyre burst into flames and smoke grew acrid in her throat until she coughed. They weren't going to make it.

She could feel the thunder of her pulse as the sweat ran down her face. They were going to be too late and Yusuf would burn. She'd really grown used to having him around.

'Fear is your worst enemy,' she muttered, and gritted her teeth as Zafar caught the rope and twisted it with the tyre lever to tighten it slowly. The rope creaked, the car creaked she watched him strain against it to shorten the rope. She ran back to him and heaved as well. Between them it finally shifted.

In the end it didn't need much, just enough to change the centre of gravity, and when it happened she wasn't prepared for it and the car swayed and then fell with a whoomph.

Yusuf cried out as he was bounced around like a cork in a bottle. Zafar wrenched open the door. A now unconscious Yusuf half fell out onto the road and she ran to help Zafar as the rear of the car filled with smoke. Flames began to lick along the interior roof lining as they dragged him free.

It was going to blow. She could hear the words in her head and she kept pulling, yanking, cursing this heavy lump of a man who had uselessly fainted on them, until he was partially sheltered behind a rock.

That was when she heard the sound of an approaching vehicle. The outcrop that almost protected them was too small to hide behind. Zafar pulled her behind him. Would this day never end?

The low throbbing rumble distracted them just as the vehicle erupted into a fire ball and she ducked her head into Zafar's back. A blast of heat singed the hands she held over her head and then it settled to a steady roar of heat.

The rumble became a throb from an armoured car, which slowed and then stopped beside their outcrop. Good guys, she hoped. Please let it be Zafar's back-up.

Two young men with machine guns jumped out of the armoured truck. One ran to the front of the vehicle and the other to the back as they guarded the road. A third climbed down and approached her with obvious relief. 'Excellency. Are you well?'

He turned a blackened face to Carmen and no doubt she looked just as much a disaster. He grinned and she realised he'd almost enjoyed himself. Men! 'It seems so.' He raised his singed eyebrows. 'Carmen?'

She nodded and after one searching look at her he stood up. Then he pulled her into his arms and kissed her. Thoroughly. 'I must go.'

Strange thing to say. She wasn't planning on staying either. 'Me, too.' A few minutes earlier for the cavalry would have been nice, she thought sourly as she peered through the smoke. Carmen sat up beside the unconscious Yusuf, bedraggled, singed and over it all.

'Miss O'Shannessy?'

'Yes.'

'His Excellency said we were to transport you to the airport.'

Now? Like this? A vehicle drove off. Of course he did. 'Yes. But what of your prince?'

'He has already left.' He reached down and helped her up. 'Our orders are clear. We have matters in hand and you must catch the flight.'

He gestured to the front soldier, who'd run in a crouching position towards the rise and after a brief surveillance had returned. 'His Excellency wishes you a safe journey.'

Carmen flew back to Australia first class from Dubai. After she'd been given fresh clothes. The strangeness of being greeted by name and with deference was both unexpected and uncomfortable. Yet all was overshadowed by the desolation she felt as the distance widened between her and the man she should hate. Even the engines seemed quieter up here, which didn't help drown out the ache in her heart.

On arrival Coogee was filled with memories of Zafar, and everywhere she turned made her want to run. And hide. She needed to get away. Maybe one day, when it didn't hurt any more, she would return here. She almost wished she could return to her double-shift working life so she could fall exhausted into bed and sleep, instead of gazing out the window and thinking of Zandorro.

Instead, the next week dragged by as she tidied up the loose ends of her life, paid the last of her husband's debts, attended exit interviews, finalised the lease on her flat, applied for and accepted a job in the new birth centre in Yalara, the access town beside Ayers Rock in Central Australia.

She had to go somewhere remote, unfamiliar, safe from memories, for the next few months.

When some time had passed then she'd see where she ended up. For the moment she told herself she needed to meet her need for escape. She'd arranged for the few sentimental possessions she had left to be stored in a box at Tilly's and she spent the last night here before she flew out.

Donna, the concierge, had arranged with Tilly a farewell morning tea at the baby hotel with a few friends from both workplaces. It was the last thing Carmen wanted but she smiled and nodded her way through the morning until her head ached as she waited for the time she could pick up her bags from her room and head for the airport.

When she could finally escape towards her suite,

compliments of the management and ironically on the seventh floor, her head throbbed with memories of another time as the lift doors opened. At least the lift hadn't jammed.

Her room lay only a few doors down from so many memories and the corridor seemed strangely empty without a man standing guard outside the tiled entrance to the presidential suite.

Carmen's door lock clicked behind her and she crossed the room to drag open the heavy sliding door to let the stiff breeze from the ocean beat against her. The wind was up and she staggered a little as it whipped the curtain from beside her and flapped it against her head. The sting of salt lifted her face and she asked herself again why on earth she'd chosen the furthest place in Australia from any beach for her new job. But she knew why. She hated the weakness she hadn't realised she would be a party to. Her hands gripped the cold metal as if to soak in as much of the sea as she could before she left.

Zafar let out his breath. She was here. She hadn't left. He'd been to her flat, peered through the windows into the empty room until he'd driven to the hotel to hear she had resigned.

He'd managed to wrangle her room number from the staff, but not access. He'd also known she was checking out today.

He'd seen her downstairs, but talking to her there was impossible. How could he get privite time with her.

'If you take a room on the same floor, you're almost neighbors,' the receptionist had purred, giving way to his charm. 'And you can see each other on the balcony.'

It made sense. He'd known she couldn't leave without her baggage; couldn't leave without saying goodbye to the sea.

So here he was, and here she was.

'I'd prefer you to move back a little. I've had bad experiences with heights.'

She didn't turn her head but he knew she'd heard him. Felt her stillness. Prayed she would forgive him for taking so long to claim her. But he'd needed to finish it. Once they'd threatened Carmen he hadn't been able to rest until it was done. For the future, they would face it together, but for the past he had needed to finish alone.

Carmen felt his presence. Memories fluttered around her like butterflies in the sunlight. His eyes on hers, his wicked mouth curved and coming closer, his angled cheeks beneath her hand. She could see it all without turning her head. So he'd come back to haunt her.

She turned to see Zafar leaning uncomfortably around the privacy screen two rooms up. If he hated heights…'Then why are you out here?'

He moved back a little to safety now that he had her attention. 'I need to see you. You won't answer the phone in your room.'

'I haven't been in the room. What do you want, Zafar?'

One word. 'You.' One command.

'Still giving orders? Another quick romp?' She had to finish this. 'Go away.'

He crossed his arms. 'Not until I have had the chance to explain.'

Of course he wouldn't go away. 'No.'

'The flight was long.'

Tough. 'I'm sure there were other business affairs of state you need to do here.'

He'd had enough. 'Your room or mine?'

Impossible man. She needed to get this right. 'Give me a moment to think.' She turned and stared at him and his smile glinted.

'As you wish.'

See, that was the problem. She ducked into her room again. She had to bite back a smile. It had to be his room. Hers was so much smaller and he would be too close no matter where he stood. When the phone rang, still she hesitated. Was she agreeing to more disillusion or should she just get it over with? She let it ring again. But he would come if she didn't, she knew that, and she hated being a coward.

She picked it up, said, 'I'll come, but must leave for my flight in twenty minutes,' and put it down again.

It seemed strange to know he was there and no guard stood outside in the corridor. Zafar opened the door himself and stood back to allow her to enter.

She slipped past carefully and he didn't try to touch her.

She positioned herself in the middle of the lounge area, creating as much space as she could from anything that could hem her in. She saw by his face that he knew what she was doing.

The silence wasn't comfortable. 'Where's your staff?'

'I came on my own.' He smiled and the warmth in his eyes almost blinded her. 'Except for Yusuf, who is downstairs in the car. He does not dislike you any more.'

'Should you be here without protection? Are you safe?'

He shrugged. 'Yes, we are all safe. At last my country will have peace.' His eyes bored into hers. 'Alone is best for this goal I seek.'

She frowned. 'And what is your personal goal?'

He took a step closer. 'I believe you know.'

'No idea.' She crossed her arms protectively across her stomach and he stopped. 'But I do have a plane to catch.'

He spread his hands. 'Your flat was empty. Moved from. I was too late.'

'For what?' She was so distant. Yet incredibly beautiful. How could he have forgotten the way she twisted his chest until it hurt? He wanted to pull her into his arms and bury his face in her hair. Breathe her in. Tell her that his fears had overcome him, so afraid he could not save her. Yet she had been the one to risk all by his side so they could all be safe.

He smiled at her. 'I'm sorry I bundled you out of Zandorro.'

'You bundled me out of a speeding car.'

His chest shook with silent laughter at her indignation. 'Because I discovered a plan to use you against me. I thought you were not safe.'

'And would their plan have worked?'

He took a step closer. 'Because of that? Like a shot.'

'Don't talk about shooting.' She shuddered. 'Why are you here? It's a long way to come to say you're sorry.'

Just what was he asking? For her to make a bigger fool of herself? 'I need to leave here and decide on my future.'

'I have no quarrel with that.'

She blinked. Then he came closer until he was right beside her. Until his warmth seeped across the tiny gap of air between them. If she wasn't careful, he'd thaw her protection. 'I would like you to leave here and come back to my country. Then decide on your future.'

'I'm not going back to Zandorro.'

'You must. I wish to show you my desert.' He took her hand, and she tried very hard not to shake. 'Most especially the desert. We spoke once before about the desert but still we haven't slept there.'

The desert. 'I tasted the desert. When the sand flew into my mouth after...'

'Yes, I know. I threw you out of the car. Tsk tsk. So unforgiving. Where is that famous sense of humour?'

He was rubbing her neck. Smiling into her eyes, and the warmth was melting her heart. She stepped back.

'You're doing it again.'

'What?'

'Playing me.'

'Come play in the desert with me.'

'You come to the desert with me. I'm due in Central Australia this afternoon.' Sure now that he wouldn't.

She'd love to see his desert. Properly. With him. But she wasn't that much of a fool. 'Better yet. Don't.' She needed to get away. Just standing here talking to him was killing her.

'Is it too much to ask that I at least try to leave you with good memories of my country? Of me?'

She had to get away. Even if she had to lie. 'I have no wish to see the desert with you. I just want you to go.'

He stared at her, narrowed-eyed, and she remembered how he'd measured her when they'd first met. In the hotel. As if he was looking under her skin, into her brain. She tried not to fidget as she forced herself to hold his gaze.

Then he nodded. 'I see.' He glanced at the window and the brightness outside. 'Then at least let me drive you to the airport. I will place my jet at your disposal to fly you to your central Australia.'

'I have my own ticket. Thank you.' So he wasn't going to fight for her.

It was over. Her shoulders dropped. It was relief. Honest. She blinked away sudden dampness in her eyes and chewed on her lip. She wasn't sure why she'd thought he would stop her, and she certainly hadn't wanted him to. Had she? He'd only come to apologise.

'I insist. Change the ticket you have for another day. Cash it in. I don't care.'

'Thank you.' She wouldn't but he could think what he liked.

Zafar watched her. This was not what she wanted. This woman who had walked unaided from an ambush. Who had helped him save his man. Had he discovered his amazing Carmen's only fear—that he might not love her enough?

Ungrounded fear. He would give up his life for her.

He did not know why she had decided she wasn't going to give him time to woo her. Then, perhaps, she would have to do without the wooing. He wanted her. Badly. More desperately than he could remember wanting any woman. And he knew she wanted him. He prayed she did.

Ridiculous to be so obsessed with her, with the dream, Carmen with him always. The life he wanted, return to his real work, for the rest of his life. But life would be nothing without his Carmen. He needed her by his side.

'Or you could come back with me.'

'Why? So you can send me away again when you've satisfied yourself? Or when you decide it's too dangerous for me?'

'I would not send you away again. This time I will go where you go.' His fear had almost cost him that. She needed less protection than he'd anticipated. He would always protect her. His lips twitched, and he supposed if needed she could protect him. He did not like the thought but she was no fragile flower. His brave Carmen.

'I know it is different for you in Zandorro. As it was for me when I lived in Australia. There are good facets of all cultures and the world will be a better place when we learn to meld and bring the best out of both worlds.'

She looked back at him. 'Do you think that will ever happen?'

'Slowly, but surely.' He smiled and it wasn't fair. He melted her with those smiles. The chameleon. 'When people work together, miracles happen.'

The more he talked the more he wore the persona of the man who had attracted her so much here at Coogee beach.

The smiling god in the water.

The man after the storm with his head thrown back and his eyes filled with laughter.

Seeing him today had been worth it to leave her with these memories because those glimpses were lost in the prince. They were the dream man, not the reality. The reality had driven away from her in an armoured car. Sent her home. Gave her no choice.

'I did not have a voice,' she said. 'I can never live like that.'

'I know. I understand more than you can guess. I'm sorry you felt excluded. Forgive me?'

'No.'

He sighed but wasn't as downhearted as she'd thought he'd be. Typical. It was all probably a ruse to seduce her anyway.

'If that is your last word then I will drive you to the airport.'

She frowned. He was up to something.

CHAPTER ELEVEN

YUSUF held the car door open for her, and this time he bowed low to her. His face was still inscrutable but his body language was different. She touched his shoulder as she passed. 'Good to see you are well, Yusuf.'

'Madam.'

She slid in and Zafar slid in behind her. The leather smelt familiar, the tinted windows reminded her of another limousine, and how she'd thought Yusuf would die. How Zafar could have. Her pride was nothing to that fear.

He took her hand and kissed the inside of her wrist. Her skin remembered. It felt ridiculously right to feel her hand covered by his. She was hopeless. With his other he gestured to the space around them. 'Now we are alone.'

'Really? Must be a remote-controlled car.' She raised her brows and glanced at their driver.

'But that is Yusuf. He is with me always.'

'I noticed.'

He shrugged. 'I have decided to accompany you on your flight.'

She struggled to keep the shock from her face. Now more than ever he mustn't know her thoughts. 'When did you decide that?'

'When I said I would accompany you to the airport.'

It had seemed too easy. 'Why am I not surprised? It seems my instincts to run from you are better than I believed.'

He was amused. Nice. 'Then why did you get in the car with me?'

Stoke up that anger. It was a good defence against the urge to put her head on his shoulder. 'What choice did I have?'

Now he was openly smiling. 'True. None.'

Too handsome. Too charismatic. Too close to her heart. 'So where are we going?'

He lifted his head and though he wasn't smiling she could sense his deep love of the destination. 'I had planned to propose to you in the desert but cannot force you to leave the country with me. So we go to your oasis. Your desert camp instead of mine. I believe they have luxury tents in the desert that watch over the ancient rock of yours. There I will woo you until you have agreed to be with me for ever.'

'As what?' She raised her brows. Fighting back the excitement as she drummed up some form of defence. 'Am I to be your concubine? Your midwife for nieces and nephews?' His bride? She was fighting a losing battle and she wasn't losing it with him but with herself. She loved him, had from the first, and she suspected she always would, even if she never saw him again.

She tried again. 'I have to work.'

He shook his head. 'Not for a few days yet. I wish to share the desert with you. At night. To show you the stars.'

She raised her brows. 'Is that all you want to show me?'

His strong hand stroked her wrist. 'What can you possibly mean?'

The conversation like foreplay. Like a teasing breathe on her cheek. Like the squeeze of his fingers against hers. 'Are you sure you're not going to try to seduce me again?'

He leaned closer. 'I certainly hope so. But you would still have the option of refusal. Or you will have agreed to be my bride.'

His bride?

The word hung. Loaded with meaning. Loaded with promise.

So belovedly arrogant. 'You have tickets on yourself.'

'Ah. Colloquialisms. We must teach our children.'

She laughed. Gave up. Leant across and kissed him, and he drew her into his arms. She was home. 'Let's not go to the desert here. I will see your desert first and another day I can show you mine.'

He leaned forward and pressed the button to lower the window between them and Yusuf.

'Stop the car.'

The limousine glided to a stop beside a children's playground. A little like the park where their unexpected baby was born all those weeks ago. Swings, a slippery slide, two little girls and their mother on a park bench.

The door opened and he stepped past Yusaf and held his hand in to her. 'Come. This is what I wish to show you.'

His hand closed over hers and she gave it and herself into his keeping. She had no idea what he was doing but she would follow this man anywhere. Anytime. And that was the measure of it.

He crossed the little park to the play pit. A small

boxed area with white sand and a fogotten plastic spade. He drew her into the square and she glanced around, saw the bemused interest on the mother and the two little girls until she turned back to him and fogot everything else.

He went down on one knee. Her mouth opened to tell him to get up but she shut it again. The love that shone from his face, the way he held her gaze, the unwavering strength as his hand held hers ordered her to listen, ignore distraction, and hear his need.

'In this bed of sand, that symbolises my heartland in some tiny way, I, Zafar Aasim Al Zamid request your answer.'

He paused and the sun beat down up on her hair, his eyes smiled, though his mouth was firm and solemn, and she could feel the trickle of sand as it filled her shoes, and crazily, never had there been anywhere as romantic as this.

'Will you, Carmen O'Shannessy, be my soulmate, my lover and my wife, be by my side, bear my children, and love me until the day we close our eyes together for the last time?'

Her eyes stung and she blinked away anything that could spoil this moment. What miracle had brought them to this? Him to this? This arrogant, generous, tender, tyrannical, amazing man she'd been destined to meet.

'Of course.' It came out less definite than she intended.

He deserved more than that. And more strongly so that it carried across the sand in a wave of truth like an arrow to his heart—like he had pierced hers. 'I will. Of course I will.'

She loved him. He knew it. Zafar watched her breathe in and moisten her lips.

'I love you, Zafar, have done for weeks now, and offer you all of my heart, all of my soul, and if we are blessed, my dearest wish is to hold your babies in my arms.'

His heart surged in his chest and he rose, brushing the sand from his knees. 'My love.' He needed her in his arms.

His lips met hers as they stood in a square box of sand and the giggle of children drifted in the breeze until they both pulled back with smiles.

'Come.' He grinned down at her with the giggles of children warm between them. 'Now let us begin our life together.' They strolled arm in arm back to the car where Yosuf held the door open.

'Return to the hotel.'

Zafar handed her in and slid in after her. The car started and she caught Yusaf's smile in the rear vision mirror.

CHAPTER TWELVE

THEY married quietly in the presidential suite of the baby hotel. Tilly and Marcus acted as witnesses and then they flew back to Zandorro with barely two hours to celebrate.

They stopped overnight for the formal part of the Zandorran wedding, a civil ceremony attended by dignitaries and the King, but finally Zaraf could carry his bride into the desert. It took an hour to reach the oasis in his helicopter.

Late afternoon saw them come upon a circle of tents on the sand beside a stand of tall palm trees, ridiculously like a movie set with shaded pool and tethered camels. An outsized tent sprawled in the centre of the oasis as large as a six-room house, and Carmen couldn't keep the smile from her face.

'You did tell me?

He frowned. 'When?'

'In Coogee.'

He smiled as he remembered. 'Before the birth in the park.' He nodded. 'That is when I fell in love with you.'

He stroked her cheek. 'Tonight I hoped we could share a traditional wedding night Bedouin style. Our official Zandorron wedding will take place in a month, when I can introduce you as a married woman. This night is just for us.'

A woman approached, vaguely familiar, bowed to Carmen and more deeply to Zafar. 'I am Kiri's mother. And Yusuf's wife. My allegiance is yours.'

Zafar smiled at Carmen's shock. 'See, others love you as I do.'

He took Carmen's hand, turned her wrist and kissed her as if the caress belonged only to them. 'We will meet again an hour before sunset. Sheba will help prepare your bath.'

Bath? She shivered. More delay. Rituals and traditions that she must now learn. Lessons for the future. She nodded, glad that she had spent some time with the Zandorran women and had an idea of what was ahead, but inside she held a little trepidation. She wasn't good at being pampered and by the smile in Zafar's eyes he knew it.

She gazed at her husband, a man she had already wed twice, and still he hadn't taken her to bed.

'Patience,' he said.

Patience would kill them both. But she had to smile. She loved him, would always do so, and she knew, without the shadow of a doubt, he would always love her. But after tonight they would live, wonderfully, she hoped prolifically, between their two countries, and his strong face framed that light in his eyes as he watched her go. Dark eyes that promised the wait would be worth it.

In the two hours that followed she discovered she could learn to cope with the hardship of luxury but the slowness of it would take some getting used to.

Kiri's mother, Sheba, took her robe and helped her

settle into a claw-footed bath strewn with rose petals and scented with oils that seemed to shimmer in the water. When she left there she was gently massaged with more aromatic oils and her toes and fingernails painted with colourless shimmer. Her ankles and wrists were traced with henna-coloured flowers and her hair dried and dressed in a coil on top of her head.

Then came the veils. Layer after layer, promise after promise to lie waiting for her husband to remove. Even the one that covered her face and left just her kohled eyes to stare back at herself, this stranger, this Eastern princess she had never planned to be but could never regret. Enough. She just wanted Zafar.

Memories of the caresses from their one time together, the promise of a night in his arms with nowhere to rush off to. She could feel awareness gathering in her belly and finally it was time to go through to Zafar's rooms. The impatience grew until it consumed her and she tried to slow her steps, but too long she'd been a doer, used to being busy. This had all taken so long when she knew where she wanted to be.

Zafar's heart squeezed. Finally she was here! He'd been ready to tear down the tent to get to her. But the wait had been worth it.

The veils, her eyes, her shapely body. How he loved this woman. He could see her impatience, she made him smile. He too had been impatient and he would leave her in no doubt about that but seeing her like this…loving her like this, loving her as a midwife, loving her naked, loving her any wat she'd accept, as long as it was forever.

'You are so beautiful, my wife. Like a vision!'

The relief was there in Zafar's voice and she smiled at him. So he felt it too.

'Thank goodness you are, too.'

'My impatient wife.'

'My frustrating husband.'

He laughed out loud. 'Now I will introduce you to our traditional wedding feast.'

She rolled her eyes and he laughed again. 'Come, eat with me on cushions, drink from my cup and I will drink from yours. We will climb to the top of the dune and you will see the stars from the safety of my arms.'

Now that she had Zafar by her side, time passed swiftly. The wine they sipped tasted incredibly sweet, almonds and honey and no doubt secret ingredients she'd never discover, but its nectar left a trail of heat that coiled in her belly and spread back up over her breasts until time slowed to a second-by-second beat of the distant drum.

Tiny bells tinkled in the tent, discordant yet mesmerising music played softly in the background, and Zafar offered her morsels of flavoursome meat, tiny slivers of candied fruit and spoonfuls of rice so aromatic she closed her eyes. Each touch of his fingers to her mouth fired the flame that grew inside her.

When she returned the favour, he sipped from her fingertips, his eyes burning into hers, but his physical restraint was a more powerful aphrodisiac than if he had taken her finger into his mouth.

Never had she felt so aware of a man, so eager to feel his arms around her, so needing to be crushed against him, to be as one…

Zafar rose and held out his hand. His heart was bursting with wonder at this woman who had saved him from a darkness he had never thought would lift. Together they would achieve whatever goal was set before them.

'Come, wife. It is time we begin our life together.' She followed him to a platform of cushions set with candles, and outside a shadow guarded silently as they began a new dynasty that promised health and happiness to their kingdom.

* * * * *

DR CINDERELLA'S MIDNIGHT FLING

BY
KATE HARDY

*For Fiona—my very best friend and the sister I wish I had—
with much love*

All the characters in this book have no existence outside the imagination
of the author, and have no relation whatsoever to anyone bearing the
same name or names. They are not even distantly inspired by any
individual known or unknown to the author, and all the incidents are
pure invention.

First published in Great Britain 2012
by Mills & Boon, an imprint of Harlequin (UK) Limited.
Harlequin (UK) Limited, Eton House, 18-24 Paradise Road,
Richmond, Surrey TW9 1SR

© Pamela Brooks 2012

ISBN: 978 0 263 89158 4

Harlequin (UK) policy is to use papers that are natural, renewable
and recyclable products and made from wood grown in sustainable
forests. The logging and manufacturing process conform to the
legal environmental regulations of the country of origin.

Printed and bound in Spain
by Blackprint CPI, Barcelona

Kate Hardy lives in Norwich, in the east of England, with her husband, two young children, one bouncy spaniel, and too many books to count! When she's not busy writing romance or researching local history, she helps out at her children's schools. She also loves cooking—spot the recipes sneaked into her books! (They're also on her website, along with extracts and stories behind the books.) Writing for Mills & Boon has been a dream come true for Kate—something she wanted to do ever since she was twelve. She's been writing Medical™ Romances for nearly five years now, and also writes for Riva™. She says it's the best of both worlds, because she gets to learn lots of new things when she's researching the background to a book: add a touch of passion, drama and danger, a new gorgeous hero every time, and it's the perfect job!

Kate's always delighted to hear from readers, so do drop in to her website at www.katehardy.com

CHAPTER ONE

'CINDERELLA, you are *so* going to the ball,' Sorcha said as Jane opened her front door.

Jane stared at her best friend. 'But I've only just got in from late shift.'

'Perfect timing, then.' Sorcha glanced at her watch. 'The taxi's going to be here in thirty minutes, so you don't have time to argue.'

'I don't have anything to wear.'

'Yes, you do. Right here. It's an unbirthday present from me because I saw it when I was in town and thought the colour was just perfect for you.' Sorcha waved a carrier bag at her. 'Go and have a shower and wash your hair. I'll dry it for you and do your make-up.'

'But—' Jane began, and then subsided. She knew from past experience that, once Sorcha was in full bossy mode, there was no stopping her.

'It's not as if you've got anything better to do tonight,' Sorcha added. 'And ironing and cleaning your bathroom don't count. You didn't go to a single one of the Christmas nights out, you're always switching your duty so you can avoid team nights out, and it's well past time you stopped letting Shaun ruin your life.'

Jane didn't have an answer for any of that. She knew it was all true.

Sorcha hugged her swiftly. 'I know he hurt you badly, Janey, but you can't hide behind work for the rest of your life. Look, I'm not telling you to go and have a wild fling with the first man you meet. Just come out with me tonight and enjoy yourself. Have some fun.'

Jane wrinkled her nose. 'There's a teensy problem. I don't actually have a ticket for the ball.' She'd given a donation toward the funds instead.

'Actually, you do have one. From Maddie and Theo, with their love—and she says if you say you can't accept it, then she'll accept a promise of babysitting one evening in return, but you're coming to the ball and that's final. And Theo echoed the lot.'

Jane knew when she was beaten. 'I can hardly argue with my boss,' she said wryly.

'Attagirl.' Sorcha smiled at her. 'You've got twenty-seven minutes. Go, go, go!'

By the time the taxi arrived, Jane hardly recognised herself. She normally kept her hair tied back in a pony-tail at work, but Sorcha had blow-dried it into a sleek bob. Her make-up was light but still managed to emphasise her hazel eyes and make them sparkle. And the dress was the prettiest she'd ever seen, with a swishy skirt that made her feel light on her feet; it fitted as if it had been made to measure.

'Perfect,' Sorcha said with an approving nod. 'Let's go.'

'What do you mean, you can't make it?' Ed asked.

'I'm stuck in Suffolk,' George explained.

Ed's heart skipped a beat as a nasty thought hit him. 'Is Dad all right?'

'As far as I know. I'm not at the hall.'

'Uh-huh.' So there could only be one other reason why his older brother was standing him up, Ed thought. He'd had a better offer than a hospital charity ball. 'A girl,' he said with a sigh.

'No, actually. My car had a slight argument with a tree.'

'*What*? Are you all right?'

'I'm fine. Nobody's hurt, except the car. Stop fussing,' George said. 'Metal's easily fixed.'

'I'm a doctor. If you tell me you've crashed your car, of course I'm going to fuss,' Ed retorted.

'Honestly, I'm fine. Not a scratch on me—unlike my poor car. I'll be back in London later in the week. I'm just sorry I've let you down.'

'Just as long as you're really OK. What happened?'

'I took the corner a bit too fast,' George said cheerfully. 'But I've learned my lesson, so don't nag. I spent *hours* polishing that chrome to perfection. I'll be more careful in future.'

Ed could see exactly why his stepmother had begged him to talk some sense into his older brother. Not that he thought George would actually listen to him, but maybe some of Ed's seriousness and common sense would rub off on George and he'd steady down a bit. 'OK. I'll see you when you're back. Try not to break your neck.'

George just laughed. 'Have a good time tonight.'

Ed replaced the receiver and straightened his bow tie. Well, it wasn't the end of the world that he had to go to the ball on his own. It was a chance to meet some of his new colleagues and have some fun, as well as

raising money for specialist equipment at the London
Victoria.

He'd liked Theo Petrakis, the senior consultant, at
their first meeting. And the photograph of the three little girls on his desk had sealed the deal: Theo was very
clearly a family man. Just as Ed was, too; his decision
to move back to London from Glasgow was less to do
with being promoted and more to do with being nearer
to his brother and his sisters. Prompted partly by a quiet
phone call from Frances saying that George desperately
needed someone to talk sense into him before he broke
his neck doing some extreme sport or other.

That was Ed's slot in the family: the younger son of
Lord Somers was the sensible, serious one who fixed
things. George, the heir to the barony, dated a different gorgeous girl each week and would be the first one
down a double black diamond ski run, making him a
firm favourite with the paparazzi. And sometimes Ed
really worried that his brother was going too far. Still.
There was nothing he could do about it tonight. Once
George was back in London, he'd take his brother out
to dinner and see if he could talk him into calming
down just enough to stop the rest of the family worrying themselves sick about him.

'Jake's over there—and he's on his own,' Jane pointed
out as she and Sorcha walked into the ballroom.

'And?'

'Sorcha, this is the *ball*. It's your chance to get him
to notice that you're stunning as well as good at your
job.'

Sorcha shrugged. 'Some other time. I'm not abandoning you on your first night out since…' Her words tailed off.

Jane met it head on. 'Since Shaun.' Her ex-fiancé. Who'd cheated on Jane with her twin sister and shattered every illusion Jane had. 'I know. But it's not as if I don't know most of the people here. I can look after myself.' Jane smiled at her. 'And anyway, I need to find Maddie and Theo to thank them for the ticket. Go and talk to Jake.'

'Are you sure?'

'Very sure.' Jake and Sorcha would make a great couple; Jane thought he just needed to wake up and see what was right under his nose. 'Go for it. I'll see you later. Good luck!'

Once Sorcha was on her way over to Jake, Jane sought out her boss and his wife. 'Thank you so much for the ticket.'

'Our pleasure, Janey,' Maddie Petrakis said, hugging her. 'I'm just glad Sorcha talked you into it.'

'But I'm definitely babysitting for you. Two nights,' Jane added.

'Janey, you look lovely.' Theo, the senior consultant on the maternity ward, gave her an appreciative smile. 'If I was single, I'd be sweeping you off your feet.'

'Yeah, yeah.' She flapped a dismissive hand. Everyone knew that Theo only had eyes for his wife. But the compliment still pleased her.

'I love your shoes,' Maddie said. 'And have you had your hair done? It's gorgeous.'

'Sorcha nagged me into letting her blow-dry it,' Jane confessed.

'Good for her. Keep it like that,' Maddie said. 'Even

if it means getting up twenty minutes early. Because it really suits you.'

Again, the compliment warmed Jane. Maddie was one of her favourite colleagues, and had been a real rock when the hospital grapevine had been buzzing about her last year. Having been through a similar thing with her first husband, Maddie understood exactly how Jane felt about Shaun's very public betrayal. And she'd joined with Sorcha in helping Jane keep her head held high and ignoring the gossip.

'Have you bought your tombola tickets yet?' Maddie asked. 'The prizes are brilliant this year.'

'If there's a balloon ride among the prizes, Dr Petrakis,' Theo said, 'then we're buying every single ticket until we get it.'

Maddie actually blushed, and Jane laughed. 'I won't ask you what *that's* about. But, yes, I'll buy tickets. And I'll do a stint selling them, if you want.'

'No backstage stuff for you, Dr Cooper. You're here to dance your feet off,' Maddie said. 'Tonight's all about having fun.'

'And raising money for hospital equipment.'

'That, too. OK, you can go and buy loads of tombola tickets—and then you get on that dance floor,' Maddie said. 'Actually—that's senior consultant's orders, isn't it, Theo?'

'Certainly is,' Theo agreed with a smile. 'Actually, I'm trying to keep an eye out for our new consultant. He doesn't start officially until next week, but Maddie bullied him into buying a ticket for the ball.'

'I was off duty when he met everyone else in the department,' Jane said. 'What's he like?'

'A nice guy. He'll fit in to the department, no problems,' Theo said. 'You'll like him. Which is just as well, as he's going to be working with you.'

'So if I don't see him tonight, I'll meet him on Tuesday morning.'

'Yes. Now, go and enjoy yourself,' Maddie ordered with a smile.

Jane had got halfway over to the tombola table when her phone beeped. She looked at the screen automatically— the senior midwife had promised to get in touch if there were any complications with Ellen Baxter, a patient Jane was worried about—but the message wasn't from Iris. It was from her twin, the one person Jane didn't want to hear from tonight. She groaned inwardly. Right now, she was feeling good about herself, and Jenna always managed to change that within the space of ten seconds.

Even the title of the message stung: PJSB. Short for 'Plain Jane, Super-Brain', the nickname Jenna had coined when they were ten and Jane had won a scholarship to the local private school. Jenna had inherited their mother's genes and was tall and beautiful and effortlessly skinny; compared to her, any woman would look plain. But Jenna had always been quick to point out that Jane was six inches shorter than her, plain and dumpy— especially during their teenage years, and Jane's confidence in the way she looked had reached rock bottom. Jenna had spread the hated nickname among the popular girls at school, to the point where Jane had simply retreated into her books to avoid them.

She meant to close the screen without reading the message—she'd learned the hard way that Jenna only ever contacted her when she wanted something, so it could wait until tomorrow—but she accidentally pressed the wrong button and the words came up on the screen.

Soz it came out lik dis. U shda dun da i/view.

Interview? What interview?

Then Jane remembered. Jenna's publicist had wanted her to be interviewed a few months ago for a *Celebrity Life* feature about twins, along the lines of Jenna being the beauty and Jane being the brains. Jane had been in the middle of exams and simply hadn't had time to do an interview, much less spend a day on a photo shoot. She'd explained why, and thought that was an end to it—but clearly they'd gone ahead with the idea anyway.

Even though she knew it was a bad move, she couldn't help clicking on the attachment.

And then she really wished she hadn't done it. She definitely hadn't posed for that photograph. It looked as if it had been taken after she'd been at the tail end of a busy week on night shifts. She was wearing ratty sweat pants and an old T-shirt under a zipped hooded jacket that had seen better days, with her hair tucked under a woolly hat—clearly ready to do her daily run before crashing into bed. There was nothing in the article about what Jane actually did for a living; it was all about Jenna and unidentical twins.

Worse still, the magazine was going to be on sale in the hospital shop, where everyone could see it. She'd better warn Theo, because it wasn't going to look good for the department. But not right now; it wasn't often that he and Maddie had a night out, and Jane didn't want to spoil things for them. There wasn't anything anyone could do about it right now in any case, so leaving it until tomorrow was the right thing to do.

She closed the phone, but the question buzzed round

her head. Why did Jenna hate her so much? Jane had tried and tried and tried to be supportive to her twin. She knew it wasn't easy, being a supermodel. You were always in the public eye; you had to watch what you did and said and ate and drank, and whatever you did people would twist it to suit their own ends. Plus there were always new models coming along, ready to take your place in the spotlight. Not to mention those who were quick to take advantage. It was a lonely, precarious business that had left their mother fragile and prone to bouts of serious depression. Jenna, too, suffered from headaches and what she called 'nerves', whereas Jane had the constitution of an ox and hardly ever caught so much as a cold. But she'd tried to be kind. She'd looked after them both. She'd never complained, never said or done anything to make them feel they were a burden to her.

And yet nothing she did could ever please Jenna or Sophia. They seemed to resent her and look down on her in equal measure, and Jane had no idea how to change that.

She blew out a breath. Sorcha had talked her into coming to the hospital ball and Jane wasn't going to let her twin get to her tonight. All the same, instead of going to the tombola table, she went to the bar and drank a glass of champagne straight down before ordering a second. The bubbles, to her relief, hit immediately. They didn't take the magazine picture out of her head, but they did at least dull the edge of her misery.

She'd just bought her second glass of champagne and was turning back to the dance floor to go and find someone she knew to chat to and dance with when someone jogged her arm and the entire glassful went over the arm of the man standing next to her, soaking his white tuxedo.

'Oh, no! I'm *so* sorry,' she said, horrified. 'Please excuse me.'

'It was an accident. It's not a problem.' He took a handkerchief from his pocket and mopped up the spill.

The handkerchief wasn't enough; she knew the champagne was going to leave a stain over his sleeve.

'Please, send me the cleaning bill.' She was about to grab a pen and pad from her handbag to scribble down her details for him when she realised: she didn't have either. The dinky little bag she'd brought tonight was less than an eighth of the size of the bag she normally used—the one that Sorcha always teased her was big enough to carry the kitchen sink as well as everything else. In this one, Jane could just about cram her door key, her wallet and her mobile phone into, and even that was pushing it. She was about to pull out her phone and offer to text him her details when he smiled.

'It's fine,' he said. 'Really. But if you want to make amends, you could dance with me.'

She blinked. What? The guy looked like James Bond. Dark hair, piercing blue eyes, and a smile that made her feel as if her temperature had just gone up six degrees. He was the kind of man that attracted third glances, let alone second. 'Dance with you?' she asked stupidly.

He shrugged. 'It's what people are supposed to do at a charity ball, isn't it?'

'I...' Yes. But this man was a stranger. The epitome of a tall, dark, handsome stranger. 'Well, if you're sure. I'm J—'

'No names,' he cut in, smiling to take the sting from

his words. 'I rather like the idea of dancing with a gorgeous stranger. Cinderella.'

Gorgeous? Even Sorcha's skill with make-up couldn't make her look as stunning as her mother and her sister. Jane knew she was just ordinary. All the same, she smiled. 'If I'm Cinderella, does that make you Prince Charming?'

'Are you looking for a Prince Charming?'

'No. I don't need rescuing,' she said. Though it wasn't strictly true. Right now, she could really do with dancing with the best-looking man in the room. To take the sharpness of that article away. Honestly compelled her to add, 'Besides, your toes might really regret that offer later. I have two left feet.'

'I don't. So dance with me anyway,' he said, his eyes crinkling at the corners.

'If you have bruised toes tomorrow, don't say I didn't warn you,' she said.

He laughed. 'Somehow, I think my toes will be just fine.'

And then Jane discovered that Prince Charming could dance. *Really* dance. Moving round the floor with him was like floating. Effortless. He was guiding her, so her footwork couldn't possibly go wrong. She'd never, ever danced like this before, and it was a revelation. This was what it was like not to be clumsy.

When the music changed to a slower number, he didn't let her go. It felt completely natural to move closer. To dance cheek to cheek with him.

His skin was soft against hers, with no hint of stubble—clearly he'd shaved just before coming out tonight—and she could smell the citrus tang of his aftershave. She closed her eyes, giving herself up to the moment. Right now she really could imagine herself as Cinderella, dancing with her Prince Charming as he spun her round the floor.

And then she felt him move slightly. His lips brushed against the corner of her mouth.

If she pulled away, she knew he'd stop. All her instincts told her that her gorgeous stranger was a gentleman.

But what if she moved closer? Would he kiss her properly?

Even the idea of it made her pulse rate speed up and her breathing become shallower.

And then she did it. Moved just a little bit closer.

His arms tightened round hers, and his mouth brushed against hers. Sweet, tempting, promising: and it sent a shiver all the way through her. It had been way too long since she'd been kissed; she couldn't help responding, tipping her head back just the tiniest bit to give him better access to her mouth.

She kept her eyes closed, concentrating purely on the touch of his lips against hers. The way it made her skin feel super-sensitised; the way he coaxed her into responding, kissing him back. Tiny, sweet, nibbling kisses, almost like a dance in itself, leading each other further and further on.

She couldn't help opening her mouth, letting him deepen the kiss. And either that glass of champagne had seriously gone to her head, or Prince-Charming-meets-James-Bond was the most amazing kisser she'd ever met, because he made her feel as if she were floating. As if there was nobody else in the room, just the two of them and the music.

He kissed her through the rest of the song. And

maybe the next, too, because when he broke the kiss she realised that it was a fast dance, and they were swaying together, locked in each other's arms as if it were still a slow dance, even though the band was playing something uptempo.

He blinked then, as if he were just as shocked.

'Wow. It's been a long time since someone's had that effect on me, Cinders,' he said softly.

'You're telling me.' She couldn't remember reacting like this to anyone, ever. Even to the man she'd once planned to marry.

He leaned forward and stole a kiss. 'Let's get out of here.'

Leave a ballroom where she knew most of the people there, to go to some unspecified place with a complete stranger she'd only just met and whose name she didn't even know? She'd have to be crazy.

Or very, very angry and hurt. Enough to think that going off with the most gorgeous-looking man she'd ever seen—a man who'd kissed her to the point where she'd forgotten where she was—would make her feel much, much better.

'What did you have in mind?' she asked.

'I have a room here,' he said. 'So I was thinking room service. More champagne. Freshly squeezed orange juice. And a toasted cheese sandwich.'

If he'd said caviar or lobster, she would've said no. But the homeliness of a toasted cheese sandwich… Now that was seriously tempting. 'Yes. On condition.'

'Condition?'

'No names. No questions.'

His eyes widened. 'Just one night? Is that what you're saying?'

'Yes.' Tomorrow morning she'd be back to being Plain Jane, Super-Brain. Well, not quite, because she was off duty and she'd actually be Plain Jane who needed to catch up with cleaning her flat. But he'd just made her feel beautiful. Cherished. And she wasn't quite ready to let that feeling go. 'One night.'

'Allow me one question. You're not involved with anyone?'

That was an easy one to answer. 'No.' Though she appreciated the fact that he'd asked, because she needed to know the same thing. The fact that he'd asked first made it easy for her. 'Are you?'

'No.' He caught her lower lip briefly between his. 'Then let's go.'

She walked with him into the hotel reception; while he collected his key, she texted Sorcha. *Bit of a headache, having an early night. Enjoy the rest of the ball, J xx*

It wasn't that far from the truth. She was having an early night. Just…not at home. And the headache excuse was enough to make sure that Sorcha didn't ring the flat to see how she was and worry when there was no answer.

'Everything all right?' Prince Charming asked.

'Fine.' She smiled back at him. 'Just texting my best friend to say I'm leaving, so she doesn't worry that I've disappeared.'

'Which means you're all mine. Good.'

CHAPTER TWO

ED USHERED his Cinderella over to the lifts. Her face was incredibly expressive; as the doors closed behind them, he could see that she was starting to have second thoughts. And third.

She was definitely the responsible, thoughtful type, because she'd made sure that her best friend wasn't worrying about her rather than disappearing without a word. And she was clearly wondering whether she was doing the right thing now.

He took her hand, pressed a reassuring kiss into her palm and curled her fingers over the imprint of his lips. 'Stop worrying,' he said softly. 'You can say no and it won't be a problem. Just come and have a drink with me.'

'I don't normally do this sort of thing,' she muttered, and more colour flooded into her face.

'Me, neither,' he said. 'How shockingly bold of us.'

To his relief, she responded to the teasing note in his voice and smiled back. 'I guess so.' And she made no protest when he unlocked his room and gestured for her to go inside.

'Take a seat,' he said. Though he wasn't surprised that she pulled the chair out from under the dressing table rather than sitting on the bed. 'Shall I order some champagne?'

She gave him a rueful smile. 'I think I've already had enough. So unless you're planning to drink the whole bottle yourself...' She wrinkled her nose. 'Probably not.'

'You spilled most of your glass over me,' he pointed out.

She winced. 'I know, and I'm sorry.'

He shook his head. 'I didn't mean *that*. I wasn't intending to make you grovel, just pointing out that you haven't had a drink tonight.'

'Actually, I have.' She bit her lip. 'This is going to sound terrible, but I drank one glass straight down before the one I spilled over you.'

Now that did surprise him. She'd looked slightly vulnerable when she'd first met him, but he'd assumed that was simply embarrassment at spilling her champagne over him. 'Why? Didn't you want to come to the party?'

'No, it's not that. The hospital ball's always fun.' She blew out a breath. 'We said no questions, remember.'

He shrugged. 'Fair enough.' Though he still wondered. Why would a woman with such beautiful eyes and such a perfect mouth need to bolster her courage with champagne?

'Why do you have a room here?' she asked.

He smiled. 'And who was it who just reminded me, "no questions"?'

'Sorry.' She bit her lip. 'I'm not much good at this. I never go off with complete strangers whose name I don't even know.'

Neither did he. But then again, he hadn't responded so powerfully to someone for a long time; if he was honest, he hadn't felt like that about his wife. And he'd avoided dating since his marriage had disintegrated.

His sisters were all nagging him to have some fun and start dating again. And the way Cinderella had kissed him back on the dance floor had really stirred his blood. He had the feeling that this was something they *both* needed. Except she was clearly worried about him being a stranger. 'That's an easy one to sort. My name's—' he began.

'No,' she cut in. 'We're at a charity ball for the hospital. So the chances are, if you were a complete snake, you wouldn't be here. Or else someone would've warned me about you beforehand and I'd know to avoid you.'

He blinked. 'The grapevine's that fast?'

'Yup.'

'So you work at the hospital,' he said thoughtfully.

'No questions,' she reminded him.

He smiled. 'It wasn't a question. It was a logical deduction. This is a charity ball for the hospital, and you clearly know people, plus you've been to the ball before and you know how fast the grapevine works. QED.'

'And you had an expensive education.' She smiled at his raised eyebrow. 'Again a logical deduction. Most people don't use Latin abbreviations in everyday speech.'

'So the fact you recognise it says the same about you,' he parried.

'Not necessarily. I might be a crossword addict.'

'I like fencing with you,' he said. 'Almost as much as I like dancing with you.' His gaze held hers. 'And almost as much as I like kissing you.'

Colour bloomed in her face, but this time it wasn't shyness. The way her lips parted slightly and her pupils grew larger told him that she liked remembering the way they'd kissed, too.

He took her hand; this time, instead of kissing her palm, he kissed her wrist right where her pulse was beating madly. The longer his mouth lingered, the more her pulse sped up. Her skin was so soft. And she smelled gorgeous—some floral scent he couldn't quite place, mixed with something else. Soft and sweet and gentle. Irresistible.

'You do things to me, Cinders,' he said softly. 'But I'm not going to push you. Do you mind if I…?' He ran his finger round the collar of his shirt and grimaced.

'Slip into something more comfortable?' she asked, raising an eyebrow.

He laughed. 'Hardly. I just want to feel a bit less— well—formal.'

'Sure.'

'Thank you.' He stood up and removed his jacket, hanging it in the wardrobe. Then he undid his bow tie and the top button of his shirt and let the tie hang loose, and rolled the sleeves of his shirt up.

She sucked in a breath.

'What?' he asked.

'Forget Prince Charming. You're all James Bond,' she said.

He raised an eyebrow. 'Is that a good thing?'

'Oh, yes.' Her voice was husky. 'My best friend and I saw the last film three times at the cinema.'

'Well, just for the record, I hate martinis.'

She smiled. 'So do I.'

'And I don't have a licence to kill.'

She spread her hands. 'The only licence I have is a driving licence.'

He laughed. 'Snap. I like you, Cinderella.' His voice deepened, softened. 'Come here.' It was an invitation, not an order. She paused, clearly weighing it up, then nodded, stood up and crossed the short distance between them.

He cupped her face with both hands. 'A perfect heart shape,' he said softly. 'And right now I really, really want to kiss you. May I?'

'Yes.'

Ed smiled and lowered his mouth to hers. Teasing, enticing, more of those little nibbling kisses that had her twining her fingers through his hair and opening her mouth so he could deepen the kiss.

And, just like it had been between them on the dance floor, he felt desire lance through him.

He pulled away slightly, spun her round and undid the zip of her dress. She arched back as he stroked his way down the bare skin he uncovered. Her skin was so soft; and touching her like this wasn't enough. He wanted more. A hell of a lot more.

Gently, he slid the dress from her shoulders and let it fall to the floor. He drew her back against him, his hands splayed across her midriff and his thumbs stroking the undersides of her breasts through the lace of her bra.

'I want you,' he whispered. 'I want to be with you, skin to skin.'

'Me, too.' The admission was low and throaty, and sent a kick of sheer need through him.

She turned to face him, untucked his shirt from his trousers and undid the rest of the buttons of his shirt. Her hands were gentle and yet sure as she slid her palms across his pecs. 'Nice,' she said appreciatively.

'Thank you.' He inclined his head, acknowledging the compliment. 'I like it when you touch me.'

She smiled back, and pushed the cotton from his shoulders; his shirt pooled on the floor next to her dress. She traced the line of his collarbone with one finger.

Good, but not enough. He needed more. He kissed her again, his mouth teasing and demanding at the same time.

He unsnapped her bra, tossed the lace to the floor and then cupped her breasts properly. 'You're beautiful, Cinders.'

No, I'm not. Her thoughts were written all over her face.

Someone—presumably her ex—had really done a number on her. Just as much as Camilla had made him wary of trusting anyone.

'Whoever he was,' Ed said softly, 'he was an idiot.'

'Who?'

'Whoever put that look in your eyes.'

She shrugged. 'You're wearing too much.'

She'd said 'no questions'. And now he had a pretty good idea why. This was starting to look like rebound sex. For both of them.

But they'd agreed from the start that this was one night only. A night out of time. The new hospital was big enough for their paths never to cross again. And if he could make her feel good about herself again tonight, the way she was making him feel good about himself, then that would be a bonus for both of them.

He took her hands and drew them down to his belt. 'Since you think I'm wearing too much, why don't you even things up?' he invited.

Her hands were shaking slightly as she undid his belt,

then the button of his formal trousers, and slid the zipper down.

'You are beautiful, you know,' he said softly. 'Your eyes—I'm not sure if they're green or grey or brown. The colour keeps shifting, and it makes me want to know what colour they are when you're really aroused. And your mouth.' He traced her lower lip with one fingertip. 'It's a perfect cupid's bow. It makes me want to kiss you until we're both dizzy. And here…' He dipped his head and took one hardened nipple into his mouth.

She gave a sharp intake of breath and tipped her head back in pleasure.

Part of Jane knew that this was a seriously bad idea. He was a stranger. And she'd never had a one-night stand before.

Then again, this wasn't a relationship. She didn't have to take the risk of trusting him and then discovering that he had feet of clay, the way she had with Shaun. In a weird kind of way, this was safe—because this man wasn't going to get close enough to her heart to break it.

His mouth teased her lower lip, demanding and getting a response. Jane wasn't sure which of them finished undressing whom, but then he'd lifted her and was carrying her to the bed. She felt the bed dip with his weight, and then the mattress shifted again as he climbed off. She opened her eyes.

'Condom,' he said in answer to her unspoken question.

At least one of them was being sensible. It hadn't even occurred to her. How reckless and stupid was that?

He rummaged in his trousers for his wallet, took out the foil wrapper and placed it on the bedside table.

'You look worried.' He stroked her face. 'If you've changed your mind, I'll understand. I've never forced a woman, and I don't intend to start now.'

'I just…' She hadn't even dated anyone since Shaun's betrayal, let alone slept with anyone. She'd turned down the couple of offers she'd had, not wanting to risk the same thing happening all over again. 'I'm not used to this kind of thing,' she admitted.

'Then let's get used to it together.' He bent his head to kiss her again; his mouth was gentle and promising, rather than demanding. Until she responded, when suddenly the kiss turned hot, turning her into a mass of sheer aching need.

This time, when he touched her, the shyness was gone. She gave herself up to the sensation as he stroked her, teased her, let her touch him in return.

His hand slid between her thighs and she gasped in pleasure.

It really shouldn't be this good for a first time. They didn't even know each other's names, for pity's sake. But it felt as if Prince Charming knew exactly where she liked being touched, exactly how to make her respond to him.

She was near to babbling when she heard the rip of the foil packet and the snap as he rolled on the condom to protect her. Then he eased, oh, so slowly into her. And it was heaven. This was a man who knew exactly what to do—how to give pleasure, how to take her right to the edge and keep her there until she was practically hyperventilating.

And then wave after wave of pleasure surged through

her as her climax hit. He held her tightly, and she felt the answering surge of his own body against hers.

Gently, he withdrew. 'I'd better deal with the condom. Excuse me a moment,' he said softly.

Jane pulled the sheet back over her, the pleasure replaced by a rush of awkwardness. What did you do on a one-night stand? Did you stay for the whole night, or did you get dressed and leave straight after having sex? She didn't have a clue. She'd never done this kind of thing before; she'd always hung out with the nerdy students, not the wild ones.

He reappeared from the bathroom—still naked, and looking completely unembarrassed about the situation. Clearly he had some idea of the rules; whereas she felt totally at sea.

He climbed into bed beside her and drew her against him. 'What's wrong?'

She sighed. 'If you really want to know, I don't have a clue what the rules are. What you're supposed to do next on a one-night stand.'

'Once you've had sex, you mean?' He stroked her hair. 'I don't think there are any rules. What we do next is entirely up to you.' He smiled. 'Though my vote would be for you to stay a bit longer and for us to order something from room service.'

'Your toasted cheese sandwich?'

He shrugged. 'Or whatever you like from the menu.'

Funny how something so homely could make her feel so much more at ease. 'Toasted sandwiches would be lovely, thank you. And orange juice.' She smiled at him. 'And can I be really greedy and ask for coffee as well?' The champagne she'd gulped down was still fizzing through her and she really didn't want to spend the next day with a hangover. OK, so she was a lightweight, hardly ever drinking more than a single glass of wine; but she didn't need alcohol to have a good time.

He smiled back at her. 'Coffee sounds great to me.'

'And of course I'll pay my half,' she added.

He shook his head. 'My room, my idea and my bill. Don't argue.'

There wasn't much she could say to that, unless she offered to treat him some other night. Which would definitely be breaking the rules—by definition, a one-night stand was for one night only. 'Then thank you,' she said.

'You know,' he said, 'when I came out tonight, didn't think I was going to end up sitting in bed with a perfect stranger, eating comfort food. But I'm really glad I met you, Cinders.'

'Me, too,' she said softly, meaning it.

The sandwiches, when they arrived, were gorgeous. The orange juice was freshly squeezed. And the coffee was among the best she'd ever tasted.

'That was fabulous. Thank you,' she said when they'd finished.

'My pleasure.'

He really was gorgeous. Those piercing blue eyes made her heart skip a beat.

But she didn't want to overstay her welcome. 'And I guess this is my cue to leave.'

'If that's what you really want.' He stole a kiss. 'Or you could…' He paused. 'Stay. Tonight.'

The heat was back in his expression. How could she resist? 'Yes.'

CHAPTER THREE

THE next morning, Jane woke with a start. She was in an unfamiliar bed, in an unfamiliar room, with a body curled protectively round hers.

For a moment she thought she was having some peculiarly vivid dream, remembering what it was like being part of a couple and waking up in her man's arms. But then the body next to hers shifted and pulled her closer.

She was definitely in bed with someone else. And she'd split up with Shaun eight months ago. Which meant that the body curled round hers belonged to... She swallowed hard. She was still in bed with the handsome stranger she'd spilled champagne over last night.

Talk about out of the frying pan and into the fire. What a stupid thing to do: spending the night with a complete stranger, without telling anyone where she was. Even if he did have lovely manners and had given her more pleasure in one night than her ex-fiancé had given her in two years, he was still a stranger. Anything could've happened.

Oh, for pity's sake. Dr Jane Cooper was known for being ultra-sensible. She didn't *do* this sort of thing.

Except...she just had.

At least she hadn't told him her name. Hopefully their paths wouldn't cross so they could avoid an embarrassing situation. Even if they both worked at the London Victoria, the hospital was big enough for her not to know at least half the staff; and she definitely hadn't met him before, or she would've remembered those beautiful eyes.

She'd needed practically no persuasion to spend the whole night with him. And they'd spent most of the night making love. They'd actually run out of condoms, and she'd felt like the bad girl she'd never actually been.

It wasn't that she had regrets about last night—how could she regret the way he'd made her feel?—but she really didn't have a clue how to face him this morning. What to say. How to deal with the situation. Plus she needed to be somewhere. So the best thing she could do would be to slip quietly away before he woke. It would avoid embarrassment on all sides. Gradually, she worked her way out of his arms; when he moved to pull her back again, she gave him the warm pillow she'd been lying on, and he cuddled that closer.

Cute.

Jane smiled regretfully. Maybe if they'd met under other circumstances... But there was no point dwelling on it, and she really needed to check on a patient and talk to her boss.

She picked up her clothes from the floor and quickly dragged them on, rescued her handbag and her shoes, tiptoed over to the door, and unlocked it very quietly. When she glanced back towards the bed, she could see that he was still sleeping. 'Thank you,' she mouthed silently. 'For making me feel beautiful.'

Then she remembered. His jacket. Considering it

had been her fault, the least she could do was pick up the dry cleaning bill.

There was a leather folder on top of the dressing table, with the hotel's crest stamped on it. Just as she'd hoped, it contained paper and a pencil. She slid the top sheet quietly out of the folder and scribbled a quick note on it. Then she took some money from her purse and left it on top of the note, then put the pencil on top of the banknotes to weigh them down. Finally, she closed the door behind her and fled.

Back at her flat, Jane showered—trying not to think about what Prince Charming had done with her in his shower last night—and changed into jeans and a plain T-shirt. Once she'd downed a mug of coffee, she flicked into her phone and read the article again, just to be sure that she wasn't making a fuss over nothing.

She wasn't.

She sighed and closed her eyes briefly. There was no point in trying to call Jenna to task over it. Her twin would simply open her big brown eyes and claim innocence, say it wasn't *her* fault the journalist had written it that way. And then somehow their mother would get wind of the row and she'd have a panic attack; and the blame for that would be laid firmly at Jane's door. Been there, done that, worn the T-shirt until it was in rags.

So instead of asking Jenna what her problem was and why she couldn't play nicely for once, Jane sent her a very polite email, saying simply, *Thank you for letting me know.* Even Jenna couldn't twist that.

And now she was going to have to do some damage limitation, as well as check up on how Ellen Baxter was doing this morning.

'You're supposed to be off duty, Jane,' Iris, the senior midwife, said as Jane walked into the department.

Jane smiled. 'I know. Thanks for sending that message through Theo last night.'

'Did you have a good time at the ball?'

'Yes, thanks.'

'Are you sure?' Iris gave her a concerned look. 'You're looking a bit…well, worried, this morning.'

'You know me. Always worrying about my patients,' Jane said lightly. She knew Iris would be sympathetic if she told the midwife about that horrible article, but she needed to tell Theo first. And if anyone was too nice to her right now, she might just bawl her eyes out—from frustration as much as hurt. 'Talking of patients, I'm just going to see Ellen.'

Ellen Baxter was listlessly flicking through a magazine, but she brightened when Jane walked into her room. 'Dr Cooper!'

'Good morning, Ellen.' Jane's smile was genuine. 'How are you doing?'

'OK. I hope.' Ellen grimaced. 'I'm trying to relax.'

'But it's hard when you're on bed rest and you want to be at home.' Jane patted her hand sympathetically. 'Let me have a look at your charts.' She read through them swiftly. 'OK. Can I check your blood pressure and your temperature?'

'You can stick as many needles as you like in me, if it means I can go home!' Ellen said.

Jane laughed. 'You're safe from needles today.' She checked Ellen's blood pressure and temperature, then marked them on the chart. 'That's good. Any twinges or spotting?'

'None. And, believe you me, I'd say if there was,'

Ellen said feelingly. 'I don't want anything to go wrong. I can't lose this baby.'

'I know,' Jane soothed. 'We're all rooting for you.'

'Everyone's being so nice here, but it's just not home.' Ellen flushed. 'And I know it's wet of me, but I can't sleep properly without Rob.'

'It's not wet. It's perfectly understandable.' It had taken Jane weeks to get used to sleeping on her own after she'd split up with Shaun. Luckily she'd been the one to move, so at least there were no memories of him in her flat. 'Ellen, I'm happy with your obs. If Rob can come and pick you up, then I'll discharge you this morning. With conditions,' she added firmly.

'Anything,' Ellen said, her eyes shining.

'Firstly, you take it easy. Secondly, any worries at all—no matter how small or how silly you think they might be—you call me. Thirdly, any twinges, you get straight here to the department. OK?'

'OK.' Ellen's eyes filled with tears. 'You've been so lovely. If it wasn't for you…' Her voice cracked.

Jane squeezed her hand again. 'That's what I'm here for.' She smiled at Ellen and got off the bed. 'You call Rob, and I'll get the paperwork sorted with Iris.'

'Thank you. Thank you so much.' Ellen's eyes glittered with tears.

Warm and soft in his arms… Ed snuggled closer, then realised drowsily that he wasn't holding someone, he was holding some*thing*. He opened his eyes. A pillow.

She'd left him asleep, holding a pillow.

Unless maybe she was in the shower? He listened, but he could hear nothing from the bathroom. And the sheet on her side of the bed was stone cold. She'd been gone for a while.

Well, he supposed it was one way to avoid the awkwardness. Though it stung that she hadn't waited for him to wake up.

On his way to the bathroom, he saw the note on the dressing table.

Dear Prince Charming, Thank you for last night. Hope this covers the dry cleaning bill. Cinders.

So she'd played the game right to the end. He damped down the surge of disappointment that she hadn't left him her number or told him her real name.

And there was the fact that she'd left him some money. He knew she'd meant it to cover the cleaning bill for his jacket, but it still made him feel cheap.

Still, it was his own fault for acting on impulse. He was better off being his usual sensible, serious self. And he wouldn't make that mistake again.

Once the paperwork was done, it was time to start the damage limitation. Jane knocked on Theo's open office door.

He looked up from his desk. 'Janey, you're supposed to be off duty. What are you doing here?' He raised one hand to silence her reply. 'Oh, don't tell me. Ellen Baxter.'

'Yes. I'm discharging her this morning. She'll call me if she has any worries and she'll come straight back here if she has the slightest twinge.'

'And did you come in to tell me that, or to bring me coffee?' he asked, looking hopeful.

'Actually, a large brandy might be more in order,' she said ruefully.

He frowned. 'What's up, Janey?'

She dragged in a breath. 'I need to show you something. I'm sorry, I had absolutely no idea about it until I got the email last night.' She pulled the article up on her phone and handed it to him.

Theo read through it, his mouth set in a grim line; when he'd finished, he looked up at her. 'I've never seen such utter spite in my entire life. I can't believe this is focused on something so shallow and it doesn't even say what you do! Are you all right?'

No. She was ragingly angry and desperately hurt. She yanked the emotions back. No more tears. Just smiles. 'I'm fine,' she fibbed. 'But this is going to look really bad for the department. If you want me to resign, I understand.'

'Resign? You must be joking. Janey, you're an excellent doctor and this rubbish has got nothing to do with you.' He flicked out of the screen. 'When does the magazine go on sale?'

'I'm not sure. This week, I think.'

'Right. I'll have a word with the shop manager and make sure it's not on sale in the hospital this week. If necessary, I'll buy their entire stock of the magazine myself. I can't do anything about people who buy it elsewhere and bring it in, but my guess is that anyone who knows you—staff or patient—will be fuming on your behalf.' He looked grim as he handed the phone back to her. 'And those who choose to spread gossip or make stupid comments to you—well, their opinions are worth nothing in the first place, so just ignore them, OK?'

'Thank you.' She felt humble beyond belief that her

boss was prepared to buy up the entire stock of magazines to try and spare her from an awkward situation.

'I take it that—' he said something in Greek that she didn't understand, but from the expression on his face it definitely wasn't anything complimentary '—sister of yours was behind this?'

Jane spread her hands. 'She asked me to do the interview months ago. It was meant to be a feature about twins, "the beauty and the brains". Except I was up to my eyes with work and exams, so I said I couldn't do it. I thought she'd just forgotten about it.'

'More like she used it to have another dig at you, because she's incredibly jealous of you.'

'She can't be. There's absolutely nothing to be jealous about. She's a supermodel,' she reminded Theo.

'She's also heading towards thirty and she's not going to get the same kind of work opportunities she had when she was eighteen. Looks don't last, but education does. You're clever, your career will be going from strength to strength while hers is starting to go more slowly, and everyone who meets you really likes you. *That's* why she's jealous,' Theo said. He sighed. 'Do your parents know about this?'

'Probably not. But I'm not going to say anything. You know my mum's fragile.'

'I know depression's tough to overcome,' Theo said gently, 'but it doesn't mean you can just give up on being a parent to your children. When have either of your parents ever put you first?'

Jane didn't want to answer that. 'It's OK.'

Theo gave her a sympathetic look. 'You've got more patience than anyone else I know.'

'It's not easy for Mum. She was right at the height of

her career when she fell pregnant with Jenna and me and had to give it all up.' According to Sophia, pregnancy had ruined her skin and her figure; and, with the crippling post-natal depression she'd suffered afterwards, she'd never been able to return to her modelling.

'You know, Maddie could say the same thing. Being a mum means that she's had to give up some of her career choices, and I've turned down offers as well because I don't want a job that'd mean I can't give her and our daughters enough time. But neither of us would change a thing, because the girls have brought so much joy to us,' Theo said softly.

Jane had to swallow hard. What would it be like to have a family who loved her unconditionally, the way Maddie and Theo felt about their children, instead of making her feel guilty for being born? What would it have been like if Jenna had supported her and cheered her on through the long years of studying medicine, instead of pulling her down and mocking her all the time?

Though it was pointless dwelling on it. She couldn't change the way they were. All she could do was try to love them as best as she could—and, since Shaun had betrayed her with Jenna, that had meant from a safe distance. Which, she supposed, made her just as bad as them.

Theo reached out and squeezed her hand. 'Sorry. I'm overstepping the mark. It's not my place to criticise your family. Though I wish they'd appreciate you for who you are.'

He paused. 'Do you want me to call Maddie? Or Sorcha?'

'No. I'll be fine.'

'Hmm.' He looked at her. 'Is that article the reason why you disappeared from the ball so early last night?'

'No.' Not exactly. She definitely wasn't telling him the real reason behind that.

'Sure?'

'Sure,' she confirmed.

'I'll believe you—for now.' He smiled at her. 'Now, go and have two nice days off, forget about that stupid article, and come back all bright-eyed on Tuesday morning, yes?'

'OK, Theo.' She dragged in a breath. 'And thank you.'

'Any time.'

On Tuesday morning Jane had just checked up on her first patient when Theo walked in. 'Janey, have you got a moment?'

She looked over at him, saw the man in the white coat next to him, and her knees went weak as she recognised him.

Oh, my God.

He couldn't possibly be... Could he?

Theo's next words confirmed it. 'I'd like to introduce you to our new consultant.'

If Theo said his name was James or Bond, she was going to collapse in a puddle of hysterical laughter.

'Edward Somers,' Theo continued. 'Ed, this is Jane Cooper, one of our F2 doctors, but it's not going to be long before she makes registrar.'

She could feel her face going bright red and there was a tiny, tiny smile lifting the corner of Ed's mouth. Oh, please, don't let him say anything about Saturday night...

'Good to meet you, Jane,' he said politely.

Then she realised she'd been holding her breath, waiting for him to spill the beans. Clearly he wasn't going to do that: because it wouldn't reflect too well on him, either. She smiled at him in relief. 'You, too, Edward—or do you prefer Ed?'

For a second, she could swear he mouthed 'James Bond', but then he said, 'Ed. May I join you in your rounds?'

'I—well, sure.' She spread her hands. 'You're the senior. I guess you should lead.'

Ed smiled at her. 'Patients are much more important than protocol. You already know them, so I'm happy for you to lead and introduce me while we're there.'

'I'll leave you in Jane's capable hands,' Theo said, and headed back to his office.

'Very capable,' Ed said softly.

Oh, help.

'I, um… Look, we probably need to talk, but for now can we keep this…well, just work?' Jane asked.

'For now,' he agreed.

Before she could take him to the next patient, Iris hurried over. 'We've just had a call from the ED. The mum's twenty-four, she's eleven weeks pregnant and she can't stop being sick. Marina thinks it's hyperemesis.'

'We're on our way,' Jane said.

In the emergency department, she swiftly introduced Ed to Marina Fenton, the specialist registrar.

'I'm pretty sure it's hyperemesis. Poor woman—morning sickness is bad enough,' Marina said. 'I've already done bloods and sent them off for electrolyte levels, blood count and renal.'

'Thanks, Marina—that's great.'

'Mrs Taylor's through here.' She showed them to the cubicle where a young woman was retching miserably into a bowl.

'Mrs Taylor? I'm Jane Cooper and this is Ed Somers. Dr Fenton asked us to come down and see you. Can I get you a drink of water?' Jane asked.

Mrs Taylor shook her head. 'I can't keep anything down.'

'Taking small sips might help you feel a little bit better,' Jane said gently, and stuck her head out of the cubicle for long enough to ask one of the auxiliaries to bring in a glass of water.

'How long have you been feeling like this?' Ed asked.

'About a month. I knew you got morning sickness, I just didn't expect it to be all day and all night and as bad as this.' She retched again. 'Sorry.'

'You don't have to apologise,' Jane said, squeezing her hand.

The auxiliary brought in the water Jane had asked for, and Mrs Taylor managed a small sip. 'Thank you. That's made my mouth feel a bit less disgusting,' she admitted.

'Good. Have you talked to your family doctor or your midwife about your sickness?' Ed asked.

'I didn't want to bother them.' She shook her head. 'My sister had it bad, too. She lost weight and felt lousy all the time for the first bit.'

Jane and Ed exchanged a glance; hyperemesis was known to run in families. But it was also more common in women carrying twins—or, more rarely, it could be caused by something more sinister. They needed to run some tests to rule out the nasties.

'My boss made me come in. I was sick over a client.

It was her perfume that set me off—it was so strong.'
Mrs Taylor bit her lip. 'I really hope he forgives me.'

'I'm sure he will. He sent you in because he was
worried about you,' Ed reassured her. 'So, you're about
eleven weeks. Have you had a scan yet?'

'No, that was meant to be next week. My Jason's
getting the day off to come with me.' Worry skittered
across her face. 'Is there something wrong with the
baby? Is that why I keep being sick like this?'

'I think you have something called hyperemesis—it's
basically really bad morning sickness,' Ed said. 'I've
treated mums before who've had the same thing. It's
really miserable for you, but you're in the right place
and we can do something to help you feel a lot better.'

'Really?' Mrs Taylor looked as if she didn't quite
dare believe them.

'Really,' Jane confirmed.

'And it won't harm the baby? Only my nan said she
knew someone who took stuff to make them stop being
sick and the baby was…' She shuddered. 'I feel like
death warmed up, but I'd rather put up with that than
risk anything happening to the baby.'

'We won't give you anything that's not safe for the
baby,' Ed reassured her. 'Dr Fenton told us she's already
done some blood tests, so we need to wait for the results
of those. But in the meantime we'd like to give you a
scan and see how the baby's doing.'

'Has anyone called your husband, or would you like
us to call someone to be with you?' Jane asked.

'Jason's on his way,' Mrs Taylor said.

'That's great. We'll to take you up with us to the maternity unit, then,' Jane said.

'And, because you're quite dehydrated from being

sick, I'd like to keep you in for a little while and put you on a drip to replace the fluids you've lost. That'll make you feel a lot better, and we have one or two things that will help you stop being sick but won't affect the baby,' Ed reassured her.

By the time they'd taken Mrs Taylor up to the maternity unit, her husband had arrived. Ed ushered them in to the consulting room with the portable scanner, and Jane noticed that he was careful to make sure that the Taylors couldn't see the screen, in case it was bad news.

'What I'm going to do is to put a bit of gel on your stomach—sorry, it's a bit cold, whereas down in ultrasound it's always warm. All it does is help us get a better picture of the baby,' Jane explained. 'It's not going to hurt you or the baby—I'm sure your midwife's already told you this, but it's all done by sound waves.'

Mrs Taylor retched again, and her husband held the bowl for her; when she'd finished, Jane wiped her face with a damp cloth.

'This baby's going to be an only child,' Mrs Taylor said. 'I'm not going through this again. Ever.'

Jane made a soothing noise and glanced at Ed. Please, don't let it be a molar pregnancy causing the sickness, she thought.

Ed returned her glance; as if he could read her mind, he gave her a reassuring smile and the tiniest nod.

Thank God.

'I'm pleased to say that the baby's doing fine.' Ed turned the screen to show them. 'I did wonder if you might be having twins, because that sometimes makes the sickness much worse; but you're having just one. Here's the heart, beating nicely.' He pointed out the baby's heart. 'Everything's looking just as it should do.'

He made some quick measurements. 'And you're eleven and a half weeks.'

Mrs Taylor brushed back a tear. 'The baby's really all right?'

'The baby's absolutely fine,' Ed reassured her.

'Can we have a picture?' Mr Taylor asked.

'Unfortunately, this is a portable scanner, so we can't print anything from it. But when you have your proper scan next week, they'll be able to give you pictures then,' Jane explained.

Ed ran through the treatment plan, explaining what they were going to try and why; Jane found herself chipping in from time to time. It was as if she'd worked with him for years, instead of only half a morning. Whatever the complications caused by their fling on Saturday night, she was definitely going to able to work with this man. He fitted right in to the team, and he treated the mums with respect and dignity. And she liked that. A lot.

'I like your bedside manner,' she said when they'd left the Taylors.

He raised an eyebrow. 'Funny, I find sometimes women run from it.'

Jane felt the colour shoot into her face. 'I didn't mean *that* kind of bedside. I meant how you are with the mums. In my last hospital, I worked with a consultant who was incredibly brusque and treated everyone like idiots, mums and staff alike. He had all the social skills of a piranha, and I swore I'd never become like that myself or be forced to work with anyone like that again.' She gave him a wry smile. 'Though I guess I knew you wouldn't be like that, or Theo would've refused to appoint you.'

He smiled. 'I was teasing you, Jane.'

Her face was burning. 'Sorry. Everyone says I'm too serious. I'm afraid you drew the short straw and you've got the nerdy one to work with.'

'Nerdy's good,' he said. 'I like clever people. Come on, let's finish our rounds.'

She introduced him to the rest of her patients. When they'd finished, he said, 'I think we need to talk. Probably not where we're likely to be overheard, so do you know a quiet corner somewhere?'

Here it came. Retribution for her acting so madly, so unJanelike, on Saturday. And Sunday. 'Believe it or not, the most private place is probably going to be the hospital canteen; it's noisy and people don't get a chance to eavesdrop.'

'Good. Let's go.'

CHAPTER FOUR

'I'M BUYING,' Jane said, trying not to think of the last time they'd had coffee together. 'Black, no sugar, isn't it?'

'Yes, thanks. You have a good memory.'

'Doctors are supposed to be observant,' she said with a smile. She ordered a black coffee, plus a cappuccino for herself. 'Do you want a muffin with that?' she asked.

'No, I'm fine with just coffee, thanks.'

When she'd paid, she found them a quiet corner. 'Thanks for not bringing up what happened on Saturday in the department.'

He shrugged. 'No problem. But we do need to talk about Sunday.'

'Sunday?' She'd expected him to talk about Saturday and how they needed to set some boundaries. They were colleagues, nothing more, and what happened on Saturday wasn't going to be repeated.

'Sunday,' he confirmed. 'I was kind of expecting to see you when I woke up.'

She stirred her coffee, avoiding looking him in the eye. 'You were still asleep when I woke, so I thought it might be less awkward if I just left quietly.'

'Maybe. But when you wake up and someone's left

you money after they spent the night with you, it tends to make you feel a bit like a gigolo.'

She nearly choked on her coffee. 'The money was to cover the cleaning bill for your jacket. I didn't mean it to—oh, help. OK.' She blew out a breath. 'Theo didn't introduce me properly. Dr Jane Cooper. Good with patients, but her social skills need a bit of polishing.'

'Want to know how I see it?' Ed asked softly. 'Dr Jane Cooper, who's charming and warm and kind; and, even more charmingly, clearly doesn't have a clue just how lovely she is.'

It was a far cry from Shaun's damning assessment of her when she'd asked him why he'd cheated on her with Jenna. He'd said that she was twenty pounds too heavy and six inches too short. Jane knew it was ridiculous—she couldn't change her height and she had no intention of tottering around in uncomfortable high heels just to please someone else—but it had knocked her confidence as well as destroying her trust. He'd homed in on exactly the same criticisms that Jenna and her mother had always made about her: everything was about appearances, not what lay beneath. She'd thought Shaun was different, that he'd love her for who she was. How rubbish her judgement had turned out to be.

She frowned. 'Look, I'm not fishing for compliments, Ed. I know who I am and I'm comfortable with that.'

'Which is just how things should be,' Ed said.

This was crazy, Ed thought. He didn't do mad things. He was sensible. But on Saturday night he'd swept Jane off her feet and surprised himself. And he wanted to do it all over again.

According to his sisters, he was too reserved and needed to get a life. If he could swap a bit of his common sense for some of George's recklessness, they'd both be a lot more balanced.

Since the divorce, Ed hadn't even dated. He hadn't trusted his own judgement. And it looked as if Jane too had an ex who'd hurt her badly and had made her wary of relationships. Which left them...where?

He'd felt that they'd had a real connection on Saturday night. Not just the sex—there was something about Jane. Something that made him want to get to know her better. Something that made his customary reserve feel totally wrong where she was concerned. Something that made him want to take a chance.

He'd seen her work. She was calm, competent and knew how to work as a team. So it wouldn't be that much of a risk...would it?

'Given that I didn't get to see you on Sunday, how about you make amends this evening?' he asked.

She looked surprised. 'How do you mean?'

He shrugged. 'Have dinner with me.' He could see the panic skittering across her face. 'Unless you'd rather go and see a film or something?'

The teeniest twinkle of mischief appeared in her eyes. 'Would that be a James Bond film?'

Just how he'd hoped she'd respond. He grinned. 'If you know where one's showing, sure. Or, if not, we could go and find a DVD—though we'd have to watch it at your place. My hotel room doesn't have a DVD player.'

'You're still staying at the hotel?'

He nodded. 'I do have a flat lined up, but I can't move

in until the weekend. So the hotel was really the only choice.'

'Don't you have family or friends you can stay with?' Then she grimaced. 'Sorry. I'm being horribly nosey.'

He spread his hands. 'I don't think our "no questions" rule applies any more—and of course you'd want to know more about a new colleague. I was working in Glasgow, but I came back to London to be near my family.'

She frowned. 'So why are you staying in a hotel rather than with them?'

He smiled. 'I love my family. Dearly. But they'd drive me crazy if I went back to live with them after fourteen years of being away—there'd be questions all the time. Far more questions than you ask,' he added, seeing the colour rise in her cheeks. 'And living with my older brother's a definite no-no.' He'd thought about it, on the grounds that maybe he'd be a steadying influence. But then again, George was too strong a character to be influenced by anyone.

'Because you don't get on with him?' Jane asked.

Ed laughed. 'No. I get on fine with George. It's just that I'd never be able to keep up with him. He tends to burn the candle at both ends.'

'And you disapprove of that?'

'Not disapprove, exactly. I worry about him overdoing things. So I guess I'd drive him crazy, the same way the girls always nag me about working too hard.' He paused. 'What about you?'

'I have my own flat.'

Sidestepping again, he noticed. OK. He'd ask her straight out. 'Do you have family in London?'

'No.'

And he noticed she didn't say where her family was. 'You really don't like talking about personal stuff, do you?' he asked softly.

She spread her hands. 'What do you want to know? I'm twenty-eight, I'm working towards being a specialist registrar and I love my job. My parents used to live in London, but they're retired now and they have a place in Cornwall overlooking the sea.' She paused. 'And that's about it.'

Her body language was definitely telling him to back off. So he changed the subject to something he thought she'd find easier. 'What made you want to be a doctor?'

'I'm a fixer,' she said. 'I like to make things better. So it was the obvious career choice.'

'Me, too,' he admitted. 'Why obstetrics?'

'I was interested in IVF,' she said. 'I loved the idea of being able to give people hope, give them the family they'd dreamed about and longed for. Really making a difference.' Giving them the dream family she'd so wanted herself. She pushed the thought away. 'But then I did my rotation on the maternity ward, and I discovered just how much I like babies. There's absolutely nothing to match seeing those first magical seconds of a newborn taking in the world. Oh, and I'd better warn you in advance—it makes me cry every single time.'

He'd guessed she was soft-hearted. From what he'd seen of her at work so far, she really cared about her mums.

'But Theo knows I'm interested in IVF and I worked with the specialist team for a while, so my list tends to include more IVF mums. It means I've got the best of both worlds—I get to deliver babies, and I also get to look after mums who need a bit of extra care.' She looked at him. 'What made you choose obstetrics?'

'The same thing, really. I'm the fixer in my family, too. Right from when I was small, I used to bandage the dogs' paws and pretend I was making them better.'

'So you wanted to be a vet?'

'When I was that young, yes.' He laughed. 'Luckily the dogs were very indulgent. They'd let me listen to their heart with my stethoscope and stick a bandage on their paw. I was forced to use them as my patients because George—my older brother—was never still for long enough for me to bandage him.' He turned his coffee cup round in his hands. 'My sister Alice got meningitis when she was two. Luckily she was fine, but we spent a lot of time at the hospital, and I was desperate to make her better and make everyone in the family happy again. That's when I decided that I wanted to be a doctor. I thought about being a children's doctor, but then Frances had Bea. She was this little red-faced squeaky thing—just like Alice was—and everyone was smiling and so happy. And I knew then that was what I wanted to do—bring little red-faced squeaky things into the world and spread all that joy around.'

She laughed. 'Do your sisters know you call them red-faced squeaky things?'

'Yes.' He grinned. 'And I'm not going to tell you what they call me. Or what Charlotte calls me, for that matter.'

'Alice, Bea and Charlotte. You're Edward, and you have a brother George,' she mused. 'So who are the D and F?'

He liked the fact she'd picked that up. 'My father's David, and my stepmum's Frances.'

'Are there an H and an I, too?'

'No. And I really hope the girls aren't planning to make me an uncle to H and I before they've finished their education.'

'They're a lot younger than you, then?'

He nodded. 'I'm six years older than Alice. She's just about to be called to the bar, Bea's training to be an architect and Charlotte—the baby—is in the last year of her degree. She's on course for a First, so she's planning to do a PhD in a really obscure bit of Roman history.'

'So you're all clever.' Jane smiled. 'What does George do? Is he a professor of astrophysics or something?'

'He's—' Ed stopped. How much had Theo told the team about him? Or had Jane worked it out for herself that Ed's older brother was the Hon George Somers, heir to the barony? From what he'd seen of Jane, she was very straightforward and absolutely everything showed in her face, so it would be obvious if she read the gossip rags and knew who George was.

'He works in the family business,' Ed prevaricated.

Jane knew a sidestep when she saw one. Probably because she'd learned to be so skilled in sidestepping herself. Ed didn't want to talk about his brother as much as she didn't want to talk about Jenna. And yet he'd sounded affectionate when he'd said he worried about his brother. Something didn't quite add up, here. Though it was none of her business and she didn't want to pry—in case he started asking questions back.

She glanced at her watch. 'We need to be getting back to the ward.'

'Of course. So are we having dinner or going to the cinema tonight?'

Help. She'd hoped that getting him to talk about himself would've distracted him enough to make him forget the idea of going out. 'It's really nice of you to ask, but I can't make tonight. Some other time?' Though she was careful not to give an excuse that he could easily topple over, or to suggest anything specific—like an actual date when she could go out with him.

'Sure.'

Back on the ward, they were both kept busy, and the rest of the day shot by.

'See you tomorrow,' Ed said. 'Have a nice evening, whatever you're doing.'

Dinner for one and a pile of textbooks. But she liked it that way. 'You, too,' she said with a smile.

Even so, she couldn't get Edward Somers out of her head all evening, and she caught herself mooning over him when she was supposed to be studying. Which was ridiculous. And she was glad when the phone went and the caller display showed her best friend's number.

'Am I interrupting your studies?' Sorcha asked.

'I was about to take a break anyway,' Jane said.

'Hmm. Just checking on how you're doing.'

Jane knew exactly why Sorcha was calling. Because today was the day that horrible magazine had come out. 'I'm fine. Honestly, I am. Nobody on the ward's mentioned that article, and Theo's gone well above the call of duty and arranged that the hospital shop won't sell the magazine this week.' She bit her lip. 'Actually, I think he bought all the copies.'

'If he hadn't, Maddie and I would've clubbed together and done it,' Sorcha said. 'I'm not going to nag you about Jenna, because I know it's hard for you.'

'Good.'

'But I still think she's incredibly mean to you and you're a saint to put up with it.'

'Do you mean doormat?' Jane asked wryly.

Sorcha sighed. 'No, because you don't do it because you're weak. You do it because you're nice, and I guess family relationships are complicated. Though I'd disown her if she was mine. You know, just because you're related to someone, it doesn't mean you have to like them—or put up with them behaving badly towards you.'

Jane just coughed.

'OK, OK, I'll shut up. So what's your new colleague like?'

The gorgeous stranger I spent the night with on Saturday, and still haven't told you about, Jane thought. My guilty secret. 'Fine.'

'Come on. Deets.'

'There aren't any.'

'Well, is he nice?'

'Yes.'

'Single?'

Yes, but she didn't want to tell Sorcha that. Or that Ed had asked her out to dinner tonight. Because then Sorcha would nag her about letting Shaun's betrayal ruin her life. And Jane already knew her best friend's 'the best revenge is living well' speech by heart. 'It's hardly the first thing you'd ask a new colleague.' She really needed to change the subject, now, before she ended up telling Sorcha more than she intended. 'How's Jake?'

'He's wonderful.'

'Good.' Jane smiled. 'It was about time he noticed you. I'm so glad it's working out.'

'I just wish I had a magic wand and could find someone nice for you,' Sorcha said.

'There's no need, honestly. I'm fine on my own.'

'Really? Because I worry that you're lonely. I think what happened with Shaun last year broke something in you.'

It had. 'I guess I learned my lesson the hard way,' Jane said lightly. 'I'm sticking to friendship from now on. It makes life a lot easier.'

'Not every man's as shallow as Shaun was.'

'I know.' Ed definitely wasn't shallow. But she didn't want to analyse her feelings about him too closely. She'd thought she had a future with Shaun, that with him she'd make the close family she'd always wanted, filled with unconditional love. And she'd been so wrong. What was to say that she wouldn't be wrong about Ed, too? One night was just one night, and she was fine with that. 'I'm fine, Sorcha. Really.' Protesting a little too much, perhaps. But she'd get there.

'Well, you know where I am if you need to talk. Even if it's stupid o'clock in the morning.'

'I know, and thank you. I'm just glad you're my best friend.'

'Me, too. Now, don't study too late.'

'I won't,' Jane promised.

'And I'll see you for lunch tomorrow. Call me if you get held up, OK?'

'Will do. See you tomorrow.'

CHAPTER FIVE

'ED, I'VE got one of my mums on the way in. She's bleeding. And I could do with another view on the situation,' Jane said. 'Would you mind?'

'Sure. Fill me in on the background. Is she one of your IVF mums?'

Jane nodded. 'Pippa Duffield. She had a low-lying placenta at her twenty-week scan.'

'Nearly a third of women do. You know as well as I do, in most cases, it stops being a problem as the uterus develops further,' Ed said. 'I take it you're thinking placenta praevia in Pippa's case?'

Jane nodded. 'She's got more than average risk factor. IVF increases the chances of her placenta growing in the lowest part of the womb and covering the opening of the cervix, plus she's having twins.'

'OK. How many cycles did she have, and how old is she?'

'This was the fourth cycle, and she's thirty-eight.'

'So her age is another risk factor.' He looked grim. 'Let's hope for her sake that it's praevia and not an abruption.'

Jane hoped so, too. An abruption, where the placenta tore away from the uterus, could be life-threatening for both the babies and the mum.

Ed looked thoughtful. 'How far is she?'

'Thirty-two weeks.'

'So we'd be considering delivery at thirty-five weeks anyway. Provided we can get the bleeding under control, if the ultrasound shows it's praevia, I'd like to keep her in the ward on bed rest until delivery, so we can keep an eye on her and monitor the babies,' he said. 'Are you happy with that?'

She spread her hand. 'Hey, you're the consultant. It's your call.'

'She's one of your mums. You asked me for my opinion—I'm not muscling in and giving orders you're not happy about.'

'Thank you. Though, actually, my clinical decision would be the same as yours.'

'Good.' He smiled at her. 'I'm glad we're on the same wavelength. It feels as if I've worked with you for years, not just for a day or so.'

Funny how that warmed her. 'Me, too. And that makes life so much easier for our mums.' She smiled back at him. 'I should warn you, Pippa's desperate for a natural birth—the way she sees it, it'll make up for the fact she couldn't conceive without help.'

'That really depends on the ultrasound,' he said. 'If the placenta's within ten millimetres of her cervix, then it's too much of a risk to go for a normal delivery—both for her and for the babies.'

'Agreed,' Jane said.

Jane had asked one of the porters to meet Pippa's taxi and bring her up to the department in a wheelchair; just as she and Ed were sorting out the consulting room, Joe brought Pippa's wheelchair in.

'Thanks, Joe. I appreciate your help,' Jane said with a smile. 'Pippa, how are you doing?'

'I'm so scared, Jane. I can't lose my babies. Not now. Not after all we've been through. I just *can't*.' Pippa's face was blotchy with tears. 'When I started bleeding...' She dragged in a breath. 'I'm just so scared.'

'Of course you are. Any mum-to-be would be worried, in your shoes, and you did exactly the right thing by coming straight in,' Jane soothed, giving her a hug. 'But first of all remember that you're thirty-two weeks now, so even if the twins arrived today there's a very good chance of them being absolutely fine. And secondly, there are all sorts of reasons why women start spotting or even having quite a big bleed. Until we've examined you, I can't tell you what's happening, but you're in the best place right now. And the best thing you can do for your babies is to take some big, deep breaths for me.'

She coached Pippa through the breathing until the other woman was calmer. 'Brilliant. That's got your blood pressure back down a bit. Now, I'd like to introduce you to our new consultant, Mr Somers. Ed, this is Pippa Duffield.'

'Oh, my God.' Pippa's eyes widened. 'The bleeding's serious enough for me to see a *consultant*?'

'No. I'm just the new boy, it's my first week here, and I'm working with Jane,' Ed said cheerfully.

'And he's very good,' Jane said. 'More experienced than I am. So between us you're in great hands.'

Pippa gave her a wan smile.

'May we examine you, Mrs Duffield?' Ed asked.

'Call me Pippa,' she said. 'Yes.'

'Thank you, Pippa. And I hope you'll call me Ed.'

She nodded.

Gently, he examined her. 'Are you feeling any kind of pain?'

'No.'

'Good. Are you having any kind of contractions, even practice ones or tiny ones?'

'I don't think so.'

He nodded. 'Jane, would you mind checking the babies' heartbeats?'

Jane did so. 'The good news here is that their heartbeats both sound normal. Now, at this stage, we're not going to do an internal exam, Pippa.' Until they were sure it was placenta praevia and not an abruption, she didn't want to take the risk of causing a much worse bleed. 'But we'd like to do an ultrasound so we can get a better idea of what's causing the bleeding, if that's OK with you, Pippa?'

'The babies are all right. Thank God.' Pippa closed her eyes briefly in seeming relief. 'Do whatever you need to, Jane.'

'I'll also need to take some blood,' Jane said.

She swiftly took blood samples and assessed how much blood Jane had lost, before putting a line in for IV access; meanwhile, Ed had gone to locate the portable ultrasound scanner.

The scan showed exactly what she and Ed had expected.

'Your placenta's right near the bottom of your womb and it's partially blocking your cervix,' Ed said. 'What happens in the last trimester of pregnancy is that your cervix starts to get thinner and stretch, ready for the birth, and in your case some of the blood vessels have broken—that's what caused the bleeding. Jane tells me you haven't lost a huge amount of blood, so I'm not too worried. We can keep an eye on you. The good news is that there's a really strong chance that we can deliver the babies as originally planned, at thirty-five weeks.'

'And the bad news?' Pippa asked.

'Jane tells me you were hoping for a normal delivery.' He took her hand and squeezed it. 'I'm sorry, we can't do that, because the placenta's going to be in the way. You could end up losing a lot of blood, and we just can't take that risk—for you or for the babies.'

A tear trickled down Pippa's cheek. 'I couldn't conceive normally and I can't even have a normal birth. I'm going to be a rubbish mother.'

'No, you're not,' Ed said. 'Lots of women need help with conceiving, and lots of women end up having a Caesarean. But the good news is that we can plan it, so you won't have to go through a trial of labour first, then end up in emergency surgery because the babies are in distress and you're exhausted. It's tough enough being a mum to twins without all that on top of it.' He smiled at her. 'Right now, I'd guess you're feeling disappointed and relieved and worried, all at the same time. In your shoes, I think I'd be bawling my eyes out. So I'd say you're doing just fine.'

Pippa bit her lip. 'So what now? I go home and have to rest?'

'No. We'd like to keep you on the ward,' Jane said, 'so we can keep an eye on you.'

'Overnight?'

Ed shook his head. 'Until you have the babies.'

'Three weeks? But—I can't.' Pippa looked horrified. 'I haven't sorted out the nursery yet! I only went on maternity leave last week.' She shook her head in distress. 'I've been so careful not to overdo things and rush around like I normally would. I've taken it really easy and waited for Mike to paint the walls instead of grabbing the step ladders and doing it myself. And now...' She rubbed a hand across her eyes, scrubbing away the tears. 'I don't want Mike's mother taking over and making the room what she thinks it should be like, instead of what I want.'

'Can your mum maybe step in and bat your corner for you?' Ed asked.

'No. She died from breast cancer, two years ago.' More tears slid down Pippa's cheeks. 'I wish she was here. I wish she was going to meet my babies. She would've been such a brilliant grandmother. She wouldn't take over and try to boss me around all the time, like Mike's mother does.'

'Ed, would you mind calling Mike for us while I sit with Pippa for a bit?' Jane asked.

'Sure.' Moving so that Pippa couldn't see his face, he mouthed, 'I'll give you a yell when he gets here and we'll talk to him.'

Jane sat with Pippa, holding her hand and soothing her until she'd calmed down. 'I know this is rough on you, but we can work round things. Ed and I are happy to talk to anyone you need us to, so they know exactly why you're in and that you need a bit of TLC.'

'I don't think Mike's mother knows how to give TLC,' Pippa said wearily. 'And he never stands up to her.'

'You'd be surprised how much it changes you, becoming a parent,' Jane said softly. 'Where you might not stand up for yourself, you suddenly find that you do for your children.' At least, you stood up for your favourite one. But Pippa didn't need Jane dumping her own inadequacies on her; she needed support.

Rosie, one of the midwives, came in. 'Jane, sorry, Ed needs a quick word with you in his office.'

'Sure. I'll be back in a minute, Pippa.' She smiled at the midwife. 'Rosie, would you mind sitting with Pippa for a bit?'

'Of course I will.'

When Jane got to Ed's office, Mike Duffield was sitting on the chair at the side of Ed's desk.

'Jane, is Pippa all right? And the babies? Ed's just been telling me what happened. Can I see her?'

'They're all doing OK,' Jane reassured him. 'Mike, I know you're worried and you want to see Pippa, but we wanted a word with you before you go in.'

'Why? Is there something you haven't told her?'

Jane shook her head. 'We want to keep her in so we can keep an eye on her, and she's really upset about it.'

Mike frowned. 'So there *is* something wrong.'

'I've told you everything, Mike,' Ed said gently. 'We want to keep an eye on her because she might start bleeding again. We can monitor her and the babies here; if things get sticky and we need to deliver the twins, then there won't be any delay. Pippa's upset because she hasn't finished decorating the nursery.'

Mike's face cleared. 'Well, I can sort that out for her, and my mum will help.'

Just what Pippa had been afraid of. Jane steeled herself for a difficult conversation. 'Mike, there isn't an easy or tactful way to put this, and I apologise in advance if I'm stepping over the line here, but that's one of the things that's worrying Pippa—that she'll end up having the nursery your mum wants, not the one that *she* wants.'

Mike looked taken aback. 'You what?'

Ed glanced at Jane and gave a tiny nod. 'Is there a chance maybe you could talk to your mum?' he asked. 'Maybe you could tell her that Pippa's upset about being in hospital and not able to do things the way she wants, and ask her if she'd consider helping you carry out what Pippa planned. But most importantly she needs to come and see Pippa, to reassure her that it's going to be *her* choices that matter.'

'I...' Mike blew out a breath. 'To be honest, Mum and Pip tend to clash a bit. They both have strong ideas. If Mum thinks that Pip doesn't want her help, then it'll put her back up.'

And clearly Mike didn't relish being stuck in the middle. Jane's father was like that, so she understood exactly why Pippa hated the fact that Mike would never stand up for her. 'Is there someone else you can ask to help with the nursery? A friend, another relative?' Jane asked. 'Because Pippa needs to rest and be as calm as possible, for her sake and that of the babies. People who haven't gone through IVF often don't really understand the kind of emotional and physical strain it involves, and maybe your mum doesn't appreciate what Pippa's gone through.'

Mike grimaced. 'Mum doesn't actually know we had IVF. Pip didn't want her to know. She's got this thing about how people are going to think she's not a proper mum because she couldn't conceive without help.'

'She did say something like that,' Ed said, 'and I told her that of course she's going to be a good mum—it's got nothing to do with the way the babies were conceived or how they're going to come into the world.' He looked thoughtful. 'What about Pippa's dad? Or does she have a sister who can help?'

'Her dad's a bit frail, and her sister…' Mike wrinkled his nose. 'They're not close. I really don't think Pip would want me to ask her.'

Jane could appreciate that. She knew all about difficult sisters, too. Jenna would be the last person she'd ask for help—because she knew the answer would be no. 'What about her best friend? That's who I'd want to help me, if I were in Pippa's shoes. And if that would reassure Pippa, then as her doctor my advice to you would be to talk to her best friend.'

'Well, I could ring her,' Mike said slowly. 'Shelley's a bit bossy.'

'So's my best friend,' Jane said with a smile. 'It's one of the things I love about her. She gets things done.'

'All right. I'll call her,' Mike said. 'And I'll tell Pip not to worry about the nursery. I'll make sure it's how she wants it.'

'Thanks. Taking something big like that off her mind will really help a lot. I'll take you through to her.'

Jane ended up spending the rest of the morning with the Duffields; when she went to collect her handbag from the rest room at the beginning of her lunch break, Ed was there, too.

'How's Pippa?' he asked.

'Much more settled. And thanks for having a word with Mike. That really helped.'

'Any time.' He smiled at her. 'Got time to have lunch with me?'

She shook her head regretfully. 'Sorry, I'm already

meeting someone.' She glanced at her watch. 'And I'm going to be late! Gotta go. Catch you later.'

Jane didn't see Ed for the rest of the afternoon. She did a last check on her patients, making especially sure that Pippa had settled, at the end of her shift. She was about to leave the ward when she passed Ed's open door.

'Jane? Can I have a word?'

'Sure.'

'Close the door.'

She frowned, but did so.

'Tell me honestly, do I have a personal hygiene problem?'

She stared at him, puzzled. 'No. Why on earth would you think that?'

'Because, unless I'm also suffering from a bad case of paranoia, you seem to be avoiding me.' He sighed. 'Jane, I like you. And on Saturday I thought you liked me, too.'

She did. But she didn't want to risk getting hurt again.

Not knowing what to say, she stayed silent.

'So do I take it you've had time to think about it and you want to be strictly colleagues?' he asked.

'Yes.' She saw the disappointment in his eyes just before he masked it.

Oh. So he *did* really like her.

'And, if I'm really honest, no,' she admitted. 'Look, I don't want to go into details right now, but I don't exactly have a good track record when it comes to relationships.'

'Join the club. I'm divorced,' he said, surprising her. From what she'd seen of Ed, he was thoughtful and kind and charming. Not to mention the way he made her feel physically. So why on earth would someone want to break up with him? Unless he, too, had completely lousy judgement when it came to relationships, and had picked someone who really wasn't suited to him.

'I won't pry,' she promised.

'There isn't much to tell. We wanted different things.'

'I can identify with that,' she admitted. She'd wanted a family, and Shaun had wanted Jenna. 'Except I didn't get quite as far as marriage.'

'Sounds to me as if we have a lot in common,' Ed said. 'Including not wanting to get hurt. So how about it? We go for a pizza, somewhere really crowded with lots of bright lights, and I walk you home and kiss you very chastely goodnight outside your front door?'

'You actually want to go out with me?'

'Yes.'

He meant it. OK, so Jane's track record in judging men was pretty rubbish, but she'd seen the way he was with their patients. Totally sincere, kind, taking the time to listen. Ed Somers was a nice guy, as well as being the hottest man she'd ever met.

'Pizza, and a chaste kiss goodnight outside my front door,' she checked.

'There might be two chaste kisses. But I promise they'll be chaste. Unless—' there was a glint of mischief in his eyes '—you decide to kiss me unchastely. In which case all promises will be on hold.'

It was tempting. So very tempting.

Dared she trust him, let him get close to her? Maybe her best friend was right and she needed to just get out there, enjoy herself, and put the past behind her. Dating Ed, maybe ending up back in bed with him, didn't mean that she was going to fall in love with him. He'd been hurt, too. They didn't have to rush this or make any promises, just see where it took them. They could both enjoy this and keep their hearts intact.

'OK. I'd love to go for pizza.'

'Great. Give me five minutes to save this file and shut down the computer, and I'm all yours.'

All yours. Jane rather liked the sound of that. 'See you in five, then.'

CHAPTER SIX

JANE knew exactly the place to go: a small trattoria that was busy and brightly lit, and the food was fantastic.

'Excellent choice,' Ed said after his first taste of the pizza. 'The food's fantastic.'

'I normally come here with Sorcha—my best friend,' she explained. 'Because of the food.'

They spent the whole evening talking, discovering that they had similar tastes in music and books and films. And when Jane finished her third coffee and glanced at her watch, her eyes widened in surprise. 'Blimey! We've been here for four hours.'

Ed looked awkward. 'Sorry—I didn't mean to keep you that long.'

'No, I've really enjoyed it.' She was aware how surprised she sounded—and how bad that was. 'Sorry. I didn't mean to imply I thought I wouldn't enjoy your company. Just that it's been a while since I've gone on a date and I thought it might be a bit, well, awkward.'

'Snap. Except it wasn't,' Ed said softly. 'I've enjoyed tonight, too.'

He walked her home, escorted her up the steps to the entrance to her block of flats, and gave her a chaste kiss right at the corner of her mouth.

'Wasn't that meant to be my cheek?' Jane asked.

'Technically, it *is* your cheek,' he pointed out.

'Hmm.'

He kissed the other cheek, but this time Jane moved slightly and Ed ended up kissing her on the mouth. He pulled back and looked her straight in the eye. 'Jane, are you going to kiss me?'

'Would it be a problem?'

He smiled. 'No. It'd be a delight.'

And it was a delight for her, too. Hot enough to let her know that he found her attractive, but not so pushy that she felt pressured.

Finally, Ed broke the kiss. 'I'd better go back to the hotel.' He stroked her cheek. 'I'm not going to ask you to let me come in, even though I'd like to, because I don't quite trust myself to behave honourably.'

Was this his way of letting her down gently? she wondered.

He stole a kiss. 'You know, your face is really expressive. Never play poker, will you?'

Jane could feel her skin heat. 'Sorry,' she mumbled.

'This isn't because I don't want to come in, because I do. But we started this all the wrong way round. It might be a good idea to give us time to get to know each other properly, this time,' he said softly. 'See where it takes us.'

'I guess.'

His kiss was sweet and warm. 'See you tomorrow. Do any of your windows overlook the street?'

'The kitchen. Second floor, middle window.'

'Good. Put the light on and wave to me when you're in, OK?'

'OK.' Jane had never dated anyone who was quite

that gentlemanly before. And she loved the fact that he actually waited until she was safely indoors and had waved to him before he sketched a salute back and left for his hotel.

'Mr Somers—do you have a moment?' Jane asked the following afternoon, leaning against the jamb of Ed's office door.

'Sure. Want me to come and see one of your mums?'

'No. I was just wondering, are you busy tonight?'

'No.' He looked pleased that she'd asked. 'What did you have in mind?'

'You said yesterday about watching a film. I was wondering, maybe you'd like to come over to my flat and see a film this evening. Say, about eight?'

'I'd like that,' he said.

'Comedy or serious drama?'

'I'll leave the choice to you.'

'You might regret that,' she warned.

He grinned. 'You said that about dancing with you. I didn't have any regrets then, so I doubt I'll have any regrets tonight, either.' He winked at her. 'See you later, Jane.'

At precisely eight o'clock, Ed walked up the steps to Jane's apartment block and pressed the buzzer.

'Come up. Second floor, first door on the left next to the stairs.' Her voice sounded slightly crackly through the intercom.

By the time he reached the second floor, her door was already open and she was waiting for him. 'Hi.'

'For you.' He handed her the flowers he'd bought on the way back to the hotel from the hospital.

'Oh, they're lovely, all summery and...' She buried her nose in them and inhaled deeply. 'I adore the smell of stocks. Thank you, Ed. They're gorgeous.'

'My pleasure.' He'd thought that roses might be too obvious, and was glad he'd opted for the pretty, scented summer flowers instead.

And he'd also guessed that she'd like crisp white wine. She beamed at him when he handed her the chilled bottle of Chablis. 'This is my favourite—and you really didn't have to, you know.'

'I know. I just wanted to.'

'Come in. I'm going to put these gorgeous flowers in water—make yourself at home,' she said. 'The living room's through there. I take it you'll have a glass of wine, too?'

'Thanks, that'd be lovely.'

Her flat was exactly what he'd expected it to be: small, but warm and homely. The living room had an overstuffed sofa and soft furnishings in rich autumnal colours. He couldn't resist browsing her bookshelves; there was an eclectic mix of thrillers, poetry and medical textbooks, and another shelf held a selection of films, a mixture of serious dramas and comedies.

On the mantelpiece there were several framed photographs. Ed knew he was snooping and Jane was cagey about her personal life, but he looked anyway. One of the photographs was of Jane on her graduation day with an older couple he guessed were her parents, though they didn't look much like her; another was of Jane with a bubbly-looking redhead he guessed was her best friend. There was also a photo of a much younger version of Jane with a Springer spaniel draped all over her and the widest, widest smile, and another of Jane with an elderly woman.

'Gorgeous dog,' he said when she came into the living room, carrying two glasses of wine.

'That's Bertie. He was my great-aunt's,' she said. 'I always wanted a dog, but my mum didn't really like them. She said they were too messy and she always moaned about dog hair on her clothes whenever we visited Sadie.' She shrugged. 'Sadie had a quiet word with me and told me that I could share Bertie with her, and she'd look after him between visits.'

'And I guess, working hospital hours and living in a flat, you can't really have a dog here,' he said.

'No.' She looked regretful. 'I adored Bertie. He was the sweetest, gentlest dog ever.'

'Is that Sadie?' he asked, pointing to the photograph of the elderly woman.

She nodded. 'Sadly, she died last year. But she was lovely. I was privileged to have her in my life.'

'That's how I feel about my sisters,' he said. 'And George.'

For a moment, he could've sworn that she flinched. And her smile didn't quite reach her eyes when she said, 'It's good to have people like that around.'

'Are these your parents?' He indicated the picture of her with the older couple.

'Yes.'

'And I'm asking too many questions?'

'No, it's OK.' She shrugged. 'It's an old picture now, but my mum's barely changed in the last thirty years. I guess that's the thing about supermodels—they have wonderful bone structure.'

'Your mum was a supermodel?'

She nodded. 'She's retired now.'

He studied the photograph, and it made him wonder. Jane's mother was classically beautiful, but there was something remote about her. Plus by Jane's own admission her mother was fussy about dog hairs and mud. He had the strongest feeling that Jane's childhood hadn't been anywhere near as happy as his own. He couldn't remember that much of his own mother, but his stepmother Frances had always been warm, welcoming and loving—not to mention completely unbothered about the amount of hair their assorted dogs and cats shed. Clearly Jane's mother wasn't like that; she didn't sound like the easiest of people to be close to.

'I think you have her eyes,' he said eventually, trying to be diplomatic.

'Maybe.' She handed him one of the wine glasses. 'Here.'

'Thanks.' He took the hint and put the photograph down. 'So what did you pick, in the end? Serious drama or a comedy?'

'Comedy,' she said.

'Sounds good.'

When she sat next to him on the sofa, he slid one arm round her shoulders and she relaxed into him. The film wasn't bad, but he couldn't take his attention off Jane. So much for his good intentions. But they'd spent hours talking last night, getting to know each other better. One kiss wouldn't hurt, would it?

He shifted slightly so he was half-lying on the sofa. When she leaned into him, he shifted further, and moved her so that she was lying on top of him.

'Hello,' he said softly, and reached up to kiss her.

He had meant it to be soft and sweet, but then she

opened her mouth, letting him deepen the kiss, and his
control snapped. His fingers slid under the hem of her
T-shirt, moving further up until his hands were splayed
against her back. And the way she was lying, she'd be
in no doubt of how much she turned him on. He could
feel the softness of her breasts against his chest, and
also the hardness of her nipples; so he had a pretty good
idea that it was the same for her, too.

'Sorry. That wasn't meant to happen,' he said when
they surfaced from the kiss. 'I was trying to be a gentleman. But you leaned into me.'

'Hmm,' she said.

But there was a twinkle in her eye, so he grinned
back, moving so that he was sitting upright and she was
still straddling him.

He wrapped his arms round her. 'You know what I
was saying about taking it slowly and getting to know
each other first? I've had a rethink.'

'And?'

'I reckon we need to do some speed dating.'

She frowned. 'Speed dating?'

'So we get to know everything about each other. Like
now. And then I can do…' He paused. 'What I think
you'd like me to do, too.'

He loved the fact that she blushed spectacularly.

'Before I met you, I never behaved like this. For pity's
sake, we haven't even known each other for a week,'
she said.

'No. It's completely illogical and irrational…and irresistible.' He kissed her. 'Your eyes are very green.'

'What does that mean?'

'I noticed on Saturday. You know I said your eyes

change colour? When you're turned on, your eyes go green.'

Her blush deepened even further. 'You make me sound like—I dunno, some kind of siren. I'm ordinary. Plain Jane.'

'If you were ordinary,' he said softly, 'I wouldn't be reacting like this to you.' He kissed her again, just to prove it. 'I was intending to go home. To be gentlemanly.'

'But?' Her voice was very, very soft.

'But what I really want to do right now is carry you to your bed and drive you as crazy as you drive me.' He shook his head. 'I don't do this sort of thing. I'm the serious one in the family, the one who plays by all the rules. But something about you makes me want to be different. To take a chance and follow my feelings instead of my head.'

'Like James Bond.' She stroked his face. 'You already know I think you'd give him a run for his money.'

Actually, he thought wryly, the James Bond-alike would be George, not him. 'Thank you for the compliment, but hardly.'

'Come off it. Half the hospital's swooning over you.'

'Since when?'

'I told you, the grapevine works fast at our place.'

He raised an eyebrow. 'Would you mind very much if they talked about us?'

She grimaced. 'I don't like being the hot topic.'

Of course. She'd probably been there after her ex. 'Did he work at the hospital?'

'No.' She sighed. 'I guess I ought to tell you what happened. Though it's not pretty. I came home early one day—I'd forgotten to tell him I was on a half-day—and found him in our bed with someone else.'

Ed sucked in a breath. How on earth could the guy have betrayed Jane like that? 'I'm sorry he hurt you like that. That's…' He couldn't find the words to describe it, but he needed to say something. To let her know he was on her side. 'That's a really shoddy way to treat someone.'

She shrugged. 'I'm over it now.'

'Are you?'

She nodded. 'But I will admit that Saturday was the first time I'd felt beautiful since it happened.'

'How long ago?'

'Eight months,' she admitted.

'Then I'm glad I could do that for you.' He paused. 'Just for the record, I don't believe in cheating. While I'm seeing you, I won't be seeing anyone else, and that's a promise.'

'Same here.'

'Good.' He stroked her hair. 'I don't know what to say.'

She shrugged. 'There's nothing to say. I gave Shaun his ring back and moved out that same day.'

She'd been *engaged* to the guy when he'd cheated on her? What the hell had been wrong with him?

'Sorcha was brilliant and let me stay with her until I found this place.'

'The more you tell me about your best friend, the more I like her.'

Jane smiled. 'She's the sister I wish I had.'

'The best kind of friend. Since we're sharing difficult stuff, I should tell you…' He sighed. 'My family's, um, fairly well-to-do. And my ex thought she'd have the lifestyle that goes with that kind of family.' Camilla had come from the same kind of background as his own, and she'd had definite expectations. 'I don't think she realised the kind of hours that junior doctors work—or how important my job is to me. I think maybe she expected me to...' How could he put this without scaring Jane away? 'To give it up and join the family business,' he finished. He knew it was selfish of him, but he was truly glad that being the second son meant that he'd never had to face that choice—that he was able to follow his real calling and make a difference to people's lives, instead of doing his duty and trying not to let his family have any idea how trapped he felt.

He sighed. 'I guess I'm selfish. Or I didn't really love my ex enough, because I just couldn't give up medicine for her. Being a doctor, helping mums through tricky pregnancies and helping make their dreams of a family come true—that's who I *am*, not just what I do.'

She kissed him. 'That's how I feel about it, too.'

'But it's not fair of me to put all the blame on Camilla. I dragged her off to Glasgow because I had the chance to work with a top specialist and I wanted to take the opportunity to learn from him. It didn't occur to me how cut off she'd feel from London, and I should've taken her needs into account a lot more than I did,' he said. 'So I'm very, very far from being perfect.'

'You and me both,' she said softly. 'I had this dream and I was so sure that Shaun was the one to make it all come true for me. I expected too much from him. And I guess he couldn't take the fact that I was never going to be tall and skinny and elegant. So he found someone who was.'

'Which is incredibly shallow. It's not what people

look like, it's who they are that's important. And anyway, not all men want a stick insect. Some men happen to like little, cute, curvy women.' He punctuated every adjective with a kiss. Just to make sure she knew he meant it. 'He really doesn't know what he's missing.' He kissed her again, and her hands slid into his hair. He splayed his palms over her spine. 'Jane. Shall we skip the rest of the film?'

Her eyes were very green. 'Yes.' She kissed him back.

He had no idea how they got off the sofa, but the next thing he knew he was on his feet, he'd scooped her into his arms, and he was carrying her out of the living room. 'Which one's your room?'

'First door on the right.'

He nudged the door open and smiled. 'I'm so glad you have a double bed.'

'It's good for spreading papers out on.'

'True.' He stole a kiss. 'But I have other plans.' He set her down on her feet. 'Starting here.' He unbuttoned her jeans, and she sucked in a breath.

'I was in too much of a rush last time. This time I'm going to enjoy it.'

Her eyes widened. 'Ed—the curtains.'

'Wait here—and stop thinking,' he directed. He swiftly closed the curtains and switched on her bedside lamp, then came back to her side. Gently, he encouraged her to lift up her arms, and drew her T-shirt up over her head.

God, her curves made him ache. He didn't know whether he wanted to look at her first, touch her, taste her, or all three at once.

He dropped to his knees in front of her and gradually

peeled her jeans down, stroking her skin as he bared it. He let her balance on him while he helped her out of the denim completely, then sat back on his haunches to look at her. 'Wow, you're gorgeous. All curves.'

She looked shy. 'Do you think you could take some of your clothes off as well? I'm feeling a bit...well, exposed, here.'

'I'm in your hands,' he said, standing up.

She peeled off his own T-shirt, then shyly undid the button of his jeans. He helped her remove them, then traced the lacy edge of her bra. She shivered and tipped her head back in invitation. Smiling, he unsnapped her bra and cupped her breasts. 'You're gorgeous. Lush,' he whispered.

She coloured, but something in her expression told him that he'd pleased her.

Gently, he hooked his thumbs over the edge of her knickers and drew them down. She did the same with his boxers.

He picked her up, loving the feel of her skin against his, and laid her against the pillows. He paused to grab his wallet from his discarded jeans and ripped open the condom packet.

Her hand slid over his. 'My job, I think.'

It thrilled him that she'd refound her confidence with him—just as he was finding his with her. He shivered as she rolled the latex over his shaft. And then he was right where he wanted to be, kneeling between her thighs and buried deep inside her.

Her pupils widened with pleasure, and her eyes were the clearest green.

He took it as slowly as he could, until finally her

body tightened round his, pushing him into his own climax, and his body surged into hers.

Afterwards, Ed went to the bathroom, and returned to see Jane sitting in bed, looking slightly wary.

'I'm not expecting you to let me stay the night, but leaving right now would feel completely wrong,' he said. 'Can I stay for a bit longer?

She smiled. 'I'd like that.'

'Thank you.'

He climbed back into the bed and drew her into his arms; she held him close and he relaxed, enjoying the companionable silence and the warmth of her body against his. He waited until she'd fallen asleep, then wriggled out of the bed without waking her and dressed swiftly.

As he left the bedroom, he realised that the DVD player and TV were still on; they'd been so caught up in each other that neither of them had noticed. He turned them off, took their glasses into her kitchen, then took the top sheet from the jotter block next to the phone and left her a scribbled note propped against the kettle.

Hope you slept well. Can't wait to see you at work this morning. E x

Then he quietly let himself out of her flat.

CHAPTER SEVEN

THE note Ed had left her made Jane smile all the way through her hated early morning run and then all the way in to work.

When she walked into the staff kitchen, Ed was already there, spooning instant coffee into a mug.

'Good morning.'

He glanced round, gave her a sultry smile, and kissed her swiftly.

'Ed!' she said, shocked. 'Supposing someone had walked in on us?'

'They didn't,' he reassured her. 'Though would it really matter if they had?'

'I guess not. I mean, we're seeing each other, but we're both professional enough not to let it get in the way at work.'

'Exactly.' He smiled again. 'Good morning. Did you sleep well?'

'Yes. Did you?'

'Oh, yeah.' The expression in his eyes heated her blood. 'Especially as I had a very, *very* nice dream.'

'Funny, that. So did I.' She glanced at her watch. 'Rounds in ten minutes?'

'Suits me fine.' He gestured to the kettle. 'Want a coffee?'

'No, thanks. I'll pass.' She gave him a sidelong glance. 'I've already had coffee this morning. With a very nice side order.'

'You saw the note, then.'

'Indeed I did, Mr Somers.' And she loved the fact he couldn't wait to see her again. 'See you in ten.' She winked at him, and sashayed out of the kitchen.

Their rounds were routine; Pippa Duffield's condition was stable, and Mrs Taylor was responding so well to treatment that Ed planned to let her go home on Monday, provided she managed to continue eating little and often over the weekend.

But the afternoon saw Iris sending Rosie, one of the more junior midwives, to grab them both. 'Iris says she need a forceps delivery *right now*,' Rosie said. 'Prolapsed cord.'

Rare, and scary, Jane thought.

'And it's not a breech or a footling presentation.'

Rarer still. Jane looked at Ed, knowing how serious the situation could be; given that it wasn't a breech presentation, it meant that the umbilical cord was probably longer than normal and part of it had passed through the entrance to the uterus. There was a real risk of the blood flow being restricted during contractions so the baby wouldn't get enough oxygen, and the baby could be in distress—or even stillborn.

'How far down is the head?' Ed asked.

'The mum's in the second stage, fully dilated, and the head's pretty far down,' Rosie said.

'Too late for a section, then. OK. Iris is absolutely right. We'll need to try forceps,' Ed said, looking grim. 'But if the baby isn't out within three sets of traction, we're talking emergency section under a general.'

As soon as they went into the delivery suite, Iris introduced them to the mum, Tilly Gallagher, who was kneeling with her bottom in the air and her shoulders lowered to slow down the delivery. Iris was clearly following established procedure, pushing the baby's head back up between contractions to avoid extra pressure on the umbilical cord. Pushing the cord back behind the head wasn't an option, because handling the cord could cause the blood vessels to spasm and reduce the amount of oxygen coming to the baby.

Tilly's husband Ray was holding her hand and looking as if he wished he was elsewhere.

'Try not to panic, Tilly,' Ed said, 'but the umbilical cord's causing a bit of a complication and the safest way to deliver your baby is if we give you a little bit of help.' He glanced at Jane, who nodded and took over.

'We're going to use forceps to help deliver the baby. We'll also need to give you an episiotomy.' She talked Tilly and Ray through the procedure while Ed checked the monitor to see how the baby was doing and Rosie went to fetch one of the senior paediatricians, ready to check the baby over after delivery.

They helped Tilly into position for delivery, in stirrups. 'I know it's not very dignified, but it'll help us deliver the baby quickly,' Jane said. 'Ray, if you'd like to stay here by Tilly's side, hold her hand and help her with her breathing?'

Ray looked grateful that they weren't expecting him to view the birth.

Ed administered a local anaesthetic and gave Tilly an episiotomy ready for the delivery. Jane put the forceps together and was about to hand them to him when he mouthed to her, 'It'll be good experience for you to do it.'

Prolapsed cords weren't that common, and Jane knew that he was right about this being good experience for her. Warmed that he had faith in her—and knowing that he would be there to help and advise her if things started to get tricky—Jane smiled at Tilly. 'OK. What I'm going to do is help guide the baby's head down with every contraction. If you're at all worried at any point, just say and we'll do our best to reassure you. Are you ready?'

Tilly took a deep breath. 'I'm ready.'

As Tilly's contractions progressed, Jane synchronised traction with the forceps, guiding the baby's head downwards. She was aware of Rhys Morgan coming into the delivery suite, but was concentrating too much on Tilly and the baby to exchange any pleasantries with him.

She was relieved when the baby was finally delivered; while Rhys and Iris checked the baby over, she and Ed checked Tilly over.

The baby was silent, and Jane was aware of every second passing, every pulse of blood in her veins.

Please let the baby cry. Please let them have been in time. Jane had her back to Iris and Rhys so she couldn't see what they were doing, but she knew they were probably giving the baby oxygen to help inflate the lungs and encourage the baby to breathe.

Please let the baby cry.

Just as she was starting to panic inwardly, she heard a thin wail.

At last. She exchanged a relieved glance with Ed.

She herd Iris calling out the Apgar score, and then

finally Rhys came over with the baby wrapped in a warm blanket and placed the infant in Tilly's arms. 'Congratulations, Mr and Mrs Gallagher, you have a little boy.'

'Oh, my baby.' A tear slid down Tilly's cheek. 'Ray, he looks just like you.'

'He's— Oh, my God,' Ray whispered. 'Our baby.'

Jane couldn't hold back the tears trickling down her own face. 'He's gorgeous.'

'Congratulations,' Ed said warmly. 'There is a little bit of bruising, but that will go down in the next couple of days.'

'And he's going to be all right?' Ray asked.

'He's doing fine,' Rhys reassured her. 'The scary stuff is all past. I'll be in to see you later today, but in the meantime if you're worried about anything you're in very safe hands here.' He nodded acknowledgement to Ed and Jane. 'Catch you both later.'

Ed looked at Jane. 'You're crying.'

'I told you, I always do when I deliver a baby,' she said softly. 'Because it's such a perfect moment, the beginning of a new life, and it's such a privilege to be here.'

Iris put her arm round Jane and hugged her. 'You did well.'

'Hey. Tilly's the one who did most of the work, and your call was spot on,' Jane said.

'I just wish I'd picked it up earlier.' Iris sighed. 'But there were no signs, not until her waters broke and the monitor bleeped to say the baby was in distress.'

'Nobody could've predicted it. And your assessment was perfect,' Ed said.

He and Jane left Iris and Rosie with the Gallaghers

and their newborn son, and Ed shepherded her through to his office. He opened the bottom drawer of his desk, extracted a bar of chocolate and handed it to her.

She blinked. 'What's this for?'

'Sugar. I think you need it.' He blew out a breath. 'That was a scary moment back then.'

'You're telling me.' She broke the chocolate bar in half and handed one piece back to him. 'I was getting a bit worried when I couldn't hear the baby crying.'

'Rhys says he's absolutely fine. They were lucky. And you were a star with the forceps.'

'Thanks for letting me do it. I mean, I've done forceps deliveries before, but they've been where the mum was so exhausted that she needed a bit of help.'

'This wasn't so much different. I knew you'd be fine—and if it had got tricky, I was there,' he said. 'We're a good team.'

Inside *and* outside work. Not that she should let herself fall for Ed too quickly. Even though she knew he wouldn't hurt her the way Shaun had, she also knew it wasn't sensible to rush into this.

'Are you busy tonight?' he asked.

'Don't think I'm pushing you away, but I'm studying.' Which was also a good excuse to keep him at just a tiny distance. Just enough to stop her being as vulnerable as she'd been with Shaun. 'Sorry. I did tell you I was nerdy. And boring.'

'No, you're being sensible and advancing your career. It's much better to study little and often than to cram it all in. You remember it better that way.'

'You're moving to your new flat tomorrow, aren't you?' she asked.

'Yes.'

'I could help, if you like,' she offered.

He smiled. 'I'd like that. Shall I pick you up at ten?'

'That'd be great.'

At precisely ten o'clock the next morning, Ed rang the entryphone, and Jane buzzed him up. Even dressed for moving and unpacking boxes, in soft ancient denims and a worn T-shirt, he looked utterly gorgeous.

'What?' he asked, tipping his head to one side.

She raised an eyebrow. 'Just thinking about Mr Bond.'

'Good.' His smile turned sultry. 'Hold on to that thought.'

'So do we need to go and pick up your things from a storage place?'

'I've already done that. The van's full,' he said. 'If I carry the boxes in, would you mind starting to unpack them?'

'Sure—actually, before we go, do you have coffee, milk and a kettle?'

He looked blank. 'It never even occurred to me. I've been living in the hotel for a week, and my kettle's packed in one of the boxes.'

'So I take it you don't have any cleaning stuff, either?'

'I'm using an agency,' he admitted. 'They bring their own cleaning stuff. And they cleaned the flat for me yesterday. All we need to do is unpack.'

'I'll bring my kettle until we find yours,' she said. She grabbed a jar of coffee, took an opened carton of milk from the fridge, and emptied out her kettle. She put the lot in a plastic bag, locked the door behind her, and followed him outside. He opened the passenger

door of the van for her, then drove her to a new apartment building in Pimlico, overlooking the river.

'Want to look round before we start?' he asked.

'Love to.' The flat was gorgeous, really light and airy.
There was a large reception room with French doors,
containing a couple of bookshelves, a small dining table
and four chairs and two pale yellow leather sofas. Next
to it was a decent-sized separate kitchen; there was a
large bedroom overlooking the river, and an immaculate
pure white bathroom. But the best bit for Jane was the
riverside terrace leading off from the reception room.

'Oh, now this is gorgeous. You could have breakfast overlooking the river,' she said, gesturing to the
wrought iron bistro table and chairs.

'That's what made me decide to rent it,' Ed said.

'If you had some tubs of plants out here for a bit
of colour and scent, this balcony would be perfect,'
she said. Not to mention eye-wateringly expensive; she
knew what prices were like in this part of London, and
the river view would add an extra chunk to the rent.

Ed had labelled his boxes sensibly, so it made unpacking much easier. He'd wrapped the crockery and
glassware in newspaper to protect it for the move, so
everything needed washing. 'Shall I do this while you
put everything else where you want it?' she suggested.

By the end of the afternoon, Ed's flat looked a bit
more lived-in. Though it was still very much a masculine bachelor pad; the soft furnishings were skimpy in
the extreme, and the place had the air of being designed
rather than being home.

'You're brilliant,' he said, kissing her. 'Thanks so
much. I'd still be doing this at midnight if you hadn't
helped.'

'That's OK.' But she was warmed by his appreciation.

She wandered over to the mantelpiece. 'Can I be nosey?'

'Sure.'

All the photographs were in proper silver frames, she noticed. And there was a really nice picture of him with a man who looked so much like him that he had to be Ed's older brother, plus three girls who had the same colouring but finer features and she guessed were his half-sisters. There was a very posh garden in the background; given the way they were dressed, she guessed that they'd been at some kind of garden party.

They all looked close-knit, with arms round each other and affectionate glances, and she suppressed a sigh. Ed was clearly close to his family. How could she explain to him that she wasn't particularly close to hers?

And she really, really didn't want to tell him about Jenna. It had been hard enough telling him about Shaun.

'They look nice,' she said.

'They are. They're noisy and they're nosey and they drive me to distraction, but I love them to bits.'

The warmth in his voice told her that he meant it. Jane felt another pang. She loved her family, too, but they didn't make it easy for her. She'd thought for years that maybe she was the problem—the nerdy, quiet, clumsy one who didn't fit in. She had so little in common with them that it was hard for them even to like her, let alone love her.

But then she'd met Sorcha. The way Sorcha's family had taken her to their hearts, making her feel like one of them—plus the easy camaraderie she had with her colleagues on the ward—made her rethink the position. Maybe she wasn't the difficult one, after all. And you could still love someone without actually liking them, couldn't you?

'Penny for them?' Ed asked, obviously noticing her distraction.

No way. Wild horses wouldn't drag these thoughts from her. 'Nothing important,' she said.

To her relief, he changed the subject. 'How about I order us a takeaway? After making you slave all day, the least I can do is feed you.'

She smiled. 'Thanks. That'd be lovely.'

Jane spent Sunday studying. And it hadn't been as bad a week as she'd expected; nobody at the hospital had said a word to her about that awful article. Jenna had been remarkably quiet, too, though Jane supposed that her twin was probably busy on a shoot somewhere. It was when Jenna wasn't busy that trouble tended to happen.

And she ended up seeing Ed every other night for the next couple of weeks. He took her dancing; for the first time ever she found herself actually enjoying it, because he led her through the moves and was there to catch her before she fell. It turned out that he liked the same art-house cinema that she did; Shaun had always been bored if it wasn't an action flick, and he'd never discussed the films with her afterwards. Ed was different; he insisted on going for an ice-cream sundae afterwards and talking about the film.

He whisked her off to Cambridge one Saturday afternoon, punted her all the way down the river to Grantchester Meadows, then lay in the long grass with her, her head pillowed on his chest. And when he kissed her in the middle of the river on the way back and whispered, 'You're beautiful,' she believed him. The more time she spent with him, the more she liked him; she'd never felt so in tune with someone before.

And maybe, just maybe, Ed was the one she could trust with her heart.

CHAPTER EIGHT

ON TUESDAY Jane was having lunch with Ed when his mobile phone rang.

'Excuse me a second,' he said. 'I'm going into the corridor where there's a better reception.'

He came back white-faced.

'What's wrong?' she asked.

He sighed heavily. 'That was Alice. George has had an accident.'

A road accident? And, given how pale Ed looked… 'Oh, no. Is he OK?'

'He'll live. Would you believe, he crashed into a cliff?'

She blinked. 'Into? Not off?'

'Into,' Ed confirmed. 'It wasn't a car accident.' He rolled his eyes. 'God knows what he was doing. Jet skiing or something like that, I suppose. He's going to be an inpatient for a week, at least. He'll be stir crazy by tonight, so I hate to think what he'll be like by the time the plaster comes off. He loathes being cooped up. The girls and I are going to have a rota to visit him, but he's still going to be bored rigid.'

'Is he in London?'

'Yes, over at the Hampstead Free—they're pinning

his leg right now, so there's no point in me dropping everything and going over, because I can't be in Theatre with him.' He bit his lip. 'I'm going straight after work.'

He looked worried sick. Jane reached across the table and took his hand. 'Do you want me to come with you?'

He looked at her. 'It's a bit of an ask.'

'You'd do the same for me, if my brother had had an accident—not that I've got a brother, but you know what I mean.'

'Thanks, I appreciate it.' He grimaced. 'I'd better warn you in advance, George is a bit of a charmer and a terrible flirt. But I guess even he's going to be held back by having a broken leg and two broken wrists. Not to mention concussion.'

She squeezed his hand, guessing what he was worrying about. A bang on the head could turn out to be very, very nasty indeed; and, as a doctor, Ed would have a pretty good idea of the worst-case scenario. 'Don't build things up in your head. It might not be as bad as you think it is.'

'Yeah, that's the worst thing about being a medic. It's years since I did my emergency department rotation, but I remember seeing head injuries and—oh, God, if he ends up with a subdural haematoma or something...'

'You're building bridges to trouble,' she said gently. 'Alice has probably already told you the worst: a broken leg, two broken wrists and concussion. And, as you said yourself, right now there's nothing you can do.'

'No.' But Ed clearly felt too miserable to finish his lunch.

She was relieved mid-afternoon when they were called in to do an emergency Caesarean section, knowing that concentrating on their patient would take Ed's mind off his worries about his brother. She let Ed close the wound after delivery rather than asking to do it herself, knowing that he needed the distraction.

Finally, it was the end of their shift and they caught the Tube over to Hampstead. On the way, Ed responded to a stream of text messages from his sisters, father and stepmother. He paused when they got to the hospital shop. 'This is crazy, but I've got no idea what to take him. The girls have already stocked him up with grapes and chocolates, there's a no-flowers rule in place and George isn't exactly a flower person anyway.'

'Why not go and see him first?' Jane suggested. 'Then you can ask him what he wants you to bring in for him.'

'Good idea.' He grimaced. 'Sorry. I'm not usually this dense or indecisive.'

'Of course not. You're just worried about your brother.'

He hugged her. 'Thank you for being here—I do appreciate it. Even if I am being grumpy and unapproachable.'

She stroked his face. 'You're worried,' she repeated. 'Come on. Let's go up to the ward and see how he's doing. You'll feel a lot better then.'

'You're right.' He released her from the hug, but twined his fingers through hers as they walked through the corridors. 'Thanks, Jane.'

'May I see George Somers, please?' Ed asked the nurse who was sorting out paperwork at the nurses' station.

'George?' The nurse looked up and then smiled at him. 'Oh, from the look of you, you must be his brother Ed. He's been talking about you.'

'How is he?'

'A bit sorry for himself, bless him,' she said. 'I'll take you through to see him.'

'Thank you.' Ed paused. He knew he was about to break protocol, but he really needed to know, because he was close to going crazy with worry. 'Can I be really cheeky and ask, would you mind me having a quick look at his notes, please? I'm not going to interfere with treatment or anything, but you know how it is when you're a medic.' He gave her an apologetic smile. 'You always start thinking the worst and worrying about the complications.'

'And seeing it all written down stops you panicking.' The nurse looked sympathetic. 'As long as George gives his permission for you to see them, yes—as long as you know that even then it'll be a favour, not a right.'

'Thanks. I won't abuse it,' Ed promised.

She took them through to the small room where George was lying on the bed, his eyes closed and his face covered in bruises.

Ed's fingers tightened round Jane's. Oh, God. He'd known on an intellectual level that George would be in a mess, but actually seeing it for himself made everything seem much more real. If George had been one of his patients, Ed would've coped just fine; he would've been brisk and cheerful and supportive. But seeing his older brother lying there after surgery, with all the associated tubes and dressings, made him feel as if he couldn't breathe. His lungs felt frozen with fear. What if there were post-op complications? What if there was a subdural haematoma they hadn't picked up? *What if George died?*

'Since he's asleep, is it OK to wait here until he wakes up?' he asked the nurse.

'Of course.' She patted his arm. 'Try not to worry. He's doing fine. If you need anything, come and find me.'

Ed sat down on the chair next to George's bed and pulled Jane onto his lap. He really needed her warmth, right now. Thank God she had such a huge heart and wouldn't judge him.

'Do you want me to go and get you a cup of hot sweet tea from the café?' Jane asked.

'No, I'm fine,' he lied. More like, he didn't want her to move. He needed her close.

'You're not fine, Ed,' she said softly.

He sighed. 'I'm better with you here.' He leaned his head against her shoulder. 'Thanks for coming with me. And I'm sorry I'm such a mess right now.'

She stroked his hair. 'Hey. Anyone would be, in your shoes. It's always worse when it's one of your family lying in that hospital bed.'

'I hate to think of how much pain he's been in.' And the fact that George could've been killed... His brother's death would have left a huge, unfillable hole in his life. Not just his, either: his father, stepmother and sisters all loved George as much as Ed did, even when he was driving them crazy with one of his escapades.

He sighed. 'Why does my brother always have to take such stupid risks?'

'Wasn't stupid. Had protective gear on,' a slurred voice informed them.

Guilt rushed through Ed. George needed his rest, and his voice had been too loud. 'Sorry. I didn't mean to wake you.'

'Wasn't asleep. Just resting my eyes. Knew you'd be here.' George gave him a slightly sheepish smile. 'Alice already nagged me, so don't bother.'

'There's no point in nagging you. You won't listen anyway,' Ed said.

'Who's this?' George looked questioningly at Jane.

'Jane. Jane, this is my brother George.'

'She's sitting on your lap. Hmm. She the girl you wouldn't tell me about?'

Ed sighed. 'Yes.' He could see on Jane's face that she was wondering why he'd kept her quiet. Once she'd met his family, she'd understand: they were incredibly full on, and he wanted to be sure where this was going before he let her meet them. He'd explain later. But not in front of his brother.

''Lo, Jane,' George said.

'Hello, George. Nice to meet you, even though it's not in the best of circumstances,' she said politely.

'And you.' George smiled at her, and looked at Ed. 'Jane. Ex'lent. I can call you "Tarzan" now, Ed.'

Jane laughed. 'You can try, but he'll frown at you.'

George grinned. 'She knows you well, then.'

'Yeah, yeah.' Though it heartened Ed that George was feeling well enough to tease him. 'How are you feeling?'

'Bit woozy,' George admitted. 'Gave me enough painkillers to fell a horse.'

'Probably because you needed them, and you've had a general anaesthetic as well so you're going to feel woozy for a day or so.' Ed meant to be nice. He really did. But the fear turned to anger, and the question just burst out. 'What the hell did you do, dive-bomb the cliff or something?'

'No, got caught out by a gust of wind.'

'*Wind*? What the hell were you doing?'

'Paragliding.'

That was a new one on him. Though he knew that George had been looking for another outlet for his energy, since their father had banned him, absolutely, from racing cars.

'How did it happen?'

George grimaced. 'My fault. Not concentrating properly.'

Thinking of a girl, no doubt. 'You could've killed yourself, George.'

''M still here,' George said mildly.

'With what looks like a broken femur, two broken wrists and some broken fingers.' Ed sighed. 'Can I read your notes?'

'Yeah. Can you translate 'em for me?'

'Tomorrow, I will, when you're more with it,' Ed promised. 'Right now, you won't take much in—you're still too woozy even to string a sentence together properly.' And he really hoped it was the combination of pain and the after-effects of the anaesthetic making George slur his words, rather than being a warning signal of something more sinister.

He fished the notes out of the basket at the head of George's bed. 'Yup. Two broken wrists, one broken femur—and…' George had hit the cliff face on, and pretty hard. He'd automatically put his hands up to save his face, which was why both wrists and some fingers were broken; but he'd also damaged his leg. And he'd sustained a blow to his testes, according to the notes. Hard enough to put a question over his future fertility.

Which meant that, even though George was the heir

to the barony, he might not be able to have children. And that in turn meant that at some point Ed could have to give up the job he loved and do his duty for the family. Not that that was uppermost in Ed's mind. All he could see was his brother crashing into the cliff. Lying on an ambulance trolley. On the table in Theatre. How nearly they'd lost him. 'You *idiot*. You could've killed yourself.'

George shrugged. ''M OK. Could be worse. Didn't break my head, did I?'

'No, just your leg and your wrists. I know you're a thrill-seeker, and I get that you love the adrenalin rush. But, for pity's sake, can't you do things the *safe* way?' Ed asked plaintively.

'Nagging.' George wrinkled his nose. 'Pointless.'

There were times when Ed really, really wanted to shake his older brother. But maybe not while he still had concussion. 'Give me strength.'

'Powered paragliding's not dangerous.'

'Says the man who's got a metal rod holding his leg together and both wrists in plaster.'

'What's powered paragliding?' Jane asked.

'Awesome,' George said, and smiled. ''S a motor like a backpack for take off, then you glide on the current. Show you pictures later.'

'I take it you need training to do that?' Ed asked.

'Yes. 'M certified.'

Jane smiled. 'Judging by the look on Ed's face, I think you might mean *certifiable*.'

George laughed. 'Prob'ly.' Then he sobered. 'Gonna be stuck here f'r a whole week.'

Given that George barely sat still for five minutes, this was going to crucify him, Ed thought. 'Think yourself lucky you're not in traction—you'd be stuck there for a lot longer than that,' he said.

'What'm I gonna do for a whole *week*?' George asked plaintively.

'The girls and I will visit. And Dad and Frances.'

'You're working. Charlie and Bea've got exams. Alice'll nag me. Frances worries.' George sighed. 'Dad's fuming.'

Ed just bet he was. 'So am I,' he pointed out.

'Didn't do it on purpose.' George grimaced. 'Uh. A whole *week*.'

'There's the television,' Jane suggested.

'Can't switch channels.' He indicated his casts. 'Six weeks till the plaster comes off.' He grimaced. 'Can't wait to go home.'

Home? He seriously thought he was going to get up from his hospital bed and go *home*? Oh, for pity's sake. 'Be sensible about this, George. You're going to be here for at least a week. And you'll need physio on your leg and your shoulders when you leave here,' Ed warned. 'How exactly are you going to manage at home, anyway?'

George shrugged. 'Voice-controlled laptop. Don't need to type.'

'I didn't mean work.' Ed already knew his brother couldn't sit still at a desk; he paced his office and did everything with voice control. 'I meant with simple little things like washing, eating…going to the loo.'

'*Ed!*' George rolled his eyes. ''S a lady present.'

'I'm a doctor,' Jane said with a smile. 'I don't get embarrassed about bodily functions. And Ed does have a point. It's going to be hard for you to manage personal care with both wrists in plaster—and I'm not quite sure how you're going to manage a crutch, actually.'

'There's one very obvious solution,' Ed said. 'Come and stay with me until you're properly mobile again.'

'Not 'nuff room.'

'Yes, there is. I'll sleep on the sofa bed and you can have my bed—it'll be more comfy for you with your leg.'

'Thanks, bro.' George shook his head. 'But best not. We'd drive each other mad. You nag too much. I play too hard.' His face softened. 'Love you, Ed.'

Yeah. He knew. Because George had always been there for him. *Always.* George had read story after story to Ed in the nights when he couldn't get to sleep after their mum had left; and, twenty years later, his older brother was the one Ed had turned to after the night shift from hell, a miserable night that had caused him to question whether he was really cut out to be a doctor.

'I love you, too,' he said, his voice thick with emotion. 'But you give me grey hairs. I thought the oldest child was supposed to be the sensible one?'

George smiled. ''M sensible. Sometimes.'

Yeah. Ed knew. It was just the rest of the time.

'I just like doing—'

'—dangerous things,' Ed finished wryly. 'I know.' Though sometimes he wondered. Was George such a thrill-seeker because he was stuck as the heir to the barony and hated it? It was something they'd never, ever discussed. He'd always assumed that George was fine with it. Maybe he was wrong. He'd been so wrapped up in his career that he hadn't even considered that George might've had a vocation, too. They needed to talk about this. Not right now, while George was still feeling rough from the crash and the anaesthetic, but soon. And maybe they could work something out between them.

'The girls said they'd already fixed you up with chocolates and grapes. What can I bring you?'

'Dunno. Can't do a lot with these.' George nodded at his casts, then grimaced. 'Feel sick.'

Jane slid off Ed's lap, grabbed a bowl and was just in time.

'Sorry. Not good to be sick over Ed's new girl,' George said sheepishly when he'd finished.

'Anaesthetic has that effect on people sometimes,' she said. 'Don't worry about it. I'm used to this sort of thing. Really.'

'Thank you. Still sorry, though.' George looked contrite.

She smiled. 'No worries.'

'Look, I'm going to see one of the nurses and ask if they can give you something for the sickness,' Ed said. 'Jane, would you mind staying with George until I get back?'

'Sure.'

'Sorry to be a nuisance,' George said when Ed had gone.

'You're not a nuisance. I think Ed's a lot happier now he's seen you for himself.' Jane gave him a rueful smile. 'It's just as well we had a busy afternoon, because he was going through all the possible complications in his head and worrying himself si—' Given that George was feeling queasy, that wouldn't be the best phrase, Jane decided, and changed it to 'Silly'.

George clearly guessed, because he smiled. 'Sharp.

You'll be good for Ed.' He paused. 'Best brother I could ever have.'

'If it makes you feel any better, he feels the same about you,' Jane said.

'Yeah.' George closed his eyes. 'Sorry. Tired.'

'Hey, that's fine. Just rest. I'm not going anywhere—if you need anything, you just tell me, OK?'

''K,' George said.

Ed came back with one of the doctors, who gave George an anti-emetic and wrote it on the chart.

'Your brother really needs to get some rest now,' the doctor said.

'Of course.' Ed put an affectionate hand on his brother's shoulder. 'Reckon you can stay out of trouble until I see you tomorrow, George?'

'Can't go abseiling, can I?' George said lightly.

'I wouldn't put it past you,' Ed said. 'I'll be back tomorrow night after work. Do you want me to bring anything?'

'Chess set, maybe?' George asked. 'Move the pieces for me.'

'Sure. Get some rest, and I'll see you tomorrow.'

'You'll come back too, Jane?' George asked.

'Maybe not tomorrow—Ed might want some time with you on his own—but yes, I'll come back. And I'll play chess with you, if you like,' Jane said with a smile. 'Take care.'

Ed was silent all the way to the Tube station, and barely said a word until they got to her stop.

'I'll see you home,' he said.

Jane was perfectly capable of seeing herself home, but Ed was clearly upset and she was pretty sure he needed some company. 'Thanks.' She didn't push him into a conversation, but she noticed that he held her hand tightly all the way to her front door.

'Come up,' she said softly.

'I'm not going to be good company,' he warned.

'It doesn't matter.' She stroked his face. 'I hate to think of you going home and brooding. You saw something bad in his notes, didn't you?'

'It's not fair of me to discuss it.' He sighed. 'There's a potential problem, yes. Hopefully it'll sort itself out.'

'OK. I'm not going to push you to tell me. But if you do decide to talk, you know it won't go any further than me, right?'

'I do.' He kissed her lightly. 'And thank you.'

She put the kettle on and made herself a coffee and Ed a mug of tea, adding plenty of sugar.

He took one mouthful and almost choked. 'Jane, this is disgusting!'

'Hot sweet tea is good for shock.'

'Yeah.' He sighed. 'That's what George made me drink, when I decided I couldn't be a doctor any more.'

She blinked. 'You were going to give up medicine?'

He nodded. 'I was on an emergency department rotation. There was a major pile-up, and—well, you know what a majax is like. I wasn't used to losing patients. Kids, some of them. And I just couldn't handle it.' He blew out a breath. 'When I got home the next morning, I knew George had been out partying all night and had probably only just crawled into bed, but he was the only one I could talk to about it. So I called him.'

'And he made you a mug of tea like this?'

'Yeah. He came straight over and cooked me a fry-up.' He smiled wryly. 'George is a terrible cook. The bacon was burned and the eggs were leathery. I had to cover everything in ketchup to force it down. But it was the best breakfast I've ever had. He made me talk until it was all out. And then he told me it was just one shift in a department that wasn't right for me, and if I gave up medicine I'd regret it and I'd make everyone around me miserable. He said I'd be a great doctor, as long as I found the right department for me.'

There was a huge lump in Jane's throat. What must it be like to have a sibling who supported you like that, instead of taking and taking and taking all the time? 'He was right,' she said softly.

'Yeah.'

'And he's in good hands. The Hampstead Free has a really good reputation.'

'I know.' Ed sighed. 'It's just…'

'He's your brother. And you worry about him.' She walked over to stand behind him and slid her arms round his neck. 'I don't have the right stuff in the fridge to cook you a fry-up, but I have the makings of other comfort food. Like a toasted cheese sandwich.'

'Thanks, but I'm not sure I could eat anything.'

'Trust me, some carbs will help you feel better.'

He lifted her hand to his mouth and kissed her palm. 'You're wonderful. I hope you know that.'

'Sure I do,' she said. She kept her voice light, but the fact that he felt like that about her made her feel warm from the inside out.

'I'm not sure I could've got through seeing George like that without you there.'

She gave a dismissive shrug. 'Of course you would.'

'But you made it better. Only you,' he said softly.

'Hey.' She kissed him lightly, and busied herself making toasted sandwiches before she did something really stupid—like telling him she thought he was pretty wonderful, too.

'George liked you,' Ed said. 'Though he's going to torment me about the Tarzan thing. As soon as his hands have stopped hurting, he's going to start beating his chest and doing the yell.'

'And are you telling me you wouldn't do the same to him, if he was seeing a girl called Jane?'

Ed looked faintly sheepish, and she laughed. 'He's very like you, you know.'

'Apart from being in plaster and covered in bruises, you mean?'

'No. I mean, he's like you but without the brakes. He must drive his girlfriends crazy with worry.'

'Not to mention his parents and his siblings,' Ed said dryly. 'He did go through a spell of racing cars, but Dad had a word with him.'

'And that stopped him?'

'Surprisingly, yes.' Ed frowned. 'He wouldn't tell me what Dad said to him, but it must've been pretty tough.'

'So he's always done dangerous sports and what have you?'

Ed nodded. 'You know you were saying I remind you of James Bond? That's actually how George is. He thinks nothing of skiing down a double black diamond run.'

'As I know nothing about skiing, I take that means it's a really hard one?' Jane asked.

'Yes. But he's been crazier these last six months,' Ed said thoughtfully. 'He's taken a lot more risks.'

'Did something happen six months ago?'

Ed thought about it. 'Yes. I should've made him talk to me. But I guess I was still getting over the divorce and I wasn't paying enough attention.' He sighed. 'Now he's stuck in a hospital bed, he's not going to have any choice—he'll have to talk to me. And maybe I can help him sort out whatever's going on in his head.'

Ed relaxed more after they'd eaten, though he seemed more comfortable in the kitchen than anywhere else, so Jane didn't suggest moving. Eventually, he squeezed her hand. 'You were going to study tonight. I'd better go. I've held you up long enough.'

'It's OK. I can catch up some other time—it's not as if I've skipped studying for weeks on end,' she said lightly. He looked so lost. She couldn't possibly make him go back to his flat where he'd be on his own, brooding and worrying all night. 'I think tonight you could do with not being on your own. So if you want to stay…' She took a deep breath. 'There are no strings. Just—if you want to stay, you're welcome.'

'I'd like that. I'll have to leave at the crack of dawn so I can get some clean clothes before work, but if you're sure?'

She smiled. 'I'm sure.'

CHAPTER NINE

ED LAY awake; he was brooding, but not as much as he would've done had he been alone in his flat. Jane was sprawled all over him and it just felt better, being here with her. She had a huge heart and, even though he guessed that asking him to stay had put her in a vulnerable position, she'd seen exactly what he needed and hadn't hesitated to offer.

He held her closer and, in response, her arms tightened round him.

Their lovemaking that night had been so sweet, so tender, and he felt that Jane really understood him—far more than anyone he'd dated before. OK, so they'd only known each other for a month, but it was long enough for him to have worked out that there was something special about her. Not just the calm, confident way she was with people at work, treating everyone with respect and kindness. Not just the physical stuff that made his heart beat faster. He liked her instinctively. He'd never felt so in tune with someone like this before. And he really hadn't expected to fall for someone so fast.

He couldn't tell her. Not yet. She'd come out of her shell a lot with him, but even so he didn't want to take this too fast for her and risk her backing off again. But he was starting to hope that this was more than just a rebound fling—for both of them.

The next morning, Ed woke early; for a moment, he was disorientated, but then he remembered where he was. In Jane's flat. In Jane's arms.

Last night, he'd leaned on her. This morning, it was time to even up the balance. He gently disentangled himself from her arms, climbed out of bed and made coffee for them both.

'Thank you for last night. For being there,' he said softly, kissing her as he climbed back into bed.

'It's no problem. You would've done the same for me,' she said.

'Of course I would. You're on the list of people who could call me at three in the morning and I wouldn't yell at you for waking me up—I'd come straight to your side. And it's not that big a list,' he said. His parents, his siblings and his very closest friends. And Jane.

She smiled. 'Snap.'

Funny how something so simple as drinking coffee in bed with her made his world seem brighter. He finished his coffee. 'I'd better go back to my flat and get some clean clothes, but I'll see you at work, OK?'

'OK. And if you're not busy at lunchtime,' Jane said, 'perhaps you might like to have lunch with Sorcha and me.'

He realised immediately what she was saying. Yesterday, he'd asked her to meet the closest person to him; and now she was returning the compliment. Letting him that little bit closer. 'I'd like that,' he said simply. 'Very much.'

* * *

The ward was incredibly busy, that morning; Jane called Ed in to help her with a difficult delivery.

'Just after his head emerged, his neck retracted and his cheeks puffed out.'

It was a classic symptom of shoulder dystocia, where the baby's shoulder was caught on the mother's pubic bone so they couldn't deliver the baby.

'Is the baby big for his dates?' Ed asked.

'And ten days overdue. But there weren't any indications that it was going to be a problem.'

Shoulder dystocia was always a tricky situation, with the risk of the baby dying during delivery from not getting enough oxygen. Even if the baby was delivered alive, there was still a risk of a fractured collarbone or damage to the nerves in the baby's neck.

Quickly, Jane introduced Ed to the mum and her partner and explained the situation to them.

'If we can change your position,' Ed said, 'it'll move your pubic bone and that should give us enough leeway to deliver the baby safely. Try not to push just yet, OK?'

'OK.'

Gently, he and Jane guided the mum onto her back, with her bottom to the edge of the bed and her thighs guided back towards her abdomen.

'Jane, do you know the Rubin manoeuvre?' he asked.

'I know the theory.'

'Great.' Though it meant that she'd yet to put it into practice. Well, that was what he was here for. He directed her where to put suprapubic pressure over the baby's anterior shoulder so it moved towards his chest and would slip free. 'I'll tell you when to press,' he said. 'Rosie, can you get the neonatologist down?' This baby would definitely need careful checking over in case of nerve damage or fractures.

He really, really hoped the manoeuvre would work; otherwise, given that the mum already had an epidural and wasn't mobile, it would mean giving her an episiotomy and moving to more advanced intervention.

At the next contraction, he said, 'Now,' and gradually applied traction to the baby's head.

To his relief, it worked, and the baby finally slipped out.

'Well done,' Ed said to the mum.

The neonataologist checked the baby over, then came over with a broad smile and gave the baby to the mum for a cuddle. 'I'm pleased to say that he's a very healthy little boy—he had a bit of a tough time coming into the world, but he's absolutely fine.'

Ed and Jane exchanged a loaded glance. The outcome could have been so very different. Luck had definitely been on their side.

The mum was in tears of relief. 'Oh, my baby.' She looked at Ed. 'Thank you both so much.'

'It's what we're here for. Congratulations,' Ed said with a smile.

'He's gorgeous,' Jane added. She stroked the baby's cheek, then wiped the tears away from her own. 'Sorry. Newborns always make me cry. They're so perfect.'

'I think I need some sugar after that,' Ed said.

'Me, too.' Jane blew out a breath. 'That was a scary one. Thanks for talking me through it.'

'I barely needed to do that—you already knew the theory.'

'Which isn't *quite* the same as doing it in practice, knowing what could happen if you get it wrong.'

'But you got it right. And you're a quick learner—you won't need a word from me next time.'

'Hopefully not.' Jane glanced at her watch. 'Perfect timing. Lunch.'

In the canteen, a gorgeous redhead was already waiting for them—a woman Ed recognised from the photograph in Jane's flat.

'Caught up in the delivery room?' she asked.

'Yup. And it was a scary one.' Jane introduced them swiftly. 'Sorcha, this is Ed, our new consultant; Ed, this is Sorcha, my best friend—she's a rheumatologist.'

'I hope you don't mind me gate-crashing your lunch,' Ed said, shaking Sorcha's hand.

'Not at all. It's nice to meet you,' Sorcha said.

During lunch, Ed could see her watching him and trying to work out what his relationship with Jane was—whether it was strictly work, or if there was more to it than that. So had Jane been keeping him as quiet as he'd been keeping her? he wondered. And for the same reason?

He could see the second that Sorcha worked it out. Because she smiled very sweetly at her best friend. 'I am *so* desperate for a cappuccino. And a tiny, tiny bar of chocolate.'

'And it's my turn to fetch the coffee,' Jane said, getting up. 'OK. See you in a second.'

'So how long have you been seeing Jane?' Sorcha asked when Jane was out of earshot.

'Seeing her?' Ed asked.

She sighed. 'Don't play games. It's obvious in the way you look at each other—apart from the fact that she already knows exactly how you take your coffee and whether you're a chocolate fiend or not. I noticed she didn't even need to ask you what you wanted.'

'Right. Not long.'

Sorcha's eyes narrowed. 'I see. And this is a casual thing, is it?'

Well, if she was going to be that open with him, he'd give her the same courtesy. 'No, I don't think it is. And I'm glad she has someone to look out for her. My brother was still woozy from anaesthetic when he met her last night, or he would've been asking exactly the same questions. And, believe you me, my sisters are going to be every bit as careful as you when they meet her.'

'You're close to your family?'

'Yes. My family's great.'

Sorcha looked approving. 'Jane's like a sister to me.'

'So she told me.'

'She's got the biggest heart in the world,' Sorcha said, her gaze challenging.

'Absolutely.' He knew that first hand.

'And she's vulnerable.'

He knew that, too. 'Thanks to Shaun.'

'*Him*.' She rolled her eyes. 'I tell you, if he had a heart, I'd be first in the queue to remove it with a rusty spoon.'

Ed got the message. Very firmly. Hurt Jane, and Sorcha would be on the warpath.

'So she actually told you about him?'

'Yes.' He could see in Sorcha's face that she hadn't expected that. Clearly Jane didn't usually talk about what had happened. 'Look, I know Jane's special. I'll be careful with her, Sorcha. You don't have to worry.'

'Good.' Sorcha bit her lip. 'I can't believe she actually told you about Shaun and J—'

'OK, Sorcha, you can stop doing the guard dog act now,' Jane cut in, carrying a tray with three mugs of coffee. 'Sorry, Ed.'

'Nothing to apologise for. I think Sorcha and I understand each other. Which is a good thing. We know we're on the same side.' He held Jane's gaze. 'Yours.'

'Thank you. I think. But no more discussing me, OK?'

'Unless we need to,' Sorcha said.

Ed laughed. 'I'm so tempted to introduce you to my brother, Sorcha. I think you might be the only woman in the world who'd have the ability to keep him under control.'

'Too late. She's already spoken for,' Jane said.

'Shame. You don't happen to have a clone?' he asked Sorcha hopefully.

Sorcha laughed. 'No. But I think you and I are going to be friends.'

Jane didn't go with Ed to visit George that evening, knowing that he needed some time alone with his brother so he could start persuading George to open up about whatever was bothering him. But she made it clear that Ed was welcome to drop in on his way home if he needed a hug and someone to talk to. As always, a hug turned to something more, and Ed ended up staying the night again. And she somehow ended up staying at his flat after they'd visited George on Friday night.

This was all going crazily fast; and yet she trusted Ed instinctively. She knew he wouldn't hurt her. He wasn't like Shaun. He had integrity, he thought of others and he learned from his mistakes.

On Monday, she had a day off, and dropped in to see George in the morning.

'I thought you could do with a fresh challenger at chess,' she said.

'Janey! How lovely to see you.' He brightened when he saw what she was carrying. 'Are they for me?'

'Yup. Fresh English strawberries. And I've already washed and hulled them.'

'Oh, wow. Has anyone told you lately that you're wonderful?' Then he looked at his hands. 'Um, think they might be a bit cross with me if I get the casts covered in strawberry juice, and I'm not very good with cutlery right now.'

'No. Breaking your wrists *and* your fingers is pretty harsh.' She produced a spoon. 'Bearing in mind that I'm a doctor, I think it might be OK for me to feed them to you. As I would do for any of my patients if they were in this state.'

'I don't expect any of your patients would end up with all these breaks,' he said.

'Not usually, though I did once deliver a baby where the mum had a broken ankle,' she said with a smile, and set up the chess board on the table that slotted over his bed. 'And I'd better check before I give you these— you're not allergic to strawberries, are you?'

'No. And I *love* strawberries. Thank you.'

She sat on the edge of the bed, so it would be easier for her to move the chess pieces according to his directions, and fed him the strawberries.

'I can see why Ed's so taken with you,' he said when she'd finished. 'He tends to be a bit cagey about letting us meet his girlfriends. Probably because we're all so full on and we've been nagging him about…' His voice tailed off. 'I'll shut up. I was about to be really tactless.'

'Nagging him about it being time he got a life after his divorce?' Jane asked.

George raised his eyebrows. 'He told you about Camilla?'

'Yes.'

He blew out a breath. 'I told him he was making a huge mistake, but she'd told him she was pregnant, and Ed *always* does the right thing—so he married her.'

'Pregnant?' Ed hadn't told her that bit.

It must have shown in her expression, because George grimaced. 'So he didn't tell you everything. Sorry. I didn't mean to be tactless.'

'That's OK. So are you telling me that Ed has a child?' But there hadn't been any photographs of a baby in his flat. He hadn't mentioned a child. And she just couldn't see Ed turning his back on his child. He wasn't that kind of man.

'No. She lost the baby just after they got married.' George left a very significant pause. 'Or so she said.'

Ah. Now Jane understood. And she was relieved that she hadn't been wrong about Ed. 'And you think she was lying to him in the first place, to get him to marry her?'

George nodded. 'Even though she was from the same kind of background as us, they really weren't suited. She wanted different things and she definitely didn't want to be a doctor's wife. But Ed thinks it was all his fault for not giving her the life of luxury she wanted, and he's been wearing a hair shirt ever since.' He looked at her.

'You've been good for him. You're definitely helping him lighten up.'

Jane couldn't help laughing. 'That's so ironic.'

'How come?'

'They used to called me "Plain Jane, Super-Brain" at school.' Jenna had managed to get the whole school to chant that one. Especially the popular crowd she hung around with; Jane's refusal to wear a ton of make-up or give up her studies to fit in with them had gone down very, very badly.

'So you're a nerd? Nerdy's good,' George said with a smile. 'My sisters are all nerds. Have you met the girls yet?'

'No.'

'You'll like them. They boss Ed around, and he...' George grinned. 'Well, he just lets them. He's putty in their hands.'

She could just imagine it. And she'd just bet that the girls adored both their brothers. 'Do they boss you about?'

'They try—but, until one of them can beat me down a double black diamond ski run, they're not going to get very far.'

She laughed. 'Right now, even I could beat you down a nursery ski slope. You can't ski when you've got a pin in your leg.'

'Tell me about it.' He rolled his eyes, looking disgusted. 'The doctor said I can't ski until the end of the year, at least. Ed says they'll take the pin out when I'm healed, because I'm under forty.'

'Ed's been, how shall I put this?' She gave him a wicked smile. 'Well, he's been boning up on ortho-paedics.'

George laughed. 'Oh, I *love* that you do bad puns. So will Charlotte. Actually, the girls will all love you.'

To be part of a big, noisy, warm, close family… Jane would give a lot for that. But she knew she was already presuming far too much. She and Ed had known each other for only a month. Yes, they were getting on well. Really well. But, given her track record in relationships, she'd be foolish to let herself hope for too much.

She pushed the thought away. 'Have you met your physio yet?'

George grimaced. 'Yes. He made me get up and walk about the day after the op.'

'Absolutely. You need to keep you moving so your muscles don't seize up—it's going to drive you mad, but you really need to do what he says, to save yourself a lot of pain and hard work in the future.'

'I can follow directions, you know.'

'Can you?' she asked.

He gave her a rueful smile. 'OK, so I like to run my own life.'

'At a hundred miles an hour.'

He laughed. 'That Queen song was made for me.' He sang a couple of bars from the chorus of 'Don't Stop Me Now'.

'I think you might be right.' She smiled back at him.

'I'm glad Ed's met you. You're definitely more his type than the debutantes who used to throw themselves at him.'

'Debutantes?' What debutantes?

George frowned. 'You mean he hasn't told you?'

'Told me what?'

'Forget I said anything,' he said hastily.

'No. Especially as you're in check. Told me what?'

He ignored the chessboard. 'What do you call him at work?'

'Ed.'

'No, I mean, do you call him Dr Somers?'

'No, he's a qualified surgeon. He's a Mr.'

'Uh-huh.' George paused. 'Did he tell you what I do for a living?'

'He said you're in the family business.' And that his family was well-to-do, though Jane hadn't paid any real attention to that. It was Ed she found attractive, not his bank account.

'I am. But I'm guessing he didn't tell you what the business was.'

She frowned. 'No.'

'I'm learning to run the estate. Which comes with a country pile whose roof just *eats* money.' He paused. 'And, as the eldest son, that makes me heir to the barony as well as being the future custodian of said money-eating roof.'

Barony? Jane felt the colour drain from her face. Their father was a baron. Which meant that Ed, George and their sisters would all be targets for the paparazzi. The kind of people *Celebrity Life* was desperate to run stories about—the magazine that had judged her so very harshly, just recently.

George's eyes widened with dismay. 'Oh, God, I've really messed things up now, haven't I?'

'No.' She dragged in a breath. 'I suppose you get snapped a lot by the paparazzi.'

'Usually doing something dashing, with my arm around a leggy blonde,' George said ruefully. 'I'm afraid I'm a bit of a stereotype. Well, I hope there's more to me than that, but that's how the press sees me. The playboy with a taste for blondes.'

Jane thought of Jenna, and felt sick.

As if he guessed part of what was worrying her, he said softly, 'Jane, they tend to leave the rest of the tribe alone. They're scared Alice will skewer them in court. Bea's learned to turn it round so they end up being wowed by her architecture instead of her private life and give her the right sort of column centimetres. And Charlotte…well, she just speaks Latin to them and they don't understand a thing she says, so they can't get a story out of her. And Ed, they can't work out at all. The only stories they can dig up about him tend to be him as the hero doctor, and he downplays it, so they can't get a quote. Honestly, it's just me they go for, normally.'

'So am I going to get snapped on my way out of here, because I'm visiting you?'

'I very much doubt it,' he said. 'I can hardly do anything scandalous with both wrists in plaster and a pinned leg.'

'Oh, I think you could.'

He smiled. 'Teasing me back—I like that. You'll fit in to the family just fine.'

'Ed and I are just good friends.'

'Are you, hell. I haven't seen him like this about anyone, and that includes Camilla. He moons about you.'

She rolled her eyes. 'No, he doesn't.'

'Yes, he does, when you're not with him. And that's good.' George looked solemn, for once. 'I worry about him being too serious, and he's way too hard on himself.'

'He worries about you going too far.'

'I might have learned my lesson. Almost a week of

being stuck in here has given me an awful lot of time to do nothing but think.'

'So you're going to settle down? Every cloud has a silver lining, hmm?'

'Something like that. He's serious about you, Jane. Don't hurt him. He's a good man—the very best.'

'I know.'

'You're in love with him, aren't you?'

No way was she admitting to her feelings. 'Can we change the subject? And, by the way, you're in check again.'

'Why didn't you warn me how good you are at chess?' George grumbled. But to her relief he changed the subject, and the conversation stayed light for the rest of her visit.

That evening, Ed said, 'You've made a real hit.'

'How do you mean?'

'George. It was your day off, and I gather you spent half of it playing chess with him. And you took him strawberries. Hand-fed them to him, I hear.'

'Well, he can hardly feed himself, given that his fingers are splinted and his wrists are in plaster as well. Wielding a spoon for him isn't a big deal.' She paused. 'Do you mind?'

'No.' Though he didn't meet her eye. 'George talks a lot,' he muttered.

So that was what was bothering him. He was worried that George had told her things he'd left out. Which was pretty much the case, she had to admit. She brought Ed's hand up to her mouth and kissed his palm, then curled his fingers round the kiss. 'He told me a lot about you. Probably things you'd rather I didn't know, and I'm not breaking his confidence. But I can tell you that he really loves you.' And she'd guess it would be the same with his sisters and his parents. How she envied him that. Knowing that he was loved for being himself.

She paused. 'So when were you going to tell me what the family business was?'

Ed grimaced. 'Sorry. I know I should've said something to you myself. But…how do you tell someone that you're the son of a baron, without sounding as if you're a huge show-off?'

'The same way you do when your mother used to be a supermodel thirty years ago.' She shrugged. 'So do I need to start watching out for paparazzi?' That was the one thing that had really worried her. George had said it wouldn't be a problem, but she couldn't imagine George being upset by the press, the way she was. Ed knew her better—not well enough to know about the reasons why, but he'd guess that her childhood had been partly in the spotlight because of her mother. And not always in a good way.

'No, you don't need to worry about them,' Ed confirmed. 'Something you should know,' she said carefully. 'I'm really not good with paparazzi.'

'They must've been so intrusive when you were young, with your mum being a model.'

'Something like that.' She knew she ought to tell him about Jenna, about the article and the full story about what had happened with Shaun—but she just couldn't bear to see the pity in his eyes.

'I'm only the second son. They're not interested in me,' Ed said, kissing her. 'I'm boring Mr Edward Somers, consultant obstetrician, who doesn't even have a private practice delivering babies to the stars and minor royalty. So they leave me alone. George is far more interesting.' He sighed. 'Sometimes I think that George only does what he does to draw their fire away from us. But I could put up with a bit of annoyance from the paparazzi if it meant he'd stay in one piece.'

The following evening saw Ed sitting at George's bedside. 'I gather you ratted me out to Jane.'

'Ah. Sorry about that.' George looked faintly guilty. 'When she said you'd told her about Camilla, I thought you'd told her the lot. Including about the baby.'

Ed blew out a breath. 'Oh, *great*. She didn't mention that.'

'Because she's tactful and I talk too much.'

'Actually, no, you don't talk enough,' Ed said, seizing the opening.

'Why do I get the distinct impression that I'm not going to like this conversation?' George asked.

'Because I want you to tell me what's wrong.'

'Nothing's wrong. I'm just grumpy about having to be more sedate than I usually am.'

'No, I mean before that.' Ed paused. 'I've been thinking. Are you feeling trapped?'

'In this hospital bed, and knowing I can't drive for weeks?' George rolled his eyes. '*Totally*.'

'I mean trapped by all the expectations on you. You've grown up knowing everyone expects you to take over from Dad. But if there's something else you'd rather do—maybe there's something we can work out.'

George shook his head. 'Ed, you don't have to worry about that. It's not the barony stuff. I'm just an adrenalin junkie, that's all. I'm fine with taking over from

Dad. Actually, I'm beginning to see what he likes about managing the estate.'

'Really?'

'Really,' George confirmed.

'And you'd tell me if something was wrong? Even if I couldn't help you fix it, I'm always here to listen. You know that, don't you?'

'Of course I do. Just as I'm here for you, Tarzan.' George raised an eyebrow. 'You're serious about Jane, aren't you?'

'Don't try to change the subject.'

'I like her,' George said. 'She gets what makes you tick. She wouldn't make you miserable, like Camilla did.'

'That's not fair, George. I made Camilla just as miserable as she made me.'

'But you're taking the blame for it. And that's not fair either. She trapped you into marriage. She lied her face off, knowing you'd do the right thing by her.'

Ed waved a dismissive hand, not wanting to talk about it. Or about how much he'd loved the idea of being a father. Or how something in him had broken when Camilla had made it very clear that she didn't want to try making another baby, and he realised he'd married completely the wrong woman for him. 'I still think something's up. Something you're not telling me.'

George just laughed. 'You'll turn into a conspiracy theorist next! I'm fine. Let's set up the chess board.'

He wasn't fine, Ed thought. But clearly his brother wasn't ready to open up yet. Ed had a strong suspicion that it was something to do with their mother and the meeting George had had with her solicitor, but he

was just going to have to wait until George was ready
to talk. And when he was ready, Ed would make sure
he was there.

CHAPTER TEN

'I KNOW it's a big ask, and it's not really a "come and meet the folks" thing,' Ed said on the Friday night. 'George is bored out of his mind, you're the only person who's managed to beat him at chess in five years, and he's desperate for a rematch.'

'And it's going to be easier for us to go and visit him than for you to bundle him into your car and bring him here, especially as he's probably not going to be too comfortable in a car,' Jane finished.

Ed looked relieved that she understood his worries. 'Yes.'

'So is your whole family going to be there?' she asked.

'Um, yes. George is staying with our parents until he's out of plaster. But I'll tell them to back off and keep their questions to themselves. And there won't be any paparazzi. Though I can guarantee that lunch will be good—Frances is a fantastic cook.' He looked beseechingly at her. 'So will you come with me on Sunday?'

To meet the rest of Ed's family. But she'd already met George and liked him; plus the heat would be off her, because everyone's attention would be on George and they'd all be trying their hardest to persuade him not to do anything reckless once he was out of plaster again. 'So am I going as your colleague who just happened to beat George at chess?' she asked carefully.

'Um, no. George has told them all that my new nickname's Tarzan. And why. And I can't even shake him for it because he claims he might still have concussion.'

Ed looked so disgusted that Jane couldn't help laughing. 'Poor George. He really is bored, isn't he? Of course I'll come.' She paused. 'Um, what do I wear?' Fashion had never been her strength. What did you wear when you met a baron? Was she going to have to grab Sorcha for an emergency clothes-shopping trip?

'Wear anything you like. It's the country pile, so I'd suggest something dogproof. If it helps, I'm wearing jeans.'

On Sunday morning, Ed drove them to his family home in Suffolk. It didn't take as long as Jane had expected before Ed turned into a long tree-lined drive. Finally, the house came into view and Ed parked on the gravel in front of it. The hall was a huge redbrick building with stone mullioned windows; at each corner there was a narrow tower, each capped with a leaded domed roof.

'Wow, it's gorgeous,' she said. 'And I take it that's the money-eating roof George was telling me about?'

'It certainly is,' Ed said with a rueful smile.

'Has your family lived here very long?' She grimaced. 'Sorry, I'm being nosey. I didn't look you up on the Internet because—well, it felt a bit too much like spying.'

'Ask whatever you like. And it's not spying.' Ed took her hand and squeezed it. 'Yes, the Somers family has lived here ever since the house was built, nearly five centuries ago. Dad's the fifteenth baron. There is a little bit of family money left, but back in Victorian times there was a baron who dabbled in scientific experiments and rather neglected everything else, and my great-grandfather lost a small fortune in the Wall Street Crash. So I guess we're like a lot of old families—land-rich and a bit cash-poor, because the maintenance is crippling and everything's entailed.'

'Meaning you can't sell because it has to go to the next generation?'

'Exactly. Dad says we're custodians and we're privileged to have grown up here. And he's right. We are.' He stole a kiss. 'We have a maze. I am *so* showing you that.'

'A maze. Like Hampton Court?' she asked.

'Sort of, but on a much smaller scale. And the rose garden. Dad's got a thing about roses. But it's fabulous—at this time of year, you walk through and you just breathe in the scent and it's like drinking roses.'

'So it's a big garden?'

He nodded. 'It's open to the public on Wednesdays and Saturdays, and whatever national garden open days Dad wants to do. The estate has to support itself. Frances got the hall licensed for weddings five years ago, so we can offer packages; and there's a minstrel's gallery in the Great Hall, so we sometimes hold concerts here.' He shrugged. 'Most summer weekends, there's something on; we're lucky that this weekend it's just us. Come on. Dad and Frances are expecting us.'

She followed him over to the front door, feeling ever so slightly out of her depth. As soon as Ed opened the front door, three dogs bounded down the hallway, barking madly and their tails a wagging blur. Jane crouched down to greet them and had her face thoroughly licked by the chocolate Labrador.

'That's Pepper,' he said. 'The Westie's called Wolfgang, and the setter's Hattie, short for "Hatter" because she's as mad as one.'

'They're lovely.' She continued making a fuss of them. How lucky Ed had been, growing up in a sprawling place like this. She'd just bet that the children had all been encouraged to run around the garden, with no shouting if they got grubby because it would all come out in the wash. Her own family had lived in a smart London apartment with too much glass and all-white furniture you didn't dare touch in case you left fingermarks. Which was fine for Jenna, who'd perfected elegance at a very early age, but Jane had always been in trouble for breaking things and making a mess. Even in her parents' new home in Cornwall, the furniture was so carefully arranged that the rooms felt ready for a photo shoot; you didn't dare relax in case you moved a cushion out of place.

'Ed, we're so glad you could make it.' A tall, elegant woman hugged him.

Jane got to her feet, aware that she was already covered in dog hair and slightly dishevelled. Not exactly the best impression she could make on Ed's family, but never mind.

'And you must be Jane. I'm Frances.' The older woman looked at her for a moment, as if considering shaking her hand, and Jane felt even more intimidated; and then she was enveloped in as huge a hug as Ed had received. 'It's so lovely to meet you. Come into the kitchen. It's a bit manic around here—but, then, George is home, so of course it's going to be manic.'

All her nervousness vanished instantly. Everything was going to be just fine. Ed's parents weren't in the slightest bit snobby; they were warm and welcoming, like Ed himself. As she followed Ed and Frances into the kitchen, Jane was shocked to realise that she already felt at home here—far more so than she did in her own parents' home. Here, she knew she'd be accepted exactly for who she was; and she didn't feel like a disappointment, the second-best child.

The man sitting at the table with the Sunday papers spread out before him looked up. Even before they were introduced, Jane could see that this was George and Ed's father; he had the same colouring and strong features.

Ed's father stood up and hugged him. 'Ed, my boy.' Jane received the same warm greeting. 'It's so nice to meet you, Jane. Welcome.'

'Um, shouldn't I be curtseying or something?' she asked.

'Good God, no!' David smiled at her. 'Don't even think of standing on ceremony. We're perfectly normal. Well, possibly except George, and you've already met him—and you're just as he described you.' He gave Ed a speaking look. 'At least *one* of our sons tells us things, Tarzan.'

'Oh, no—he's got you at it as well,' Ed groaned, but he was laughing. 'And may I remind you that one of your sons doesn't also spend his time narrowly avoiding avalanches or paragliding into cliffs? You can't have it both ways, Dad. Sensible and silent, or mad and gossipy. Your choice.'

'Oh, stop it, you two.' Frances flapped a tea towel at them, laughing. 'Jane, you've just come all the way from London, so you must be gasping for some coffee.'

'I'd love some, but I can see you're up to your eyes.' Jane gestured to the pile of broad beans that Frances had clearly been podding. 'Shall I make the coffee for everyone, or would you prefer me to help you with the beans?'

Frances gave her an approving smile. 'Making the coffee would be lovely. Thank you.'

'So where's George?' Ed asked.

'In the library, plotting,' David said. 'He's thinking about setting up some ghost walks for the winter. And just talk him out of this fireworks idea, would you? It terrifies me that he's going to take a course, get qualified and start blowing things up.'

'Since when does George listen to me?' Ed asked.

'You'd be surprised. And he's set up the chess board, Jane; he's desperate for that rematch with you.'

'So Ed told me.' She smiled back at him.

'Are the girls here yet?' Ed asked.

'Bea's got a meeting but she'll be down just after lunch. Alice is bringing Charlotte with her from the ivory tower,' Frances said. 'They'll be here any time now.'

Jane made the coffee, and Ed added milk and sugar to various cups. 'We'd better take one of these to George.'

'With a straw,' Frances added. 'He's not coping very well with losing his independence.'

'I did warn you he'd be a terrible patient,' Ed said dryly. 'If he gets too fed up, he can always stay at my place.'

'In your flat, he'd be too cooped up. At least here

he can limp around the garden with the dogs and mutter that he's never going paragliding again,' David said with a smile.

Ed ushered Jane through narrow corridors to the library—a light, airy room with more bookshelves than Jane had ever seen in her life, with several battered leather sofas scattered about, a grand piano and a huge, huge fireplace.

George was reclining on one of the sofas with a pair of crutches propped next to him, and a small table on his other side with a chessboard set out on it.

'Janey. Lovely to see you. Excuse me for not standing up; I hurt a bit, today. And, yes, Ed, I have done my physio today, before you ask.'

'I didn't say a word.' Ed spread his hands. 'I know better than to nag.'

Pepper had sneaked in beside them, and curled up on the sofa between George and his crutches.

And Jane was happy to curl up on one end of the other sofa next to Ed and play chess with George, with Hattie's head resting on her knee. This was the most perfect Sunday ever, she thought. In a place where she felt as if she belonged.

She beat George again, much to his chagrin; but before he could ask for another rematch, the library door burst open.

'Georgie-boy. You have—'

'—done my physio, yes, Alice.' He rolled his eyes. 'It's Sunday. That means no nagging, OK?'

'You wish,' Alice said with a grin.

Ed introduced his sisters to Jane. She liked them on sight; Alice was as brisk as she'd expected and Charlotte looked like a scatty academic, but Jane already knew not to be fooled by that.

'Lovely to meet you, Jane. George tells us you're a doctor, too,' Alice said. 'Please tell me Ed didn't tell you about the red-faced squeaky business.'

Jane smiled at her. 'No comment.'

George gave a crack of laughter. 'Well, he's right. You were red-faced and squeaky. You still are.'

'I might be eight years younger than you, Georgie-boy,' Alice said crisply, 'but I at least have the sense not to fly into a cliff.'

'Yes, m'lud,' George teased.

'Milady,' Alice corrected. 'Except I'm not a judge. Yet.'

Jane could see exactly why the paparazzi were scared of Alice. Though she also had a feeling that Alice had as big a heart as her brothers.

Lunch was in the dining room. The table was set with porcelain, solid silver cutlery and what looked like ancient Venetian glassware; Jane was terrified she'd drop something priceless and break it.

Ed moved his foot against hers so she glanced at him, then gave her a reassuring wink as if he understood what she was worrying about and wanted to put her at her ease.

The meal turned out to be full of laughter and noise and teasing—good-natured teasing, not the stuff with a nasty edge that she was used to from Jenna—and Jane was most definitely included as part of the family. The food was fantastic, too; Ed hadn't been exaggerating when he'd said that Frances was a great cook. 'Thank you. This is the best roast beef I've ever had,' she said, meaning it.

'It's from one of our farms. And all the vegetables are from our kitchen garden—I'm making a proper potager,' Frances said, 'before David takes up the whole of the garden with his roses.'

She and David shared an affectionate glance, and Jane realised that was another thing missing from her own childhood. Her father had always been tiptoeing round her mother, careful not to upset her, but there had never been that look of affection or adoration between them.

Alice was taking full advantage of the fact that George still couldn't manage cutlery and was making a big deal of spoon-feeding him.

'That's it—Frances, from now on I'm living on soup, custard, and anything else you can stick through a blender and I can drink through a straw,' George said with a pained look.

'No, you're not. This is such sweet revenge for all the times you spoon-fed me when I was a toddler and deliberately got yoghurt up my nose,' Alice said.

'Behave, children,' Frances said, laughing.

Alice gave George a hug. 'You can't get Mum to stick roast beef through a blender. It'd be disgusting. And you know I love you, really.'

'Love you, too, even though you're the bossiest woman I've ever met. Ruffle your hair for me, will you? I can't do it with these mitts. Not without cracking your skull, anyway,' he said wryly.

Jane was aware of a rush of envy as well as wistfulness. How wonderful it must've been, growing up in this kind of atmosphere, laughing and joking and secure in the knowledge that you were really, really loved.

After lunch, Ed took her for a stroll round the gardens. They were utterly beautiful and she could see why the public flocked there. The rose garden in particular was fantastic. 'Wow. You were right about the incredible scent,' she said, inhaling appreciatively.

'Do tell Dad. He'll be pleased. These are his babies, now we've all left home,' Ed said with a smile.

The promised maze was small, but big enough to be very private, and Ed kissed her at every corner before finally taking her back in to join the family.

Bea arrived mid-afternoon. 'Sorry I'm late. I'm up to my eyes in meetings, right now—but it's going to be *such* a good commission. I think it's going to be the one that'll make my name,' she said. And then she proceeded to grill Jane over coffee at the kitchen table, abetted by Alice and Charlotte.

'Charlotte, do you want me to fetch the spot-lamp from Dad's office so you can really make this an interrogation?' Ed asked in exasperation.

But Jane didn't mind at all. 'It's great that you look out for Ed.' She smiled at them. 'Anyway, my best friend did exactly the same thing to him, the first time she met him.'

'Don't you have any brothers and sisters to look out for you?' Alice asked.

'No.' Technically, she had a twin sister; but Jenna had never looked out for her. It had always been the other way round.

'Hmm. In that case, you can borrow us,' Charlotte said.

Looking at her, Jane realised that she meant it. And there was a huge lump in her throat as she hugged Ed's sisters.

'Your family's just *lovely*,' she said on the way back to London that evening.

'I know. And I told you they'd love you,' Ed said.

She could see the question on his face: when was she going to let him meet her family?

'Mine aren't like yours,' she said carefully. 'I'm not close to them.' She made regular duty phone calls home, but she hadn't actually seen her parents since Shaun had cheated on her with Jenna. And she most definitely hadn't seen her twin. She'd needed to take a step back and put some distance between them.

Ed reached across to squeeze her hand briefly. 'I can't imagine you not being close to anyone. My family loved you straight away.'

She dragged in a breath. 'You know I told you my mum was a model? Well, she didn't plan to have children. Pregnancy was hard for her.' Especially as she was carrying twins. Not that she could bring herself to tell Ed that, because then she knew he'd ask her about Jenna. 'She wasn't able to work during her pregnancy. Then she had really bad post-natal depression. And she couldn't go back to her career.'

'Why not?'

'Cover shoots and stretch marks don't mix,' she said dryly. It had been one of her mother's mantras. Though at least one of her daughters had been able to get her back into that charmed world. Going on photo shoots with Jenna had brought a small measure of happiness back to Sophia. Whereas Jane's world was alien to her. Disgusting. Particularly as it involved working with babies…the things that had ruined Sophia's life. She sighed. 'Appearances are really important to my mother.

I'm never going to be tall, thin and elegant—and I'm clumsy. I drop things.'

'No, you don't.'

She coughed. 'If you remember, the very second I met you I spilled a whole glass of champagne over you.'

'Which wasn't your fault—someone knocked into you.' He paused. 'So your mother blames you for the end of her career?'

'If she hadn't been pregnant, she wouldn't have had stretch marks. Or had PND. She could've carried on doing what she loved.' Jane shrugged. 'And I can understand that. I know how I'd feel if I had to give up my job. It's who I am—just as modelling was who she was. She's fragile.'

'Fragile?'

'She has depression,' Jane said. 'On bad days, she doesn't get out of bed. Bad days can last for weeks. And, yes, she's seen doctors about it. Depression's tricky. It doesn't always respond to treatment.' She sighed. 'It's a matter of keeping her on as an even keel as we can. I guess seeing me upsets her, reminds her too much of what she's lost.'

Ed pulled off at the next layby.

'Ed? Why have we stopped?'

'Come here.' He pulled her into his arms. 'I'm sorry that your mum can't see you for who you are. And blaming you for losing her career—that's really not fair. You didn't ask to be born. What about your dad? Can't he help her see things differently?'

'He…' How could she put this? 'He's a bit like Mike Duffield. He likes a quiet life. Which is ironic, considering he used to be in advertising—that's how he met Mum. She was a model on one of his campaigns.'

Ed stroked her hair. 'I'm sorry. I wish I could fix this for you.'

'I don't think even a superhero could fix it. But it's fine. I'm used to it.'

The expression on his face said that he didn't think it was something you got used to. But he kissed the tip of her nose. 'Come on. Let's go home.'

CHAPTER ELEVEN

OVER the next couple of weeks, Ed and Jane grew closer still.

On the Friday night, Ed told Jane to dress up. 'A prom-type dress,' he said, 'seeing as you always ask me about dress codes. But I'm not telling you where we're going—it's a surprise.'

The first surprise was that he picked her up in a vintage sports car.

'It's George's. I'm taking full advantage,' Ed told her with a grin. 'He says he's going to inspect it minutely when I take it back on Sunday, and if there's a single speck of dust on it, I'm toast.'

She laughed. 'We'd better get a chamois leather and beat him to it.'

He opened the door for her and helped her inside.

It was the first time she'd ever sat in a low-slung sports car. 'Wow. I feel like a princess,' she said.

'Good. You look like one.'

'Thank you.' She felt colour seeping into her cheeks.

He stole a kiss. 'You're so sweet.'

'I haven't missed your birthday or anything, have I?' she asked.

'No. I just wanted to make you feel a bit special and have some fun.' He squeezed her hand, then drove her to a very swish hotel, handed the keys to the valet, and ushered her inside.

'Doesn't this place have three Michelin stars and you have to book up months in advance?' she asked.

'Yes to the first, usually to the second, but they had a last-minute cancellation. I had to book the tasting menu in advance. I hope that's OK?'

She smiled. 'That's more than OK. I've always wanted to do something like this. Ed, this is such a treat.'

'Good.' He looked pleased that she liked his surprise.

Ed stuck to mineral water because he was driving, but he ordered her a glass of champagne.

'One's definitely enough,' she said softly. She smiled at him. 'And I'll try not to spill this one over you.'

He laughed. 'Good. But I'm still taking you dancing, afterwards.' His eyes glittered. 'And I have plans after that.'

Repeating the night they'd first met. Except this time they really knew each other. A thrill of pure desire skittered through her. 'That,' she said, her voice husky, 'sounds just about perfect.'

The food was amazing; she savoured every mouthful.

And the dancing turned out to be very similar to that of the night of the hospital ball. Just like before, Ed made her feel as if she were floating when she danced with him.

'That was the perfect evening,' she said when he'd driven her home. 'Thank you. You made me feel really special.'

'That,' Ed told her, 'is because you are.'

And then he proceeded to show her exactly how.

* * *

At work, too, Jane found that she and Ed were completely in tune. When Pippa Duffield started bleeding in the shower and Iris came to fetch them from the patient they were seeing, they spoke in unison: 'We're going to need the anaesthetist and the neonatologist, and we need Pippa in Theatre now.'

Jane got one of the nurses to call Mike Duffield and put him on speaker phone for her while she scrubbed in. 'Mike, it's Jane Cooper from the hospital. Unfortunately, Pippa's started bleeding again, so we need to deliver the twins now.'

'Are they going to be all right?' he asked anxiously.

'I'm sure they will be,' Jane said, 'but the bad news is that we have to give Pippa a general anaesthetic, so you won't be able to come in with us and see the twins being born as we'd planned. But you can see them as soon as they've been checked over.'

'Tell Pip I love her,' Mike said, 'and I'm on my way now.'

Pippa was in tears. 'I didn't do anything out of the ordinary. I've been taking it so easy ever since I've been here. I can't understand why I started bleeding like that. And there was so much of it!'

'I know, and it's not your fault,' Jane soothed. 'We did say this might happen, and you're in exactly the right place for us to help you.'

'Two days before the babies were going to be delivered anyway. Why couldn't I have hung on for just two more days?' Pippa asked despairingly.

'That's just the way it goes sometimes,' Ed told her gently. 'Pippa, there's something else we need to talk about. If we can't stop the bleeding, we might have to give you a hysterectomy. We'll only do that if there's no other way, but may we have your consent?'

'So...then I won't ever be able to have another baby? Even with IVF?'

'No,' he confirmed quietly. 'I know this is a lot to take in, and it's unfair of us to dump this on you right now when you're worried sick about the babies, but we do have to think about you as well.'

Pippa swallowed hard. 'And if I don't have a hysterectomy, would that mean you can't stop the bleeding and I'll...?'

Jane squeezed her hand, realising that Pippa knew exactly what the consequences were but just couldn't say it. If they couldn't stop the bleeding, she would die. 'Yes.'

Pippa dragged in a breath. 'If it's the only way, then do what you have to. Just make sure the babies are safe.'

'Thank you,' Ed said.

She bit her lip. 'I so wanted Mike to cut the cords.'

'I know,' Jane said.

'Nothing's gone to plan.'

'But the babies will be here safely soon, and Mike's on his way. He told me to tell you that he loves you,' Jane said, and held Pippa's hand while the anaesthetist counted her down.

In Theatre, Ed swiftly made the incision; he delivered the first twin into Iris's waiting hands, ready to be wrapped in a towel and checked over by the neonatologist.

Just after he'd delivered the second twin, the anaesthetist said, 'Blood pressure's still dropping.'

Just what they'd wanted to avoid: Pippa was haemorrhaging.

Although they were prepared for it and had ordered cross-matched blood, the transfusion didn't seem to be helping. Jane went cold. Please don't let Pippa go into DIC. Disseminated intravascular coagulation meant that the clotting factors in the blood were activated throughout the body instead of being localised to the site of the injury, so small blood clots developed through the body, using up the blood's clotting factors so it couldn't clot where it was really needed.

If they couldn't get her blood to start clotting, there was a very good chance they were going to lose her, and she'd never get to meet the twin girls she'd wanted so desperately.

They continued pumping blood into her.

Please, please, let her start clotting, Jane prayed silently.

After what felt like a lifetime, the anaesthetist said softly, 'We're there. Blood pressure rising nicely.'

'Thank God,' Ed said softly.

Finally they managed to close the incision ready to take Pippa through to the recovery room.

'How are the babies doing?' Ed asked.

'I'm going to take them to the special care unit for a while; I want them on oxygen for a bit. But they're fighters, like their mum. They'll be fine,' the neonatologist said.

'We need to take pictures of the babies for her, for when she wakes up,' Jane said.

Iris grabbed the camera they kept for this kind of situation and took pictures of the twins. While Ed sat with Jane as she started to wake up, Jane went out into the corridor. Mike was there, pacing.

'What's happened?' he asked desperately.

'You have two beautiful girls, and Pippa's waking up now,' she said, smiling.

'Can I see them?' he asked.

'The babies are going down to Special Care—not because there's a major problem but at this age they often need a little bit of help breathing.' There would be time enough to let him know that they'd been close to losing Pippa; for now, she wanted him to enjoy the first few minutes of being a dad.

She took him through to the recovery room; he held Pippa tightly. 'I was so worried.'

'I'm fine. But the babies…they're in the special care unit.' A tear trickled down her face.

'We've taken pictures for you for now, until you're ready to go and see them,' Iris said, and handed over the photographs.

Mike and Pippa were both crying. 'They're so tiny.'

'They're good weights for thirty-five weeks,' Ed said. 'I know it's easy for me to say, but try not to worry. They're doing just fine.'

Back at Jane's flat that night, they collapsed into bed.

'What a day,' Jane said.

'Mmm. I had a few bad moments,' Ed admitted. 'If she'd gone into DIC…'

'But she didn't. It was a good outcome. Twin girls, both doing well, and with luck they'll be out of Special Care within the week.'

'We did well today,' he said with a smile. 'Great teamwork.'

'Absolutely.' Jane curled into his arms. Funny, she'd never thought she could ever be this happy. Neither of them had actually declared their feelings, but she knew.

She'd fallen in love with Ed, and she was pretty sure that Ed loved her all the way back. Just the way she was.

Life couldn't get any better than this. She just hoped it could stay this way.

The next morning, Jane called in to see how Pippa was doing, to find her in floods of tears.

'I'm just so tired—and I'm dreading Mike's mum coming in to see the babies and taking over,' Pippa confessed.

Jane sat next to her and took her hands. 'You've been through an awful lot, Pip. And, the thing is, Mike's mum doesn't know the half of it. I reckon if you tell her what's been happening, she'll be a lot gentler with you than you expect. She'll realise that you need support and help, not someone taking over and telling you what to do.

'But we've never been close. She always made it clear she felt I took her son away.'

'Maybe,' Jane said softly, 'that's a defence mechanism. Mike's her only child, is he?'

Pippa nodded.

'Maybe she always wanted a daughter as well—and, now she's got one, she's scared she's going to get it wrong because she's used to just having a son, and she's too proud to tell you. Just like you're too proud to tell her that you went through IVF,' Jane said, 'Right now, I think you could do with a mum to lean on, so why don't you talk to her? Tell her how you feel.'

Pippa bit her lip. 'It's hard.'

'But it'll be worth it if it lets you build that bridge.'

'Do you think so?'

'I know so,' Jane said confidently.

* * *

Later that afternoon, she dropped in to see Pippa again, and was surprised to see an older woman sitting on the side of the bed, cuddling one of the twins and talking animatedly to Pippa.

'Jane, this is my mother-in-law,' Pippa said, introducing them almost shyly.

'Pip's told me so much about you,' Mrs Duffield said. 'She says you've been so supportive, right from the moment she had the pregnancy test after her IVF.'

So Pippa had taken her advice, Jane thought. And clearly that bridge had been built from the other side, too. She smiled. 'That's what I'm here for. And it's lovely to see the babies getting stronger and stronger every day.'

Mrs Duffield beamed. 'I'm so looking forward to being a hands-on granny. But things have changed a lot since my day, so I'm taking my lead from Pip.'

Jane looked at Pippa, who mouthed, 'Thank you. You were absolutely right.'

Jane had to blink back the tears. 'Well, if there's anything you need, any questions you have, just ask. And congratulations on being a granny of twins.'

'They're beautiful. Just like their mother,' Mrs Duffield said. 'Though I think they both have Mike's smile.'

'Yeah.' If only she could find a way to build a bridge like this with her own mother, Jane thought. But she pushed it aside. Brooding wasn't going to help anyone. 'I'll see you later,' she said with a smile.

CHAPTER TWELVE

A COUPLE of weeks later, Ed dropped in at his brother's flat on his way home.

'How are you managing, now the plaster's off?' he asked.

'Fine.' But George's smile didn't reach his eyes.

'What's up?'

George sighed. 'Nothing.'

'Come off it. Fed up with being stuck in the slow lane?'

'I guess.' George shrugged.

'OK. Let's take your car,' Ed suggested. 'I'm not breaking the speed limit for you, but a quick drive up the motorway with the top down might make you feel a bit better.'

George dragged in a breath. 'Sometimes I wish you weren't so nice. It'd be easier.'

'What would?'

'Nothing.'

Ed took his brother's hands. 'Is this about the fertility stuff? Look, they said it takes time. Don't write yourself off just yet. You took a hard knock when you hit the cliff. Wait until the next test. And even if the motility of your sperm doesn't get much better than it is now, it doesn't mean you can't ever have kids. There's a special form of IVF called ICSI that could work for you—they pick out the best sperm and use them.'

'It's not that.' George looked bleak. 'Forget it.'

'No. George, I can see that something's wrong.' He'd been sure of it when George had been in hospital, too. 'You're my brother. You've always been there for me. Let me be there for you.'

George's face was full of anguish. 'What if I'm not your brother?'

Ed frowned. 'Of course you're my brother.'

'I might not be.'

'How do you work that out? We have the same parents.'

'Not necessarily. Supposing Dad isn't my father?'

'Of course he is.' Ed frowned, too. 'George, you and I look alike. We've got the same colouring, the same cleft in our chin—exactly the same as Dad's.'

'We're not *that* alike,' George said.

'Where's this all coming from?' Ed asked, mystified.

'I've read her diaries.'

Ed didn't have to ask whose. Because something was becoming nastily clear. He'd been right about the unfinished business. 'Is that the package you had to collect from the solicitor's, earlier this year?' The meeting that only George had been invited to after their mother's death; Ed had pushed aside the hurt at the time. Of course it would be George. He was the eldest of her two children.

'Her diaries, letters and photographs.' George gave a mirthless laugh. 'I knew Dad used to send her photographs of us on our birthday. Stupidly, I thought she might've kept them. She didn't—the photos were of the men in her life. But I started reading the letters and the diaries.' He shook his head. 'I really don't know how to tell Dad. Ed, I know it for sure. I'm not his.'

'But *how* do you know?'

'She had an affair. Well, more than one, while she was married to Dad. And…Dad just isn't my biological father.'

'No way. You look like Dad. You look like me,' Ed said again.

'Maybe the guy looked a bit like Dad—maybe he had the same colouring and build and what have you.' George blew out a breath. 'I hate to think the girls aren't really my sisters.'

'They're your sisters, all right. The same as I'm your brother. Nothing's going to change that.' Ed paused. 'Is this why you've been taking more risks than usual, the last few months? Since you first read her papers and came to that completely crazy conclusion?'

'It's not crazy. It's the truth.' George sighed. 'Yes.'

'And this was what was distracting you when you crashed?'

George nodded.

'And you've kept this to yourself for months? You *idiot*. Why didn't you tell me?'

'Apart from the fact that you were in beating yourself up over your divorce and I didn't want to dump yet more burdens on you, I guess I didn't know how. And I kept hoping that maybe I'd got the wrong end of the stick. When I woke up after the crash, I thought maybe I'd got it all wrong and I was being an idiot. But I've read the diaries again, since I've been back home. And the letters.' He limped over to the dresser, pulled out a thick envelope, rummaged through it and brought out a diary and a handful of letters. He dumped them on Ed's lap. 'Read them and tell me if I've got it wrong.'

He'd marked the pages with a sticky note. Ed read through them, and went cold.

'She doesn't say you're definitely not Dad's. She says she's not sure.'

'Which is the same thing.'

'No, it's not. Look, we can do a DNA test. That'll prove it for sure.'

'But what if,' George whispered, 'what if a DNA test proves I'm not who I always thought I am?'

Ed could see the demons haunting his brother. He was afraid of being the cuckoo in the nest, unwanted by their family. Just as they'd both been unwanted by their mother. 'It won't matter at all,' he said softly. 'I don't give a damn about genetics. You're my brother and I love you. I know the girls will feel the same. And Dad and Frances.'

'Maybe.'

'No, *definitely*. You're ours, and you always will be.' He gave George a hug. 'I love you.'

'And I love you, too.' George looked bleak as Ed put the papers on the table and came back to sit beside him. 'But if I'm not Dad's, that means legally we're talking about a whole new kettle of fish. It means I'm not the heir. *You* are, Ed,' he said softly.

Ed was glad he was sitting down. If he was the heir... It meant he'd have to give up the job he loved to run the estate. He couldn't be selfish; he'd have to put his duty first. Of course he'd do it.

But this didn't just impact on him. How would Jane react to the idea of such a change in his life—and what it would mean for her, if their future was together?

'Oh, hell,' Ed said.

'You get it now?' George asked dryly.

'I get it.' Ed ran a hand through his hair. 'So how are we going to deal with this?'

'I don't know. I've got to think of a way of breaking it to Dad. Without hurting him.'

'We need to do the DNA test first.'

'Right, and I can really say to him that I need a sample of his DNA for a quick paternity test. Not.' George rolled his eyes.

'Maybe they can test you and me, to see if we have parents in common.'

'And what if we both have different fathers, and neither of them's Dad? Or if we do have the same father, and he isn't Dad?'

Ed hadn't thought about that. 'This is one hell of a mess.'

'You're telling me.' George swallowed hard. 'All these years, I've tried to tell myself that it doesn't matter. That I have Dad and Frances and you and the girls, and it doesn't matter that she left us. I tried to feel sorry for her, because I knew she was unhappy. But now...' He shook his head and grimaced. 'I just wish I'd never seen those bloody papers.'

'So do I,' Ed said. 'Not just for me, but because you've been going through hell ever since you read them. I hate to think you've been brooding when I could've been there for you. I *knew* there was something wrong. I even asked you about it. And you still didn't tell me.'

'You know what they say about a problem shared being a problem halved? It's completely untrue. I just told you and it's double the misery.' George looked bleak. 'I have no idea how we're going to sort this.'

'We need DNA testing. You, me and Dad. There isn't any other way.' Ed thought about it. 'I know people in the lab at work, but they don't do DNA testing. We'll need a specialist lab. Maybe Alice knows a reliable, discreet one?'

'I don't want Alice involved,' George said immediately.

'Then we're going to have to tell Dad and get the test done. There's no other way round it, George.'

'How long does testing take?' George asked.

'I have no idea. And it'll depend on the workload of the lab as well as the physical time it takes for the test to run,' Ed warned.

'This feels like all the exams I've ever taken, rolled into one,' George said. 'Except this time I don't have a clue what the results are going to be. And I don't know if I'm going to pass.'

'Whatever the results say, you're my brother and that's never going to change. Dad, Frances and the girls won't stop loving you, either.'

'Damn, I'm so bloody wet,' George said, closing his eyes and rubbing his forehead.

'No, I'd feel the same.' Ed gave him a wry smile. 'Actually, now I think about it, it's the same for me, too. How do I know that Dad's my biological father? And if he's not…then who the hell am I?'

'This weekend,' George said, 'is going to be one of the worst of my life. And yours.' He limped over to the table to collect his laptop. 'Right. Let's find ourselves a lab.'

'You start looking them and I'll make us some coffee,' Ed said. 'We'll sort this out. Together.'

'Yeah.' George gave a deep sigh. 'Thanks.'

'Well, what did you think I was going to do? Make you the worst breakfast in the universe and make you drink tea with too much sugar in it?'

'It worked for you,' George said. 'But please don't do it to me. Coffee's fine.'

Ed laughed, then sobered slightly. 'I know we're keeping this quiet for now, but I do need to let Jane know what's going on.'

'Because it's going to affect her as well. If it gets messy, she'll end up under the spotlight because she's your girl,' George said.

'She won't leak it.'

George rolled his eyes. 'State the obvious, why don't you?'

'Yeah.' Ed was heartened that his brother could see it, too.

In the kitchen, he texted Jane swiftly. *Running a bit late. Don't wait dinner for me. Still OK to call in later?*

Her reply was almost instant. *Course it is. Is everything OK? George?* she texted.

I'll explain later, Ed replied. *Don't worry.*

Though not worrying was a lot easier said than done.

When Ed left George's flat, he headed straight for Jane's flat.

'You look like hell,' Jane said when she opened the door, and wrapped her arms round him.

He leaned his cheek against her hair, breathing in the comforting, familiar scent of her shampoo. 'Sometimes life really sucks.'

She shepherded him inside. 'Come and sit down. Have you eaten?'

'I'm not hungry. But I wouldn't say no to a mug of tea with about ten sugars in it.'

'That bad?' She stroked his face. 'Tell me about it.'

'It's a long and very messy story,' he warned.

'I'm not going anywhere. And whatever you tell me won't go any further than me.'

'I know that.' He trusted her. He knew she wouldn't lie to him.

He let her lead him into the kitchen and sat down. When she'd switched the kettle on, he scooped her onto his lap. Just holding her made things feel a bit better.

'So what's happened?' she asked softly.

He sighed. 'You know Frances is my stepmother.'

She nodded.

'My biological mother left Dad for someone else when I was four and George was six. She never said goodbye, and she never sent either of us so much as a Christmas card or a birthday card after she left.' The fact that she hadn't wanted them: Ed was pretty sure it was half the reason why George wouldn't settle down with anyone. His brother didn't want to risk being abandoned again.

He'd made that mistake himself, with Camilla. He'd thought he was doing the right thing by her. That together they'd make a family, a strong one like his father and Frances had. But when he'd turned out to be completely wrong and Camilla had left, it had brought back some of the old hurt, the stuff he'd thought buried and forgotten about.

He sighed. 'I know Dad would never have done anything underhand like not giving us her cards. George said he used to send her photographs of us every Christmas, trying to build bridges that she just knocked down every time. And I once overheard him ranting about her to my godfather. He said he could forgive her for leaving him, but he couldn't forgive her for how she'd behaved to me and George.'

'Oh, Ed. How could she possibly…?' She swallowed hard. 'I just can't imagine walking away from my children. Not that I have any, obviously, but… How could she do it?'

'Because she was damaged,' Ed said softly. 'Dad's love wasn't enough for her. Her children weren't enough for her. And all the men she flitted between—they were never enough for her, either. Sometimes I think that maybe she did love us really—that she realised Dad would be able to give us a happy, loving childhood more than she could, and she stayed away because she didn't want to wreck that.'

And now for the biggie. 'George thinks he's not Dad's.'

'Why?'

'She died earlier this year, and her solicitor gave George her diaries and some old letters. He read them, and he's convinced himself that all the evidence says he isn't Dad's.'

'Could he be right?'

Ed sighed. 'I don't know. But that's why he's been so reckless, these last few months. He was thinking about it when he had the accident. And he's been brooding about it ever since.'

'Poor George. But he does have you.'

'That's what I told him.' Ed sighed again. The only

way to be sure of the truth is to take a DNA test. We're telling Dad this weekend and taking the test kits with us.'

'What can I do to help?'

He'd known Jane would say that. She had the biggest heart of anyone he'd met. He held her tighter. 'Nothing.'

'Even if all I can do is listen or give you a bit of moral support, I want you to know I'm here.' She kissed him lightly. 'Anything you want me to do, just say. If you want me there with you at the weekend, that's fine. Though it's pretty sensitive. So if you'd rather leave it as just you, your dad and George, that's also fine—I won't go huffy on you.'

'Thank you.' He gave a tired smile. 'I have to be honest with you. I don't have a clue what's going to happen next. If the test proves that George and I really are Dad's, then that's brilliant and we can stop worrying. But we have to be prepared for it not to go our way. If we're *not* Dad's, then the papers are going to drag up some truly horrible stuff. Things about my mother flitting from man to man, things about George never dating anyone more than three times because he's a chip off the old block.' He paused. 'I hate to think of you being dragged through what could end up being a real mess. So if you'd rather walk away now, I understand.'

She shook her head. 'No chance. I don't care what the papers say and I don't care what the DNA test says. I know *you*, and that's all that matters.'

She was standing by him. Regardless. Ed's chest felt tight. 'Thank you. But if you do change your mind, then I'll understand that, too.'

'I'm not going to change my mind.' Jane held his gaze. 'I'm not Camilla. Just as you're not Shaun.'

Camilla might have sat it out until the DNA test results came through, especially if there was a chance that Ed could be the heir to the barony. But if the tests had shown him not to be David Somers's son, he knew how she would've reacted. The complete opposite from Jane.

And there was a subject he'd been avoiding. Since they were talking about difficult stuff already, they might as well add this to the whole mess, he thought. 'I know George told you about the baby. And he probably told you his theory.'

'That she lied to you about being pregnant in the first place.' She nodded. 'Is he right?'

Ed shrugged. 'Maybe. But you know as well as I do how many pregnancies end up in an early miscarriage. And, once you're in the middle of wedding preparations, it's not that easy to say you've changed your mind and call a halt to everything. Especially when it's a society wedding and there'd be so much talk.'

She could understand that; and for Ed to give his ex the benefit of the doubt like that just showed what a huge heart he had. 'Did Camilla know about your mum?'

'Her family have known mine for years.' He shrugged. 'I guess they must have talked about it at some point.'

'So she knew you wouldn't walk away from her if she was accidentally pregnant,' Jane said softly. 'Because you're a good man and you do what's right.'

'I tried. But I wasn't what she really wanted. And I *was* selfish, Janey. It wasn't all her fault. I didn't give her the choice about moving to Glasgow,' he reminded her.

'She didn't give you a choice about getting married,'

Jane pointed out. 'Or about the baby.' She paused. 'I'm not going to ask you if you wanted a family. I've seen you with your sisters, and I've seen you with the babies on the ward. You never miss a chance to chat to a mum and cuddle a baby.'

'Busted,' Ed said with a wry smile. 'Yes. I wanted a family. But later, when I suggested we try again, she made it clear that the baby had been a mistake and she didn't want to try again.'

Jane swallowed. 'You don't think she…?'

'Had a termination?' He shook his head. 'She wasn't that hard-bitten.' He stole a kiss. 'I've seen you with the babies on the ward too, Dr Cooper. Is that what you wanted with Shaun?'

'A family. Like the one I didn't grow up in,' she said. 'But I don't think that was what he wanted.'

'More fool him.' Ed stole another kiss. 'Jane—I know we only met a couple of months ago. It's probably way too soon for me to say anything. And I shouldn't be saying anything at all when my family's in such a mess. But I know how I feel about you, and I just…' He swallowed hard. 'I love you. Ever since I've met you, I've felt so in tune with you. I told myself I'd be sensible and I wouldn't repeat my mistakes with Camilla, that I wouldn't let anyone get close to me again. But I can't help myself; with you, I feel complete.'

'Oh, Ed.' Her eyes filled with tears. 'I…I never thought I'd let myself feel like that about anyone, either. That I'd learn to trust again. But you—you're different. And I love you, too.'

'Thank God,' Ed whispered, and kissed her.

CHAPTER THIRTEEN

ON Saturday morning, Ed felt as if he was driving the condemned man to the gallows—except George might not be the only one who was condemned.

He half wished he'd asked Jane to come with him. Her calm, quiet support would have helped. Then again, given the bombshell that he and George were about to drop on their father, maybe it did need to be just the three of them and Frances.

He drove on through the rain with a heavy heart.

Jane reached for the entryphone. Had Ed changed his mind and wanted her to go with him to Suffolk after all? 'Hello?'

'It's me.'

Jenna. Jane recognised the voice instantly, and ice slid down her spine. What did her twin want? Given the radio silence since that article had hit the news stands, she guessed it wouldn't be to apologise.

'Are you going to let me in, or what?' Jenna asked. 'It's peeing down out here and my hair's getting wet.'

For a moment, Jane wondered what would happen if she said no. Then she remembered what she'd said to Pippa Duffield about building bridges. It had worked for Pippa. Maybe this time it would work for her. 'Come up,' she said, suppressing a sigh and pressing the button to let Jenna in through the building's front door.

The kettle had boiled and Jane was infusing peppermint tea by the time there was a knock on the door.

Jenna looked cross. 'You kept me waiting for *ages*.'

Oh, great. It looked as if her twin was spoiling for a fight. Jane tried to defuse the atmosphere. 'I made you some peppermint tea.' She didn't drink it herself, but she knew Jenna did, and she kept a stock in for her sister. 'I'll put some honey in the cup in a second.' She nodded at Jenna's luggage. 'Have you just come back from a shoot?'

Jenna rolled her eyes. 'Why else do you think I'm here?'

To get a convenient bed for the night. Not to see how her twin was and spend some quality time together. Jane suppressed the hurt. 'Where was the shoot?'

'The Big Apple.'

'A night flight home, then. You must be tired.' Jane tried to be conciliatory. 'Can I get you a late breakfast or something?'

Jenna rolled her eyes again. 'Little Dr Perfect.'

What? Jane frowned. 'What's this all about, Jenna?' OK, she could understand that her twin was tired and grumpy after travelling, but why did Jenna have to take it out on her?

'You always have to *nag*, don't you?'

Normally, Jane let it go and tried to avoid a full-on fight. But today she was keyed up, worried about Ed, and the question just burst out. 'Why do you hate me so much?'

'Why do you think? You and your perfect job and

your perfect life.' Jenna scowled at her. 'You have no idea what it's like to struggle.'

Jane couldn't believe she was hearing this, from Jenna of all people. Her childhood had been a lot tougher than Jenna's. The only time she'd ever really felt loved had been at Great-Aunt Sadie's. 'That's unfair. I've always tried to look after you. When we were kids and Mum was too ill, I used to cook dinner for us.'

'Exactly. Dr Perfect,' Jenna sneered. 'Always doing everything right. So *perfect*.'

'Perfect? Give me strength. You made my life a misery all the way through school. You and your friends laughed at me because I'm clumsy and I was always picked last for sports. You sneered because I studied instead of partying, and you made sure the whole school called me that horrible name.'

'Oh, you *studied*.' Jenna made exaggerated quote marks with her fingers. 'And don't we all know that you always got straight As? You're the clever one. I had it rammed down my throat all the time by the teachers—why couldn't I be more like you? The good twin, not the bad one.'

Said the girl who'd made her feel bad for not being like her. And now she was complaining? Jane saw red. 'If you'd made the slightest bit of effort in class instead of spending all your time fiddling with your hair and make-up, you could've done well in your exams, so don't you dare throw that at me. You made your choices and I accept that, so why do you have a problem that my choices were different? Why can't you just accept that we're different? I don't whine all the time that I'm not as tall and skinny as you. I accept myself for who I am. Why can't you do that?'

Jenna curled her lip. 'You're just jealous because I take after Mum.'

'No. I'm fine with who I am. But I'm tired of you putting me down all the time. Like having that horrible article printed.'

'It's not my fault the journo wrote it up like that.'

Jane doubted that. Jenna's publicist would've insisted on approving the copy.

'It's not just the article, it's been my entire life. Even my first boyfriend—I'd had a crush on him for months and I could hardly believe he wanted to go out with me. The day after our date, it was all round the school that he'd lost a bet with you and his forfeit was to date me. That's the only reason he asked me out.'

Jenna shrugged. 'It never seemed to bother you.'

No, because Jane had been determined not to let Jenna see how much it hurt. Or how it had felt when she'd discovered during her teens that half of her boyfriends were only dating her in the hope they'd meet Jenna, and the other half saw what they were missing as soon as they met her twin and dumped her. Before Ed, she'd had lousy taste in men.

'And Shaun.' Jenna had never apologised for that. 'I could've understood it if you'd fallen for him, if you really loved him—but you dumped him as soon as I left him.'

Jenna shrugged again. 'I didn't want him. It wasn't my fault. He came on to me.'

Jane had no idea if Jenna was telling the truth or twisting it. 'Couldn't you have said no?'

'He wasn't right for you—so, really, I did you a favour. If you'd bought a flat together or even got married, it would've been harder for you to walk away, with all the legal mess and expense.'

Jane blinked. 'You slept with *my* fiancé, in *my* bed, and you're telling me you did me a *favour*?'

Jenna lifted her chin. 'You know I did.'

'What kind of weird planet do you live on?' Jane shook her head. She'd had enough. 'Jenna, I've tried and tried and tried to be a good sister to you. But I just can't do this any more. I'm tired of you pulling me down all the time and making me feel bad when I've done nothing wrong. I'm sure you have plenty of other people you can stay with in London. I'm going out now, and I'd prefer you not to be here when I get back.' Jane grabbed her coat and bag, and walked out of the flat before she said anything she'd *really* regret.

Jenna stared after her twin, absolutely furious. Little Doctor Perfect was throwing her out?

She wasn't in the mood for dragging down to Cornwall to stay with the parents. And now it looked as if she was going to have to find somewhere to stay.

She used Jane's landline to ring round her friends. Half of them were away on shoots, but she finally found someone who could put her up for the night. She was about to leave when the phone rang and the answering machine clicked in.

'Janey, it's Ed. I said I'd ring you when I got to the Hall. You're obviously out. I wish I was with you instead of here in Suffolk.' There was a sigh. 'George and I are going to talk to Dad about the paternity test stuff now. I'll ring you later, OK?' A pause. 'I love you.' And then the beep as he ended the message.

I love you? Jenna frowned. As far as she knew, Jane wasn't even seeing anyone. Who was this Ed person?

Whoever he was, he lived in Suffolk, he'd gone to some hall or other, and there was someone called George.

Intrigued, she flicked into the search engine on her mobile phone and typed in *Ed, Suffolk, Hall, George.* Just to see what would come up.

Right at the top of the list there was a link to 'Visitor Information, Somers Hall'.

Jenna skimmed through it. Interesting. David Somers, fifteenth baron, and his sons Edward and George. Hmm. It looked as if Jane was dating the younger son of a baron.

But why would Ed Somers be talking to his father about a paternity test?

Jenna thought about it a bit more, then smiled. Her contact at *Celebrity Life* would just *love* this story. And it would serve Jane right for being such a bitch and refusing to give her a bed for the night.

'What's all this about, Ed? You both look as if you haven't slept in days.' David frowned.

'You need to sit down, Dad. And you're going to need tea with about ten sugars,' Ed said.

'You're both here, so it's not as if George has finally managed to break his neck,' David said. 'What else could be that bad?'

'This.' George tossed the packet of letters and the diary onto the kitchen table. 'And I'm sorry, Dad, there's no way of softening it.'

'That's your mother's handwriting,' David said as he saw the open diary.

'Tea with ten sugars coming up,' Frances said with a sigh.

George told his father what he and Ed had worked out.

David looked in shock by the time George finished.

'I knew about the affairs, but it never occurred to me that you might be another man's child. Either of you.' His eyes narrowed. 'This doesn't change anything, you know. You're *mine*. Both of you.'

'And mine,' Frances chipped in. 'I know I'm not your biological mother, but you've both been my sons for more than a quarter of a century. I hope you two haven't been worrying about that.'

George and Ed exchanged a guilty glance.

'Idiots, the pair of you,' David said, rolling his eyes.

'Dad, there's the legal side to consider,' George said. 'I'm sorry, this is going to sound horrible and I'm certainly not wishing your life away, but we have to face it. If neither of us is yours, then the hall, the title and everything else reverts to another branch of the family when you die. Which means Frances loses her home and we all lose our childhood. Given this evidence...' He gestured to the papers.

'Which is all circumstantial, as Alice will no doubt tell you,' David cut in.

'No. It sheds enough doubt on the matter to mean that we need to do a DNA test,' Ed said gently. 'We've found a lab.'

'And paid for the kits. They came to my place yesterday,' George added.

'All you do is swab the inside of your mouth so you get cells and saliva, let it dry out, send the samples off in labelled envelopes and their machines do the rest,' Ed explained.

David sighed. 'Right. Let's get it over with.'

'We can't eat or drink for half an hour beforehand,' Ed said.

'Then tea is on hold,' Frances said, removing the pot from the middle of the table.

'There's a set procedure to follow,' Ed continued. 'We need to use gloves to make sure that none of the samples are contaminated, and the samples all have to dry out in separate glasses.'

'This is where it's really useful to have a scientist in the family,' George said, patting Ed's shoulder.

'How long does it take before we get the results?' David asked.

'About five working days. So that means we have a week to wait,' Ed said. 'And, no, they can't do it any faster. George already asked.'

'Whatever the results, *nothing* is going to change the fact that you're my sons and I love you,' David said softly.

'I love you, too,' George and Ed echoed.

Ed left George in Suffolk, knowing that his brother could get a lift back to London with one of their sisters the next day, and drove back to London late that afternoon. Back at his flat, he rang Jane. 'I'm home.'

'How was it?' she asked.

He sighed. 'Difficult.'

'Do you want me to come over? Or do you want to come here?'

'Can I come to you? I could do with your warmth.' And his flat didn't feel like home, the way hers did.

'Come over now,' she said. 'I've been baking. The choc-chip cookies are fresh out of the oven.'

'Now there's an offer I can't refuse.' He smiled despite himself. 'See you in a bit.'

She buzzed him up as soon as he rang the entryphone. He took the stairs three at a time, and wrapped his arms round her. 'That's better,' he said softly.

'How are George and your dad bearing up?' she asked.

We're a united front,' he said. 'In private as well as in public. Dad says that whatever the results show, he doesn't give a damn about the barony or the hall. We're his, and nothing's going to change that. Frances said the same.'

'And so will your sisters. I could've told you that,' she said. 'It's so obvious in your family, the love and affection—the way you talk to each other, the way you look at each other.' She swallowed hard. 'A million miles away from the way my family is.'

He held her closer. 'Oh, Janey. I'm sorry they give you such a hard time.'

'Some things you can't fix, and you have to learn not to beat yourself up about it,' she said. 'Remember that. And love…love can fix an awful lot of things. I'm not giving up on them quite yet.'

Monday morning started in a rush, with a breech birth where they needed to try turning the baby into a better position for delivery; and then a patient with all the symptoms of pre-eclampsia but with the addition of jaundice, meaning that it was more likely to be acute fatty liver of pregnancy. The only treatment was to deliver the baby; though, at thirty-five weeks, it was better for the baby to stay where he was for a while longer, until his lungs had matured properly.

Although the mum was on a drip to maintain her glucose levels and stop hypoglycaemia, routine monitoring of the baby showed that the foetus was in distress, and they ended up needing to take her straight into Theatre for an emergency section.

'We can't risk an epidural in case there's a bleed at the anaesthesia site. It'll have to be a general anaesthetic,' Ed said grimly.

Luckily the delivery was fine, without the mum having any of the clotting problems Jane and Ed had worried about. And he caught her eye at the end of the operation, mouthing, 'Well done.'

They worked so well as a team. So in tune.

Jane was writing up the notes at her desk when the phone rang.

'Janey? It's Sorcha. I've just seen the papers on the ward and it's not good. There's a story about Ed and his family. About how there's a paternity test going on.'

Jane went cold. How could the press possibly have got hold of the story?

'And it's worse than that, Jane. The source—they say it's close to Ed Somers. His girlfriend.'

'No. That's not true. I don't understand.' Jane blew out a breath. 'Thanks for the heads-up, Sorcha. I'd better take a look online and find out just what they're saying.'

The story was all over the place. *Somers: who's the real heir?*

Oh, hell. She needed to talk to Ed. Right now.

He was in his own office, talking on the phone; he acknowledged her with a gesture, then finished his conversation and replaced the receiver.

'Ed, do you have minute? There's something you really need to see,' she said urgently.

He looked grim. 'If it's what I think you're going to say, I already know the story's leaked. George just called me. He's been trying to get hold of me all morning, except we were in Theatre.'

'I haven't talked to anyone about this, Ed. Nobody at all. But the one I read—' she felt sick '—it says the source is me.'

'Maybe someone overheard you talking to me about it.'

She shook her head. 'I don't see how. And if they had, then surely they would've said that you were the source, not me.' Then a seriously nasty thought hit her. 'Your phone message.' She closed her eyes. 'Oh, my God. Saturday, when you and George went to see your dad. When you called me and left a message. Jenna must've still been in my flat. On her own.'

He looked mystified. 'Who's Jenna?'

Her throat felt dry. 'Oh, God. Can I close your door?'

'Sure.' He looked concerned.

She did so, and sat on the edge of his desk. 'I'm sorry, Ed. I should've told you about her before. You know I said my mum couldn't model any more once she was pregnant? It's because she was having twins.'

'You have a *twin*?' Ed looked at her in seeming disbelief. 'But you said you were an only child.'

'No,' she corrected, 'I told Charlotte I didn't have a brother or sister to look out for me.'

His expression went hard. 'That's semantics.'

She knew what he must be thinking—she'd lied to him, just as much as Camilla had. 'Ed, it's complicated. My family's not like yours. And you have no idea how much I envy you having George and the girls. They love you. I've never had that.' Her eyes pleaded for him to understand. 'The thing is, Jenna's like Mum. She's a supermodel. And she takes after Mum emotionally as well as physically. She's fragile. Any cold or virus, she always gets it. She had glandular fever the other year, and couldn't work for six months. Whereas I've got the constitution of an ox and I'm almost never ill.' She sighed. 'I tried to look after her. When we were kids and Mum was ill, I'd cook dinner for us. Jenna can't so much as boil an egg. But she told me at the weekend that she's always hated me for it. She called me Little Dr Perfect.' She dragged in a breath. 'I thought I was being caring and kind and nurturing, looking after her, and she thought I was just showing off.'

Ed stood up and put his arms round her. 'Oh, honey. You're very far from being a show-off. If anything, you hide your light under a bushel.'

'She wanted to stay at my place on Saturday—she lives out of a suitcase most of the time, so she normally expects to stay with me if she's in London—but she was spoiling for a fight, the second she walked through the door. I shouldn't have risen to it, but...' Well, she wasn't going to blame Ed for the fact that she'd been worried about him. 'I just snapped. I told I was going out and I didn't want her there when I got back. She must've heard your message and worked everything out.' She swallowed hard. 'I haven't told her or my parents that I'm even seeing you and I'm so sorry. I never wanted you to get mixed up in all this. I'll understand if you don't want to see me again, and I'll write an apology to your family.'

'Jane, you don't have to do that. And no way am I dumping you. It's not your fault that the story leaked.' He sighed. 'But I wish you'd told me about her before.'

'My relationship with my entire family is rubbish,

and I'm not very good at being a failure. I guess she's right about me wanting to think I'm perfect.'

He stroked her hair. 'Nothing of the sort. It isn't you.'

'I'm the one who doesn't fit into my family. So it feels like it's me.'

'What does Sorcha say?' he asked.

She rolled her eyes. 'You don't want to know what she calls Jenna. Especially after...' She stopped.

'After what?'

Given that her sister had hurt his family like this, she owed him the truth. 'Shaun.'

He blinked. 'Your *twin* was the one you caught him with?'

'Yes.'

Ed shook his head, looking stunned. 'Wow. That's seriously... I'm not sure I could forgive George if he'd done that to me.'

'George would never do that to you. He loves you.' She shrugged. 'Jenna hates me.'

Ed looked her straight in the eye. 'Please tell me you weren't worrying that the same thing would happen with me? That I'd meet her and go off with her?'

'No, of course not. Jenna might have tried it on with you, but you're not Shaun. You have integrity. I know you would've turned her down if she'd come on to you. I didn't tell you about her because...because no matter what I do, I can't get close to her, and she makes me feel bad. And I hate that.'

'What a mess.' Ed leaned his forehead against hers. 'And I hate that you're feeling bad when none of it's your fault.'

'It is. Because if I hadn't blown up at Jenna and

walked out, I would've been there to answer your call and she wouldn't have overheard the message. And she wouldn't have been mad at me for telling her to leave, and...' She shook her head. 'I need to talk to her and find out what the hell she was playing at. And then maybe I can call Dad and find out the number of Mum's old publicist, see if she can help with some damage limitation.'

'George is bound to know someone. So will Alice. Don't worry about it.'

Jenna wasn't answering her mobile, and her parents didn't answer their landline. Jane sighed. 'I'll try again later.'

'Janey. It's really not your fault.' Ed took her hand and kissed the back of her fingers. 'I know it wasn't you who leaked it. When I said to George I wanted to tell you, he said immediately that he trusted you, too.'

But, thanks to her family, she'd let him down. Broken their trust in her.

'You know, before all this blew up, I'd been thinking,' he said. 'You know I love you.'

'Even after this?'

'It's only talk. We can just ignore it. I'm sure worse things have been said about my family over the centuries.' He took a paperclip from his desk and began fiddling with it, then dropped to one knee in front of her. 'This is quite possibly the worst timing in the universe. I have no idea what the DNA results are going to show. If it's the wrong result, a lot of sticky stuff's going to hit the fan. All that "for richer, for poorer" stuff—I could be asking you to take an awful lot more of the rough than the smooth. And I know you've had a bad experience before, being engaged to someone who let you down badly. But I love you, Jane. I want to be with you, and life's a million times better with you than without you. And you're the one who's taught me I can put the past behind me and believe in the future. So will you do me the honour of marrying me, Jane?'

She caught her breath. 'Are you sure about this? I mean, with my mum and Jenna the way they are, it's never going to be easy with my family.'

He shrugged. 'They're difficult and they don't appreciate you. That's their problem. I'm not asking them to marry me—I'm asking you.' He reached up to stroke her face. 'For what it's worth, my family's got enough love to support us both through anything that happens in the future. But at the end of the day it's you and me. And I'll be right by your side, through the bad times as well as the good. So will you marry me, Jane?'

He was asking her to take a chance on him and join her future with his. To risk having a lot more rough times than smooth times.

She'd been here before, full of hopes and listening to a speech that turned out to be a piecrust promise, empty and easily broken.

But Ed wasn't Shaun. He wasn't saying that life would be a perfect paradise and offering her the moon and the stars. He was offering her something better: something realistic and solid. A life that wasn't always going to be easy, but he'd always be by her side.

She bent down to kiss him. 'I'd be honoured. Yes.'

'Good.' He slid the makeshift ring onto the ring finger of her left hand and kissed her. 'Let's go shopping after work tonight and choose the real ring together.'

He smiled. 'And it really doesn't matter if the paps follow us. It just means they'll have a nice story to print about my family instead of a pile of spite. And we're going to celebrate.'

CHAPTER FOURTEEN

JANE tried ringing Jenna's mobile and her parents' land-line several times more before the end of her shift, and at last her father answered.

'Dad, is Jenna there?' she asked.

'Yes. She's in bed.'

Which meant that Jenna could be feeling guilty enough about what she'd done to push her into depression. Normally, Jane would be sympathetic about her twin's depression, but not after what she'd just done. This time, Jenna had gone way, way too far.

'I need to talk to her.'

'Is something wrong?'

You could say that again. But Jane also knew that Martin Cooper would go into protective father mode and make excuses for Jenna. He always did. And this time her twin had to face up to what she'd done. Jane made her voice sound as light as she could. 'I just need to talk to her about something, Dad.'

'She's resting. Can't it wait?'

'It's important.'

His voice hardened. 'She told me you threw her out.'

Jane sighed. Of course Jenna had got her story in first. And she wouldn't have said *why* Jane asked her to leave; she only ever told the bit of the story that made her look a victim. 'Dad, there are two sides to every story, OK? Please. I really need to talk to her.'

'To apologise?'

If that was what it took to get Jenna on the phone... 'Yes,' she fibbed.

Jenna took her time coming to the phone. 'What do you want?'

'The story in the press.'

'What story?'

'The one about Ed. I know you were the leak. You must've heard his message and worked it out for yourself.' Jane sighed. 'Look, I get that you hate me, but this time it isn't just me you hurt, Jenna—you've hurt some really nice people, none of whom deserved this.'

'I was trying to help,' Jenna said defensively.

'Help? By spreading scandal in the tabloids? How do you work out *that's* helping?'

Jenna said nothing.

'You have to stop hurting people, Jenna. Or you're going to end up destroying yourself.'

Jenna's response was to hang up.

Two minutes later, Martin was on the phone to Jane. 'What the hell did you just say to her?' he demanded. 'She's breaking her heart down here.'

'Nothing like what I wanted to say, believe you me.' She put her father in the picture about exactly what Jenna had done, the people she'd hurt.

'It's a pity you don't think more about your *own* family,' Martin commented. 'You haven't even bothered seeing us this year.'

And they'd bothered coming to London to see her? Not. Jane finally saw red and everything she'd never said before came pouring out. 'Actually, Dad, have you ever considered things from *my* point of view? That Jenna expects and demands and takes all the time? And you let her get away with it. You never, ever tell her no. She can put the vilest stuff in the press about me, and it's fine, because it all boosts her career and that's far more important than not hurting me.'

'Jane! How can you say that?' He sounded shocked.

'Because it's true, Dad. You and Mum value looks above everything else. You've always made it clear that I'm the disappointment—the one who can't strut down a catwalk and be like Mum. But I'm doing just fine in my own field. You're the ones missing out. And in future you can just count me out. I'm tired of bending over backwards, being nice and saying nothing, no matter how badly Jenna behaves or how nasty she is.'

His silence gave her the courage to continue. 'And do you want to know why I've backed off from you all, why I haven't visited you this year? Then let me tell you why I gave Shaun his ring back last year. It's because I came home early and found him in bed with Jenna. My fiancé. In my bed. With my sister.'

'I had no idea.' He sounded stunned.

'Well, you do now. And this week she's leaked that story to the press—a private message that was on my answering machine—and claimed she was trying to help. If you can work out how the hell hurting people she doesn't know—nice, genuine, kind people—is helping, then do let me know. Have a nice day.' Gritting her teeth, she replaced the receiver.

She'd well and truly burned her bridges, now, so she might as well make it complete. She sent her father an email with a link to the *Celebrity Life* interview. *When the journalist wanted to do the interview and photo shoot, I was doing my exams. I said I couldn't do it and explained why. This is the result. Perhaps now you'll understand why I've had enough. I just can't do this any more. And if you can't accept that, then perhaps I'm better off without all of you.*

She was brushing the tears away when Ed walked in. 'Janey? What's happened?'

She told him about her conversations with her father and Jenna. 'I think I've well and truly done it now. I've as good as given him an ultimatum.' She sighed. 'I guess it's been a long time coming.'

'Maybe it'll make a difference, now you've told them how you feel. Sometimes it takes a crisis and some hard words to make things work properly,' he said. 'Look at Pippa Duffield and her mother-in-law. You're the one who persuaded her to try building bridges, and her mother-in-law responded brilliantly.'

'I know, but I don't think this is going to work out for me,' Jane said.

He wrapped his arms round her. 'I'm so sorry, Janey. If it helps, you're most definitely part of my family, and they all love you to bits.' He kissed her. 'And we're going to make it official tonight.'

After work, Ed took Jane to choose the ring: a single diamond in a pretty platinum setting.

'Now you're officially mine,' he said, and kissed the back of her ring finger before sliding the diamond on to it. 'Do you mind if we call in to see George and share the good news?'

'No, I'd like that.'

Except when they got to George's flat, the whole of Ed's family was there; so were Sorcha and Jake, and champagne was chilling in the fridge.

'Ed? Did you organise all this, just this afternoon?' she asked.

'After you said yes?' He smiled. 'Yup. I thought we could all do with some good news to celebrate. Do you mind?'

'No—I'm just...' She swallowed hard. He'd done this to surprise her, to make her see that his family would drop everything at incredibly short notice to come and celebrate their engagement, because they considered her one of them.

He kissed the single tear away. 'I know. Your family should be here, too,' he said softly, guessing her thoughts accurately. 'That's why I asked Sorcha.'

Her best friend. 'The sister I wish I had.' And who would never, ever hurt her the way her biological sister had. 'Thank you.'

'I love you, and you love me. And whatever lies ahead, we're going to cope with it,' Ed said, holding her close. 'Together.'

The next morning, a huge hand-tied bouquet arrived for Jane at the hospital.

'How lovely. Your family works fast,' she said to Ed. Then she opened the card. 'Oh.'

'Who are they from?'

'Jenna.' Jane sat down. 'She's never apologised to me before. Ever.' She paused. 'Then again, they might not actually be from her.'

'How do you mean? Isn't her name on the card?'

'Dad likes a quiet life. I know the way his mind works.' She sighed. 'He thinks that if I believe Jenna's apologised, I'll let it go and things can carry on as they were.'

Ed looked surprised. 'You think your father sent them?'

She nodded. 'With the best of intentions. But it somehow makes everything feel worse.' She put the card back in the envelope and left it on her desk next to the flowers. 'We have rounds to do.'

'OK.'

It was a busy morning on the ward; halfway through their rounds, Rosie called them to come and look at a mum whose labour wasn't progressing.

'Why it's taking so long is that the baby's turned round and his back is against yours,' Jane explained.

'You've done a wonderful job, but you've been in labour all yesterday afternoon and all last night, you're tired now, and the baby's starting to get a little bit distressed. I think it's time to say enough,' Ed said gently. 'I'd recommend a section.'

'I'd so wanted a natural birth,' the mum said, looking miserable. 'I was going to do this with just gas and air. But I might as well make my birth plan into a paper plane.'

Ed squeezed her hand. 'Babies don't read birth plans. They have their own ideas,' he said with a smile. 'Come on. You've done brilliantly. If you really want to keep going for another half an hour, then I'll go with that, but if you haven't progressed any further then it's time to call it a day, for the baby's sake. Then we'll ask you to sign the consent form for a section.'

She sighed. 'It's not going to work, is it?'

Jane squeezed her other hand. 'I'm sorry, I don't think it will.'

'OK. I'll sign the form now.'

Half an hour later, she was cuddling her baby, and Jane was wiping away her usual tears of joy at helping a new life enter the world. She went to her desk to write up her notes, and realised that there was a registered post envelope on her desk. And she recognised the handwriting: Jenna's.

Warily, she opened the envelope.

Jane,

I'm sorry. I've always been jealous of you—you're the clever one, the strong one, and I'm as flaky and hopeless as Mum. You always make me feel as if I'm not good enough.

Jane stared at the words, barely taking them in. She'd made Jenna feel useless? But—that wasn't at all what she'd intended. She'd tried to make Jenna feel cherished, looked after.

I'm sorry I gave you a hard time when we were growing up. And I'm sorry for what I did to Ed and his family. I hope he doesn't dump you because of me. I'll apologise to him in person, if you want me to.

Jenna was actually apologising. Sincerely.

I hope you like the flowers. I sent them, not Dad.

So Jenna, too, knew how their father's mind worked.

I've had time to think about it. I know it's a lot to ask and I haven't been good to you, but can we start again? This time, as equals?
Love, Jenna.

Ed came over. 'Janey, are you OK?'

Wordlessly, she handed him the card.

He read it swiftly. 'Wow. I would never have expected that.'

'Me neither. I don't…' She shook her head. 'I don't know what to think, how to react. I mean, it's the first time she's ever offered me any kind of olive branch.'

And then Gwen, one of the junior nurses, came over with another huge bouquet of flowers. 'Janey, is there something you're not telling us? Like it's your birthday or something?'

Jane exchanged a glance with Ed. There was something they weren't telling, yet, but they were waiting until the DNA results came back before they told the rest of the world. 'No, it's not my birthday. I had a fight with my sister.'

Gwen rolled her eyes. 'Tell me about it. I have those all the time—my sister never sends me flowers, though.'

'This is a first for her,' Jane said dryly. She opened the card and read it.

I'm sorry. Jenna's fragile, like your mother. You're like me, the one who gets on with things. I never meant you to feel second-best. You're not, and it won't happen again. I'm so proud of you, Jane. And I love you.
Dad.

* * *

'They're from my dad,' she said.

'Did you have a fight with him, too?' Gwen looked surprised. 'You've never fallen out with anyone since I've known you. And then you had two fights in one night?'

Jane gave her a wry smile. 'I guess it's a bit like buses. You wait for ages, then two come along at once.'

'Well, they're lovely flowers,' Gwen said with a smile. 'Enjoy them, you lucky thing.'

When Gwen left, Jane handed the card to Ed.

'Judging by that card and all those flowers,' he said when he'd finished reading it, 'I think your family's finally started to see you for who you are—and realised your worth.'

'Maybe.' There was a huge lump in her throat. 'I'd better ring them. I have some making up to do.'

'Go for it. And come and grab me if you need me,' he said, and kissed her.

CHAPTER FIFTEEN

THE results of the test were due back on the Monday. Jane and Ed had both managed to swap shifts so they had a day off to wait in for the post; David and Frances had come up from Suffolk to stay with George; and the girls were all on standby to come straight over to Ed's flat as soon as the post arrived and he called them.

Ed couldn't settle to anything and was pacing the flat. There were lines of tension on his face, and he glanced at the clock every couple of seconds and then looked shocked that so little time had passed since he'd last looked.

'Oh, honey.' Jane kissed him lightly. 'There's not much longer to wait.' If only she could take this strain from him.

'This is worse than waiting for exam results to come. George said the same thing. You've always got a good idea how you did in your exams. This...this is completely out of my control.' He shook his head in obvious frustration. 'I know who I am right now, but that envelope could tell me I'm someone completely different.'

Jane squeezed his hand. 'Ed, whatever the results are, you know they won't change how I feel about you.

I love you for who you are, not for who your biological father is. And David will always, always see you as his son, regardless of what the test says.'

'I know. And thank you. Sorry. I'm being difficult.' He sighed. 'This waiting is killing me. I can't *breathe*, Jane. My chest feels tight and my head hurts, and it feels as if someone swapped my blood for ice.'

There was nothing she could say, nothing she could do, to make things better. Only hold him.

When the intercom buzzed, he froze. 'Oh, my God— the results are coming by registered post. That must be the postman now.' He rushed over to the intercom. 'Yes?'

'Can you *please* let us in before I start threatening the paps with my crutches and Alice has to bail me out in court?' George asked plaintively.

Ed buzzed him up and went to open his front door. Jane switched the kettle on and busied herself making coffee.

'The results aren't here yet,' she could hear Ed say. 'I said I'd call you the minute they came.'

'I just couldn't stand the wait any longer.'

'Even when they do turn up, you know we can't open them until the girls are here,' Ed warned. 'We promised.'

'True, but I'd still rather wait here with you.' George limped into the kitchen and hugged Jane. 'Hello, Janey. How's my favourite sister-in-law-to-be?'

'As nervous as you lot are,' she said. 'Ed can't settle to anything.'

'Me neither. I'm not good at waiting at the best of times, and this is driving me crazy,' George said.

'Especially as he had to put up with me driving us

here from his flat,' David said wryly as he walked into the kitchen. 'Trust me, we're all desperate for his leg to be good enough for him to drive himself again, so we don't have to put up with all the instructions and comments.'

Frances ruffled George's hair. 'Don't listen to your dad, love. He's a worse passenger than you are—which is why I never drive him anywhere!'

Jane handed round mugs of coffee. Although she'd put cookies on a plate, nobody was hungry and they just sat there in the middle of the table.

'I wish there was a way you could just wind time forward,' George said.

'Me, too,' Ed agreed.

'We need to talk about something else. *Anything* else,' David said.

'The wedding?' George suggested. 'We can plan it all now. I mean, we have the bride here, the groom, the best man…'

'Do you seriously think we'd let you loose on the planning?' Jane asked. 'You'd have us getting married in mid-air on one of your paragliding things!'

'What a great idea, Janey.' George dimpled at her. 'Maybe we could offer that as one of the wedding packages in Suffolk.' Then he frowned. 'Well. Maybe not. It might not be my place to suggest that any more.'

'Of course it will be.' David rolled his eyes. 'I already told you. I don't give a damn what the genetic specialists say; you're both my sons.'

'And mine,' Frances added. 'You don't have to be biologically related to be someone's parent.'

'Frances, you've been a much better mother to us than ours could ever have been,' Ed said quietly.

'Actually, George and I have thought of you as our mum for years.'

Jane could see Frances' eyes mist over with tears. 'Oh, Ed.'

'It's true,' George said. 'And, Dad—we couldn't have asked for anyone better than you.'

'I couldn't have asked for better sons. Even though you give me grey hairs with those damned extreme sports, George.' David patted his shoulder. 'Ed, how does this DNA thing work exactly?'

'They look at genetic markers. With every pair of genes, you inherit one from each parent. Obviously we couldn't give the lab a maternal sample, but if your DNA profile matches one of each pair of alleles in our DNA profile, then it proves you're our father.'

David was white-faced as he asked, 'And if it doesn't match?'

Ed took a deep breath. 'Then the results will say that they exclude you from the possibility of being our father.'

The minutes ticked by, slower and slower; none of them felt like making small talk, and the kitchen was filled with a silence so heavy that it weighed down on all of them. Ed resumed pacing, George drummed his fingers on his crutches, and David turned his cup round and round in his hands.

Finally, the intercom went again; this time, it really was the postman.

Ed buzzed him up, then said, 'George, ring the girls while I sign for the letters.'

When he came back, George said, 'They're all getting taxis. They'll be here in twenty minutes, tops.' He blew out a breath. '*Twenty more minutes*. Do we really have to wait for them?'

'Yes, we do—this is a family thing, and we're all in it together. Right, Jane?' Frances said.

It warmed Jane that Frances had included her. 'Right,' she agreed.

Finally the girls arrived; they all refused coffee and just leaned against the worktops in the kitchen, looking grim.

'OK. This is it,' Ed said, and swallowed hard. He ripped the first envelope open and unfolded the sheets of paper.

'And?' George asked impatiently.

Ed scanned the paper. 'Yours and Dad's markers match—it says there's a 99.9 per cent probability that Dad's your father. Which is as good as it gets.' He looked up and met his brother's gaze. 'Thank God.'

'And you?' David asked.

Ed took a deep breath and opened the other envelope. He looked at the sheet swiftly, and sagged in apparent relief. 'Me, too.'

'So all that stuff in her diaries and those letters… She was completely wrong,' George said.

'Your mother was completely wrong about an awful lot of things,' David said. 'I'm sorry that you both had to go through this.' He hugged both his sons. 'And now we tell the press the truth, and they'll can go and find someone else to write their stories about.'

'If this is an official statement, Dad, do you need it written down?' Alice asked.

'It'll be short and sweet,' David said. 'And, no, I don't need to write it down. What I'm saying comes straight from the heart.'

The whole family, united, went down to the entrance to the flats. David stood between his sons. Flashes started popping, and there was a barrage of questions until it became very obvious that David had something to say and he wasn't going to answer a single question until they'd given him a chance to speak.

Eventually the hubbub died down.

'Thank you,' David said. 'I'm aware that you've all been interested in the paternity of my sons, George and Edward. So I'm delighted to announce that the DNA testing has conclusively...' His voice cracked, and he stopped.

George put his hand on his father's shoulder to bolster him.

'Conclusively proved that my sons are...' David stopped again.

Clearly their father had been bottling up his feelings all week. Despite his assertion that he hadn't needed to write anything down, emotion had robbed David of his voice and he couldn't make the announcement.

George widened his eyes at Ed and gave the tiniest nod.

Ed decoded the message: *you're the scientist—it's better coming from you.*

He lifted his chin. 'The DNA testing proves without a shadow of a doubt that George and I are our father's biological sons.'

There was murmuring from the press pack. Obviously this was robbing them of the scandal story they'd been hoping for.

Maybe it was time to give them something else instead. Something much, much more positive. He held out his hand to Jane.

She gave him a tiny nod, and stepped forward to take his hand.

'We also have some other news,' Ed said. 'I've found the love of my life and she's agreed to marry me. I know she'll mean every word of those vows, because she agreed to marry me before we knew the results of the testing, and she didn't care whether they'd make me a prince or a pauper. Dr Jane Cooper and I are going to get married as soon as possible.'

'So is there a third bit of news, Ed?' one of the journalists called out.

Ed laughed. 'You mean, are we getting married because we have to?' But this would be nothing like his marriage to Camilla. 'No.'

'We're getting married quickly,' Jane said, 'simply because we don't want to have to wait for the rest of our lives to start.'

'Exactly.' Ed pulled her into his arms, bent her back over one arm and kissed her. Thoroughly. And the flashing lightbulbs felt like stars exploding in his head.

The headlines the next morning ran, *George is the boy.*

And Jane smiled at the caption beneath the photograph of Ed kissing her speechless: *Ed with Dr Cinderella.*

The following Sunday afternoon, she and Ed headed down to Suffolk, with Sorcha and Jake following them; Alice had the task of driving George, and had threatened to ask Bea to bring gaffer tape to shut him up if he said a word out of place.

'We could've had a big party, you know,' Ed said.

'A marquee, a band, a chocolate fountain and lots of champagne.'

'I just wanted the important people there,' she said softly. 'A small, intimate family lunch to celebrate our engagement.'

Ed reached over to squeeze her hand. 'I spoke to your dad on Friday night. If they don't come, *don't* take it personally. It's at least a seven-hour drive from Cornwall to Suffolk, and that's assuming they don't get stuck in traffic.'

Which meant that they would've needed to drive up the day before and stay nearby. Jane was pretty sure that Frances would've offered to put the Coopers up, but she was equally sure that her mother would've refused the invitation.

Her father and Jenna had wished them well. Jenna had even said the photos in the press of Ed kissing Jane were gorgeous, like a fairy-tale. But there had been a resounding silence from Sophia.

Well, OK. Maybe her mother would thaw out by the wedding, next month.

Though Jane wasn't going to hold out much hope.

When they finally arrived at the hall, Frances greeted them warmly. 'Come through to the rose garden. David's spent all morning putting a gazebo up.' She glanced up at the skies. 'And it looks as if the weather's going to be kind, so we won't have to make a run for the house.'

George and the girls were already there, Sorcha and Jake were only a couple of minutes behind, and Jane was very, very aware of the empty places that would be at the end of the beautifully laid table. Where her family should've been.

'I thought a cold buffet might be best,' Frances said. 'Though I have hot new potatoes in the Aga, and the bread's still warm.'

Jane's eyes widened as she saw the spread. 'Wow. That's fabulous. Frances, you've gone to so much trouble. That's an awful lot of work.'

'It was a labour of love,' Frances assured her. 'We're so pleased you're going to be part of our family.'

If only her own family felt the same way. But she damped down the disappointment and forced herself to smile.

It was only when Ed nudged her and said softly, 'More guests to greet,' that she turned round and saw her parents walking across the lawn towards them, along with Jenna.

'Jane.' Sophia, as always, greeted her daughter with an air kiss. Jane tried very hard not to mind.

But Jenna surprised her with a warm hug. 'You look beautiful,' she said. 'My little sister.'

Jane blinked the tears back. 'Only by five minutes.'

And Martin surprised her further by holding her really, really tightly. 'Janey. My clever, special girl,' he whispered. 'I think your mother and I have got a lot of making-up to do to you.'

She swallowed hard. 'It doesn't matter, Dad. Not any more.'

'No, because you and Ed have each other. This one's going to do right by you.' He smiled at her. 'I never liked the other one in any case. He wasn't right for you. But Ed...he's the one.'

'He certainly is.'

She caught Ed's eye, and he mouthed, 'I love you.'

David tapped a wine glass with a fork. 'Now we're

all here, I think we should have the official business before lunch.'

'Absolutely.' Ed took Jane's hand and led her to the middle of the gazebo. 'We already know Jane agreed to marry me when everything was going wrong and it looked as if she was going to have a lot more of the rough than the smooth. But that's all behind us now, and I think it's made all of us stronger. So today I want to do this properly and get engaged officially, with the people we love most in the world around us, and in a place that's special to both of us.' He dropped to one knee and opened the velvet-covered box, just as he'd done in her kitchen. 'Jane Cooper, I love you with my whole heart. Will you do me the honour of being my wife?'

There was only one answer she could possibly give. 'I love you, too. Yes.'

And as Ed slid the ring back on her finger, everyone cheered and George opened the champagne with a very, very loud pop.

* * * * *

A sneaky peek at next month...

Medical Romance

CAPTIVATING MEDICAL DRAMA—WITH HEART

My wish list for next month's titles...

In stores from 6th April 2012:

☐ *Georgie's Big Greek Wedding?* – Emily Forbes

& *The Nurse's Not-So-Secret Scandal* – Wendy S. Marcus

☐ *Dr Right All Along* – Joanna Neil

& *Summer With A French Surgeon* – Margaret Barker

☐ *Sydney Harbour Hospital: Tom's Redemption*
   – Fiona Lowe

& *Doctor on Her Doorstep* – Annie Claydon

Available at WHSmith, Tesco, Asda, Eason, Amazon and Apple

Just can't wait?

Special Offers

Every month we put together collections and longer reads written by your favourite authors.

Here are some of next month's highlights— and don't miss our fabulous discount online!

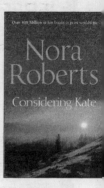

On sale 16th March   On sale 16th March   On sale 6th April

Save 20% on all Special Releases

Find out more at
www.millsandboon.co.uk/specialreleases

Visit us Online

The World of Mills & Boon®

There's a Mills & Boon® series that's perfect
for you. We publish ten series and with new
titles every month, you never have to wait
long for your favourite to come along.

Blaze®	Scorching hot, sexy reads
By Request	Relive the romance with the best of the best
Cherish™	Romance to melt the heart every time
Desire™	Passionate and dramatic love stories